THE HERO WITH A THOUSAND EYES
A historical novel

B orn in the alpine district of Bumthang, Karma Ura went to Yangchenphug High School and Kanglung Junior College in Eastern Bhutan. While he was in St. Stephen's College in Delhi studying Indian History, he got the JCR Third World Scholarship from Magdalen College, Oxford to read Politics, Philosophy and Economics (PPE). He continued his education in the University of Edinburgh where he gained an M. Phil research degree in Economics. He was a staff of the Ministry of Planning from 1989 to 1998 He works now for the Centre for Bhutan Studies. In December 2006, he was conferred the title of Dasho by His Majesty the King.

KARMA URA

THE HERO
WITH A THOUSAND EYES

A historical novel

This novella is set in the Himalayan Kingdom of Bhutan in the recent past. Nevertheless, it reflects an age and a set of manners - mostly set about the Court and central administration - which is now almost completely changed. This is a book about a courtier, who represented a mode of life and living which had vanished overnight, and not about the kings he served, but the reader will find rich detail on all aspects of life in Bhutan.

The plot is a relatively simple one. A reincarnation is born in central Bhutan with prospects of a quiet and uneventful religious life in a small but lively rural community. By happenstance, he is allowed to serve first at the Court of the second King, and later in the wider administration of the country. He achieves high position. By the time of his voluntary retirement, Bhutan was already caught up in increasingly rapid economic, social, political, and cultural changes.

Within this outline, the author weaves a sensitive and detailed account of daily life and court ritual, of loves and intrigues, with an abiding nostalgia for an era from which even the shadows are fading daily. The reader leaves this book feeling enriched by the sheer vitality of the lives, emotions and landscapes so faithfully portrayed, but tinged with sadness for the passing of such a vigourous sense of community. Long after the volume is put down, *The Hero with a Thousand Eyes* remains hauntingly with us and teases all our senses, like the early morning scent of juniper smoke from a temple in that far-away land. For young Bhutanese especially, the volume stands like an old *thangkha* backdrop to contemporary life, while for older generations it will be savoured for the bitter-sweetness of a full yet gentle life in the midst of often unexpected complications.

For the international audience which can also access this volume, the tale can be read on its own merits as a biographical novel; but it can also be read as both a record and an exploration of aspects of Bhutan's recent past, reminding us of how novel is the material aspect of much of our development, and how its foundations often are laid through the forethought and imagination of outstanding leaders such as the late and revered third King of Bhutan, Jigme Dorji Wangchuck.

THE HERO
WITH A THOUSAND EYES

A historical novel

KARMA URA

First published in 1995, reprinted in 1999, 2004, 2007

by Karma Ura, Centre for Bhutan Studies,

P.O. Box 1111, Thimphu, Bhutan

Fax: 975-2-321001

E-mail: drphilos@yahoo.co.uk

ISBN 81-7525-001-1

Cover Illustration: *Views from Mule Tracks*

by Lharip Dorji and Karma Ura.

*To the Royal Institution of Bhutanese Monarchy,
who brought order, progress and
international recognition of state sovereignty,
and is the source of all good and great things
that have come to this mountain-state.*

**His Majesty Jigme Dorji Wangchuck,
the Third King of Bhutan (1928-72).**
Photograph taken in 1950

CONTENTS

Photograph   *ix*
Preface   *xiii*
Acknowledgements   *xix*
Maps   *105,199*

1.   A Priestly Grooming   1
2.   Summoned to Wangdecholing Palace   19
3.   Early Years as a Retainer   29
4.   The Great Fair of Wangdecholing   59
5.   The Court Leaves for the Winter Palace   69
6.   To Have a Betel Nut by the Stream   85
7.   To Haa, the End of the Sky   95
8.   Entangled Web of Taxation   111
9.   Men Who Ruled   129
10. An Epidemic and a Festival   139
11. No More Fragrant Smoke from Donkarla   151
12. The Door Closes   163
13. A New Era Begins   171
14. Years in Trongsa and Trashigang   189
15. Views from Mule Tracks   201

16. Freedom of Serfs and PM Nehru in Paro   219
17. On the Fast Lane to India   229
18. Tumultuous Mid-sixties   237
19. Two Sublime Visitors   247
20. Coming Home at Last   253
21. The Fifth Speaker   259
22. The Thunderbolt from Kenya   279
23. A Funeral and a Coronation   295
24. Hanging up the Sword   303
25. Envoi   315

Annexes
Biographical Milestones   *321*
Glossary of Dzongkha Terms   *325*

PREFACE

I began collecting fragments of notes on the life of Shingkhar Lam first in May 1990. While I worked in the office at the Ministry of Planning on anything that came my way, I went to him to take notes on countless evenings between May and December 1990, as he reminisced about his past in the dialect of Bumthang. Listening to him in the dialect of Bumthang and writing at the same time in English might have allowed idioms of the dialect of Bumthang to creep into the book.

Three succeeding years - 1991,1992,1993 - were completely lost as far as the progress of this novel was concerned. Only in late 1994 was I able to come back to pick up the thread of the historical novel. I got three months leave from the Minister of Planning, Lyonpo C. Dorji, under whose direct guidance I have been working since I joined the civil service. I am grateful to Lyonpo C. Dorji for the sympathetic gesture of granting leave.

I did not ask Dasho Shingkhar Lam, out of the well deserved respect he enjoys, more than what he wished to tell me. There is much, I am convinced, that he kept to himself, and a large part of memory which he did not want to delve into and stir. When this happened, readers may find that certain parts of narrative skirts the subject. This book does not purport to be a critical biographical novel, but I hope that it breaks away a short distance from the hagiographic mould of Bhutanese biographies.

While recollecting his experiences, he did not have any diary or paper, which could have been prompts, to help him or me. I noted by hand whatever occurred to him and whatever he chose to disclose to me. Although everything is narrated in first person, a great deal of information was given by his contemporaries whose help I have acknowledged. Moreover, I have taken the artistic licence to add, to the extent logic would permit, to the personal incidences he described. I have embellished several personal experiences related strictly to his feelings and relationships, by imagining how he perceived the experiences within a certain context. But fundamentally, the experiences are narrated as he told me. I have not on my own subjugated the truth of the experience to the design of the novel when it comes to public events. I have ensured that all public events mentioned in the story are factually reliable by consulting many other sources.

I have retained a sketch on the administrative and tax information, found in Chapter 8 and 9 entitled "Entangled Web of Taxes" and "Men Who Ruled" respectively. They can be skipped by western readers, though the younger generations of Bhutanese may probably find the account of administrative units and taxes that existed then dissimilar to the present ones, and therefore perhaps interesting as historical background.

I have revisited many places that occur in the novel, to rekindle the experiences vicariously, and to attempt to capture the atmosphere that probably prevailed in that period. Often, direct observation of the site and houses where the event took place helped. That included the mule tracks, which are increasingly out of use or are seldom traversed. I have also visited some of the houses and palaces of those years. Three main palaces of the novel, Kinga Rabden, Wangdecholing and Domkhar are now more deserted than the mule tracks. I hope to see them regain their former glory in some form, as they were not only hub of activities then but also represent architecture of that era.

I must say very clearly that this is a book about a courtier, who represented a mode of life and living which had vanished, and not about the kings he served. Thus, if the book gives only an incidental picture of a king or kings, it is only because it is not meant to do otherwise. Yet it may be tempting to criticise the shortcomings in terms of portrayals of the kings and other personalities of those years. They appear in the story only in so far as the situation that is associated with the courtier demands. Nevertheless, some of the deeds of the kings naturally come through, most of it for the first time in writing. If there is frequent reference to a king, then it is because the subject of the novel was at all times at the disposal of the king and others higher than himself. The king was, after all, the hub in their wheel of existence, and what happened in his life was only a radiation of the movement at the hub. A courtier's life was only a partial reflection of the experiences in the life of the king he served.

The story of Shingkhar Kunzang Wangchuck will enable the readers to get a broad-canvas view of the crucial period of Bhutanese history when modernization, which started with in-kind tax reforms, burst upon Bhutan. Some aspects of the process of modernization are explained through the unfolding of the life of Dasho Shingkhar Lam. He and his contemporaries participated in Bhutan's path of development as it was conceived and executed by kings whose subjects were over-awed, even while they deeply adulated them.

The reader will find that the life in the court was very hectic, a circumstance which the kings did not wish to escape because of their reformist attitudes and dreams. All through the late forties till the end of his reign, the second King was quite preoccupied with lowering of the tax burden, chiefly by abolishing various local offices that required the support of the people through a quité arbitrary system of taxation. Reading of the Epic of Gesar (legendary King of Ling), prolonged games of archery, a priceless collection of horses and visits to hot springs were only the few private pleasures he sought. He kept his country out of internal and external strife in a period when both Tibet, China and India were in a tumultuous state.

The second King was determined to reform taxes, and it remained his life-long interest and concentration. A brief examination of his reasons for the reform suggests that he saw the many offices, like that of dungpas, as a drain on the rural economy, which could be abolished without any deleterious effect on national interest. Among many other landmark contributions the second King made, he sent many Bhutanese for professional courses to India, laid the foundation of modern health service and education systems, and established the armed force. Prominent among his achievements was his statesmanly steering of Bhutan's relationship with India and other neighbouring countries, when many dangers to Bhutan's position could have arisen in an unsettling period in this part of the world. The reader will also find that the engrossment with tradition and ceremonies in the court of the second King tended to take on a life of its own. However, it had the effect of refining etiquette, protocol and discipline.

Things were to change radically when Paro Penlop Jigme Dorji Wangchuck became the King in 1952. Until then, he gave no indication of the changes that he would bring immediately upon the demise of his father, including the shifting of the capital from Bumthang to Thimphu. He pursued with breath-taking shrewdness, consolidation of the sovereignty of Bhutan, while initiating the process of modernization, and making the country undergo a sea change towards development goals.

As the subject of the novel told me "all succeeding generations of Bhutanese may wonder whether a small country could produce such a great person!" He transcended the rational and the logical aspects of living, and responded deeply to the aesthetic side of life offered by the arts. He found great solace and self-expression in folk dance, songs, poems, mask dances, architecture, folklore and painters. He cut through frequently and very easily the people who usually surrounded him, and reached Bhutanese peasants in rural areas. He was personally able to participate in the collective ethos of Bhutan, represented in these spheres of the laymen's arts. This partly explains his enduring appeal, in addition to being father of modern Bhutan, to the collective memory of the Bhutanese.

ACKNOWLEDGEMENTS

Very little is usually done all on ones own. I must express my most sincere gratitude to a large number of people for their warm encouragement and kind support. I wish to acknowledge my debt especially to:

Agay Khila, Khoma; Agay Kuenga, Sha Samtengang; Aum Gogay, Sha Kashi; Aum Pedon, Khoma Pangkhar; Aum Pema Choden, Bartsham; Aum Tshering Doma, Thimphu; Aku Tongmay, Thimphu; Dr. Brian Shaw, Hongkong University; Dasho Karma Gayleg, Dorjibi; Dasho Lhaderla, Chumey Nangar; Dasho Pasang Wangdi, Sha Khemseling; Chief Justice Dasho Sonam Tobgye, Dungsam Nangkor; Dasho Pema Wangchen, Ura; Dasho Drukpon Kinzang Wangdi, Pra; Gup Chewang Rinzin, Pangrey; Mr. John Tyson and Mrs. Phebe Tyson, Cumbria; Jow Thinley Tshering, Haa Talung; Lopon 'Geshey' Jampa, Chumey Nangar; Lopon Kunzang Dorji, Bongo; Lopon Minjur Dorji, Shingkhar; Lyonpo Dawa Tsering, Thimphu; Lyonpo Chenyap Dorji, Haa; Monpa Taula, Phrumzur; Ms Jamie Zeppa, WWF, Thimphu; Mr. Mingma Norbu Sherpa, WWF, Thimphu; Mrs. Rinchen Doma, Thimphu; Mr. Pema Nadik, Thimphu; Lopon Ugyen Tackchu, Monggar; Aum Ugen Zangmo,

Rangshikhar; Professor Fredrik Barth, Oslo University; Tshewang Darjay, Ura; Mr. E. Werner Kulling, Zurich; and Paro Penlop Prince Namgyal Wangchuck. In one way or other, all of them have contributed to the book.

I would like to acknowledge my continued debt to Lyonpo C. Dorji, for his understanding and help in ways too numerous to be recorded. I would like to express my special thanks to Prof. Fredrik Barth who has been an inspiration to me. I have come to value his stimulating friendship. To Mr. E. Werner Kulling and Paro Penlop Prience Namgyal Wangchuck, I owe an enormous debt for their warm encouragement and for making the printing of this book possible. Dasho Sonam Tobgye gave invaluable help in directing and recommending me to people who proved to be rich sources of information. I would like to thank both Jamie and Brian for their generous help with editing and proof reading. In the final stage, Brian did the proofs. But nobody is responsible, by association, for any mistake. This includes the subject of the novel. I am fully responsible for any kind of mistake that remains in the book.

1

A PRIESTLY GROOMING

I came from a hereditary lamaist family that stood out from the community. Its status lay halfway between households of the commoners and of the nobility. Such families were considered higher than households of the commoners, who had to pay taxes, but lower than aristocracies who received some of the taxes. Hereditary lamaist families are a vanishing social institution, if not already extinct. Its distinctive privileges were annulled some three decades ago. In my youth, such families could claim special dispensations.

Like other such families, our family of Shingkhar Lam was exempt from a variety of taxes which were levied on ordinary households. Being a part of the network of lamaist families did not free us from other obligations and specialized responsibilities. The eight lamaist families in the province of Bumthang were obliged to perform periodic rituals in Kurje and Jakar. Almost all taxes were honoured in either services or goods, and rarely in coin-money. The type of taxes our family faced involved performance of rites in the temples of Kurje and Jakar dzong, the administrative centre which was a day's walk from our village.

My father joined lamas of other families to conduct the annual Sondep Bumdi ritual in Kurje for about ten days, and read volumes of Kanjur in Jakar dzong for about seven days. Kanjur comprises a hundred or so volumes of Buddhist teachings. The ritual took place on the same dates every year. There were about forty of us representing eight lama families in Bumthang. A set of Kanjur was read for seven days, during which food was served by the administration in Jakar dzong. A week was the prescribed duration for provision of our sustenance. But it was not possible to read the complete set of Kanjur by the end of the week. The rite would end abruptly after seven days without all the volumes being read. The compulsory participation in these two annual rites was part of the taxes on cleric families.

My father and I were delayed once on the way to Jakar, and were late by a day for the rite. He had to go through a disconcerting punishment for not arriving on time. My father, who was deeply venerated as an eminent lama in several districts, had to pull his clothes up to his waist and bend, and he was flogged in public three times on his bare posterior. Then, he had to lug around rather heavy stones from one spot to another for five days, to no purpose. As I recall, my father performed this penal service with the same dignity as he would observe during a ritual to sanctify a place.

Another onus on us as a lamaist family was that my father had to call on the monarch within three days of the latter's arrival from his winter capital. The court migrated to Kinga Rabden Palace in Trongsa in winter and back to Wangdecholing Palace, Jakar, in spring. It was customary at the time of calling for each lamaist family to pay a fixed levy of one yathra, the famed woollen textile of Bumthang, with a pitcher full of araa to greet his return from the winter palace. Yathras, a textile speciality of Bumthang, were useful as gifts from the elites of Bhutan to the nobles of Tibet. Through a suitable means of communication, the royal family disclosed the choice of size and patterns of yathras they preferred, so that the nobles and lamas could bring more agreeable tributes. Quite often, the King inspected the quality of yathras. Good ones were sent as gifts to high ranking Tibetans. The tribute of one yathra and a pitcher full of araa was reciprocated by the King with three balls of tea and five metres of broad cloth. This exchange of gifts within three days of the court's arrival was bound by tradition.

Another responsibility of the lamaist families was to nurse back to health and strength emaciated horses belonging to the court stable. Scrawny and weak horses that required too much care for the Tapon (chief of stable) had to be revived by the lamaist and other well known families. Such horses were also assigned to the managers of royal estates in Trongsa district. I was intrigued by the convention, and wondered how horse rearing came to be associated with the expertise of lamaist families.

We had to go to a great deal of trouble to rejuvenate such horses. We were very wary that they might fall victim to the wolves, tigers and leopards which haunted the ranges above the village, or be impaled by oxen and yaks with whom they could not avoid contact in the narrow confines of village streets. We fattened them by feeding a raw egg or two whenever we could spare. Buckwheat, wheat and maize filled their troughs as frequently as possible, until the chief of stable asked for them. The horses were voracious and consumed a great deal of grains, which could have been used as our own food. My parents had the honour, though it now seems dubious, of rearing many sickly horses for the royal stable.

As the lamaist family of Shingkhar, we had a certain

respectability in the community. My father, Lama Kenchog Gyeltshen, was the astro-practitioner in the village as well as the main custodian of the shrine of the community. He was consulted and had a significant role during occasions of birth, death, marriage, journey and celebration. But the prestige of the family was not backed up by any tangible wealth. The members of our family wore handed-down clothes from my grandfather, who was richer than us. Our grandfather gave a set of clothes to each of us every few years.

We had no land holding of paddy fields in warmer places, which was the first conventional yardstick of the well-to-do. The size of both our herds of yaks and cattle were below fifteen head, which was the second measure of wealth in such pastoral communities. We owned yaks only after my mother was brought as a bride from Ura. My maternal grandfather gave her a small breeding stock of both yaks and cattle. But the seed stock failed obdurately to multiply and we lived within the means provided by an extremely small herd.

We had a small flock of sheep, as did most of the households in our village. Our sheep were tended by another family in the village, along with their own flock. I went occasionally with my shepherd friends. They would let their flocks out late during rough weather, or when there was snow cover on the ground. In spring and autumn, they let the flocks out only after the morning sun melted away frost.

Some of my most recurrent memories of childhood are associated with the days with my shepherd friends. Along with them, I remember chasing rams, as soon as we crossed the threshold of the village. I could catch only a few docile rams to ride, especially the spotted one. The spotted ram and I developed a sense of companionship. We would advance on our rams in a column after a great mass of sheep. We got off near the village, when we returned in the evening, so that our parents would not know that we had been riding them. We suffered from several injuries, getting tossed in the air, before we could master how to remain astride a running ram. It was generally agreed among knowledgeable shepherds that it was more dangerous to be thrown off by a ram than a pony.

The rolling slopes round the village, now thoroughly encroached by forest, provided wide foraging grounds for the sheep of our village. The flocks were usually driven in the same direction, so the shepherds could keep each other company throughout the day. We pooled our lunches, usually made up of roasted black barley, popped corns, buckwheat khurwa (a type of pancake) and keptang (wheat or buckwheat pancake). It was a great temptation to eat our lunches early and then return home with our flocks because we found ourselves hungry.

While not rounding up the flocks which strayed into fields or forests, we sang songs, spotted lice on each others' scalp and clothes, held games meets among children, fought with each other, set up fights between dominant rams, told stories, hunted for moulted feathers of pheasants to fletch arrows, collected firewood, bamboo, lichen, mushrooms and flowers to take home in the evening.

Sometimes, the news of the presence of major predators like leopards and grey wolves reached us from the next village or rangeland sheds where livestock had been maimed or killed. We had to be especially watchful over our flocks of sheep, cattle and horses during such times. But keeping patrol over flocks did not really help, for the predators frequently out foxed the child-shepherds.

For my shepherd friends, winter and lambing seasons were the most demanding part of an otherwise fun-filled time. After the ewes lambed, the child-shepherds were forewarned about the lambs who had far less sense and did not keep up with the wandering flocks. The lambs would be left behind, beneath bushes, though the ewes would then become inconsolable and bleat all the time. Foxes were a constant threat to the lambs.

The most calamitous event for one of my shepherd friends occurred one night in winter. A sheep pen made up of a stone wall enclosure stood near his house. Small gaps were kept between the roof and the wall to let in air and light, but these gaps also tempted prey. In a night raid, during which we did not feel the slightest disturbance, eighteen out of seventy-one sheep were killed, perhaps by leopards. When he went to release them in the morning, he found mangled bodies. Some were about to die, and lay with their necks stiffening with pain. My favourite spotted ram, one of the few I could catch and ride, was also a casualty.

We had a darkened, crumbling, three storeyed house. I grew up, in my first ten years, in its soot and smoke-filled rooms. It was very drafty and did not provide good protection against the fierce and frigid wind. The speed and the ferocity of the wind blowing against the windows and doors gave me the impression of someone invisible forcing them open. The death of a person in the village intensified that impression and I would not dare to get up and go to bolt the door. During such moments, I rushed to sit by my mother's side.

The ladder up to the middle storey was perilously steep and the corridor and landings did not get a ray of light. I was frequently gripped by fright when I had to go through the corridor and down the ladder on my own, a fear which was reinforced by my tumbling down the ladder several times when descending it. It is a common childhood experience among the Bhutanese that often leaves marks in the form of scaly scars and swellings on the scalp and forehead. The profusion of scars and protuberances in unlikely places left behind by numerous falls during childhood were made worse by the scars added during the handling of knives from a young age.

The thought of waking up alone at night filled me with an aching fear. I felt petrified whenever I woke up at night. During those interminable moments, I held my breath for too long out of fear, and after many such instances, I sweated and had to come up from under the heavy duvets for air. Never did I require greater courage than to push my head out of the blanket cover so that I could breath properly. But as my head popped out on the pillow, the sinister sound of snoring overwhelmed me. A priest and a shoe-maker, who often slept in our house, were champion snorers. Instead of feeling reassured by those sleeping close by, the sniffing and snoring that reverberated through the silence of the night only worsened the vivid fright I suffered. The room would become dead silent for one moment and full of snoring the next, as people spasmodically snored in unison.

I would shudder for many years afterwards when I recalled an incident I had one night. I went to bed alone in the shrine room after lighting a butter lamp there. I had gone to sleep, lying on my side, while it was flaring, with the comforting knowledge that it would last throughout the night. But it was put out perhaps by the draft soon after I slept.

There was no light when I was woken up by the noise of several things on the altar dropping one after another. Nothing could be seen as there was not a glimmer of light anywhere. I sweated, held my breath and became rigid. Then I felt the weight of something stepping on the blankets over my feet. It seemed to pace over me for ages. It even began to make a low hissing sound. It got inside the blanket, near my feet. I could feel a hot and moist sensation against my legs, as it squirmed its way up.

I realized at that moment that my bed was being invaded by a horde of snakes. I lay paralysed. The whole of my legs below the knees felt clammy with sweat and the oozy snakes wriggling against my legs. My legs became increasingly runny. I slowly moved both my hands to feel my wet knees and drew them back full of a jelly-like substance which later turned out to be blood.

My courage snapped suddenly and I shouted and jumped out of bed and groped towards the altar to light a butter lamp. I lit the lamp and in the flickering light, I saw something long and black bounce off the altar and fly across the room. Yelling, I ran to the room where my parents were sleeping.

We came back immediately to probe into the scene of my nightmare. Between my blood stained blankets and mattress were six freshly littered kittens. The long and black flying object was our own black cat.

When I was about ten years old, our house was rebuilt. On one of his regular visits to our house, my grand father, Yeshey Namgyel, promised support for the reconstruction which took place in 1938. It was rebuilt by two master carpenters - Ura Chimi and Pangkhar Nimala - and mason Nado. Chimi was keen to have a house with a facade done in wood carvings and paintings, and I was employed to do engravings in wood for him during the period of construction. I had my first wood work lessons from him. Our old three storeyed house was replaced by a two storeyed one. It took five months to build even with the contribution of labour from the villagers. The villagers very often took turns in providing food for the labourers. Our family had to provide the chief mason and chief carpenter the standard payment in-kind, which consisted of a lagho (gho to replace the one worn during work), a drupgho (gho given when the work was completed), and a replacement set of their tools.

The eldest of the three children, I was born on 1 February, 1928. I had a sister and a brother. In her bloom, my sister was known for her beauty uncommon in such a village. As a child, I was unusually fond of making idols and torma (ritual offerings) moulded out of clay and dough. I was told that as a child I was equally obsessed with painting, drawing and mask dances. My interest in carving, mask dance, painting and tailoring were to grow more intense as the years went by.

Looking back, I think that my career would have followed these particular gifts, had my life not held in store so many twists and turns. It used to be said that my talents in such things were learnt not from my parents and teachers, but transmitted from my previous life. It could not have come from my father; he was good at only stitching and rituals. Along with other indicators, it was my unusual interest at an early age in painting, drawing, mask dances and idol making that marked me as the incarnation of Lama Chokey Dorji of

Wamtshespa, a place for meditation above the Ura valley. In 1932, when I was about five years old, I was installed as its lama.

Wamtshespa became only a token spiritual home for me, for I could not stay there. My life was to lead me away from that place. Nevertheless, soon after I was accredited as its lama, I began to receive my tuition from one of my two uncles - Jigme - who lived in the retreat located on the rocky cliff of Somthrang, which looked down on the valley of Ura. My early training was to prepare me for my vocation as the reincarnation of Lama Chokey Dorji. My uncle had over a dozen followers of various ages with whom I spent two years. After teaching us for two years, my uncle left for Kurtoe Waiwai. A marriage had been arranged for him.

My father taught me after my uncle left. But my father and I visited him almost every winter, mainly to collect some food grains during our annual rounds for alms. Going to Kurtoe in winter settled into a pattern, and the alms round made our food stock both adequate and varied. The distance between Shingkhar and Waiwai was very vast. Only the thought of getting some free rice and maize from uncle Jigme spurred us on the trip. It took a week to trek to Waiwai, which stood very close to the Tibetan frontier. Both Kurtoe and Zhongar (now Monggar) were our economic hinterland, where the priests of our village and my family gathered a good amount of rice, maize and chillies each winter.

My father and his gomchens (priests) had a license for the alms round from the zongpons (fort governors) of both Kurtoe and Zhongar. As winter approached, the people of Bumthang would fan out over wide areas of Kurtoe and Zhongar to collect additional foodstuffs. Buckwheat, for which I had a strong dislike, was the staple food in our house. Despite the lack of rice at home, I had an unusual weakness for it. My mother frequently cooked rice for me and when the stock (which was a pittance), ran out, I had karchey (flour made out of roasted wheat). Though buckwheat was the staple diet of all the central Bhutanese, none of the families in Shingkhar in those days could produce enough buckwheat or wheat to last throughout the year.

In the summer of 1940, an initiation sermon on Kanjur was held in Kurje in Jakar by a Tibetan lama. Over a thousand people might have congregated there in the meadows of Kurje for four to five months in sunny, autumnal weather. A select group of people asked the Tibetan lama who conducted the initiation ceremony for an initiation into Kanjur Rochute (the essence of Kanjur).

They listened carefully to his confident effusions of inspired wisdom. One person, among the small audience, was discerning enough to find that his chants were spurious; they did not sound like the usual ones. He suspected that he might not be genuine but he could not be so bold to say aloud what he thought of him, for in the tantric setting of Bhutan, the magical and mystical priest can emerge in all moulds of personality. The lama could barely read, but he held back his suspicion that the faithful audience had become the victims of mass deception by a counterfeit lama, whose fame and reputation among the believers rose by the day.

Immediately after the lama's public initiation on Kanjur, the community of Ura invited him to their village. The lama, also an exorcist, said that he had seen in a vision that the sacred grove on the edge of village was haunted by a hostile spirit who was the cause of sickness and death in the village. He set forth, with the cooperation of the villagers, to destroy this spirit. He blessed the brawny men and spiritually empowered them to hack the old trees. Within hours, the dark and green alpine grove next to the village was decimated. He then set fire to the whole area, and from somewhere underneath a tree pulled out the embodiment of the malevolent spirit. Keeping a safe distance from the observers, he shook it vigorously. It looked very much like a mangled chicken. It might have been a dead sparrow whose feathers had been hastily plucked and hidden. An ancient grove was scorched to look for the dead chick, which he had hidden there before.

He ordered the destruction of several mausoleum-like structures (Lu) in the village. Instead of averting sickness, as foretold by the lama, this destruction caused more of it. The incidence of sickness was on the rise, and they restored these structures in their original locations after the lama left. This wandering lama, a Tibetan, had an impressive set of liturgical articles with seven monks as his close disciples. People later came to hear that he had robbed and killed another lama in Tibet to equip himself, and that the seven monks were not his disciples but his partners in crime.

After his successful visit to Bhutan he travelled to Nepal. He took more daring miracles on himself and, by then, became confident enough to extract hidden treasures. It is believed that there are certain type of religious objects like books, statues and instruments, which are kept protected for posterity in rocks, lakes, rivers beds and high mountains. These sacred goods can be discovered and extracted by pre-ordained discoverers. The Tibetan lama aspired to that role when he reached Nepal. It was said that he dived into a lake in Nepal to discover some hidden treasure he predicted could be found. He had admirable physical courage and audacity. But, not being very aquatic, he drowned himself and so he met his ignominious end. His mortal remains might still be at the bottom of that cold lake, like pieces of wreckage, after misadventure, on the bed of a sea.

Once my father, myself and four of his disciples were about to go on an alms trip to Waiwai and to other villages in Kurtoe. As I remember, I was then about nine years old. My father got an eye infection only days before we were about to leave. I had to substitute as his emissary in order to raise a substantial stock of grains and chillies. So my father's four priest-proteges, led unexpectedly by an nine year boy, left on this serious mission. During the journey it became evident that I had caught the same eye infection. Along the way, my eyes became a disgusting sight.

In every village in lower Kurtoe, my father had his traditional hosts and we went to stay with them. Whenever our party approached a village, one of the priests would blow the bone trumpet loud enough from a high vantage point to be heard by our host. He would then go ahead to inform the host of our impending arrival, in particular about the young lama - me - who was leading the group. In this case, since my father could not come, the priest who went ahead tried to establish my credential as son of so and so, before I made an entrance. The advance signal was to enable the host to clean and vacate a room for us and make any exalted arrangement they could to welcome us.

I could not have looked too impressive when we finally marched into the village and the house of our host. I was only around nine and my eyes were sticky, swollen, bloodshot, filled with pus and watered continuously. Moreover, I could not wash my face for several days. The whole occasion must have been an anticlimax for our host family, though its members tried to be as polite as possible. Our host stretched a tanned hide of a calf for me on which to sit and sleep. The host also made an altar for us upon which I could display any sacred ritual object I carried. I gave them a tantalizing glimpse of this sacred object, which was swathed in shreds of silk.

We gave our kind host and hostess some incense powder. The incense powder was made of many fragrant high altitude plants. Incense was an appropriate gift because it was used daily. Each family offered spring water early in the morning and burnt incense. It fumigated the chapel, and enveloped the whole house and the people with the aroma of alpine herbs at the start of their day. This gift of incense prepared by my father, and our old ties, ensured that the five of us were provided with free meals every evening, after we called it a day for grain collection.

Meeting ends was difficult for our family, without doing an alms round in Kurtoe for cereals and chillies. I had to aim at collecting at least one hundred and sixty dres (1.67 kg per dre) of paddy. We went to every house, as my father's group had been doing every winter; some gave us a cupful of paddy, while others gave us a little more. When we came up to the doorstep of each house, we began a resonant chant, accompanied by beat of tangti (small hand drum), extolling the virtues of transcendental generosity. At the door, when the householders came out with some grains, I was quickly introduced as my father's ambassador, to arouse greater generosity. It did not always have the desired effect. Most households doled out a phuta (333 grams) of paddy to each of us, though I would usually get a little more than others. At the end of my tour, I accumulated four back loads of rice. My father would have collected a greater amount. The loads were transported by four priests who had to do the trip twice, once for their own grain and a second time to get mine, for each segment of the road. It lengthened our return trip by about eleven days.

When I was about thirteen, I spent a summer with my father in retreat in Somthrang. The place gave us solitude which was conducive to memorizing essential texts and prayers. I had by then memorized a number of liturgical prayers and grammar texts. I did not follow all the obscure meanings of the texts I recited every morning and evening. But, the memorization of a mass of basic texts made them a part of my mental world; a collection of texts had been internalized for reference. As I grew older, all the memorized texts began to exert a sublimated but continuous influence on my attitudes and language as I revisited the texts effortlessly again and again. I was also trained to play a variety of liturgical instruments and recognize a pantheon of statues and figures on wall paintings.

The following winter, I and my father left for Kurtoe and Tsamang in Monggar. On our way back through Ongar, I got sick and fell into a coma. I was carried on a hand-made stretcher by four men to Zhongmay, still unconscious. When I got slightly better, I was carried on the backs of various people to our home to get treatment from an indigenous doctor. My hair fell rapidly and I became completely bald; a few follicles of hair stood as I convalesced at home. The illness is now diagnosed as typhoid.

One winter, my father and I were in Ganglapokto in Zhongar on our alms round. My father's brother, Uncle Sonam Tenzin, a court attendant, visited us one evening in our camp. My uncle was on his way, by royal command, further east to buy lac from the farmers and sell it at higher prices in Guwahati, the source of merchandise imports to Bhutan. It was the last time I saw my uncle, for he did not reappear again in Bhutan. His companion returned without him.

Things were soon to change forever as a result of his flight. He had abandoned his service, and his next of kin was accountable to the court. So my father and my mother went to the palace of Wangdecholing to give an explanation. For many weeks, there was no decision on whether to overlook his flight, because the royal family was preoccupied with the public benediction given by His Holiness the XVI Karmapa who was on a visit to Bhutan. Only after the return of the Karmapa to Tibet was a pardon granted to my parents for the disappearance of my uncle.

What caused my uncle's voluntary emigration we shall never know, beyond the belief that he did it to avoid a possible censure and punishment over some unacceptable behaviour concerning amorous affairs, and debt to a few people which he thought he would not ever be able to repay. He never reported back after his trip to Guwahati, India. His sudden flight, from the rank of attendants, to another country became a matter of regret for the family and a highly discourteous behaviour for the court. But the clemency was conditional: my younger brother and I must become retainers to fill his place. Substitutes were required, and as my uncle did not have any male issue, my younger brother and I were summoned to join the rank of innumerable retainers. Retainers were drawn from elite and well established families. Conscription of retainers on a hereditary basis from such households ensured their inexhaustible supply.

2

SUMMONED TO WANGDECHOLING PALACE

At the height of summer of 1944, a messenger of the court arrived in my village to take me and my younger brother as retainers. My younger brother and I thus began to prepare to go to Wangdecholing to become lowly retainers - tozep (attendants who were entitled to food from the common kitchen). I was sixteen and my brother had turned twelve.

There was much sighing and solemn words from our neighbours and villagers on the eve of our departure for Wangdecholing. As the day for my departure came close, they came to see us, each bringing some amount of the best food items they had: sun dried vegetables like slices of shrivelled pumpkin and radish; araa, buckwheat flour, wheat flour, rice, roasted and puffed rice, maize bran, butter, dried mushrooms, cheese, eggs and dried meat. Over rounds of butter tea followed by rounds of heated araa around the big mud stove, they contemplated our new occupation among the retainers and comforted my mother who was very anxious. The life of a retainer was associated strongly with discipline, etiquette and harsh regimentation. Retainers were expected to develop a sense of unswerving loyalty. Their ideal was to perform duties as the religious struggle for their faith. The duties of a retainer were conflated with the accomplishment of a seeker of religious truth.

Some people considered it a privilege to become retainer. Fortunate retainers expected to become high officials in due course. As I later discovered, many men of distinguished families of Western Bhutan chose to become retainers in the court. Their personal wealth was hardly in question and they had servants waiting on them even while they waited on the King. Having a man from the family in the court provided an added measure of standing in the society for the family members at home. It gave the family members some tacit protection against the possible rapacity of local officials and heightened the authority of the family to keep a hold on their serfs and tenants.

Some of my friends with whom I had been tutored or had together tended domestic animals invited me for meals to their houses. After meals, my friends, including girls, sang songs with brisk dances into the grey hours. I distinctly remember the girls finishing off with a particularly haunting dance. The meaning of the song, as I look back now, seemed to have resonance in my own life:

You are the high sky, I am the radiant sun.
The sky and the sun,
I wondered whether the twain shall meet
Or whether the twain shall come across each other.
We found each other, Tshering, once again today,
Ah, destined by the force of our previous lives.
No! we are not meeting to make good
The remains of deeds from our previous lives,
But because we have been comrades in dharma from immemorial times.

SUMMONED TO WANGDECHOLING PALACE

You are the snow bound mountain, I am the great white lion.
The mountain and the lion,
I wondered whether the twain shall meet
Or whether the twain shall come across each other.
We found each other, Tshering, once again today,
Ah, destined by the force of our previous lives.
No! we are not meeting to make good
The remains of deeds from our previous lives,
But because we have been comrades in dharma from
immemorial times.

You are the alpine meadow, I am the ten antlered stag.
The meadow and the stag,
I wondered whether the twain shall meet
Or whether the twain shall come across each other.
We found each other, Tshering, once again today,
Ah, destined by the force of our previous lives.
No! we are not meeting to make good
The remains of deeds from our previous lives,
But because we have been comrades in dharma from
immemorial times.

You are the wide corn field, I am the white dove.
The field and the dove,
I wondered whether the twain shall meet
Or whether the twain shall come across each other.
We found each other, Tshering, once again today,
Ah, destined by the force of our previous lives.

No! we are not meeting to make good
The remains of deeds from our previous lives,
But because we have been comrades in dharma from immemorial times.

As I now dwell on it, the folk song is an evocative declaration of love and constancy, for which there is an enormous longing, in any relationship. It describes the shattering feeling when we meet a special person. It was composed in the medieval age in a searing circumstance by a woman of western Bhutan. She married a retainer who soon left for central Bhutan on the call of duty. He promised to return to her very soon, but his absence cast a pall of gloom on her days. Her waiting and longing for him lengthened into years and with each passing year, her hope only became stronger. It had lingered on in vain. When at last she got some news about him, it was only to be told that he had remarried someone else from central Bhutan. Heart broken, she renounced the life she led and left for Tibet to become a nun. Decades later, in her old age, she returned to her country and went on an alms round from door to door in central Bhutan. Unknown to her, one of the houses she went into, turned out to be the house of her previous husband. He was now a shadow of his former self though she recognized him at once. But he did not recognize her, an old nun. She stayed for a while in the village. The New Year came, and on the day of celebration, he invited her to sing a song. The same song was sung to me by the girls of my village on this touching occasion.

The next day, which happened to be in the seventh Bhutanese month, we began our trip to Wangdecholing with a few porters. My father accompanied us. We closely followed the burdened men who carried our stock of food and cloth. They were rough-clad and had worn their dress to the thread, and had sewn on many patches, typical of people in the village in those days. Their gho was variegated with patches of different textiles and colours. Yet the colours were not visible because of overlaying grease and grime. None of us had shoes, although the track was muddy and strewn with splinters, blades of strong grass and twigs. The splayed feet of other men looked almost moulded out of steel in their ability to stamp on any injurious surface. Their gigantic toes spread like claws. They stepped over sharp gravel, mud and heaps of horse droppings lying at regular intervals on the track. Flies hummed around, disturbed by the feet that brushed aside the droppings. We took a narrow foot path, winding through the undulating slopes of buckwheat. Wheat had just been harvested, and buckwheat was ripening. Buckwheat was a crop which occupied the less productive land owned by our village. Further away from the foot path, almost erased by the encroaching growth, in the fallow meadows and young alpine stands, browsed herds of cattle, horses and sheep, half submerged in the green of bracken and thickets.

A little distance away from the foot path, around a depression in the meadow, were a group of youngsters who tended animals. As usual, they were absorbed in some home-grown game and were oblivious to the animals straying into the fields of buckwheat and wheat. A closer inspection of the game would have revealed that the boys were hauling out tadpoles from a puddle formed by rain which fell overnight. The children revelled in handling them. When the girls were unaware, the boys slipped squirmy tadpoles inside the kira collars of the girls. In mock surprise and fear, the girls screamed a bit and began to unbutton their upper part of the dress, as they dislodged the tadpoles.

As we trekked our way through grasslands, we saw other groups of children herding the animals, already gathered in a circle on the turf. Although it was quite early in the day, we noticed that they could not resist unfolding their lunch packs and making an early lunch. These usually consisted of roasted black barley or crusty loafs of buckwheat with thick chilly sauce. I watched them, my friends, play and eat. I felt a tinge of envy come over me as I vaguely felt at that moment that my unfettered boyhood was at an abrupt end. I was to enter into the severe discipline of a court retainer.

Within half an hour of our departure from my village of Shingkhar, we crossed into the extraordinarily spacious and open valley of Ura, the village of my mother's parents. Two hours later, we ascended the mountain of Korilla, stopping so often in the deep shade of fir trees, not so much to rest as to look back towards Shingkhar where I had mentally remained. The sides of the Korilla mountains were sparsely clad with pine, fir, larch and spruce. As we progressed higher up the lofty pass, light clouds glided past us.

Descending on the other side of Korilla, we saw the village of Tangsibi which was situated way down in the valley. It was much later than mid-day when we decided to have our lunches at a spot used by all travellers, from where the fort of Jakar and Wangdecholing Palace were visible as white specks against grassy plains. We renewed our journey and soon advanced to the wooden bridge over Tangchu (Tang River), which joined the Chamkharchu (Chamkhar River) a few kilometres downstream.

SUMMONED TO WANGDECHOLING PALACE

Very soon, the Choskhor valley opened to our views. We walked for a few hours up the right side of the river and approached Wangdecholing. The afternoon blast of wind, for which this part of Choskhor valley is known, started to wail through the valley. As the wind swept me from behind, I felt my stride go out of control and depend occasionally on the vagaries of the strong currents of wind. I was getting very worn out by walking, and my brother was so languid that he began to drag his feet heavily.

On our way into the village, we passed the paper factory next to the stream. The paper factory was built on purpose as an annex to a large compacted mud enclosure for oxen. The inner and outer surfaces of the mud walls were unusually even and were being used to dry hundreds of sheets of paper at a time. A group of men and women were busy taking these sheets off the wall and packing so that they could hand the bundles of paper every evening to the stationery store in the palace of Wangdecholing.

At dusk, we walked into the villages which stood outside the ramparts and tall tree hedges around the palace of Wangdecholing. I thought that a towering building loomed nearby the river. On closer observation, it turned out to be a gigantic firewood dump from which, as I found out later, firewood was issued for use around the palace. Firewood was neatly stacked as high as a tall two storey building and equally as wide. I had never seen such a collection of firewood and I could not help being amazed. But the rate at which firewood was used was also incredible as hundreds of retainers and the common kitchen were provided with the wood.

The palace of Wangdecholing had a vast array of permanent retainers: there were over hundred and fifty changgaps (butlers, valets, conveyers of orders or men in waiting), five or so kadreps (conversation companions), forty chandaaps (security squad), fifteen chashumi (personal aides), a hundred or so zingaps (menial task force), twenty silver smiths, twenty stable men or liveries (adungs), five cooks in the common kitchen and three chefs (solyoks) in His Majesty's kitchen. There was a batch of Western style soldiers, of which the highest was Zamadar Chencho, trained in Shillong. There was also a group of twelve soldiers, mostly from Kheng, who formed a brass band, led by Aku Tongmay, who played bagpipes, coronets and bass drums. The succeeding batch of soldiers, all subordinate to Zamadar Chencho, included Dungkar Namgay (later Brigadier Namgay), Khenchong, Chado, Samtenlingpa and Menji Namjay.

In addition to the aforementioned number of people, there were some thirty blacksmiths and thirty weavers. For part of the year, there were about three hundred pangoleng garpa, who came from all over eastern Bhutan to break the sod for buckwheat cultivation. Among the various classes of retainers, the changgaps (butlers, valets, conveyors of orders and men in waiting) were a select group. Some of them were men of well to do families but most rose so high because of their proven ability and appealing personality. The most impressive looking were the fifteen or so chashumi (personal aides). Because of various tasks such as propping up the King when he got on a horse or walked downhill, they had to be extremely tall and strong.

The presence of a large number of people in service at the palace meant that the surrounding villages were full of people. The villages not only had to offer places for the permanent retainers to stay, but there were also visitors coming to the palace from all over the country and they had to find accommodation. So the guests and travellers would take up temporary residence, though a little far away, in many villages scattered through the valley. It was difficult to find a place to board in the village next to the palace, consisting of about thirty houses made of a large quantity of timber and compacted mud. Every spare room, every hut and every decent attic was occupied by the retainers who worked during the day in the palace. Many retainers built huts made out of bamboo nettings as the villages ran out of rooms to spare.

3

EARLY YEARS AS A RETAINER

My father had an acquaintance, a kind, childless widow in the village just outside the rampart of the palace, and had arranged for me to stay in her house. Whenever I was in Wangdecholing, she put me up in her cramped storeroom, and I slept in the midst of wooden shelves, wooden boxes and baskets containing buckwheat and wheat flour, dry mushrooms and chillies, mature cheese and butter. Chunks of dry beef and bones hung by a string and dangled dangerously over my sleeping place. I was to sleep in this inner sanctum of her possessions during many years of my work in Wangdecholing Palace, unmindful of her coming and going to get edibles even in the middle of night. Many months after my arrival in Wangdecholing, I began to sense that she sometimes considered me as her foster son.

A day after we reached Wangdecholing, an attendant informed us that my younger brother and I would be presented to the King the next morning as tozeps - the lowest level among the retainers allowed access to food from the common kitchen.

My father accompanied both of us to the northern gate of the palace. The gate keeper did not allow us to enter any further. Although it was just after daybreak, a large number of people had gathered there to go in and call on the King. The gate-keeper queried the purpose of their visits, and in turn went in to inform a chashumi.

The chashumi on duty came to the gate to allow in those who could call on the King.

My father offered both the gate keeper and the chashumi a cup of araa each, which seemed to make them more well disposed towards us. After we got inside the palace premises, we were on our own among a vast group of people seeking audience. We stood in a single file in the courtyard and were escorted in, turn by turn. Toward the middle of the day, my brother and I found ourselves at the beginning of a column, which glancing back I found, had become as long as it was in the morning by more visitors joining its tail.

As we were about to be presented, a chashumi asked us if we were familiar with the formalities of bowing and prostrations. We were first led up the ladder to a long rectangular room in the second floor. I began to tremble with fear and nervousness as soon as I was in sight of many zingaps sitting in two long lines. My brother and I stood in front of them. After some time, a man gripped our arms and lead us to another door. As we entered that room, there was another crowd of imposing looking men - chandaaps (security men) and chashumis - sitting in three long lines in pillared recesses. Against the walls behind these men, I noticed a formidable set of whips, canes and rods of all shapes and sizes, with which I came into contact quite frequently later. We were led across this room to another one inside. This time I certainly expected it to be the chamber of the King. We were feeling quite lost, and more and more unsure of the surroundings. Yet again, it was a room full of changgaps who unlike in the other two rooms had swords at their sides. It was getting more petrifying for both of us. There was a fourth room to be crossed. Finally, a young man, also without wearing shoes, who stood by the door to the fifth room drew the door curtain and whispered to someone to usher us in. That was, as I later found out, Crown Prince Dasho Jigme Dorji Wangchuck.

I found later that the relationship between the King and his son Dasho Jigme was loving but also uncompromising as far as duties of the Crown Prince was concerned. Dasho Jigme was expected to perform all the mundane work of an ordinary changgap. He was rarely given any princely privilege. He was forbidden to wear shoes, as were all other retainers in the palace, and he was commanded, like many other attendants, to arbitrate disputes. Dasho Jigme was faithful to the wishes and commands of his father and regarded them as divine.

At his murmured signal, a changgap behind us stuck his finger at my ribs and pushed me in and we suddenly found ourselves in the presence of the King. As soon as we crossed the threshold of the chamber, I was presented to His Majesty. As was customary, we immediately performed three prostrations and made the offerings of a cane of araa and a single silver coin known as betam in front of the throne. The offering of a silver coin, which had replaced the earlier offerings of three copper coins (zangtam), was a token of my registration as a tozep.

The event was so momentary that I can not recall anything except my own nervousness about it and a glimpse of a person in a black silk gho. The silver coin was returned to a retainer who might later be dismissed for some reason. In the next moment, we found ourselves bowing out.

I can still hear His Majesty's resonant voice as we were going out. He said, "Let him be with Jigme." I was thus assigned to be with a senior attendant to Dasho Jigme. As soon as we came out in the courtyard, a senior attendant told me that I was to be deployed anywhere at the behest of the senior attendant to Dasho Jigme. My younger brother was relieved on account of his unsuitable age, and he and my father left for home.

A few days later, the senior attendant, who was my taskmaster, sent me to Kurje to help the painters of the shrine. I was paid a standard monthly allowance of a tozep while out of station: ten phuta (measure of volume approximately equivalent to 333 gm) of rice, ten phuta of wheat flour, 1.25 kg of butter, some dry chillies and a roll of dry meat, on which to subsist. But there were three hundred other pangoleng garpas who were entitled only to buckwheat flour.

The nature of my work and the hardship of my station, which can be gathered from my lowly position, contrasted strongly with my past comfort and the dignity of an heir to a lamaist estate. I was given a role I had never been brought up to assume.

The first job I was given indicated the difficulty I was going to experience, and made me realize forcefully that my ritualistic training was of no value in my new occupation. I was sent to Kurje where the temple was being restored. My task was to boil cattle skin, day after day, to make hide glue out of it. I collected firewood, which was not found nearby, and water. I woke up extremely early in the morning to get the fire going under the huge vessel of water with an ox skin in it. I tossed wood into the fire and kept it going throughout the day. The vile smell of the disintegrating hide permeated my room and my cloth.

After two days of continual cooking, the hide dissolved

indistinguishably in the water and became glutinous and transparent. The fresco painters of Kurje temple added it frequently to the paint as a thinner and medium. They asked me incessantly for hot water to clean their brushes and to clean their mixing containers. I was shouted at frequently and told to throw away dirt and clean the place. I ran frantically around.

After a week, the monotonous grimness of the work made me feel overworked, gloomy and homesick. I was both physically and psychologically unable to continue. Unable to go on, I sent desperate messages to my parents in Shingkhar. My father came to my rescue the next day, and instigated me to go to the chief attendant for leave with the usual pretext that my mother was critically ill. I returned home on leave after transferring the remains of my monthly ration to someone else who substituted for me.

I returned to Wangdecholing to a change of responsibility. My father was able to persuade the chief attendant to include me among a select group of boys consisting of Drepong Kota, Sangye Penjor, Kunzang Dorji, Kurtoe Thinley, Phub Dorji and Sangay Rinchen, to study for half a year or so the basics of secretarial grammar including composition, comprehension and calligraphy in Chumey with Lopon Norbu Wangchuck, a monk who also served as a secretary to the Elder Queen in Domkhar. I was given the opportunity to join the group in order to become part of the clerical staff in the palace. The court sponsored my secretarial training. After seven months of strengthening my clerical skills with Lopon Norbu Wangchuck, I returned to Wangdecholing and became one of the youngest of the six members of court clerical staff or secretaries, a job which was considered more befitting my birth and lineage.

Soon after I joined the court as a clerk, I got an idea of a typical day in His Majesty's life. His Majesty went to bed around 10 o'clock or later and got up early. As soon as the chamber closed, His Majesty slipped into a silk gown with chopped silk filling that would partially shield him in the event of a sword attack. This device was worn particularly when he slept in the dzongs on formal occasions. Their Majesties retired into an enclosure of cloth blinds within the chamber.

Early in the morning, following a short burst of wake up jaling (a clarinet like musical instrument), Their Majesties were served a cup of boiled water each. The door of the chamber remained closed after letting in the person who served boiled water. It would open only after Their Majesties got dressed and His Majesty put on his sword, which he kept on till he went to bed.

The day began with the opening of the door of the chamber, which also served as the audience room. This meant that all the attendants, secretaries and courtiers had to be in waiting. Immediately after opening the chamber door at around 6.30 am, the court astrologer presented his report for the day. After he bowed out, morning tea with rice and zaw (granules of sizzled rice) were served. Five mandatory cups of tea, interspersed with rice and zaw, were served, and one had to accept this fixed quantity. Kadreps would join in the morning tea.

After the morning tea, either dronyer (guest master) or a changgap reported the number of people who would be calling in the course of the day, with precise details about their greeting gifts and offerings. A meal was served at around 8.30 am, preceded by a bout of soulful jaling.

Around 9 am, the brass band came marching into the courtyard and struck up 'God Save Our Gracious King.' His Majesty got up and held his coronet high, even if he was in the midst of his meal. Their Majesties followed suit. Kadreps like Naap Sangay and Mahaguru had to likewise stand up and look solemn, with a mouthful of half-chewed rice and curry.

There was a mid-day snack, consisting of some dozen dishes, around 11 am; tea at 4 pm; dinner at 9 pm; and rice porridge with mince meat thrown in at bedtime. The leftover dishes were distributed among the attendants in a systematic way. The excess of the first morning tea was left for the stable boys. Leftovers of tea and snacks, if any, served between the first morning tea and the snack lunch were the entitlements of the changgaps. A number of people who came to call on His Majesty brought along tea and snacks to be served. The leftovers were given to the chashumis. Lastly, the surplus food prepared for dinner was left always for the zingaps.

There were five secretaries in the court. The secretaries, who were to become my friends and mentors, were Lopon Kelzang Dawa, Thinley, Sonam Penjor, Tangsibi Kesang and Yeshey Wangdi. Sonam Penjor was the oldest amongst us.

Both Tangsibi Kesang and Sonam Penjor were attendants of Ashi Wangmo, younger sister of His Majesty, and they came to work in the secretarial team when she left for Tibet to become a nun. Tangsibi Kesang was more of an astrologer by training than a court secretary, but he spoke well and stood out because of his fair complexion, good looks and size. Although he was one of us junior secretaries, he had already a successful air of self-importance. I recall quite clearly that he often mingled freely with important courtiers and sat quite close to them, something I could not dare during those days. As Tangsibi Kesang was not trained as a court secretary, he was more active in other fields. He was sent on bangchen missions (missions to levy penalty or fines to different parts of the country), and settled disputes that came to the court.

Bangchen missions were very rewarding for the changgap, as he could demand textiles, food stuffs, money and even horses and cows from the host against whom bangchen was directed. Bangchens went to the victim's house with purposeful conceit and frightful vanity. Some intentionally put their swords horizontally across their waists so that they would not be able to enter through the narrow door of a village house. The housewife and other hosts then made a fuss to welcome the bangchen, often with a gift of money or textiles at the door. Such generosity enabled him to adjust his sword so that he could enter.

A slight shortfall or excess of salt in the butter tea or curry provoked their anger and rejection of the food. A bangchen garpa complained against the inappropriate temperature of the cuisine, another pretext to harass the host or hostess against whom the bangchen garpa was directed. A number of favourite changgaps were sent on bangchen missions against people, particularly wealthy families, who had trodden on royal sentiments, exceeded their authority, or had breached the customary law.

Bangchen missions were treated with the utmost deference and hospitality during their long stay. As a final gesture during their departure they demanded mules, cows, textiles, food grains and money from their hosts. Most of these things became personal, windfall gains for the members of a bangchen mission. The untrammelled display of power by a bangchen mission made it humiliatingly clear to the hosts that no one is lord in their own house. The dividing line between the privacy of ones' own home and the state disappeared completely when a bangchen mission was imposed.

Sonam Penjor was already over fifty when I joined the secretarial team in Wangdecholing. He had an unusually gaunt and angular look. Although not very big, he was somehow quite unwieldy in his movements. He was too honest and forthright to understand the nuances that ought to be present while drafting court circulars and was frequently corrected despite his age. Once he was not mindful enough to take the most painless posture while being thrashed. He could not withstand the pain, even after a few strokes, and let out a fearful bellow: "I am dying, I am dying." Etiquette demanded that one be very stoic and not shriek in such a manner. When Sonam Penjor screamed with such abandon, everyone could not help laughing. He was never punished again. In fact, after this incident, he was not required to come for duty like the other secretaries, and he was allocated the leisurely job of hand copying the Epic of Gesar and similar books.

His Majesty had a considerable liking for Yeshey Wangdi, who was once a class mate of Crown Prince Jigme and now a junior clerk. He was always known to His Majesty by his nickname, Churey Cheo (forehead of river stone), because of his formidable looking, frontal baldness. In his ringing voice that reverberated along the corridors, His Majesty could be often heard calling 'Churey Cheo, Churey Cheo'. When I joined the secretarial team, Yeshey Wangdi had already come to acquire a taste for a high dose of good araa, a trait which at that time was also shared by Lopon Thinley, Mahaguru and several others in the court. As His Majesty looked very kindly on Yeshey Wangdi, he was frequently assigned to settle disputes and sent often on bangchen missions to levy and collect fines and penalties.

Thinley was not a batch mate of the second King, but was among the next batch of students. He was not in Thinley Rabden school for as many years as other students, but he was well brought up in indigenous scholarship by his learned father Zhongar Zongpon Tshewang Penjor. Therefore, when he joined the court service, he could draft well, an art which he constantly refined and polished as an ardent pupil of Lopon Kelzang Dawa, the chief secretary. I recall that when I first joined the secretarial team, Thinley, then known as Dungyik (clerk) Thinley, was considered the most capable secretary after Lopon Kelzang Dawa. He sang well and also enjoyed araa, like many others in the court, to the point of having to rest for a few days to recover. But he gave up drinking around 1947 or 1948, as the weight of his responsibilities grew, and as Lopon Kelzang Dawa himself started to drink, vexed by a growing darkness in his personal life. The title of lopon came to be prefixed increasingly to Thinley's name as much as Lopon Kelzang Dawa.

Lopon Thinley had the greatest respect and deference for Lopon Kelzang Dawa, who was a multifaceted man. I remember that Lopon Thinley used to forbid us and the attendants to walk noisily, if Lopon Kelzang Dawa happened to snooze a little in the antechamber. He visited Lopon Kelzang Dawa whenever he was unwell.

Of all the people in the court of the second King, none was as illustrious as Lopon Kelzang Dawa. Lopon Kelzang Dawa, son of the learned lama Penden of Geden, was chosen by King Ugyen Wangchuck to study in Thinley Rabden above Wangdecholing with King Jigme Wangchuck, then the Crown Prince. They were pupils of Haap Phentok, who later became Pasa Kutshab (Governor of Pasakha, now Phuntsholing) and died as its incumbent. Lopon Kelzang Dawa was the most brilliant of the lot. From the same batch, several other pupils, such as Jampa Wangdi, Babu Nakchung and Phajo, were retained, after their schooling, as attendants to the second King. Phajo was clownish, acrobatic, witty and agile and could leap from one running horse to another in the meadows of Kurje.

Though His Majesty, then the Crown Prince, was younger by many years, he had high regards for Kelzang Dawa since their days together as students in Thinley Rabden. Moreover, Kelzang Dawa was well educated in indigenous tradition, having been tutored by his father, a lama, as well as Dangdung Pem Tshering. Thus, it was natural for him to become the chief secretary and confidant when Jigme Wangchuck acceded to the throne. Kelzang became a trusted counsel in addition to being impeccably loyal, erudite, able, eloquent and inscrutable. When I joined the secretarial team, Lopon Kelzang Dawa was already powerful and reputed, even though he had no red scarf. That was, of course, not unusual, because no one in the court had a red scarf except Dasho Dronyer Naku, the younger brother of His Majesty. When Dasho Dronyer Naku died, the Crown Prince Jigme was appointed as Dronyer (Chief of Protocol or Guest Master), and then he was the only one with a red scarf around the palace.

Although Lopon Kelzang was never honoured with a red scarf by the second King, there were, in my opinion, only two other personalities in the country whose reputation and prestige were comparable to his: Paro Penlop Tshering Penjor and Gongzim (Chamberlain to the King) Sonam Tobgye. Gongzim had great deference for the King, and the King reciprocated it in equal measure. Gongzim was addressed as "phogema" (elder brother) in letters, and as Gongzim at other times.

Officials who were formally more distinguished than Kelzang Dawa came to call on him in the evening at his house. On those occasions, he would get up and receive them at the door before inviting them for discussions. Each evening after work in the palace, we, the other secretaries, including Lopon Thinley, took turns waiting on Lopon Kelzang Dawa.

Most of the time, Lopon Kelzang Dawa worked in his office in the top floor of the South-Eastern Wing of the palace. But sometimes, he sat, with an aura of serenity and calm, by the far window of the commodious antechamber. Lopon Kelzang Dawa kept a big moustache. He was exceptionally fair complexioned with an angular face propped up on a slender body that stood on rather thin, long legs. The commotion around the antechamber created by attendants and visitors walking in and out hardly distracted him when he sat by the window. He seemed not to pay much attention to the coming and going, although he could later recount the happenings with precise detail. He had been observant without appearing so.

He went into the chamber only when he was asked for specifically. I recall that he would not be in a hurry to go in when he was asked. He would first brush down his handlebar moustache which was usually turned fiercely upwards. He would then ponderously brush and dust off his gho before he went in. As he was about to enter the chamber, he would arch his upper body towards the front, draw his chin against his chest and walk with the crown of his head in the direction of His Majesty. Once inside, His Majesty and Lopon Kelzang Dawa always discussed things in Hindi. Lopon Kelzang Dawa could be heard uttering a stream of "haa ji, haa ji, haa ji, haa ji, haa haa ji, haa, haa, haa, haa ji, ji,..." (yes sir, yes sir, yes sir, yes sir, yes yes sir, yes, yes, yes, yes sir).

The King addressed all his favourites by nicknames he invented. I was known as Molotov. I never knew what or who Molotov was until the mid-sixties and vaguely thought of it as an amusing object. There could not have been a more obscure nickname than mine which, I was told, was the name of Stalin's foreign minister.

Sonam Penjor was Megala (one who could be better without). He was allowed to copy manuscripts on his own and did not have to report to work every day. Lopon Kelzang Dawa was known as Waadum (fox, because of his flinty mind, long face and spindly legs); Lopon Thinley as Bampuli, since he was purported to have a head like a ball. Lopon Thinley was also interchangeably known as Arabodhi as he took a lot of araa in his young days. Changgap Nagphay was known as Bep (frog) because he had a pronounced upper eyelid. Chungsep Thinley was known as Robert Clive because he was fair and had brown hair; Khemseling Kunzang as Mohammed Ghori; Khemseling Pasang Wangdi as Mohammed Ghazni; Kurtoe Menji Namgay as Homayun; Tshering as Lhaderla;

Gelong Adangpa as Goitre; Sangay Wangdi as Tsipata, the mythical mask. Thegila, the most handsome attendant of all, was generally known as Mathenla (one who had tendency to plummet lower and lower down the social ladder). Sangye Penjor was nicknamed Bamlashe as it seemed that he always wore a mask; Dasho Ugyen Wangdi was Chitshi Marm (red mouse); Darpon (Chief of attendants) Chimi was Sahib because he was as pink as a white man; Dawa Norbu was Chawchi (clown atsara in mask dance); Tangsibi Dorji was Ganapati (Hindu God with the face of an elephant). The King had a great facility for giving names to many other attendants. He also gave all the children in Wangdecholing a nickname and lavished on them food gifts, especially rice porridge once a day.

His Majesty used neither a gavel nor a bell to call the attendants. He perfected a voice signal that sounded like a bear's short and deep grunt - wooh oop - to call the attendants. There were about twenty changgaps waiting on the King every day in the antechamber. They sat cross legged with their ears perked up to listen for this sound which meant that one of them had to go in. They went turn by turn and on average, in one day, which lasted from six in the morning to ten in the evening, each changgap went in about ten times to receive and relay orders and to do odd jobs.

New attendants were sometimes perplexed when His Majesty suddenly switched to either his fluent Hindi or limited English. I remember several moments of nervous hilarity and fright when he spoke in English to the people who had never heard another language before.

Once, when the attendants heard 'wooh oop' sound, the turn fell on the young Pasang Wangdi (alias Mohammed Ghazni) to go in. His Majesty had nicknamed him Aurangzeb at one time, and then Sha Radrap (the wrathful looking guardian deity of Sha), but eventually settled for Mohammed Ghazni. Pasang Wangdi's brother, also an attendant, was known as Mohammed Ghori. Among the attendants, Pasang Wangdi was generally known as Momo Gaanji, a corrupted form of Mohammed Ghazni. Momo Gaanji, who was then a new attendant, came out of the chamber in utter panic and immediately inquired what 'bring wataar pout' meant.

At this moment, Lopon Thinley, who happened to be around, translated the phrase into dzongkha (national language) in a self congratulatory tone. His Majesty also called Momo Gaanji the 'chairman' because Pasang Wangdi minded His Majesty's chair which had to be carried back and forth between the two targets when His Majesty played archery or sat out on the lawn. His Majesty even practised English on me. I minded his stationeries and was used to being asked for his "iink pout" and "pen". His Majesty knew an extensive set of English words but he was more comfortable in Hindi which he spoke to Yeshey Wangdi, Lopon Kelzang Dawa, Lopon Thinley and Babu Tashi who responded with a torrent of "ji, ji, ji, ji, ji, ji, ji, ji,...."

After I returned from my clerical training, I found myself amidst such a disorienting linguistic world - of Hindi and English - and among such a group of knowledgeable people. All the instruments of my trade were ever on my person; in the pouch of my gho, I carried a glinting copper ink bottle, a bamboo quiver full of bamboo pens, a pen-knife to sharpen the pens and to cut bark-paper. I was apprenticed to the other senior secretaries and constantly exposed to the intricate art of drafting court letters and maintaining records.

Over the years, I learnt a great deal from my long association with Lopon Thinley, just as Lopon Thinley imbibed all the artfulness, grit and powers of Lopon Kelzang Dawa, who was then the chief secretary to the King. Thinley was with Lopon Kelzang Dawa from the days at Wangdecholing till Lopon Kelzang left for Paro as its Dzongtshab.

Later as Gaydon Thinley, the paragon of ability in the court circle, he used to often say, out of humility, that his own abilities appeared genuinely insignificant before that of Lopon Kelzang Dawa. Lopon Kelzang Dawa often drafted important Kashos (court circulars or decrees) before we made as many copies as needed. All of us were intimidated by his skill and power of articulation. As far as I remember, he drafted Kashos which needed no further change.

From my occupation as a secretary, I was to launch thousands of letters on every topic and to people in every walk of life. I was able to acquire an elegant script, the flowing style of which never deteriorated. Apt phrases and paragraphs were enhanced by my day-to-day experience. We, the five secretaries, sat in the hall on the top floor of the Palace and came down now and then to the chamber, ever poised to clothe the thoughts of our King in the most resplendent of expressions.

As the beginner among the clerks, one of my most regular tasks was to keep a ledger of daily food distribution and maintain a record of those who came to wish His Majesty well or to seek an audience. Each morning, men and women of great distinction and importance milled around the gate of the palace, waiting to call on the King, bearing gifts which ranged from a whole carcass of hog or ox, back loads of green grocery, bundles of textiles, vessels of wine, food, antiques and jewellery. We meticulously maintained a ledger of visitors and their presents. The probable worth of the presents were estimated in order for Dasho Dronyer to reciprocate the gifts in roughly equivalent value. We also recorded the daily issue of provisions and the assignments of work to the attendants. Another common task for the secretaries was writing slips authorizing someone to get a fixed quantity of goods from the stores of a certain dzong. Such slips were written and read to His Majesty before the royal maroon seal was imprinted.

The seal was zealously guarded in a box whose key was often kept near the King. It was used only with his permission. During the travels of the royal entourage, it was mostly the responsibility of either Lopon Kelzang Dawa or Lopon Thinley to carry the seal box. There was no signature on official records; all documents and letters were authenticated by the stamp of the red royal seal marked 'Choerabtsey' i.e. Trongsa. His Majesty preferred the seal of Trongsa Penlop to that of the King of Bhutan.

The seal could be easily misused if it were not guarded with the utmost vigilance. There were occasions when a secretary bent upon theft of the red seal could surreptitiously manage to impress the emblem on a blank paper while he pretended to stamp it only on a genuine circular. A small amount of graft had sustained such practices in earlier times. The blank paper became worth a lot more when it was filled with royal orders to local officials to exempt certain people from labour taxes or in-kind taxes. This was the only way that His Majesty could dispense favours of which he really did not approve or was not even aware. However, because of the severe risk such abuse carried if it was ever found out, only minor taxes of a short duration were granted exemption in this manner.

We also wrote an inundating number of letters to Tibetan high lamas and nobilities with whom the King enjoyed, in general, extremely cordial relations. He sent parcels to them very frequently and in return received letters almost every other day.

When the odd letter to British Officials and Gongzim Sonam Tobgye, who was based in Kalimpong, needed to be drafted, Babu Tashi, the tutor to the Crown Prince Jigme, wrote them. Known as Master to His Majesty, he had another regular duty besides teaching. He monitored news broadcasts and prepared a summary of news bulletin on a slate for daily briefing. Babu Tashi was quite a versatile teacher; he could read and write in Hindi, English and Dzongkha. Babu Tashi had also been tutored by well known lamas and was one of the most highly educated teachers and courtiers in those days. Babu Tashi, Phenchong, Karchung, Nakchung and Golong studied in Haa and Kalimpong. Babu Tashi then began a school in Wangdecholing and tutored two batches of students: Crown Prince Jigme's batch and later Ashi Chokie's batch. After his departure as Zongpon of Zhongar, he was replaced by Babu Chogyel.

Babu Tashi, Babu Dago, Babu Chogyel and Lopon Norbu Wangchuck were occasionally invited for morning tea with His Majesty. Lopon Norbu Wangchuck and Babu Tashi met in the antechamber both before and after the tea to resume their lively academic debate about the shape of the universe, the planetary system and the earth. Babu Tashi championed the theory that the earth is round and rotates around its axis and orbits round the sun, whereas Lopon Norbu Wangchuck's argument was based on a cosmological model found in Buddhist scriptures. Neither could convince the other fully, yet they continued to argue tenaciously whenever they met.

"The earth orbits the sun and the moon orbits the earth. The earth rotates on its own, like a mani (prayer wheel) around its axis, while it goes around the sun. The path taken by the earth around the sun is not a perfect circle but is elliptical." Babu Tashi began to draw a diagram of the solar system on the bark paper with an elliptical orbit of the earth to illustrate his point.

"The earth is stationary, but the sun and the moon go around the earth once every night and day. The path followed by the sun is not a perfect circle. It can be as you have drawn. The sun is farthest from the earth during its northerly march and southerly march, and the variable distance between the earth and the sun causes seasonal change. But the earth can not be spinning like a mani nor go round the sun. The earth is stationary; the rest of the bodies including nine planets and twenty eight commonly identified stars orbit round the earth (yu gi riwi chok raab)." Their debate widened to include the question of how the universe and life began, about which Lopon Norbu Wangchuck had a lot to say. They would conclude their session reluctantly, to meet yet another day.

After the batch of clerks that included me, he taught another six students for a short while. While teaching them, Lopon Norbu Wangchuck had one day marked a substantial portion of the texts for rote learning by his students. All of his six students were busy memorizing for the recitation test to be held in two days. But their teacher did not come to the school. When a student - Pasang Wangdi - was asked to check the lodging of Lopon Norbu Wangchuck, he found that it was fully vacated. Lopon Norbu Wangchuck had fled to Tibet via Tshampa and Monlakarchung. He wanted to study further. Pasang was sent to bring their teacher back but could not catch up with him. He followed Lopon Norbu Wangchuck, who had a lead of almost two days, up till Tshampa, the last military outpost on the Bhutanese side, but returned disappointed because he did not have enough food to last for the trek across the Monlakarchung pass into Tibet. Had Pasang Wangdi the required amount of foodstuff, he had decided on the way that he would join his teacher and escape from Bhutan! Lopon Norbu Wangchuck returned to Bhutan in late 1950's a very learned man.

Among the attendants, I recall that Gup Leki of Bemji, Parop Jaga and Gup Jangtu were the most distinguished ones. Gup Leki was always busy in the store, measuring and releasing food to be cooked during the day for hundreds of people.

Among the many stores, the one containing valuable commodities like molasses, betel nuts, araa, butter, meat, fabric and woven textiles was accessible only through the chamber of the King who occasionally kept a distrustful watch over changgaps going in and out of the store. The commodities were thus well-guarded from grasping hands.

Even the formidable entrance into the store through the chamber could not completely protect the goods from the avaricious hands of the changgaps, who pilfered in a number of ingenious ways. Some came back with sizeable blocks of brick tea, butter and molasses jammed under their naked arm pits and others with betel nuts in the folds of their ghos. Many changgaps quickly drank some araa before coming out. But Changgap Dramitsep, fast at walking and good at making tea (western tea as opposed to traditional churned butter tea) had too much to drink one day. He failed to come out for a suspiciously long time. When His Majesty went into the store, he found Dramitsep talking to the vessel of araa, drunk beyond fear.

Gup Leki was fluent in Hindu which he had picked up during his association with the Bhutanese babus. We admired him for speaking Hindi without having at all been a student. But he was highly regarded in the court for his phenomenal memory, which was considered as reliable as a land register (thram). Whenever some dates or numbers relating to events that took place years ago were in doubt, they were referred to Gup Leki. He remembered everything, as though such things took place just yesterday. Gup Leki was appointed dungpa (administrator of a part of the district) in Trongsa but died soon after getting his new post.

Soon after I joined the secretarial team, Paro Jaga was promoted to Darpon, the Chief of all the attendants, which included stable boys, cooks, security squad, and menial task force. He allocated jobs to all the attendants according to a roster, besides helping to settle disputes or litigations. The team arbitrating disputes almost always consisted of one of the secretaries and another attendant. A secretary was anyway needed to note the proceedings. Two of us often arbitrated disputes together and I came to know my partner well. He was an unruffled and reassuring person, and the arbitrations conducted by the two of us went on smoothly. However, when I worked with some others, the arbitration process occasionally got miscarried. But Parop Jaga could explain to His Majesty the course of the dispute and follow it with a clear proposal on how it could be settled fairly. Parop Jaga was appointed as Debi Zimpon Nam (Chamberlain to the Deb) by the second King and was posted in Punakha. As Debi Zimpon Nam, he became the link between the central monk body in Punakha and His Majesty.

I remember Gup Jangtu, a swarthy man of medium build, as being another outstanding attendant in the court of second King. In fact, he was the highest Gup as well as a relative of the King. He had started as a junior attendant in the court of the first King, and so he was quite old by the time I joined the secretarial team. Other attendants and dashos often referred to him on finer points of etiquette and discipline.

Among the kadreps, Babu Nakchung, Naap Sangay, Jenab Kala, Naalep and Mahaguru provided good company to the King. The function of the kadreps was to be conversational companions. Naap Sangay, a former merchant of Wangduephodrang dzong, and Mahaguru were the permanent ones in the court of the second King. Kadreps were truly chattering courtiers and they had to keep on saying something to His Majesty while he commanded them to be present. To add colour to his personality, Naap Sangay claimed that he was of the blood of a lost Mongolian Prince. He was full of stories about Tibet, western Bhutan and horses. He was a landlord of Gaselo in Wangduephodrang commanding over a hundred serfs. It used to be said that the numbers were so high that a bell had to be rung to call his serfs for their meals.

It required a certain skill to go on talking for years on end without using the position to speak invidiously against people whom a kadrep did not like and create an unhealthy atmosphere. In this respect, Mahaguru was not as harmless as Naap Sangay. Mahaguru habitually drank before he went in for the day to the chamber of His Majesty. In the course of the conversation, he inadvertently talked about some of the things that the attendants did which were best left unreported. All the attendants were very wary of Mahaguru. Kadreps were often in the chamber with His Majesty late into the evening, when I went in to resume my reading for His Majesty.

Soon after I returned to Wangdecholing after completing the course in grammar, it became known that I could read well and one more task was given to me. I was required in the evenings to read the Epic of Gesar for His Majesty's listening pleasure. The King commended the humour of my expression and made me replace another person who read badly. Reading usually took place in the evening at 4 pm for some hours. After that, I accompanied the entourage partly to read for the King on his expeditions around the valley. He was extremely fond of the Epic of Gesar and he dwelled on the verses. Perhaps it was a source of solace and helped him to stiffen his resolve to do what was politically necessary and to seek justifications for his actions. He went trotting along the river and across the wheat fields, and often he went riding to Kurje for medicinal bath, and to the pine wood of Chakhar on fine summer days, whilst I followed him on foot with a volume of the Epic. The King often chose a charming spot in the countryside, not very far from the site where his father's remains were cremated, and lay down for a reading session. It was conventional for other aristocratic families such as Lame Gonpa to bring picnic lunches whenever His Majesty went on outing.

One evening in autumn, I lay in my host's storeroom, which was my bedroom. I did not want to report for work and I feigned illness, with a touch of juvenility. But as I wriggled and pulled up my knees to find a more restful pose, I instinctually heard in the stream of my consciousness the orchestra of ritual drums, jalings and trumpets. I pressed my head deeper into the pillow, yet the sound got louder and more vivid; it gripped and enveloped my mind and then the images of my mother and sister appeared before me. I was seized with a sudden longing to see them. I had my lunch and left for my village on an impulse.

A vast and an inexplicable sense of sadness overcame me as darkness thickened around me on the way. I was descending the pass at Shaythangla, two hours away from my home, and a crow flew overhead to roost in the monastic ruins in Chungthang. The trail lengthened before me, in diminishing light, from one side of the valley of Ura valley to the other. And I began to speculate if the wholly unnatural anxiety prognosticated some misfortune.

I was approaching, in that moonless night, the edge of my village, now only indicated by the origin of excited barking and specks of light. I secured a firm footing on the stone slabs anchored in the mud which was invisible in the night and stood still for a while, and once again I heard the drums reverberating. Only this time, I was certain that it was not my imagination. I traced this sound to my house where I found that a prayer was going on for my mother. She had caught an infection and fallen ill a week ago and now she lay in a coma, unable to recognize me or my voice. But she had wrapped herself in one of my tattered ghos, in her anguish of not being able to see me during her last moments.

I arrived by eight in the evening, sat by her holding her limp hands, and by midnight my mother died. Many months later, I realized that I had irretrievably lost a part of myself in her death. That part of me which would grow under her affection would never be made up in another way. I returned to Wangdecholing to get formal leave for the funeral and cremation services. Since the news of my mother's passing away was reported to His Majesty, I was summoned to be given personally the condolence presents - a piece of textile, seven cubes of tea and ten silver coins. After the remains of my mother were cremated and ashes dispersed, I came to Wangdecholing to resume my duties as a clerk.

But the life of a junior clerk in the court was not always sedentary or bound to the palace. In summer, I had to carry out the annual census of yaks and cattle of the royal household and collect the cumulated produce of a year from the mountain camps. These herds were up over the mountains of Dur, Damthang and Shabthang. Thus, late in the summer of 1946, I was in the mountains of Dur assessing and collecting the produce of three separate yak-herds, as the assistant of Changgap Nagphay, who was an old hand at it and was in charge of this trip. It was essential for me to go with Changgap Nagphay because he could only read.

As we ascended the mountain to find the conical tent of herders, we came by a few yaks, with their luminous and mossy fur coat, and intense glistening black eyes boring through us in their startled pause. Then these animals lurched away wildly into the alpine thickets. We sighted more and more yaks on their way up. Brown, patchy, white and black yaks were gradually converging on the herder's camp in the evening. When at last we came to the camp, it was teeming with yaks, and the bass and throaty call of the cow yaks for their calves being corralled separately permeated the evening air in the wilderness. At the camp of the herders, formed in an old forest clearing, Nagphay and I were welcomed by the herder's handsome family of eight, who had ruddy cheeks, lean and hardy physiques, and ravenous hair. The family was exempt from all taxes and was allowed to graze their own stock on the King's pasture. They were paid in-kind: forty dres of buckwheat flour and a hundred dres of wheat a year.

Changgap Nagphay gave me a few tips before we started the next day. "These are the rules, boy" Changgap Nagphay went on, looking at me. "For every lactating yak with a calf, collect twenty sangs (sang is a measure of weight roughly equivalent to 333 gm) of butter and twice the amount for a lactating yak without a calf. You have to inspect each animal individually and then match its distinguishing marks with its physical descriptions found in the record." The identification marks, ages and sex of each animal were recorded in scrolls which were updated annually during such census. The scroll- records were changed completely every year to note the cattle's demographic changes from calves to heifers and heifers to lactating animals. Yaks become lactating animals in five years and cows in four years.

The records of the last census were kept attached to the new one to give a picture of year-by-year change. The description of each herd during a particular census filled up more than four large scrolls. I verified the herd physically during the day and made fair notes in the evening. The names of the dead animals were kept on the scroll for a year, though then qualified as dead. Dead animals were accounted by their carcasses' meat. To prove that the animal was dead, the herder had to produce ribs, a pair of legs with hind knuckles, a pair of shoulders with fore knuckles, a hide, a neck with crag, a head, and breastbone, with twelve sangs of lean meat carved from the bones for each missing yak. Cords of dry meat were bunched together. From those oversized bunches of meat, Nagphay deducted a few for his own consumption and reduced all of them to a uniform size.

Changgap Nagphay retired early without working too hard during the day. In fact, he left most of the work to me. He had his dramnyen (guitar like instruments with seven strings) with him; he was very jolly and he liked to hum and drum very frequently. But he had a terribly hoarse and weak voice, to which he was oblivious. I played his dramnyen so frequently when we were together on the census that I was able to pick up the basics. Our careers crossed paths several times in the decades following this census expedition. He rose to become Nubi Dungpa of Trongsa and finally the chief of the mask dancers in Thimphu.

In Dur village, Changgap Nagphay asked the young ones to come and sing almost every evening. I found company and used to get away while people were dancing. I thought I was careful and discreet. But the villagers prattled about it the next day. We had slept over the garlic shoots in the vegetable garden. The weight of two bodies had caused a deep indentation over garlic plants and spring onions.

At the end of a month-long census, Changgap Nagphay and I collected over a thousand kilograms of meat and butter, which were neatly packed in forty porter loads. With an impressively long train of forty five porters, including five carrying our personal affects, we marched to Wangdecholing Palace. Nothing was paid to the porters;

carriage of goods was their obligation. The abundant palace stocks of vintage butter and meat were built up to an even higher quantity. Such commodities were stored to last the royal household for a few years.

The day after we returned to Wangdecholing, we presented a report to the King about the cattle census. Most able people spoke freely and fluently without notes. So, in our striving to create a good impression, we tried to present our report orally. It was acceptable to refer now and then to a note, but the most brilliant and masterly presentations were done without notes. We held mock reporting sessions the night before. Mock sessions and practices were common when attendants had to sum up the litigations which they had arbitrated. A lot of people eavesdropped while we reported. They admired our mastery of the census information. We reported about various aspects: porter services used; mortality and birth trends of animals and their causes; quantity of dairy products recovered from each herd; the conditions of pastures; and expectation of dairy products in future.

Given the experience I gained in the previous year, I was again assigned to go on a cattle census of the King's herds in Trongsa with Dayok Phoje Buep in 1947. We walked extensively around Gangtey, Longtoe, Gangjela and Gongchula tracing herds of cattle and yaks. Our first task was to settle the accounts of dairy produce, and take a census of two herds of yak and one herd of cattle belonging to the trulku (reincarnation) of Gangtey, who had died many years ago. The care of these herds had lapsed into the royal household because of the delay in the lama's reincarnation. Similarly, we had to take a census of four herds of cattle owned by the King. A herd had an average output of sixty standard sized packets of butter, each weighing about 1.5 kg. There were about one hundred and twenty jatshams (a breed of cow) in each herd. Any fall in the number of the herd was replenished by livestock procurement in Trashigang and Kheng, at a price fixed by the buyer rather than the seller. The monthly output was thus not allowed to fall below a fixed quantity.

The royal entourage often clambered up the mountains of Dur for days of relaxation in medicinal baths. There was a special spring at the bottom of the mountain of Dur. I was at the resort to read to the King in the evenings. His Majesty found the time after a relaxing bath conducive to the appreciation of the Epic of Gesar. Beside this function as a reading boy, I maintained a daily record, as I was instructed, of the expenses of the day in terms of food commodities. On such excursions, the entire entourage was put on a diet of rice, a prestige food. The record had to be kept meticulously and left within easy reach of the King, who often went through it. The consumption of food at the hot spring camp had to balance with the quantity issued at Wangdecholing, at the end of the excursion.

One day, I could not retrieve the register and so could not record the quantity of food released for cooking for the entourage. The register was kept in the bamboo room made for the King and one had to cross the room by plunging into the wooden tub bubbling with hot spring. His Majesty was luxuriating in the bath with the door locked from inside when I went to fetch the register. He inquired whether I had updated the record for the last meal after he came out of the bath. In a moment of anxiety, I replied that I had, though I actually had not done it. His Majesty ran through the register and scowled gloomily at it. He was annoyed to find out that he had been misinformed by a novice attendant. A bleak sentence was delivered upon me: I was to leave and return to Wangdecholing at once. More experienced attendants told me that the sentence was not to be carried out so literally. That night I lay in my bed ruminating on my fall from grace. I passed the night in an intense terror.

Early next morning, I was summoned by the King; I instinctively felt my hands wring and sweat. A senior attendant was directed to firmly grip the whip which accompanied the entourage everywhere, and give me a good hiding. I was given prior advice as to the posture which would minimize the shock. He struck me several times with as much force as he had. My body was sore and none of the sleeping positions I tried that night was comfortable. But I was soon reinstated fortunately to the usual duty of reading the Epic of Gesar.

4

THE GREAT FAIR OF WANGDECHOLING

In the seventh lunar month every year, when the weather was at its best and farmers in Bumthang had harvested their wheat, a fair was held at Wangdecholing. The fair was first instituted to celebrate the completion of the Domkhar Palace in 1937, but it was so popular that it became an annual event. It was the biggest spectacle in Bhutan, rivalling the Punakha festival. Every year, it started on the 15th and lasted for a week. The fair was well known throughout the country. People came from far and wide, planning their journeys so that they would be in Wangdecholing during the fair. Men and women came from as far as Haa, Trashigang and Tibet, particularly Lhodrak Karchung. There might have been two to three thousand people at the fair.

Preparation for the fair took at least twenty days. The grassland near Wangdecholing Palace filled up with bamboo huts and tents which housed stalls and shops during the fair. Games and tournaments seen only in India were practised for weeks ahead of the fair. Since there was no facility for producing lottery tickets, we devised them manually. These were made out of hand written notes with imprints of the royal seal, and sold in advance for one betam (equivalent to 25 paise) each, mostly in Bumthang and Trongsa. With the proceeds, oxen and cows were bought and awarded as prizes in the lottery draw. In addition, the King donated some cattle to be distributed as prizes.

Stalls and shops for dishes, cereals, handicrafts, metal wares, and textiles and clothes were opened, all named and numbered as if they were permanent establishments. The range of food was extremely wide. The merchants from Tibet cooked their splendid, rare dishes; peasants tasted them just this one time in the year. A stall was entirely devoted to sweet tea, which was sold for the first time in Bhutan; this sugar tea (ngaja) was extremely popular. Dramitsep, an indomitable changgap who sold tea, hawked so well that he managed to draw a big crowd. He yelled, "Aho! my relatives, aho! my relatives, come and have tea here, come and have tea here." A cup of sugar tea cost one betam or twenty five paise as did a cup of milk.

A line of Tibetan priests sat at the end of the column of shops and stalls, and prayed for the enlightenment and welfare of any person who paid them. The duration of mantras and prayers they chanted naturally depended on the amount one paid.

Across the archery ground facing the stalls and stores, live animals, especially horses and cattle, were kept for sale. Among the livestock were also His Majesty's surplus cattle and horses which were disposed of during the fair.

On the first day of the fair, the royal family came in a ceremonial procession. As part of the procession, His Majesty came trotting on his favourite mount to the site, although it was only a hundred yards or so away. He was then about forty one and looked incredibly handsome and awesome with his thundering voice and piercing glare. The attendants in the procession wore their silk gho uniform and looked as sleek as possible. About thirty monks of

Trongsa, who were in Bumthang at that time of the year, were brought to join the ceremonial procession so that they could play the jalings. The whole atmosphere was glittering and exuberant.

There was a huge wooden board inscription which told, among other things, the story of the fair. Instead of a speech to open the fair, someone had to read it aloud. Although the second senior most secretary, Lopon Thinley, had done it before, the job devolved on me, soon after I joined the secretarial team. I used to rehearse my role several times. Walking along the swollen and turbulent river flowing by the palace, I pitched my voice high enough to be heard by thousands of people, over the pulsating noise of the river. I visualized a sea of faces over the greenish currents of the river. As I completed reciting the inscription, I imagined rapturous smiles among the people and a dignified nod, expressing satisfaction over my performance, from His Majesty who observed the event from the grand, silken canopy. I further visualized an immediate rush among hundreds of young ladies asking me to escort them around the fair stalls, and I chose to take around only three of them from different villages - one from Chamkhar, one from Chumey and the last one from Dur. The one from Chumey, I fantasized, won a handsome, young bull as her raffle prize, the possession of which would please her parents. With my help, she took over the leash of the nose band attached to the bull to rein him. At that point, I recall, I really went headlong into a patch of marsh, skidding on a unstable river stone.

On the opening day of the fair, my aspiration for showmanship was dimmed a little bit from the start. Other people had emptied the store of all average sized silk ghos leaving for me an oversized one. Swaddled in this huge blood red silk gho, I stood on the platform next to the wooden board inscription, until all the people congregated around me. I cleared my throat lightly and began to read the inscription at the top of my voice. It narrated the founding of the monarchy in Bhutan in order to overcome strife and disorder.

The fair began with games and sports, including dances, pillow fights, long jump, musical chairs, high jump, races, bull fights, horse racing and boxing. As most of the spectators had never seen this kind of fun and entertainment elsewhere, the whole proceedings struck them as full of surprises and liveliness.

The members of the royal family were naturally the first to visit the shops and stalls. Then, officials made their rounds. Shops and stalls were later thrown open to the crowd who poured in, an endless stream. I was most astounded to see how quickly the shops became empty. I had to run back with a senior changgap to the reserve food store in the palace to issue additional stock to the shops and stalls sponsored by Their Majesties. I had to record the changes in food stock every time some provision was released. On the very day of opening, stocks of meat, handicrafts and butter sold by several shops were absolutely depleted. People from western Bhutan bought a great deal of butter, a symptom of butter scarcity in that part of the country.

During the fair, archery was played on one side of the ground and His Majesty also participated keenly. From time to time, he sent money to buy the most expensive and acclaimed dish sold in the fair, namely shamdrel, for the players. This was a type of fried rice with numerous ingredients like meat, boiled egg, chilly, potato, etc. In fact, archery players feasted on His Majesty's beneficence during the whole fair.

I suffered from sheer gluttony when it came to shamdrel that I used to slip out once a day to buy it. The taste of shamdrel, I remember, could not ever be recreated. I have never had any dish as appetizing as the shamdrel sold in the fair. Or perhaps it was a youthful urge for a full stomach all the time that causes me to remember the mammoth banquet during the fair so vividly.

The members of the royal family and royal guests (including the Dasho and Ashi of Lame Gonpa) took part in gourmet lunches in the grand tent. In a giant silver saucer, a mound of rice for the King was served first; the quantity was excessive even for ten people but it was a custom for that amount of rice to be served, though His Majesty by no means ate so much. More than thirty other dishes were served, made out of pheasant, chicken, jungle fowl, fish, venison, yak meat, pork, bacon, sausage, chilly, hocks, tripe, frond, pumpkin, turnips, spinach, legumes, wild asparagus, chives, onion, cabbage, yam, radish, potato, bamboo and rattan shoots, tomato, cheese, wasp, golden hornet, amaranths, millet, wheat, sweet buckwheat, bitter buckwheat, pepper, black barley, mustard, kohlrabi, cucumber, rye, oat, and so forth. The variety of dishes was so great that it took as many as twenty people to transport them to the archery ground. The last course was curd.

While the royal family sat for lunch in the tent, the archery players huddled near the target to be served their lunch. The rest of us sat under the shade of willow, peach and apricot trees. Retainers, who were normally on a diet of buckwheat flour, dined upon rice throughout the fair. Cooked rice was measured by a standard ladle, and the ladler habitually counted heads loudly. At every score, he shouted "nyisho" (twenty). As I recall, he counted approximately five hundred heads.

After dinner, young women and men took turns dancing late into the night, illuminated by several gas lamps used on these rare occasions. Each song was interrupted with rounds of betel nut and araa. The second senior most secretary, Lopon Thinley, who had a soothing voice, was a magnificent and energetic singer and dancer. His performances appealed much to the King.

The excitement of archery was also augmented by a bevy of songstresses serenading their own team and distracting the other team. Because of their joking and lampooning, to which archery players retorted wittily, there was a steady crowd watching archery every day. These women dancers heckled and harassed the other team by occasionally levelling personal criticism in the form of songs. One team's dancers sang:

Your head resembles that of an ape
And from the backside you appear like a bear.
The monkey-headed bear will not find the target.
The arrow will hit away from the target.
It must be deflected! It must be deflected!
Let it overshoot and fly up to the sky.
Let it fall short and drop on the earth.

The archery players who were the butt of this provocation responded in the form of a song. Their lines were full of sexual innuendos and hinted at the liberal virtues of some dancers. The archery player with the best voice gave it back:

One who is the maid of the lady adorned with coral necklace.
Your eyes look only to the bright and colourful chambers.
Your bedroom, at the end, is a stable.
Though you vocalize as much as a parrot,
My arrow can not be swayed from the bull's eye!

Jenab Kala, a tall man of black barley complexion, was a fine archery player. He raised the tone in the archery ground during the fair by speaking often in verses. He was by far the best known instant bard, both inside and outside the archery field. He could make instantly cutting and humorous verses.

When the turn came for His Majesty to shoot his arrow, the women dancers picked on him, too. They lowered their voices by a scale so that it did not sound too much like heckling. But the words did not need to be any more reverent. They taunted him equally. One usual singing refrain, welcoming royal seduction, when his turn came was:

You will not propel your arrow on to the target,
If you must shoot, you could launch it below my navel!

On the penultimate day of the fair, the lottery was drawn. Tickets, which had the names of the buyers, were thrown into one basket. In another basket, a roughly equal number of paper pieces were kept; most of these papers were blank but some of them had a horse, an ox, a heifer, a certain piece of textile, or a piece of handicraft written on them. Her Majesty presided over the lottery draw. A girl chosen at random from the crowd was asked to pick up a paper from each of the two baskets and pass them on to a secretary for announcement. The tension in the crowd grew to breaking point: they stretched their necks to the utmost degree to hear the announcement.

A senior secretary, usually Yeshey Wangdi, read the outcome of the lottery. He used various euphemisms when he had a blank ticket in hand. He said that the person would get the prize next year or that this year was not a good one for the buyer of the lottery. When a non-blank ticket was drawn, the specified prize was presented to the winner immediately. For instance, when the ticket read 'one horse', a horse was presented at once to the winner. The peculiar system of lottery meant that every ticket holder's name was announced whether the person won a prize or not. His Majesty bought many tickets under the pseudonym Phuntsho Dorji. Though there were several announcements for Phuntsho Dorji, they were all to convey that Phuntsho Dorji's prize was postponed to the next fair, which provoked His Majesty to burst into laughter.

One evening during the fair, a silent documentary film was staged for public viewing. There was only one film and this one was shown every year. It was a film about a fight between a tiger and two dogs. The projector set was transported to Kinga Rabden and many other places, until it became battered and unusable.

On the last day of the fair, people marched from the fair ground to the palace singing 'laybey' (a song). The first song was always laybey, in contrast to the present practice of singing it at the end. Nobody could ever outdo Sha Changlung in singing laybey. He was the central figure during the laybey dance, because he had an inhumanly moving voice that could send shivers down everyone's spine and stop everyone from thinking their thoughts. I felt that only he could exploit to the full the meaning of the lyric:

Under the sky-dome of the eight-spoked wheel
The land is unfurled as an eight-petalled lotus
Between them reign the eight auspicious signs.
In the midst of the high heavens
Rests the beaming and radiant sun.
As propitious as the high blue sky
And fortunate as the radiant sun.
Both the auspicious and the fortunate
Are welcome in the colourful shrine.
The good, oh good, oh good it is
From what is good, the good may be heralded.

The lower valleys of the beloved land
The ranges of the towering mountains.
As auspicious as the main and minor continents
And fortunate as the southern continent.
Both the auspicious and the fortunate
Are welcome in the colourful shrine.
The good, oh good, oh good it is
From what is good, the good may be heralded.

In the unsullied Buddhist Kingdom of the South
There is the sacred personage: Ngawang Namgyel.
As auspicious as the chief abbot
And fortunate as the spiritual lord.

THE HERO WITH A THOUSAND EYES

Both the auspicious and the fortunate
Are welcome to the colourful shrine.
The good, oh good, oh good it is
From what is good, the good may be heralded.

At this time of a propitious day,
That which is most high is the golden throne.
How auspicious, the waxing fortune of the King.
The good, oh good, oh good it is
From what is good, the good may be heralded.

5

THE COURT LEAVES FOR THE WINTER PALACE

In the ninth month of the Bhutanese calendar year, the royal household moved to its Winter retreat in Kinga Rabden, to avoid the coldness of Bumthang. The entourage spent the next six months in Kinga Rabden. By the third month of the Bhutanese calendar, Kinga Rabden hotted up, and the heat and the humidity brought out flies and insects. This indicated the time for the King and his courtiers to move to Bumthang, where the willows were lush and its wide valleys verdant. His Majesty was quite idiosyncratic in his choice of dates to begin his trips. Defying astrology, he set out on one of the prohibited days - the 20th, 2nd or the 8th day of Bhutanese month - when it was considered inauspicious to begin a journey.

To prepare for the three day trip to Kinga Rabden, goods were packed a month in advance, and sealed and handed over to the dojab (overseer of loads) and his deputy. They were the officials concerned with removals and transportation of properties of the court. As I recall, the number of loads consisting of royal personal affects could not be less than two hundred. Every garpa or attendant could deploy a porter each, and every dasho was entitled to five porters each. I was among those who got a porter. The number of standard back loads containing the personal affects of retainers or garpas could have been about three hundred. Altogether, there were more than five hundred back loads, which, for the purpose of transportation, were divided among the four gewogs (sub-districts) of Bumthang. Around five hundred people were mustered from Bumthang district by a court circular sent to each gewog. Eventually, a combination of hundred or so pack horses and three hundred people - both men and women - from all parts of Bumthang were available to transport the loads.

My senior colleague Yeshey Wangdi and I became furiously busy in the month before the court's movement to Kinga Rabden. We had to keep a detailed description of the sealed luggage, particularly the packs containing the personal affects of Their Majesties. We had to note down the addresses and the names of the porters to whom they were given for transportation. When we arrived in Kinga Rabden, we had to issue receipts of the goods to the porters, who were paid a token wage in-kind - either maize or paddy.

On the eve of departure, porters from my own village and others who knew me pleaded discreetly for light loads to be earmarked for them. They naturally preferred to carry something light though the load might appear to be grossly bulky. On such occasions, I was glad to oblige by allocating to them big pots, water buckets made of bamboo, giant saucepans and bowls used in the common kitchen; spare bass drums and trumpets used by the bagpipers' band; personal, royal effects such as duvets and pillows. On the morning of departure, I was absolutely frantic as most porters rushed in a blitz to get lighter loads and would upset my carefully prepared load allocation plan. For a short while, the frosty morning atmosphere became acrimonious. Women sneered at men who chose lighter loads than theirs. Old men disparaged youths who did not offer to take heavier loads. Muleteers who accepted only inadequate loads for their horses were belittled by porters. But within an hour or so, the Eastern Meadow which had been filled overnight by loads, porters and pack horses, became empty and peaceful.

Only after they left the place, did I once again become aware of the beauty of the morning and the meadow. It was only then that my eyes were drawn by the bushes of marigolds and chrysanthemums, lapped in frost, that were about to wither and dry. The giant Bhutanese peach trees around the meadow stood starkly against the mountains. Although too high even for talented tree climbers, peaches were still up on the trees, shrivelling day by day. It was going to be a fine day; the sky glowed like a turquoise. A clan of ravens and several magpies landed on the peach trees: immediately they began to bob at me and became highly raucous. But I had to prompt myself to walk faster to the cloisters of the Wangdecholing Palace where morning tea and rice were being served, along with luncheon rice which each retainer had to pack for himself.

On the day of the journey, the cavalcade and five hundred or so porters formed an endless column and overcrowded the rutted tracks which usually lay deserted and lonely. The porters, families of the attendants and retainers, weavers and others left hours before the cavalcade of His Majesty. Their Majesties the Queens, Princes and Princesses also went many arrow flight's distance ahead of the cavalcade. The march out of Wangdecholing Palace began in a formal procession of about three hundred people and thirty riding horses. The most elaborate procession was formed only when His Majesty visited western Bhutan. A magnificent parade of retinues was put on at that time.

During this present modest pageantry, the column was spearheaded as usual by a drummer, a bell-man and a pair of jalingpa (those who played a coronet-like musical instrument). Some two hundred zingaps followed next, each with a gun (chagabao) and a round of magazine. After them marched the secretarial staff and changgaps (personal attendants) who carried the boxes containing the royal seals, notebooks and stationery, cameras, binoculars, keys and relics. I was part of this segment in the procession. Then came the band playing tunes which then sounded entirely out of place. The bag pipers, who were trained in North East India, were playing foreign (Scottish) tunes. His Majesty's riding steeds, ready for mounting - numbering about twenty or so on such long trips - came next. Each riding horse was immediately followed by an adung (riding assistant). The King valued good breeds, and discussed horses passionately with his horse trader Naalep. He rode at the end of this long line and a good crowd again walked behind him. The changgaps (personal attendants) walked right behind the riding steed, along with the chashumis. Among the changgaps, four men in order of presentability were Dranglab Thegila, Baleep Jampela, Shayngab Dendu and Lhaderla. They were regarded in the court circle as the embodiment of masculine harmony and balance. Their bared legs were perfectly formed, and the gho never suited anyone better than them. On the other hand, the chashumis were abnormally big men. No one qualified as a chashumi unless he was over six feet or so. A rule of thumb was that the shoulders of chashumi should at least be at the same level as the rump of riding steeds of tall equine breed.

THE COURT LEAVES FOR THE WINTER PALACE

The King usually rode his favourite and famed steed named Seerja (golden bird). Naalep was able to strike a deal with a Lhasa nobleman to acquire Seerja by bartering over 300 kg of red rice with a great deal of persuasion. Seerja possessed impressive looks even among well-known, contemporary steeds: he was bright lemon, with blonde forelock, mane and tail.

Sometime after passing by Jakar dzong, the procession broke rank so that people could travel in smaller groups. The journey at once became convivial. I overtook horses and hundreds of security squad members and porters to catch up with a group of vivacious young women porters. I took some part of a back load off a young woman despite her reluctance to give it to me. This gesture of chivalry did not go unnoticed by my colleagues and I became the butt of teasing. For some time, such attention and the idea of a high clerk of the court helping her made her feel even more uneasy. However, the journey became so lively with bantering that I forgot about the hard climb over Kikila and the descent into the Chumey valley.

The porters, all from Bumthang, had to bring their own food for the trip. The trip had two night halts on the way. For the first night, the caravan halted at Pangtsham Bungtsham, a spot that overlooked the Domkhar valley. A clusters of tents was pitched for the royal family. Further down at a distance sufficient for the noise to be inaudible to the royal family, hundreds of men and women sought their protective camp sites as the night advanced. Most took to camping under trees, some near bushes and others near rocky caverns to avoid frost. Men and women from different villages of Bumthang met in this wilderness, struck up immediate comradeship, and slept round the bonfires to keep as warm as possible from the autumnal chill. They gossiped while they took rest and awaited for sleep to descend on them.

Specks of light flickered and shone like stars overhead as I searched, after my duties were over, for my friends with whom I had walked during the day. They were lying on beds of ferns under a giant cedar tree with their belts untied, chatting around the embers of fire. Its flickering light shone on flanks of the porters covered by nothing more than the cloth they wore during the day. I once again joined them and embarked on a jaunty conversation with the winsome young porter till the grey hours. I threw my forearm over my head resting on a bundle of ferns, and saw the moon go by through a canopy of cedars. Lichens swayed in the wind; a cone landed softly in the forest. A breeze picked up, and there was a nip in the air. From far down the valley, a pheasant made a ringing whistle. A moment later, another answered its call. I knew the signs; it was already time to get up.

In the morning, innumerable plumes of smoke rose from almost every direction above the thick forest as people cooked their meals. Once every year, the heath and forest above Domkhar took on this jubilant look. Well before sunrise, the party left the camp site, leaving traces of firewood everywhere. We began our climb over the Ngangdagla (a pass) in hot sunshine. I was afraid that I would flag a little during the climb as I had slept very little at night. But I had the same enjoyable company, and with the winsome porter at my heel, I felt I could cross another mountain.

The stopover for the second night was in Zangrongpang, where the nyerpa (store-master) of Kinga Rabden came with a big reception party to welcome the entourage. He managed the estates of Brakteng and Namthere, owned by the King. The landscape changed suddenly after crossing Zangrongpang, as though we had stepped across an ecological fault. The deep trough valley of Mangdechu (the Mangde River) opened out, with hundreds of thousands of sun-drenched terraced rice fields, divided by numerous hill springs diverted partially into channels, stretching from the crest of the mountain to the shores of the Mangdechu. These terraced fields were on every spur and shoulder of the hill. I could imagine the private granaries of Trongsa dzong being filled by the harvest from royal estates found in this area. Some terraced fields extended right up to the edge of the precipice; a pair of bullocks and their ploughman could easily miss a step and go over the cliff if they could not make a timely and perfectly agile swerve. In the midst of the terraces, as we descended down, the golden pinnacle of the palace shimmered in the sun.

I looked forward, as much as any other retainer, to our stay for the next six months in Kinga Rabden in the mellow season, with harvest of sub-tropical fruits, vegetables and cereals. The last crop to be harvested was sugar cane, grown all over nearby places like Kela, Changray, Yudrongcholing and Brakteng. Molasses was bartered with yak and sheep fat in Tibet. Animal fats were used in cooking (especially by serfs), and were issued as quota food items to the serfs. Such animal fat came neatly packed in tripe.

The winter weather in Kinga Rabden was mild, and the spring water soft. One of the first things we rushed to do was wash by the spring. Within a day or two of their arrival, the retainers rebuilt their huts on the traces of earlier structures. The dismantled parts of temporary structures like the bamboo netting and poles, carefully kept under trees and in the corners of oxen's sheds, were reassembled. Overnight, numerous huts of bamboo netting, shacks and hovels sprang at a comfortable distance from the palace of Kinga Rabden.

Others tried to find lodging for the winter in the fifty or so houses. This was often impossible, and so people camped below protective rocks and towering cliffs, for a while displacing Himalayan tahrs, barking deer, wild boars and jungle fowl. Once again, Kinga Rabden became absolutely crammed with retainers, litigants, official delegates from various parts of Bhutan and other visitors. I had my own host family who put me up, year after year, in the same attic where I slept in the midst of maize cobs left to dry. I had countless opportunities to study and stare at maize cobs that greeted my sight first thing in the morning. Sometimes, the roosters and hens of my host family would attempt to park themselves in the attic, as they were used to doing during the summer, but my host family was kind enough to allow me to disperse them.

Three days after the arrival of the King in Kinga Rabden, the nobles and the notable figures of Trongsa called on His Majesty for the ritual reciprocation of gifts. My role was once again to list the names of the people and the particulars of their gifts. Each well wisher offered to the King a pitcher of araa, a large bag of rice, and sometimes, an odd basket of groceries. It was customary for the King to present each of them with five square metres of broad cloth and a ball of tea, both of which were scarce and thus highly valued. This pattern of social interaction and gift reciprocation was repeated when the King returned to the summer palace of Wangdecholing; as noted earlier, the wealthier and prominent subjects in Bumthang had to customarily present the King with a pitcher of araa and a yathra.

One could disregard this custom and a few others only at the risk of a visit by a bangchen garpa, an attendant empowered to exact the most lavish hospitality and reception from the family on whom he was imposed. One would do well to thoroughly satisfy every whim of the bangchen garpa during the period of his stay, if further retribution was to be avoided, even if these whims included the most insolent demand accompanied by extreme rudeness. For a bangchen garpa, it was the most fabulous opportunity to indulge himself, and in all probability, his wishes would be fulfilled. It was mandatory for a set of new clothes to be offered to him on his departure.

His Majesty left occasionally for Samchiling, another palace which stood close to that of Kinga Rabden. A stream and a spur divided the two palaces. For a fortnight or so he also lived within the confines of Trongsa dzong which was, at the most, a day's walk from the palace of Kinga Rabden. I found the stay in Trongsa dzong the most stifling part of the year. It was quite tedious to spend our days within its ramparts, meeting only monks and officials.

It was in Kinga Rabden that His Majesty indulged in one of his greatest passions: archery. Good breeds of horses were another of his passions. In Bumthang, bad weather often disrupted archery, but here he could go on playing for three weeks at a time. King Jigme Wangchuck was very formal and maintained the habit of wearing the sword throughout the day while playing archery. He was less fond of the scarf which he wore only on occasions. There were fifteen archers a side and fourteen dancers. The game would begin in the morning at about 9 o'clock. The teams had an early lunch break at

11 o'clock. The other players had their lunch in the courtyard of Kinga Rabden dzong while the King had his in a leafy enclosure built for him next to the play ground. In a surge of generosity, the courtiers and retainers would be fed lavishly during the period of archery. A sumptuous lunch was served to the King in the archery field. The Chamberlain to His Majesty first served rice in the gigantic silver bowl meant only for the King. Since he would not have even one tenth of what was served, the amount was totally extravagant, but correct in terms of regal protocol. A pot full of bacon was served, followed by an endless variety of curries, sauces and salads.

Archery continued for about twenty days or so at a stretch. As the days wore on, they took a toll on the vigour of the players. Bow strings snapped and arrow shafts split down the middle. Players got sore bodies and black faces. They suffered from headaches and thirstiness due to the solar radiation striking their heads over which - in keeping with etiquette - they did not wear hats. Blisters popped on the index, middle and ring fingers of the players.

Only Bao Shelngo was relatively happy, for he could hit targets as many as twenty five times a day, and often got textile pieces as gifts. He finely judged his shots, as though he had worked out intuitively the various factors affecting the arrow's trajectory such as the speed of wind, height and distance of the trajectory, gyration of the arrow during its flight, and the personalized design of his arrow. His Majesty himself was far from exhausted because he sat on a chair in the shade between bouts of shooting his arrows, and was plied on a rickshaw across the archery ground. When they were into the third week of the game, the players collected about four hundred betams amongst themselves, and with this offering, begged His Majesty to end the game for the time being. The Elder Queen often interceded on behalf of the players to bring an end to the prolonged game.

The secretarial team, including myself, kept away from such merriment. Much of our time was taken by auditing official records of Thimphu, Punakha, Wangduephodrang, Trashigang, Kurtoe and Zhongar. Both the zongpon and nyerchen (store master) of these dzongkhags came with documentary evidence in the form of two files - yongbab (income) and zetho (expenditure) - showing how they used produce from corporate land and herds belonging to their respective dzongkhags. They also accounted for the uses of goods collected as taxes - rice, flour, puffed rice, mustard oil, butter, daphne bark paper etc. They presented their final annual accounts to His Majesty in Kinga Rabden, and when he was preoccupied with archery, Dronyer Jigme Dorji Wangchuck examined the books of accounts. The expenses of Paro Penlop were exempted from the usual accounting procedures. Paro Penlop Tshering Penjor, the King's nephew, exercised independent authority over revenue he collected and did not render his account to the King.

While in Kinga Rabden, one of our routine jobs was to go to Trongsa dzong to take an inventory of food commodities (especially butter, meat and rice) derived from His Majesty's private sources. As a junior clerk, I accompanied senior attendants several times to take inventory. Butter accumulated for over five years. Butter and meat loads from His Majesty's own herds were stored in Trongsa dzong. There was an prodigious amount of it, filling cool and cavernous rooms. When new stock arrived every year, old stock had to be dug out and put on top of the fresh inventory. The quantity was so vast that sorting it took days for several people.

Likewise, there was meat stock which had to be rearranged every year. Butter remained fresh within; its rancid exterior was peeled away every year. But the meat stockpiles became susceptible to meat worms. As the neatly piled meat packs were disturbed during re-arrangement, the storeroom swarmed with black worms that had been breeding profusely and feeding lavishly on the meat, bones and hocks. Cattle hides were never stored. They were immediately treated and tanned and turned in to hide bags for packing cereals, or used for long distance transportation.

His Majesty did not permit the use of slaughtered meat in his kitchen. He preferred beef that became available through natural causes of death. People sold carcasses to the palace kitchen and in return were issued receipts for live animals to be redeemed from His Majesty's herds. Other spare rooms in Trongsa dzong were filled with cereals harvested from His Majesty's land holdings, e.g., Khawajara and Botokha in Punakha, Chebakha and Dremdi in Wangduephodrang.

The outputs from these valleys were brought all the way to Ridha by the taxpayers of Punakha and Wangduephodrang and transhipped from Ridha to Trongsa by the people of Ridha. Thus, it became known as Ridha Redo (paddy carriage by Ridhaps). More than 56,000 dres (seven khaichen) of rice were transported by Ridhaps to Trongsa every year. Some of the rice was further taken to Bumthang for quota distribution to courtiers. By imposing a so-called horse tax on households in Bumthang and Trongsa, free carriage of rice between Trongsa and Bumthang was provided for. A census of horses was taken regularly in Trongsa and Bumthang to determine the horse tax base. This tax was invoked whenever some freight needed to be moved from one place to another.

Buckwheat - both bitter and sweet varieties - was also stored in Trongsa. In Trongsa, His Majesty's buckwheat fields were in Balingpang and Taktsi. The subjects of Trongsa grew buckwheat for the King. Jakar dzong was also a granary for buckwheat and wheat grown in Bumthang in His Majesty's private estates. As I recalled earlier, the land was tilled by a special task force raised from Eastern Bhutan, collectively known as pangoleng garpa. There were over three hundred or so pangoleng garpa from the East - Kurtoe, Zhongar, Kheng, Dungsam, Trashigang and Monggar. Their position was indicated by the sword worn across their waists, instead of vertically. They travelled to and from Bumthang to their respective hamlets with a porter each, whom they were entitled to raise from their own villages. Though they came to till the land for buckwheat, they took a certain pride in this assignment and would proudly proclaim their position when they travelled.

Those pangoleng garpa who were absent were levied fines of up to a hundred betams (silver coins), or worse, they faced a bangchen garpa who could in this instance recover from the absentees more than a hundred silver coins each. A hundred betams was not a negligible sum. A cow generally was worth not more than one hundred and thirty betams in those days. At the end of preparing the land in Bumthang for planting of buckwheat, a pangoleng garpa returned home with a parting gift of betams from the King. Some years later, the harvesting of buckwheat in Bumthang previously done by pangoleng garpa was made the responsibility of zingaps.

Besides working on the tax reform, auditing the books of accounts, and taking inventory of food commodities in the stores of Trongsa dzong, I had to assist senior attendants in the preparation of offerings to be sent to Punakha on the occasion of Punakha Domchoe. Puna Domchoe, or the festival of Punakha, was a national event held in winter in Punakha. The highest officials of Thimphu, Wangdue, Paro, Daga and Wang sent customary offerings to the Shabdrung. However, if the three penlops of Bhutan - Trongsa, Paro and Dagana - could not make personal appearances, they dispatched their representatives with presents. The offering from Trongsa Penlop consisted of clothes, paper, butter, pots and pans, a milk churner, a wooden bucket, incense, yarns of various colours for ritual decoration, yathra (woollen textile), pangkhep (cotton textile) etc. There were about a hundred porter loads delivered by the representative of Trongsa Penlop alone. This vast melange of offerings was accompanied by a Ngotshab (representative of the King).

By meticulous planning, the representatives of the Penlops of Trongsa, Dagana and Paro would arrive simultaneously at the magnificent cantilever bridge of Punakha. From there, they would march and ascend three wooden staircases and go into the dzong at the same time. The three of them watched the performances during Domchoe from the balcony seats reserved for guests of honour.

Representatives of the Penlops carried a letter each addressed to the great Shabdrung Rimpoche under the pretense of his existence. The offerings and letters marked the hierarchy between the Shabdrung and the Penlops. The King in his capacity as Trongsa Penlop addressed his letter to Shabdrung as well as the Zhung

Kalyon (government chief minister) and Zhung Dronyer (government guest master). The Shabdrung was non-existent and the post of Zhung Kalyon and Zhung Dronyer were vacant. Nevertheless, once a year, the Trongsa Penlop kept up the ritual of writing these letters, which were received by much lower officials. This arcane correspondence was discontinued by the third King.

6

TO HAVE A BETEL NUT BY THE STREAM

I was getting on 20, an age which stirs matrimonial ideas among one's parents. My father and maternal uncles naturally felt that I should settle down with a suitable young woman. When they talked to me, I could often trace a hint that I might find myself with an inappropriate woman. They also alluded to the fact that I was on the brink of several relationships which they hoped would be nothing more than transitory. My friends informed me that my maternal uncles were trying to find a bride for me among the daughters of genteel families of Bumthang and Kurtoe. I was not very surprised by the idea, as I had come to know that arranged marriages were popular with upper families.

But the news, nevertheless, excited my curiosity as to who the young lady might be. I was seen as the main inheritor; my sister was at home, but my parents and my uncles preferred the eldest male to be the head of the household. They reckoned that I would resign in the not too distant future and carry on with domestic life. I would gradually be handed over all the domestic responsibilities in order to continue the family line. However, I was quite relieved when they failed to find an acceptable bride for me. For whatever the disadvantages of my youth as a retainer, I was beginning to see myself as a minute part of court life. I knew that I would be married, but for the time being, I was glad to see it as only a speck on the distant horizon. I continued my single life whose simple joys and happiness depended on fragile relationships that were struck during my brief stays around many places. At the same time, I had to cope with the strain of having to face the end of such relationships which came all too often, forced upon me by my itinerant life.

One summer, I was temporarily assigned to be the secretary to the Elder Queen who lived in the palace of Domkhar in Chumey. This palace was an exquisite replica of Kinga Rabden. It was set in the middle of wheat fields which were in full ear at the time I was there. Between the belt of wheat fields and the alpine forest was a band of buckwheat fields. From where I was, such fields appeared as strips of delicate pink, signifying that the buckwheat had flowered. On sunny days, the inspiring sight of a large buckwheat field was enough to lift my heart and fill me with a sense of greatness and optimism. Walking through a buckwheat field, I used to gulp its sweet air and listen to the drone of thousands of bees and butterflies gliding serenely over it. The atmosphere around seemed exceptionally charged and I felt then that I was on the brink of great possibilities and realization.

However, on the whole, it was a dull summer, very often with prolonged rain and gales, as had been divined by the court astrologer. The footpaths in the village and around the palace became slippery. The rivulets and streams began to overflow, bringing wooden dregs along the bed of Chumey River. Mist often hung very low and for very long.

Every morning I sat looking out of a window on the second floor of Domkhar Palace, lapsing into reverie instead of drafting letters. I recalled my friends from my village and Wangdecholing, and those I met in the mountains of Dur while I went on the expedition to take a census of cattle and yaks. I heard the voice of the soft spoken friend who talked to me all the way from Bumthang to Kinga Rabden. I saw many other smiling faces of friends, redolent of blossoms on a cloudless spring day in Wangdecholing. Each of them in their own way left an indelible memory that haunted me for a long time despite the brevity of our days together. They left me with an idea of endless happiness in the relationships I had with them.

Being a secretary hardly left me much free time during the day. Yet, memories and hopes burst upon my mind so often to distract me. Sitting by the window, I fondly recollected the lonely trails, far-flung villages and kind hosts. When I entered the later's houses on my alms round, as the emissary of my father (lama), they burnt fragrant greenery to infuse the room with sweet air. But I did not suffer from a scorn of the dirt and filth of rural life, to which I was anyway accustomed. I never felt superior to the environment of childhood or my own background.

I recalled the escapades we undertook in many places. In those places in Bumthang, Kurtoe, Trongsa and Monggar where I have been, both young women and men took in their stride the extent of youthful impulses to which we were prone. The unspoken norm was to have affairs, as long as people got along well, while not getting blinded to fall into marriages.

Rendezvous were very down to earth in those days especially among ordinary people. Young ladies would be befriended and consulted during the day. Young men were inclined to call on them in their houses at night. In most cases, the doors were firmly bolted, perhaps with extra precaution when the presence of nocturnal young men were felt. Without definitive knowledge about the structural loopholes, doors and windows could not be forced open even after hours of attempts with basic equipment like a knife and a door-fiddler. The latter implement was especially invented and improved upon by generations of nocturnal young men, out of necessity, to manipulate door bolts. Sometimes, the rickety noise of forcing the door open woke up people inside, forcing the young men to make a hasty retreat into the night. More often, the escapades were undertaken more for their adventure than for the results, which were hard to obtain.

The stream of my reverie gave way for a few moments to what was happening around me. As I cast a glance around, I saw a number of attendants sitting alongside me discussing the day's menu with exuberance. Among the many dishes, a salad would be prepared with the first crop of cucumbers from Jakar. But soon, their voices receded into a distance. My own attention shifted to the retainers moving stealthily and fast across the front quadrangle, carrying fresh groceries and water. Another retainer was squatting in the corner of the quadrangle and sharpening his all-purpose dagger.

Way down by the rivulet stood the village, and the footpath from the palace to the village was lined by hundreds of prayer flags fluttering in the gale. It was so pleasing to see the prayer flags in the breeze in spite of the rain. In the field adjoining the village, I saw the youth of the village, shielded from rain only by a square yathra, striding ahead with their bullocks and horses. As the mist was spreading along the back of the village, I could also see vague outlines of two men and a woman, who carried a bundle of hay, letting their bull out into the field. At this point, I remember hearing the poignant, fused notes of a dog howl far away and pigeons mourn while paying court to each other.

This view, of the whole setting, suddenly reduced me to tears, though it was not in any way a particularly significant sight. Unable to continue with my routine that day, I left for the house of my host family. I feigned illness for a few days. And this enabled me to stay away from work in the palace. Several people in the village, including young ladies I was acquainted with, came to inquire about my illness. In fact, several young ladies of the village kept bursting into the room in whose corner I sat affecting a slightly painful expression. But I could not get into a different frame of mind, despite their kind and sometimes amorous attention.

I walked into the pine woods and scrub clearings where cattle and horses were grazing, to seek a brighter mood. Though the gentle contours of the mountain of Chumey seemed as familiar and friendly as the ones around my own village, I felt a stranger among these hills, and, at that moment, very far from home. Suddenly, I heard a woman's sharp tune filling up the valley. It somehow struck me as being unusually sober and striking. The tune became louder and louder and also pleasing. A figure, not yet clearer than a silhouette, was weaving her way down the pine forest. I supposed that she was returning after gathering firewood, which was bit unusual on a wet day.

The situation of that afternoon is etched very sharply in my mind. For the first time after several dull and wet days, the sun came through on that evening. Through the shafts of sunlight penetrating the pines woods, I could see a young woman striding down towards the stream where I was resting. We were now at a distance from where we could see each other clearly. She had gone to her cattle herders perhaps to borrow some milk, as she carried a bucketful of it.

I can vividly see still now that she (Pedon Wangmo) wore at a jaunty angle a broad lady's buley (flat and circular lady's hat made of bamboo netting) trimmed with wild roses, primroses and primulas of many shades. Her face, with an expressive and direct stare, appeared totally flushed. She was tall and proportionate, and drenched by rain to the skin. She was about to wade into the stream when I asked her where she had been and where she was going. Stream water crashed on the stones and water flew against her robust shank and flank.

I did as much as I could to delay her with an exchange of pleasantries, and found myself quite charmed by her. In the course of our frivolous talk, I took out my pan holder and scooped a dash of tsuna (lime paste) with two rumpled leaves of pan. I recall that I did not put a quarter of a betel nut on the pan leaves as commonly done, but three pieces of betel nut, which I am sure she understood as romantic (and perhaps narcotic), lavishness. For there was no doubt in my mind, as much as hers, at that moment, that a meeting of hearts was possible between us.

Days later, Pedon Wangmo told me with much anguish that she was a married woman. But I had become irreversibly fond of her and continued seeing her covertly from time to time. I began to suffer from a measure of recklessness and inattentiveness to the hazards which the relationship posed to her marriage, and to my own status as a single man, which I valued. Yet, I thought I could find some basis for my own attitude in this matter in an old Bhutanese saying:

> If lovers and companion for life it is not;
> Fleeting, happy friendship should be sought.

It might seem extra-ordinary now: while I undoubtedly liked her, I was still too fond of bachelor's freedom to come to terms with the idea of marrying her. Perhaps I liked to believe that I was safe having a clandestine affair. Very soon, I found myself in the centre of an imbroglio. Her husband started, quite rightly, to initiate a series of discussions with me, through an intermediary. In keeping with the Bhutanese custom, the role of the woman was not discussed and she was left blamelessly out, however wayward a role she might have actually played.

Her husband had come up with the most formidable man behind him. The uncle of her husband was no less a person than Lopon Kelzang Dawa, the Chief Secretary to the King and a man of enormous reputation and insight. Her husband's uncle was in a way my ultimate chief, though I had by now very little day to day association with him. When he entered the fray, a new dimension of inconvenience was added to the case.

In order to quickly bring the offending situation to an end, Lopon Kelzang Dawa invited my father to the discussion, instead of me, from my village - at a distance of a day. I learnt later that my father asked at length for his pardon for my most regrettable and embarrassing behaviour and gave his assurance that I would not be a source of disturbance to the marriage between his nephew and his wife. The understanding, that I would cease to have anything to do with her and discontinue giving any indication for her to divorce her husband, was reached between him and my father.

Soon afterwards, I had to join the entourage leaving on a trip to Haa in Western Bhutan. The King took this trip - involving some seven days trek each way - to meet Gangtok Sahib (A. J. Hopkinson, the British Political Officer who was resident at Gangtok, the capital of Sikkim). In the grey hours of the day of my departure for western Bhutan, she turned up at my place. In a naive sort of way, she asked me if I could not stay back or take her along with me. Lowering her head down on her lap, she wept bitterly, turning away from the mustard lamp. I mopped her eyes and held her face up with both my hands. I then told her that I could not disregard the command of the King; I was bound by his command to go to Zhungda Phunsum (western Bhutan). I repeated an often quoted saying:

The command of the King:
To dismiss it, is as dear as gold,
To carry it out, is as heavy as the hills.

I continued: "Nevertheless, I am not going away forever. I am not going, as you know, to the land of no return. I shall return on the first instance I can. Will you pray for me to return safely and soon?"

"Till your return, I would like to have something, something that I can keep near my bosom and see, because I will miss you. I need something to fasten my restless heart."

"Yes, as the symbol of my love, the white empty path. Watch its length stretching from the village up to the mountain everyday to see if I am coming down."

"The white empty path, the white empty path! Please do not quip. I need..."

She opened her fist, took out a ring, and put it on one of my fingers. Then she said: "May it forever feel the human warmth."

In response, I tried to present her with the pan and tsuna holders. She turned them down. I further offered her my cup and its wrapper, both of which she again refused to accept. "Would you tell me now what is that you would like to have? I must attend to the senior secretaries. They must be looking for me" I said, little exasperated, as I was getting impatient to go to report to senior secretaries. There was much to be done by way of numbering the porter loads.

"I want to have the red shirt you are wearing. I will always cherish it. At night, I will cover my pillow with it and sleep on it. I will unfurl it on a hanger during the day for me to see," she admitted finally.

I untied my gho in a hurry to take off my red shirt. I was going to say goodbye while I gave her the red shirt. But she snatched it from me and was gone. I ran down the log ladder, almost tripping on the way, to see her. But she had vanished without a trace. I nearly broke down, and tempted myself momentarily with the desire to stay back.

But there was no time at all to linger on with such wishfulness. I packed my bedding and went to see the senior secretaries to get instructions. Soon, I was recording and numbering the porter loads, so that the train of porters and ponies could start early. Much preparation was involved for this journey, for the size of the entourage was over a hundred, leaving aside porters who equalled the entourage in numbers. The entourage consisted of twenty chandaaps, sixteen changgaps, sixty zingaps and nine members of a brass band. All the secretaries were part of the entourage, and they carried important objects like the box containing the royal seal and the sword of the legendary hero, Ling Gesar. I had the camera, and moved at the heels of the steed the King rode, in case he wanted to take pictures.

As we started our trip, an immense crowd gathered around the palace to see off the entourage. I watched surreptitiously for her in the crowd, but she was nowhere to be seen. A few hours later, we were ascending the mountain above Jakar and I excused myself from the line to go behind the bush. As I resumed my climb rather breathlessly to catch up with others, from behind the trunk of a pine tree, she rose. Before I could say a word to her, I could hear someone way up shouting for the camera and I simply ran even faster up the hill with the camera. As I recall, after a photograph was taken and the camera put into its bag, I had a chance to look back from a higher vantage point. I was able only to make out the red shirt she was waving. On this long journey, whenever I flagged, rest restored me immediately. But there was no rest that would bring serenity to my mind, at least for the first half of the journey into western Bhutan.

7

TO HAA, THE END OF THE SKY

I remember my first journey in 1947 through western Bhutan to its end, Haa, as an interminable number of tea ceremonies held around the scenic spots on the way. It was usual for the entourage to be welcomed by not less than half a dozen tea ceremonies a day. The journey was constantly interrupted by such official and private receptions, where the entourage replenished itself with food and drinks.

It was obligatory for aristocratic households like that of Lame Gonpa and Wangdecholing Ama Sonam Chodon to host tea and lunch receptions on the way. They had to bring an assortment of snacks known as lasey to the nearest high pass. For example, on this journey, the entourage received lasey at Yatongla from Lame Gonpa and the Elder Queen. The lasey pack consisted of diced dry meat; buckwheat loaves; dough made of flour of roasted wheat mixed with araa, molasses and butter; and mixed spice mash.

At Trongsa, we were bid farewell by the monks and officials of the dzong. They came till the cliff of Thomangdrak to see us off. We walked slowly down the steep incline to the cantilever bridge that spans the Mangdechu; and up the narrow, meandering mule track over the most dangerous precipice in Bhutan. From the shores of the Mangdechu, the cliff rose in upright steepness, and the mule track rose by ramps and stone steps. Those who had a horror of heights found this part of the mule track highway disagreeable, just as the medieval warriors found it appalling because they became highly vulnerable while crossing it.

In one instance in late 19th century, a well known leader of an expeditionary force tried to escape after losing the battle. But he was pursued by the enemy forces until he came to a point in Thomangdrak, which was like a blind alley. There, those who pursued him caught up with him. But he committed suicide by jumping off the cliff rather than giving himself up.

At several points along the route in a day, people from nearby villages came to welcome their King enthusiastically and see him pass by. They sent up plumes of smoke from aromatic plants, infusing the air he breathed with fragrance and 'cleansing' the earth on which he trod. Women and men lined the mule track with offerings of food, cookies, fruits and drinks. A normal offering consisted of a tiny basket of uncooked rice (about 1.5 kg) on which were perched three rubia-coloured hard boiled eggs. One or three incense sticks smouldered in the centre of the eggs. The King, with a kind word here and there, personally acknowledged all of these gifts and gracefully received the people's respect. His reciprocal gift was a coin (betam) for each person. As soon as the King passed, rice, eggs and other food offerings were quickly collected by chashumis (attendants), who were allowed to keep them as their personal benefits. Their collection increased in direct proportion to the length of the journey; during their long journey, their food collection activity thrived.

The porters from Trongsa and Bumthang returned from Ridha and porters from western Bhutan took over from there. Yeshey

Wangdi and I had to pay the wages to the porters from Bumthang and Trongsa. I went through the list of porters in front of a senior attendant. As I read the names serially, it became obvious that there were more porters than I had recorded earlier. The senior attendant was outraged by my neat but inaccurate registration and decided to give me a birching. Then, he changed his mind and decided on another form of punishment. We were to return to Bumthang the next morning.

The prospect of not being able to continue my journey to western Bhutan weighed somewhat heavily on me over the night. Only four days earlier, I would not have minded staying back, as she had asked me. But that whispered talk early in the morning seemed ages ago, as though many years had passed since that experience. I had fortunately shaken off the spell I had been under for the last few days, and found myself eager to go to unknown places and meet unknown persons.

The next morning, we handed over the documents to others and were about to go in the opposite direction, when someone advised us confidentially to disregard the punishment to return to Bumthang. He kindly told us to follow the entourage at a distance, without being seen by His Majesty for the next two days. We followed the entourage, keeping a safe distance, till Wangduephodrang. Being out of sight for two days enabled the senior attendant to once again be less objectionable towards us. We were formally readmitted into the fold and were able to rejoin the entourage.

Sha Samtengang was then considered somewhat of a threshold to western Bhutan. As the entourage approached Samtengang, all the bundles of silk ghos were unwrapped, and a number of these ghos were distributed to the garpas, who instantly wore them over the ones they already had, unmindful of the sweltering heat they felt. The garpas, with their rifles and silk ghos, marched to the tune of bagpipers playing full tilt, down the hill from Samtengang village to the camp in the open by the lake of Lutshokha.

The experience of the overnight stay near Samtengang left me with one of the few nostalgic feelings I held for a long time. The location was the most pleasing one I have come across for camping out. Even His Majesty, who slept in a tent, did not hesitate to sleep in the open at this spot. We slept in groups of twos and threes under giant chirpines that surrounded the lake and the hill. The place gave me a feeling of lightness, of standing on the clouds, and affording the most fascinating view of the Bhutanese landscape. In the afternoon sun, I walked around the edge of the swollen lake and looked towards the south and the west. In the vastness of the mountains, a human settlement appeared as a mite. The stupendous view of the chains of mountains, as though observed in a crystal clear silver mirror, seemed to draw me out of myself further and further, towards a sense of mystery. I sat down on the spur above the lake from where the villages of Kashi and Nisho came into view. I began to ponder on the mysterious quality of the landscape around the villages that moved the great bards of the last century - Sumdar Tashi and Pemi Tshewang Tashi - to muse about it in their poems.

Pemi Tshewang Tashi was from Sha Kashi, a village which was visible from the hill. He was deeply attached to the physical setting of the area and wonderfully inspired by it. He was moved in a poem to vividly describe the beauty of the rugged and diverse landscapes, their fertility and profusion of fruits and flowers. Corresponding to the imagery of productivity and warmth of the land, he evoked in his poem a gay picture of vigorous drinking and eating along the way, when he travelled from Wangdue to Trongsa leading an expeditionary force.

> Towards the rising sun, among the eastern villages
> The hamlet of the lady of Kashi:
> Like golden scriptures, its upper reaches
> Like a silver dish, its lower stretches.
> In the middle, within something of a palace:
> Brother of one, festooned with a coral necklace
> A husband and companion of Phurchung Zam
> A great father, father of daughter Lhaden Zam
> The trusted son of mother Sonam Pem
> I, the Chamberlain Tshewang Tashi
> Upper lip like a lotus petal
> Lower lip like a coral flower
> In between, what is like a temple
> The boneless tongue can turn well.
> The crests of Phangyulgang are like Tibetan hills;
> Tibetan hills and plateaus are reserves of gold.
> The foothills of Komathang are like Indian places;
> Indian places and plains are reserves of silver...
>
> As we passed through Rabuna
> The orchard keeper of Rabuna came
> With a banana off its dancing plants

Upon which oranges were heaped like offerings of a mandala
And a tangerine was arranged on top, like a golden copula...

As we clambered up the slope of Samten
And came to the village of Samtengang
The people of Nayulchem
Were watching us from their windows.
Beneath the evergreen tree of Samten
Aum Ugyen Chuzom of Jayshing
Had unfolded a golden bamboo mat
Had planted an iron tripod
Had placed on it a precious cauldron
That nectar of strong sumchang
Had stuck upright ivory white yarden.[1]
Filled pitchers of buffalo horn.
Popped and sizzled granules of zaw[2]
Were filled in brightly coloured bamboo baskets.
As these are auspicious, let me have
As these are parting gifts, let me take...

I cast back a glance once and saw:
To the right of the serpentine river
To the left of the footpath by rice terraces
The blessed hamlet of Sha Kashi.
Above it, in its golden lotus-plain[3]

---

[1] These are three fang shaped pieces of butter stuck on the edge of the cauldron which is filled with drinks.
[2] A snack made of popped rice.
[3] The modest flat area above Kashi is compared to the plain area in India.

I saw the dwelling of chablubchem.[4]
Below it, in its silver dish
I saw the place of priest phajo[5]
In between, within the turquoise parapet
I saw mine, the Lord's, own manor house...

As I turned back to see down below
The lake of Sha Lutsho was green and full
The evergreen tree at Samten was dark and deep
The lonely white track was pale and pallid
Jadaruchet itself was ashen and faded...

Whenever the entourage passed through important stretches of habitation, the garpas decked out in shimmering silk and formed a ceremonial procession with the full blare of bagpipers. For example, the entourage formed into processions from Samtengang to Chebakha, Razawog to Wangduephodrang, Simtokha to Babesa, and Jishingang to Paro Dzong. The procession signified the arrival of the entourage in important places, where the receptions were correspondingly full blown.

Our night stopovers were in Domkhar, Trongsa, Chendebji, Ridha, Samtengang, Hinglayla, Simtokha, Chimithangkha. Paro was the next stopover (see map of mule tracks on next page). On the eight day after we started from Wangdecholing, we reached Chimithangkha, where the entourage was met by Paro Penlop

Plains are associated with the lotus, as it grows only in the plains. Hence, the definition 'Lotus-plain'.

[4] A rank in the monastic organization.

[5] Refers to the local priest.

Tshering Penjor. The tents pitched at Chimithangkha were the best I saw till then; they were colourful, large and high.

Several gas lamps, which in Wangdecholing were used only during the fair and in the chamber of the King, shone at strategic points in the camp. A horde of riding ponies was brought to give respite to the ones from Bumthang.

Paro Penlop Tshering Penjor was a man of great girth and a nephew of the King. Thought to be the uninstalled and unrecognised reincarnation of Gangtey Trulku, Tshering Penjor was reputed to be quite pious and spent a great deal of time praying. He had a large collection of religious antiques. His collection was expanded by the excellent workmanship of smiths and jewellers, who were considered generally superior to those in Wangdecholing Palace. The Paro Penlop often sent parcels consisting of silver ware, swords and ornaments to the King in Wangdecholing.

Paro Penlop Tshering Penjor went ahead early in the morning to Paro to supervise the preparation of reception. Grand signs of welcome were displayed again in Jelela; there were flags of many colours decorating the hills and the pass. It seemed to me that the hospitality got more and more lavish as we advanced further into western Bhutan. The frequency and the variety of food also increased as we approached our journey's end.

The King was received at the gate of Paro dzong by the Paro Penlop with the most elaborate welcome. It was unsurpassed in our travelling experiences till then. Windows, balconies and vantage points of the dzong were filled with spectators.

The position of the Paro Penlop entailed great power and wealth. He had a free hand in the disposal of tax receipts because such resources were not accountable to the King. Like Trongsa dzong, Paro dzong was a store house of taxes collected in-kind - from rice to mustard oil. Rows of leather bags full of mustard oil, used for oil lamps in the dzong, hung on racks in the cellar of the dzong. I was amazed by the splendour of the halls and chambers occupied by the Paro Penlop in Ugyen Pelri Palace. These were more commodious and better furnished than those in Trongsa dzong, Kinga Rabden or Wangdecholing.

The entourage halted for three nights in Paro. During those three days, the high and the mighty of Paro, civil and monastic representatives, ex-officials, well wishers and dungpas came to call on the King out of courtesy, or to redress their grievances. They arrived early at dawn outside the gateway to Paro dzong and waited till they could be summoned by turn.

Also present at Paro was Gongzim Sonam Tobgye, one of the few officials with the rank of an orange scarf and something of the foreign minister of Bhutan in those days, beside being the point of contact between Bhutan and India.

Every year, Gongzim Sonam Tobgye dispatched a team of attendants with Rs. 100,000 which was paid by the Government of India to Bhutan. An amount of Rs. 50,000 was paid as compensation according to the Treaty of Sinchula, 1865, for the annexation of about 300 sq miles of Bhutanese territory. The amount was doubled by the Anglo-Bhutanese Treaty of Punakha, 1910. As there was no means except physically to transmit the money, it was carried by people on their backs to Wangdecholing. Even sure-footed horses were not trusted for the transportation of this valuable consignment. There might have been other remittances in the consignment, which came escorted all the way from Kalimpong.

The entrance of the train of people into Wangdecholing Palace with boxes of money caused much excitement there. As the escorts and attendants with money approached the palace, they hoisted a white banner and marched into the palace with acertain pomp natural to people in possession of a large amount of money (even if it was not actually theirs). Equally, His Majesty expressed his pleasure at their arrival by ordering a marchang ceremony (wine libation ritual) to be put up in the gateway to welcome the bearers of the cash consignment. Otherwise, only high lamas would be greeted with a marchang ceremony by His Majesty. Gongzim chose his favourite attendants to deliver the boxes of coins. As bearers of money, they were naturally received with generous hospitality in Wangdecholing, and sent back with two ghos each and other gifts.

The entourage finally left for Haa, though a few senior secretaries were left in Paro to reform its tax system. At Haa, Gongzim Sonam Tobgye, the host, outdid the lavishness of all the hospitality which the entourage had hitherto been accorded. Each official of the entourage was given a fully furnished room. The generosity we experienced and relative wealth we observed amongst officials of western Bhutan took me by great surprise. People in Paro seemed to be richer and were accustomed to the consumption of betel nuts as a daily necessity, whereas it was still an occasional indulgence in central Bhutan.

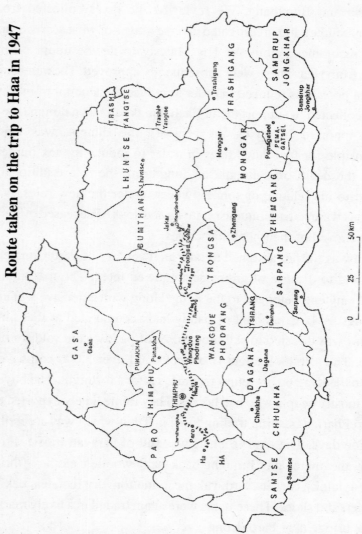

Route taken on the trip to Haa in 1947

Yeshey Wangdi, Lopon Thinley, Sonam Penjor and later

myself were assigned to restructure the taxes of Paro on the model of Trongsa and Bumthang. We reviewed the taxes collected from various sources and investigated diverse usages of what accrued, and made recommendations for His Majesty to decide upon, on his return from Haa. These were subsequently approved. The number of official posts was reduced in order to reduce the amount of in-kind taxes collected to support them. Each dungkhag had a dungpa, who was supported by taxes. In general, one dungpa was made responsible for two dungkhags in order to reduce the tax burden. Upon the death of a dungpa or dungthrim, the role traditionally passed to his relative or son. However, under the new rules, new dungpas were not appointed; relatives and sons of deceased officials were relieved of their hereditary roles.

I was further assigned to take an inventory of Paro Gangteng store and to dispose of grains accumulated there. The mansion of Paro Gangteng belonged to the King, along with extensive wetland holdings. A large amount of paddy had accumulated at that time, which I was directed to sell. Four dres of paddy were sold for one rupee. The sale took about two weeks and over 3,000 coins were paid to the King on his return from Haa after a fortnight. The buyers were mostly people who had horses. They immediately exported the rice to Phari, a bustling trading town in Tibet which was accessible in three days. The road to Phari was full of caravan traffic. From Phari, the merchants brought back salt, woollen clothes (thruk, nambu, jalok), carpets, lard, yak meat, mutton, dry fish, tea, baking powder, and shoes. These items were again traded in a lively market by the bridge near Paro dzong.

His Majesty wished to relax before the arduous journey back

and held a week long game of archery in Paro. Meanwhile, a special messenger brought the news of the death of his younger brother, Dasho Naku in Jangchubling monastery in Kurtoe. Both his brother Dasho Naku, and his younger sister Ashi Wangmo, lived in Kurtoe where she had her estates of Thimshung, Zhamleng and Dungkar. But they gradually moved to Jangchubling monastery, built for the two of them. The children of the serfs and neighbouring villages were recruited as monks and priests in Jangchubling monastery. Dasho Naku was the Dronyer before he became monk and was an ardent disciple of the Karmapa. Ashi Wangmo, sister of His Majesty, an extraordinary and resolute woman, was also a monk and a disciple of the Karmapa. The death of Dasho Naku had an unsettling effect on Ashi Wangmo; she left Jangchubling for good and spent most of her life in Tshurphu in Tibet.

The entourage hastened to Bumthang as soon as the news of Dasho Naku's death reached His Majesty. Dasho Naku's funeral was held much later in Shabthang, upstream from Kurje, because of the long period needed for the preparation of funeral rites.

On the day of the cremation, His Majesty sat on a chair next to the flaming pyre. It was apparent that the occasion had induced an emotional state in him. He was no longer the detached person which he constantly attempted to project. His Majesty could not restrain tears from dripping out in public, as he took masses of butter in his hand, raised it to his head, concentrated in prayer for a while before dumping it on the pyre in order for the wood to burn steadily. The butter crackled in the fire, glowing with a blue luminescence.

It was almost five months before I returned from Western Bhutan to Wangdecholing, via Trongsa and Kinga Rabden where I halted for several weeks. Some days after I reached Wangdecholing, I was informed most unexpectedly that Pedon Wangmo was pregnant. I was completely unprepared for this news. This was a fact which was not anticipated by anybody at the time of the earlier settlement. As it was pointed out to me, I had no option but to take her as my wife. I now had to settle the matter fully with her husband, to whom I was liable to pay a substantial sum. The amount of restitution was much beyond my capacity to pay. In this and many other critical occasions I faced, Dronyer Jigme was most thoughtful and generous. On this occasion, he gave me a present of one hundred rupees - in coins - and a pack of broad cloth. He estimated that this amount, coupled with the fabric roll, would be sufficient to pay her husband as restitution for marital dissolution. However, the level of compensation was still considered by the other party to be paltry. Since my father was unable to raise the level of payment, the discussions ran into a stalemate.

My father now went to see the Elder Queen about the case, with the same hundred coins and broad cloth originally meant for the other party. Her Majesty was gracious enough to give a patient hearing to my father and accept all the hundred coins and the cloth, as a token of her sympathy with our case. This tacitly meant that the Elder Queen would be a bulwark against further persecution by the other party. No more was said about higher payment because of the possibility of wider confrontation involving very important persons. The case was suddenly abandoned in the middle of its track. Thus, without paying even the hundred coins and the piece of cloth to her husband, Pedon Wangmo came to be my wife, and I a father. This was a turn of events I had not anticipated, as marriage and fatherhood were not what I had previously contemplated. However, the chain of events led her to my village as the housewife, a position which badly needed filling, since the death of my mother.

8

ENTANGLED WEB OF TAXATION

❝All that accrues to me is the butter tax. I was not aware that
my people have been paying so much taxes in terms of
both commodities and labour. Dzongkhags have absorbed a lot by
compelling my people to pay too many taxes. Who are the ones to
consume these taxed goods? This must be accounted for." His
Majesty voiced his concern about the burden of tax.

He issued writs directly to the people seeking accurate details
of each household's tax obligations. The writs asked them to send
their replies without consulting any officials in the dzongkhag who
might make the reports biased. The reply to His Majesty from
Khoma gewog in Kurtoe, which was probably dated 1946, calculated
the annual taxes a household in Khoma paid in those years. The
reply is as convoluted and complicated as the many kinds of taxes it
describes. The weights of tax commodities were measured in sang,
shey, joey, and jaam and the volume of tax commodities was
measured in je[6].

---

[6] Measure of volume
   10 chupar = 1 phuta (= 333 gm)
    5 phuta = 1 dres   (= 1.67 kg)
   20 dres   = 1 ba   (= 33.3 kg)
   20 dres   = 1 dos   (= 33.3 kg)
                        or 1 back-load

Measure of weight
1 sang   = 333 gms
2 sangs = 1 joey = 666 gms
3 sangs = 1 kg
5 sangs = 1 shey

The reply says:

"To the lotus feet of the most high golden throne of the ruler of the land, the Precious Kusho of the Dual System, who is the master of fortune and power:

"We the six tax paying subjects of Khoma would like to submit the list of taxes levied on each taxed person (head of the household).

"To begin with, tax payer Taula is levied one shey of butter for Punakha Domchoe and Lhamo Domchoe (Thimphu Domchoe) and four shey of butter for Tshongjur.

"Further, on each trelpa (tax paying household) is levied five boobs (a boob of textile is the length of the textile sufficient for the dress for a man or a woman) of textile for Punakha Domchoe and Lhamoi Domchoe two boobs of textile, seven sangs of butter as seemar and eight sangs of butter as tomar for Tshongjur; fifty two je of paddy towards the cost of one meat animal for Punthangpa (Desi or Shabdrung in Punakha); fifty six je of paddy towards the cost of one bullock for Punthangpa; twenty je of paddy towards the cost of one jatsa (castrated mithun ox); and fourteen je of paddy towards the cost of one calf bullock. A calf bullock is also supplied collectively by the serfs of Khoma to Punthangpa. When the monks of Trongsa move to Bumthang from Trongsa, each tax payer delivers at Gyetsa in Bumthang five je of dry chillies and five jaams of sliced and dried pumpkin. In addition, each tax payer supplies some amount of fruits, five je of green chillies and five jaams of fresh pumpkin.

"The following are taxes paid to the lower part (occupied by the administration) of Lhuntsi dzong: forty je of paddy as wangyon; one large heap of firewood; sixty baskets; ten joey of paper bark;

twenty joey of ash; a hundred joey of paddy straw in the eleventh month; three hundred joey of green fodder in the second month; one rope, one bucket and one trough for the tapon (chief of stable) of Lhuntsi; twenty one je of paddy towards the cost of one pig for Blessed Rainy Day festivity for the Khoma Sasungpa (official based at Khoma). The chipon of Khoma is responsible for the payment of one boob of textile; one pitcher of araa and one bangchung (small basket) of rice snacks towards the cost of tsendar and rudar (ceremonial standards) for the Khoma Sasungpa. Further, each tax payer has to supply to Lhuntsi one hundred and twenty zungs (pair) of shingles; and forty-six je of paddy to make up for not raising a pig for Lhuntsi dzong.

"As porterage tax (labour tax to move goods), each tax payer has to transport: forty je of rice from Lhuntsi to Khomteng Lhakhang (a Tibetan settlement across the border) and forty-four je of salt back from Khomteng Lhakhang to Lhuntsi; eight hundred and forty je of paddy collected as thojab tax from Takmachu area to Lhuntsi dzong; one hundred and eighty je of paddy for trelpa households (full fledged tax payers), and one hundred and twenty je of paddy for moringmo (partial tax payers) households from Dromshong to Lhuntsi dzong.

"Moreover, each tax payer has to pay to Lhuntsi one shey of butter as tax for each head of cattle and one je of paddy in lieu of another form of butter tax known as tsa mar (butter which might have been exchanged with salt distributed by the Lhuntsi dzong could have been commuted to a butter tax later). Whenever there are double months (e.g. two seventh months which is possible in Bhutanese calender) in a year, each tax payer has to pay fourteen je of paddy and six shey of butter as entitlements on account of the extra month to Lhuntsi Zongpon. Each tax payer pays twenty je of paddy towards the cost of a pig for Lhuntsi Zongpon.

"Each tax payer has to husk forty je of paddy (which is extremely time consuming when it is done manually) for Lhuntshi Zongpon.

"Further, each tax payer pays to the upper part (occupied by the monk body) of Lhuntsi dzong the following: four sangs of butter; one je of mustard; one hundred and five je of paddy towards the cost of meat; twenty five je of paddy towards the cost of one pig. Every six months, each tax payer has to husk one hundred and eighty je of paddy. The six tax payers of Khoma supplied collectively two hides as hide tax.

"The drami (serfs) of Khoma collectively pay twelve shey of butter and thirty boobs of textile. The serfs of Drakgong collectively pay twelve shey and two sang of butter and twelve boobs of textile.

"Ugyen, a moringmo household of Khoma, pays two sheys of butter and four boobs of textile for Punakha Domchoe and Lhamoi Domchoe; one shey of butter, two matam and one boob of textile for Tshongjur. Katala, a zurpa (not a full-fledged tax paying household) of Khoma pays one boob of textile and one shey of butter; twenty je of paddy in lieu of labour mobilized for work on shifting cultivation land of the dzong; and sixty zung (pairs) of shingles. Katala has to transport as porterage tax three hundred and sixty je of paddy from Takmachu to Lhuntsi and one hundred je of paddy from Dromshong to Lhuntsi. We are all liable also for dzongsel woola (dzong maintenance labour tax). Wherefore, we - the tax paying subjects of Khoma - submit for your gracious information."

ENTANGLED WEB OF TAXATION

Even omitting the irregular but significant amount of taxes levied on account of double months occurring in a calender, in- kind taxes were extremely oppressive. The most conservative estimate of the important in-kind taxes paid by a typical tax paying household per year could be as follows: three hundred eighty five je (462 kg) of paddy; 34 sangs (28 kg) of butter; 120 pairs of wooden shingles; 7 boobs of textile; sixty baskets; 10 joey of bark for paper; 10 joey of ash; 100 joey of paddy straw; 300 joey of dry grass; one je of mustard; 5 je of dry chillies and 5 jaams of dry sliced pumpkins.

As labour tax, every tax payer was obliged to husk over 360 je (over 432 kg) of paddy in Lhuntsi dzong. Every tax payer was also responsible for transporting over 1000 je (1200 kg) of cereal from one place to another, beside being subjected to other kinds of labour taxes. Undoubtedly, people worked half the time not for their own livelihood or welfare. His Majesty gained a clear view that people in some parts of his kingdom were being crushed by the weight of the existing tax system.

For most of the time, whether we were in Wangdecholing, Kinga Rabden or elsewhere on trips round the country, His Majesty engaged all of us (secretaries) on the huge task of reforming the tax system. After I became a part of the small secretarial team of five people, I spent much of my time also on the effort, initiated by His Majesty, to change the tax system. As I recalled earlier, the main purpose was to reduce the burden of tax on the tax payers and make taxes less iniquitous.

The results, unsung in history, were highly beneficial for the people. There was a drastic curtailment on the number of offices whose necessity was questionable, but whose burden on the people was undisputed. For example, the office of the dungpa was a drain on the manpower and resources of the community.

There were labour taxes in varying man days between summer and winter seasons. In addition to tilling the land belonging to the monasteries and local authority in one's own dungkhag and performing many other kinds of labour taxes, households also provided - turn by turn - a few workers for the dungpa as cook, herder and so forth.

In terms of in-kind tax, a whole range of edible and non-edible things were paid, as wherewithal not only for dungpas but also for officials higher than him in a dzong: such as tsanyer (fodder master), tapon (chief of stable), banyer (cattle master), shanyer (meat master), gorap (gate controller), nyerchen (senior store master or chief steward), zimpon (chamberlain), darpon (chief of attendants), dronyer (guest master), zongpon (fort-governor) etc.

All of these officials had an impressive array of staff under them. For example, a nyerchen or chief steward of Jakar usually had a staff of twelve to fifteen working exclusively in the store. A gorap had a staff of five or so, and the shanyer or meat master had a staff of eight or so. Shanyer and banyer were often substitutes and it was more usual to have only a shanyer. The posts of tapon, dronyer and darpon were filled only in important dzongs like Trongsa, Punakha and Wangduephodrang. Because of its proximity to the Wangdecholing Palace, Jakar also had a tapon.

These officials and their staff had clear responsibilities but they became blurred as soon as the third King introduced administrative reforms. But until then, a dzong had usually three layers of functionaries. The first layer consisted of the attendants, known locally as garpas. The number of attendants assigned to an official of the dzong was broadly fixed, so that it would not differ haphazardly from dzong to dzong. It was also necessary to limit the number of attendants working for an official who were fed by the nyerchen or chief steward of the dzong out of in-kind tax resources. This would ensure that they consumed only the food stock allocated to them.

In the second layer, prominent posts included gorap or gate controller, shanyer or meat master and tsanyer or fodder master. They were appointed by their respective controlling officers who were in turn appointed by the King. Tsanyer or fodder master was the warden of feed and fodder for livestock, especially horses. Horses were kept in reserve for carriage and riding, probably in many dzongs. Feed and fodder also had to be issued for the horses of officials passing through the district. For such purposes, it was the responsibility of the tsanyer or fodder master and his staff to collect hay and grass through fodder tax. The gorap or gate controller was responsible for the safety and cleanliness of the dzong compound. By enforcing a labour tax known as 'mewang', people were requisitioned to clean and guard the dzongs. The shanyer or meat master was responsible for supplying meat to the common mess in the dzong, which fed numerous monks, the staff of high officials like the gorap, shanyer, zimpon, zongpon and his own staff. He did this through a complicated arrangement which will be clear from the description of in-kind taxes paid, for example, in Bumthang.

The top layer of officials in a dzong consisted of the zongpon (fort-governor), dronyer (guest master), zimpon (chamberlain) and nyerchen (chief steward or store master) who were often the direct appointees of the King. They were of the rank of nyikem or red scarf officers. The zongpon was the chief in the district, and usually arbitrated disputes, assisted by his chamberlain.

By the time of the second King, many posts of zongpon had fallen vacant and in their places, he appointed dzongtshabs or fort-governors in-charge, instead of full-fledged fort-governors. The function of a nyerchen or chief steward of a dzong was similar to that of a housewife. The similarity went as far as the responsibility for brewing and distilling araa. He maintained food-stock, built up by in-kind taxes, and ran the dzong mess. He was the official host for calendar rituals, offerings, festivities, and visiting official delegations and messengers passing through the district.

The main goods collected through in-kind taxation during the reign of the second King were food grains like wheat, buckwheat and rice; yak-meat and beef; mustard oil and butter; textiles of raw silk, cotton and wool; bark of paper plants and ash; pig iron; lac; firewood and building timber; gun powder; animal feed and fodder (grass and hay); baskets, mats and ropes and leather bags and pelts. The type of in-kind taxes imposed on the people of an area depended on what they produced or their resource base. For example, collection of in-kind taxes like yak meat was specific to Paro and Haa; cotton and raw silk textiles to Khengrig Namsum and Trashigang; and pig iron to Paro and Thimphu.

Before I discuss about the in-kind taxes, I should explain that in-kind taxes not only varied geographically, but the entity to whom taxes were owed was not always the state through its officials in the dzong. There were enclaves in a district which did not pay any tax to the local dzong but paid instead directly to any one of the following persons: the King, the Elder Queen, the powerful aunt of the second King and the sister of the first King, Ashi Sonam Chodon, and Lame Gonpa Dasho Phuntsho Wangdi, grandson of King Ugyen Wangchuck and great grandson of Trongsa Penlop Choje Pema Tenzin. The majority of the people of Zhongar, Trashigang, Dungsam Dosum and Khengrig Namsum paid suma tax directly to one of them. In Trashigang, most of the people were suma, leaving only a few places (like Rangshikhar, Radhi and Paam) to pay taxes to the officials in the local dzong and Punakha. The households known as suma paid their dues and performed obligatory services to the families of two nationally entrenched aristocratic households of the day: Wangdecholing and Lame Gonpa.

Nevertheless, a zongpon or nyerchen found ways to tax the people more than what was stipulated, and His Majesty sent circulars frequently reminding people not to pay anything above the fixed amount. His Majesty took a serious view of reports against people who infracted tax limits. There were several cases of punishment, but one involving Howdrukjay of Tungkhar springs clearly to my mind. Howdrukjay was an attendant of Ashi Wangmo, younger sister of the King. He had taken the liberty to mobilize three porters to carry the produce of Ashi Wangmo's rice fields from Kurtoe to Bumthang. But there was no royal permission to raise these labourers in an ad hoc manner. When this came to the attention of His Majesty, Howdrukjay was summoned to Wangdecholing; he was stripped, tied to a tree and kept standing on spherical river stone for a whole day. He was going to be flogged, but was finally excused and charged a fine of Rs. 1200 which had to be paid by morning tea the next day. Through Lhuntsi Zongpon Kunzang Namgyel (cousin of the King) who acted as an intermediary, Howdrukjay borrowed Rs. 1200 from the Younger Queen and paid the amount to His Majesty the following morning.

The following morning, His Majesty was quite forgiving and returned Rs. 800. He remarked, "You have not followed my repeated injunctions not to deploy my people without permission. I have issued circulars as many as the leaves of the tree that nobody should make my people work except for the number of days I have specified in writing. I am excusing you this time, for you are a servant of my sister Wangmo. You shall remember that you will go along with Chamkharchu (Chamkhar River) if you violate my circular on porterage tax."

In a village, there could broadly be three types of households. Firstly, there were tax paying households (trelpa) who paid full taxes to local authorities of the dzong, to Punakha and to members of the aristocratic families. Secondly, there were a minority of zurpa or moringmo household. Zurpa households consisted of a couple who had broken away from their parental household and were setting up a fully fledged household of their own. Moringmo households consisted often of single mothers and widows, who were vulnerable because of lack of male workers and deserved tax relief. These households also paid partial taxes to local authorities of the dzong, to Punakha, and to the members of the aristocratic families. Trelpa and zurpa households were subjected to taxation by multiple sources of authorities, though the burden was much less on zurpa and moringmo households.

Thirdly, there were suma households who paid taxes directly to one of the aristocratic families. Suma were present, mainly in

Trashigang, in Eastern dzongkhags and Khengrig Namsum. Suma households faced the lowest burden of tax. The unequal burden of tax between suma and trelpa generated an acrimonious relationship between the people of these two households; bickering between them was not infrequent. Suma households were protected by Lame Gonpa, His Majesty, the Queens, and Ashi Sonam Chodon (alias Wangdecholing Ama), sister of King Ugyen Wangchuck, in return for their suma payment, a form of yearly cash payment or in-kind tax payment. The amount would be either about ten betams (coins) or one piece of pangkhep or thara textile. They became suma simply by declaring that they would like to pay their taxes directly to aristocratic families of Wangdecholing or Lame Gonpa. People from various parts of Eastern Bhutan voluntarily offered to become suma to either Wangdecholing or Lame Gonpa. Those who sought this station were issued a letter by whoever they approached - the King, the Elder Queen, Ashi Sonam Chodon or Lame Gonpa Dasho Phuntsho Wangdi - who had the power of remitting their taxes and other obligations to the authorities of the dzongs. When they failed to pay their suma tribute on time, attendants were sent to recover penalties in addition to the fixed tribute. People sought to become suma because this gave them a sense of belonging to a certain powerful authority. The suma of Wangdecholing and Lame Gonpa often climbed the social ladder by transferring their loyalty to the King. They offered to become the suma of the King, the highest authority.

The distinction between the tax paying households and suma was far from clear, as even the tax paying households (trelpa) in some areas paid some of the taxes directly to Wangdecholing instead of local dzongs. For example, certain grain taxes (thojab) introduced in Bumthang, Mangde and Kurtoe by His Majesty; butter tax levied in Kurtoe, Kheng and Bumthang; and textile tax levied in Kheng and Trashigang, were paid to His Majesty instead of local dzongs. Resources thus collected augmented the output of royal estates and herds and were put at the disposal of His Majesty the King.

The settlers in Southern Bhutan, then known as pahari, were not taxed in-kind. However, Gongzim Sonam Tobgye collected a certain token amount of cash from the settlers in Southern Bhutan, for he had appointed officials in Southern Bhutan to collect taxes. One of them was based in Gaylegphug. This tax income accrued directly to Gongzim Sonam Tobgye.

I should perhaps recall in some detail the in-kind taxes collected in Bumthang just before the tax reform started. The taxation collected in other districts can be inferred from the situation that existed in Bumthang. First, there were two main types of food grain taxes, namely wangyon and thojab on wheat and buckwheat. In other areas, wangyon (also known as wangtho), and thojab were collected in terms of both rice and mustard. The main difference between wangyon and thojab was that wangyon did not bear any correlation with land holding or output: a household with a small land holding paid a high amount of wangyon, compared to a household with a large land holding, and conversely, a household with a large land holding paid a negligible amount of wangyon. The meaning of wangyon might enable us to understand the anomaly associated with it: it means 'blessing-offering', and the offering of food grains might have been made in olden times in response to blessings by various incarnations of Shabdrungs and their stand-ins.

Such one-time offering might have been connivingly recorded in their thrams (registers) as perpetual offerings, and collected as a yearly tax. Wangyon existed throughout Bhutan but, as in Bumthang, it was not proportional to the land holdings of the payer.

Thojab, however, was based on land holdings. On a plot of land capable of producing twenty dres of grain, three dres were paid as thojab tax. While thojab and wangyon were levied in Bumthang, there was no thojab in Kurtoe and Mangde, although these two districts had substantial paddy holdings. His Majesty later introduced thojab on paddy land in these two districts in order to support the newly-recruited soldiers.

There were two types of butter tax in Bumthang, namely, annual and monthly butter tax. There were two sub-divisions of monthly butter tax: benda and khodrup. The annual butter tax was levied according to the number of cows in the herd. Five sangs or 1.5 kg of butter was paid for each cow in a year. There was no annual butter tax in either Kurtoe or Khengrig Namsum. His Majesty introduced it in these two areas though the rate was comparatively lower; the rate was three sangs for each cow in a year. But the two kinds of monthly butter tax were peculiar to Bumthang, and made the livestock sector in Bumthang heavily taxed. Every month, every gewog in Bumthang had to supply one hundred sangs of butter as benda butter tax, and another one hundred sangs of butter as khodrup butter tax, to Jakar dzong.

Each gewog also had to provide a certain number of bullocks every year on account of beef animal tax. The number from each gewog in Bumthang was ten bullocks for Trongsa Penlop, four bullocks for Jakar nyerchen (store master), four bullocks for Jakar zimpon (chamberlain) and one bullock collectively for Jakar gorap (gate controller), tsanyer (fodder master) and shanyer (meat master). Altogether from Bumthang, one of the smallest districts in the country, over forty live cattle were paid as meat tax to the shanyer or meat master of Jakar. These were not slaughtered but exchanged on a one to one basis with carcasses of cattle which had died through either natural or accidental causes. It was mandatory for the people to declare the death of any cattle and surrender the carcass to the shanyer.

His Majesty the King often recalled that his late father, King Ugyen Wangchuck, wanted the tax burden to be lower and made equitable throughout the country, and he therefore worked constantly towards this goal. Tax reform was first implemented in Bumthang. He engaged us - the secretarial team - to form an accurate picture of the type and the amount of taxes paid to various officials in both dzongkhags and dungkhags. We discussions on taxes with the gups of Bumthang. It took us a year just to peruse systematically and understand the existing tax system in Bumthang. Then, the King brought the rate of most taxes down to alleviate the tax burden. Some types of taxes were abolished. He made the taxes equitable and uniform among all gewogs and households in Bumthang. After we were done with the tax system in Bumthang, our energies were directed towards the study of the tax system in Trongsa dzongkhag, and gradually to rest of the country. The reform of the tax system was a task that could not be completed during his reign.

As noted earlier, it took a year for us to study comprehensively the multiplicity of goods collected and labour services requisitioned in various parts of Bumthang by both district and the sub-district functionaries. Bumthang had four gewogs: Tang, Ura, Choskhor and Chumey; and Brokpa Khasum, namely, Khangdang, Ngangpa and Durpa. The lowering of taxes inevitably required the abolition of offices which absorbed resources of the people. In Bumthang alone, there were three dungpas - Tang Dungpa, Chumey Dungpa and Ura Dungpa. All three posts were abolished to cut down the labour requisition and in-kind taxes.

The second dzongkhag to benefit from tax reform was Trongsa. There were four dungpas in Trongsa - Brakteng, Langthel, Tangsibi, and Nubi. Three of these posts were withdrawn and these dungkhags were directly administered by the former Nubi Dungpa, who was based in Trongsa dzong.

After completing the work on the tax system for Bumthang and Trongsa, our focus switched to the reform of the tax system in Trashigang district. Knowledgeable people from Trashigang were invited to Wangdecholing for consultation. The secretarial staff needed to be augmented because of the scale of the task demanded by the relatively larger size of Trashigang district. A monk from Trashigang Ramjar, Tenzin, was fortuitously and reluctantly inducted as an additional hand. He was the able preceptor of Trashigang monk body, well known for his fast and tidy script, good at geomancy and astrological forecast, and accomplished in rituals. The throne of abbot could easily have been his if he stayed on in the local hierarchical organization. But he was indispensably useful to the chief of Trashigang district, Zongpon Dopola, and was converted into his secretary. Fascinated by guns, Tenzin was toying with Zongpon Dopola's pistol one day while he was among a group of people. The pistol went off and by accident killed another person. It was a convention that the King should be informed about any killing or manslaughter, but with the connivance of Zongpon Dopola, a plausible story was fabricated about the cause of the death and certain restitution was paid to the bereaved family by Dopola. It was done to enable Tenzin to continue working for Dopola. Some two years later, the King came to know the truth and summoned Tenzin. He was still in his monk's robe when he arrived but he was commanded to change into normal clothes and enlisted as a secretarial staff member. He could write superbly at tremendous speed and his reputation preceded his arrival.

The team worked in the central tower of Wangdecholing by first preparing a draft on slate. The draft was rewritten onto bark paper and four fair copies made. Tenzin had the fastest hand and sparkled in the group. Given the same time limit, he could write four copies; I managed to do three, whereas others struggled to finish only one. Within a week of starting the work, His Majesty presented him with a sword sheathed in a silver scabbard. Still, Tenzin hoped to revert to his former monk's life. Indeed, his aim was fulfilled after he put a few years or so of work into tax reform; he took leave and never returned. He became a lama.

We investigated existing taxes in minute detail, and made room for reduction on the supposition that a number of dungpas would be relieved. We also applied certain norms for food allowances for various officials to estimate the amount of tax reduction. After the decision was made, the changes in the tax system were communicated to the officials and tax payers through a circular known as Cheta Kasho. Scores of Cheta Kasho were issued jointly to the dungpas and the people. Each Cheta Kasho ran to four big square pages of bark paper, measuring 2.5 feet by 2.5 feet. Cheta Kasho contained detailed information on the reduced tax liabilities in terms of both labour and goods.

9

MEN WHO RULED

Western and Eastern Bhutan were demarcated by the Pelela (pass), based on an ancient administrative division. On either side of Pelela, there was a Penlop who wielded almost paramount power. For the time being, the King was also a proxy for the Trongsa Penlop: his trusted nephew Tshering Penjor was the Paro Penlop. The King had consolidated his control over western Bhutan by appointing his close and loyal relative, who came from Lame Gonpa in Bumthang, to the second key position. When he left Bumthang to take up his position in Paro, Tshering Penjor was accompanied by his confidants drawn from Lame Gonpa and Tamshing. He brought along, for instance, Nohla who became the nyerchen of Paro. A host of other lower positions were occupied by the staff he had had in Lame Gonpa. However, His Majesty reserved the prerogative to appoint people to higher posts such as Druk Zongpa (zongpon of Drukgyel dzong), Dorji Zongpa (zongpon of Dorji dzong, near Dawakha), and Dronyer of Paro.

Paro (Parkor Tshodruk) was divided into six dungkhags, each administered by a dungpa. In addition, Naja Dungsum, the area that included Samtse, was controlled by the Paro Penlop through three dungpas, bringing the total to nine dungpas in Paro. Tshento was a separate administrative unit directly under a red scarf official, the Druk Zongpa. Usually, dungpas were appointed or dismissed directly by the King. The exceptions were dungpas of Paro dzongkhag, who could be appointed by the Paro Penlop himself. However, the ngikem or red scarf officers under the Paro Penlop were directly appointed by the King.

Paro had numerous state-supported monasteries and retreats. Laymen who took time off to live in these monasteries and retreats were made responsible for renovating them for being exempted from other kinds of taxes.

The district of Thimphu, then known as Tshochengay, lay between Hinglayla, Jelela and Chimithangkha. It included Kabji, Toep, Jimep, Toewang, Mewang, Kawang, Chang and Baap. Each of these areas was controlled by a dungpa, though two of these officials were oddly styled as Penlops, i.e., Toepi Penlop and Kabji Penlop.

The post of Thimphu Zongpon was left vacant. It was now governed by a dzongtshab, Rukubji Tenzin. His main function was to arbitrate disputes arising in the district. Lopon Tsamangpa, a monk turned nyerchen and man of high integrity, was responsible for tax collection, including pig iron. Iron was mined in Gey Nyenkha under Thimphu, and the people of Gey Nyenkha paid only pig iron by way of taxes. In the late 1950's, I recall that some people from Gey Nyenkha were ingenuous enough to bring pieces of railway track from North West Bengal to Thimphu dzong instead of smelting their own iron ore. They were obviously depriving the railway yards of some of their reserve railway tracks. In the northern part of Thimphu (including Laya, Lingshi, Dagala), only dairy goods were collected as taxes. Similarly, taxes of only dairy goods were imposed by the authorities of Punakha on the Lungnana yak herders. The nyerchen, or chief of store and food supplies, was Langmarp. The

Thimphu zimpon's function, which had depreciated quite a bit, was to allocate firewood which had been collected as tax. It was stored and managed systematically because of the large numbers of officers and monks who depended on its supply. Some people in Thimphu and Punakha provided rice in lieu of firewood.

Chapcha was under the jurisdiction of the dzongtshab of Thimphu, though there was a red scarf officer entitled Chapcha Penlop.

Punakha had relatively fewer people in proportion to the amount of arable land. The wealthy people of Thimphu had dual land holdings: one in Thimphu and another in Punakha, to where they moved in winter. However, since the taxes were based on land holdings, the same people had to pay taxes to two dzongkhags. The highest civil authority in Punakha was a dzongtshab, Mani of Wang, whose father was long ago the zongpon of Gasa. Another notable official was its Nyerchen, Chansher Dorji of Sha. Punakha had two Dungpas: one in Shungpa and the other in Jasop. The district would have been smaller if Gasa were not part of Punakha. Mani controlled Gasa district too. Gasa had three gups: at Goen Shari, Goen Khatod and Goen Khamed.

Wangduephodrang used to have a zongpon but had recently been put under the charge of a nyerchen, Tshewang Namgyel of Tangsibi. The post of dronyer was vacant. The zimpon was Zeko of Sha, who succeeded his father to the post. Wangduephodrang district comprised of Sha Dargay: Jena, Wachen, Ngawang, Ruep, Gaseng Tsho Gongm, Gaseng Tsho Wom and Sha Tsho Nyi that sprawled on either side of the river. In addition, there were three dungkhags: Om Nahep, Dangchup, and La Gongsum (sub-divided into

Longtoed, Phobjikha and Wangchukha). Like the Jasops of Punakha, the people of Sha had two houses; one for winter in Sha and another for summer in Phobjikha.

Bumthang was controlled by Zimpon Dandi Pem of Ura Tangsibi and Nyerchen Geom Dorji. Nyerchen Geom Dorji succeeded his father to the post. Zimpon Pema was nicknamed 'Dandi' Pema because he was big, broad, tall and strong and often carried a palanquin ('dandi' in dzongkha and Hindi). Dandi Pem often used to arbitrate cases without grasping the essence of litigation. He was easily convinced by the party who appealed to him first and accepted the force of their argument. Equally, when the other party presented their brief, he was swayed by its members.

Trongsa was governed, in principle, by the Trongsa Penlop, who happened to be the King in his dual role as Trongsa Penlop and the King of Bhutan. In his absence from Trongsa, which was almost always the case, authority was delegated to a group of officials led by Zimpon Adaap Sangay and Nyerchen Lopon Paybar of Singphu. Adaap Sangay, a just and forthright man, belonged to a well known family. Nyerchen Paybar of Singphu was a brilliant store master. He always orchestrated big ceremonies and feasts, including the annual fair in Wangdecholing, where food was prepared for hundreds of people. He stage managed all such occasions effortlessly.

Lhuntsi had a zongpon, Kunzang Namgyel. Though he was a white scarf official, he was a relation of the King and was empowered to appoint his sub-ordinate dungpas for Koor Doshi, namely, Kurtoe, Khoma, Menji and Takmachu. Takmachu was divided into Toetsho and Metsho. As with many hereditary posts, Kunzang Namgyel succeeded his father to the post.

Trashigang was the largest and most populous of all the dzongkhags. It was managed by Zongpon Dopola, son of the late Zongpon of Trashigang. Their family, based in Kurtoe Sukubji, became very wealthy.

The maximum number of yak herders was found in a part of Trashigang district, namely, in Merak and Sakteng. Annual dairy taxes on these yak herders came to about two hundred back loads of butter. The butter stock was transported from Trashigang to Zhongar by the people of Trashigang, from Zhongar to Ura by people of Zhongar, and from Ura to Trongsa by the people of Bumthang. His Majesty used the butter collected from Merak and Sakteng to offer a thousand butter lamps (tongchoe) every alternate month, either in Jambay Lhakhang or Kurje Lhakhang.

Trashigang dzong was destroyed by fire during Dopola's lifelong tenure. He masterminded its reconstruction and also built a new temple in Yonphula. Trashigang dzong took only three years to rebuild because of the abundant availability of labour.

Yangtse was a separate administrative unit and had its own administrator - zongsungpa (watchman of the castle) - who was appointed by the King. However, the zongsungpa was under the jurisdiction of Trashigang Zongpon Dopola.

Dungsam (now Pema Gatshel) comprised the Dosum, and used to be controlled by a sasungpa (sentry of the strategic pass), appointed by the King. Although there was a sasungpa in Dungsam, for all practical purpose the sasungpa was accountable to Zhongar Zongpon Kunzang Wangdi.

Zhongar (now Monggar) consisted of Kengkhar, Tormashong, Tsamang and Chaskhar. These places were controlled by a dungpa each under the overall authority of Zhongar Zongpon Kunzang Wangdi. Kunzang Wangdi succeeded his father as Zhongar Zongpon. Kunzang Apgain, father of Zhongar Zongpon, was a point of reference for etiquette, mask dances and dances. He had two other sons besides Kunzang Wangdi. One of them was Dagana Zongpon Rinzin Dorji and the other was Kengkhar Dungpa Tandin.

The original Zhongar dzong near Karbithang was destroyed by fire; Zhongar Apgain did not rebuild it in the same place because of its inhospitable heat. He decided to move it to Monggar; a mini dzong, which was subsequently enlarged, was built by Kunzang Wangdi.

There were skilled weavers in Dechencholing, at the border of Dungsam and Monggar. No taxes of any kind were levied by the local authorities on inhabitants of these areas. Instead, a form of textile tax known as trolthak was levied. The people had to pay about twenty seven porter loads of pangtshe, pendap and kamtham and other textiles a year, directly to the King. It was also a tradition to distribute yarn and spools of wool to the weavers of Trashigang who were obligated to weave aikabur and lungserma (raw silk textile).

The textile taxes were known as kapey tsatrey in Khengrig Namsum. It was a cotton textile tax which was compensated nominally by salt. Every year, two attendants led a train of porters, carrying twenty back loads of salt, to Khengrig Namsum. Each back load contained a hundred sangs of salt. For every ten sangs of cotton delivered to be spun as tax, a sang of salt was given as compensation. Then the cotton yarn was issued back to the people to be woven into thara, pangkhep or ngosham. Ten sangs of cotton yarn were given to be woven into a piece of thara or pangkhep or ngosham. The return from twenty back loads of salt was about eighteen back loads of textiles.

Daga Lungsum was under the administrative control of Daga Zimpon Rinzin Dorji and his nyerchen.

Zhemgang also had a zongsungpa with a nyerpa. Zhemgang consisted of Khengrig Namsum: Chikor, Nangkor and Tama with a dungpa each. When its Zongpon Jokarp Minjur died, the functions were discharged by a monk for several years. Later, the post was filled by Dasho Thinley Namgyel, a cousin of the Queens. There was hardly any challenging duty in Zhemgang, and so Dasho Thinley Namgyel seldom lived there.

Haa was controlled by a dungpa and the post had become hereditary. Gongzim Sonam Tobgye was a Dungpa of Haa: he was succeeded by his son Jigme, who later became the first Lyonchen of Bhutan. Haa was divided into Jewshi - Je, Katsho, Zongwog and Autsho. Haa Dungpa Dasho Jigme was awarded the red scarf when he was eight years old.

At the forefront of the dratshang (monk body) hierarchy was the Gendup (central monk body), who was in immediate association with the Je Khenpo (Chief Abbot of Bhutan). The strength of Gendup was about seven to eight hundred. The monks of Paro, Wangduephodrang and Trongsa were collectively known as Rabdey. Each Rabdey had about eighty monks. Lhuntsi, Dagana and Trashigang had about sixty monks each; they belonged to a third grouping known as Rabjungpa. The third King brought the average number of Rabdey and Rabjung to about a hundred monks and Gendup to about one thousand monks. Beside the Gendup, every state supported monastery, whether Rabdey and Rabjung, had a lama Neten as their supreme local head, who was appointed by the Je Khenpo. The exception was Trongsa Rabdey, who elected their Lama Neten from their own fold. Trongsa always enjoyed some degree of autonomy from the central monk body. Nyerchens were responsible for boarding and lodging of monks in their respective dzongs. Until the reign of the second King, admissions into the Gendüp, Rabdey and Rabjung were meticulously controlled and restrained because of its implication on in-kind taxes which had to be generated to support them. This issue was carefully assessed by Debi Zimpon Nam (Chamberlain to Desi), a position which existed even during the reign of second King. His office was closely associated with the Gendup and he was an intermediary between the Gendup and the King. In fact, in consultation with the King, he took key decisions about the Gendup, except on rituals and teachings, which were left to the monks.

There was no thrimpon (judge) at the time we were in Kinga Rabden and Wangdecholing. The King was the main dispenser of justice. The litigants appealed to him, and he assigned his courtiers, garpas and secretaries to arbitrate and resolve the disputes. The secretaries were particularly asked to resolve a dispute when it arose between important people. Each litigant submitted the grounds of dispute, on which the arbitrators made detailed comments when the case was tried. The notes of the proceedings were fi nally presented to the King who passed his verdict. Fines were imposed according to the verdict.

The procedure differed slightly when one of the litigants involved was very wealthy and powerful. As soon as a complaint was received against a wealthy family, it was conventional to send an emissary of the King to his house to summon him. The emissary was expected to be treated very lavishly. For instance, there was an adverse report on Zongpon Dopola of Trashigang about abuse of power. Zongpon Dopola had made extravagant demands on the tax payers by asking them to weave an excessive amount of textiles for him. Zongpon Dopola was a wealthy man, because of his trading activities and huge tax base. The King acted on the complaint against Zongpon Dopola by dispatching his attendants Sha Yabjee and Tangsibi Kesang. Dopola was summoned to Wangdecholing to hear the verdict, but he was made to wait in Wangdecholing for several months before he got an audience. All the while, the two attendants were Dopola's guests. To bring them to heel, the decision was delayed considerably for richer people. When he succeeded in calling on the King, he was fined several bags of betam, several cows and many loads of textiles. The two attendants lived off Dopola until the case ended several months later. Dopola was finally obliged to present each attendant with five ghos, a riding mule, five cows and two thousand betams.

Often those accused of some serious offense were stripped and whipped publicly with rods and pelts of various severity and design such as Youpam, Tayu, Zankuichem and Chabji. For a serious crime, the accused was stripped and bound and stretched on a cross for an hour before public birching. For crimes of murder, public lashing was followed by life-long hard labour.

The verdict, once pronounced by the King, could not be reversed except on appeals made through Lopon Kelzang Dawa or the Queens. If the appeals were accepted, pelts and whips were rudely brought into contact with the nose of the accused as a token of public lashing.

There was an outbreak of small pox in Trongsa, and movement between Bumthang and Trongsa was banned. The King strictly prohibited anyone from leaving Trongsa. Someone from Trongsa disobeyed the embargo, and he was caught and brought to Wangdecholing. He was tied but not too securely, for after a few intolerable strokes, he made a dash towards the Chamkharchu, the river flowing nearby. He sprinted as far as he could, ahead of a band of attendants. He came to the bank and dived into the river until he felt he could proceed no further without risking the dangerous currents. He looked back upon the posse closing in around him and out of desperation, threw himself into the currents of the foaming river, which carried him down knocking against the boulders. The men who chased him ran down the bank of the river until they could no longer keep sight of him. All the attendants were penalized by five lashings each for their incompetence in the mishap.

10

AN EPIDEMIC AND A FESTIVAL

In the summer of 1949, before the entourage left for Kinga Rabden, an undiagnosed epidemic swept through the village of Shingnyer in Bumthang. There was no medical relief that the King could mobilize. The country at that stage had an ill equipped hospital in Haa, and Kurtoe Tobgye, a compounder, operated a dispensary for the leprosy centre in Trashigang. Phub Gaytse, the only compounder in Bhutan, gave injections to the King. Phub Gaytse later moved to Wangduephodrang to open a dispensary for malarial control. The medical team was later augmented by the arrival of Dr Kabo, who had studied medicine and had joined the Indian Army. Dr Kabo was quite tall and impressive, and he resembled a European. He could have easily passed for a foreigner. He often decked himself up in his medalled uniform which accentuated his foreign appearance. His decoration and rank were subject of gossip for a while. His appearance and bearing bore the hallmarks of a soldier in the British army in which he was said to have been a captain and which he left to serve the King. There were two other persons - Babu Karchung and Phenchung - who dabbled in medicine, but they were actually veterinary compounders and more at home performing castrations on animals.

As the epidemic in Shingnyer spread throughout the village, the area was isolated by restricting contact with its inhabitants.

Approaches to Shingnyer were blockaded from both sides: at the passes in Karma Koray and Shaythangla. But a line of communication and food supply was kept open. A messenger from the King came to a fixed place everyday where he was met by an inhabitant of Shingnyer at as great a distance as they could keep between them and still hear each other. Every day, the inhabitant brought news about the number of sick and dead in the village. A monthly supply of food was dropped beneath a bough of an old tree to avoid physical contact, from where the inhabitants of the village collected it. Eight months went by, and the epidemic continued to take its toll of thirty lives or so in an oddly silent way, significantly depopulating the small village.

Soon the harvesting time for buckwheat, the staple food of Shingnyer, came. I was commanded to go to organize the harvest. I mobilized a man from each house in Ura and descended to the outskirts of Shingnyer. The village stood on a south-east slope. Pheasants, quails and partridges were sighted frequently in the woods and shrubs in the back yards of village houses. The whole slope was a vast nesting site for pheasants and the young lads of Shingnyer were skilled at setting fine snares and traps for the birds.

My work party harvested the buckwheat fields. After I got to a point from where I could be heard by the villagers, I yelled to ask each household to leave a number of bags to pack their harvest. The epidemic had disrupted the cultivation around the village on a staggering scale. Half of the buckwheat fields were virtually empty and uncontrolled weeds dwarfed the short stems of buckwheat. I and the men cut the crop, threshed and filled the bags with it, and left them in the fields to be retrieved by the owners after we left.

I then left Bumthang to join the entourage which was already in Kinga Rabden. As I recall, one of the exhilarating things I had to do that winter was join the mask dance troupe. Some thirty mask dancers were required to participate in the festival in Trongsa dzong in the 11th Bhutanese month, and athletic retainers were asked to practise mask dances in Kinga Rabden. My uncle Phuntshog Wangdi (who was a chandaap), and I were keen at mask dance, and we were selected to dance in Trongsa Tshechu. The lead mask-dancer was Nagphay, with whom I spent a summer in Dur some years earlier taking a census of the cattle belonging to the royal household. He had by then risen to become Nubi Dungpa, based in Trongsa dzong. He danced with the most elegant gestures and was later appointed the Chief of Mask Dancers in Thimphu.

The festivities in Trongsa dzong fell three months earlier than the annual festival in my uncle's village, Ura. My uncle Phuntshog Wangdi and I decided to leave for the festival in Ura. It had been many years since either of us had gone home during the festival. We excused ourselves from duty on account of a sudden illness, and borrowed a variety of dance costumes from Trongsa dzong. The two of us got to Ura a few days before the festival; but the distinguished hereditary lama, the person who was to preside over the entire celebration, did not arrive from his winter alms round in Monggar. The general enthusiasm, which had built up to an anxious level, was going to be frustrated if the festivities were delayed. Fortunately, the lama arrived just the day before the inauguration of the festival.

As I recall, in Ura, it was the perfect time of the year to stage a festival. The place had just come out of its harsh winter. Its people, ever busy eking out their survival from its unforgiving and unproductive land, were going to let themselves go for once. Though the ground was still bound in permafrost in the upper reaches of the mountain, the cold stream had by and large receded. The air was just warm enough for the people to sit, eat and drink outside and watch the festival dances and songs. The peach blossoms and willow shoots were out. The red-billed choughs were croaking and creaking in the evenings as they came to roost under the eaves. The sweep of pasture land and fields, in this open valley with its wide view, were beginning to green.

Having been away many years, my uncle first went to make a peace offering of drinks to the palace of the local deity, who was also his birth deity. It was a deity to whom the local population could expect support from, and appeal to for help. At the same time, the villagers felt fearful and threatened if it was angered. It was both a destructive and a benign force. My uncle used to pray to the deity whenever he felt baffling powers making his plans go wrong. He then felt better, just as he did before this festival, after completing this process of re-introducing himself to the deity with offerings and prayers.

On the evening before the start of the festival, the community met in the main hall of the community shrine, the venue of the festival. All the residents of the village gathered in this very impressive, pillared hall on the second floor, to discuss the organizational and logistic preparation for the festival. The hall had elaborate pictorials on the walls and statues, sculpture, and metallic casts of gods. At first, I thought there was a subtle incongruity between the exquisite artistic work on the walls and in the sculptures on the one hand, and the peasants on the other, who nevertheless seemed able to feel absolutely at home in the temple, whether they were herders, cultivators, housewives, weavers or lay priests.

On deeper reflection, there was no incongruity in this. In fact, on second thought, I realized that the same peasants were the painters, artists, designers, engineers, carpenters, masons, builders, architects and sculptors of the community shrine. They had participated in its creation, according to their respective capacities. The shrine manifested their own abilities and views. The second incongruity I felt was the buffoonery and teasing that went on in the midst of a serious discussion in a shrine. Yet again, on reflection, I found myself agreeable to the whole idea of a sacred shrine where there was no solemnity and rigidity. The unusually high ceiling of the shrine and the representation of all gods in their symbolic polarities - past and future, male and female, peaceful and wrathful, ascetic and locked in sex, all suggested to me, at that moment, an open-ended, unfathomable yet ironic situation.

The villagers were really meeting that evening to organize the festival, and to participate in the tasting of singchang (beer) to ensure the quality of the singchang was maintained from year to year. The group tasted singchang produced from wheat contributed by every household, and brewed by the four communal breweries. I found the scale of the brewery activity quite staggering. For a community of about four hundred people, some one thousand kilos of wheat were converted into about four thousand litres of singchang, which became public property. The community and its guests consumed singchang throughout the festival, so that a mood of beery revelry could be kept up. The community ensured in the same evening that the food commodities collected from individual households would adequately feed the guests, the lama and his entourage, girls' chorus, and dancers throughout the festival. Lastly, the community assigned responsibilities and festival roles, to all able people, appointing a chief curry maker, chief rice maker, chief tea maker, girls' chorus captain, bell-boy and drummer, chief of protocol, master of ceremony, law-officer, fine collector, and theatrical manager. Thus, something like a hundred people were formally organized to manage the festival.

On the inaugural day, we went to extend invitation to the lama, who lived only fifteen minutes away. There was a delegation of about fifty people to go and fetch him and his entourage; it took hours before we got there and managed to line up. Finally, we wound down the hill in a procession with the lama, with singing and a full range of ritual music. There was also a horse saddled for the lama, though he never rode it as the distance was ludicrously short (besides being gently downhill). I was quite close to the lama, as we walked down on that afternoon in the bright sunshine.

As I recall, the long column advanced down the hill buffeted by the strong breeze typical of an afternoon in spring in Ura, and people jumped and leaped over the streams we had to cross several times. Fragments of memories of the same festival I saw when I was a child resurfaced time and again and faded repeatedly. The procession first stopped at a site near the stream. Centuries ago, the sculpture-treasure, now held by the lama, exorcised a nine-headed serpent from the site and thus brought an end to the epidemic of some disease which was troubling the community of Ura. The myth of the miraculous appearance of the sculpture-treasure and the exorcism of the nine-headed serpent was commemorated in the festival. It is believed that the miraculous appearance of a small sculpture-treasure, which was held by the family of the lama, had beneficial effects in the area.

Then, the procession was constantly stopped, on its way to the community shrine, by groups of women offering wine to the lama and entourage, and making pine and cypress smoke.

That evening, I witnessed a ritual chant to the accompaniment of the bellowing of long trumpets and the beat of big drums and cymbals. All the people in the village were also present and joined at one stage in an intensely moving session of mass prayer, and prostration facing the giant alter. The shrine was large enough for twice the population of the village to fit in quite easily. Yet the ritual instruments and deep sonorous chants filled the big room so that we felt drowned in melodious noise. We were very struck and moved by the droning vibrations of the deep horns, the sharp sound of the cymbals and the hand bells, the rhythms of the drums of all sizes. From time to time, the music was brought to an end by a sudden and staggering silence, so that I began to sense the silence itself as a part of the music and prayer.

Late in the night, there was a spectacular fire dance in the temple (and later around a bonfire) by a horde of ferocious-looking mask dancers holding torches. They went into various parts of the village carrying torches, dancing and working themselves up to a climax. They were cleansing the temple and the village with fire. The dancers threw fire at the backs of the people. It was a powerful image of cleansing the community of accumulated bad feelings and acts, and was an expression of the intention to maintain good social relations.

Going on almost simultaneously with the fire dance was a brief play of fully armoured warriors going to battle. This began in the shrine and concluded around the bonfire. I can still remember the warriors in their full armoury: iron hat with panache, chain mail, shield, lance, sword, winter boots, and sashes of silk. They went into the battle with the perfect courage of a warrior which is needed to live life righteously and meaningfully. As the bonfire died, all the people walked back late at night singing boisterously about the triumph of good over evil.

The next day, the mask-dances in which I also participated were started. But the first item was a dance by about a dozen clowns lead by the main clown with a black mask. He began introducing himself to the audience, while he paused breathlessly between his feverish dance, waving a big wooden phallus:

From the peak of the white mountain, when I came down
To light incense, a hundred people were there;
Not a single plume of smoke did I see.
From the peak of the white mountain, when I came down
To offer welcome tea and chang, a hundred people were there;
Not a cup of tea and chang did I drink.
From the peak of the white mountain, when I came down
I was the owner of a hundred cattle;
With my meal, I lack even a cup of butter milk.
From the peak of the white mountain, when I came down
I was the friend of a hundred young ladies;
When the night fell, not one companion did I have.
My eyes are a pair of soap-nuts

That have seen much merriment and show;
Not a young fellow did I see.
My nose is a pair of golden trumpets
That have savoured all aroma;
Not a whiff of fart have I smelt.
My ears are elongated into fan-like coronets
For I have listened to many holy sermons;
Neither Ka nor Kha[7] did I hear.
My teeth are dungso[8] white-teeth
That have masticated a vast quantity of pork;
I crunched it: 'mur-mur' and 'chop-chop',
Not a single piece of bone did I come across.
My breast is like the scriptures's golden cover
That has pressed and crushed many girls;
Not a single child did I beget.
My spine with its golden suppleness
Did push and press;
Not a single child did I beget.

The head is sheeted in copper
It is known as the Copper Mountain[9]
The waist is encircled in skin[10]
It is known as Shakya Thupa[11].
The root is covered in forest[12]

---

[7] The first two letters of alphabet.
[8] Teeth which grow once again during old age.
[9] The abode of Guru Rinpoche.
[10] Sha in dzongkha.
[11] Lord Buddha.

It is known as Naro Penchen[13].
It had fought a battle long ago
There is a remnant of gun shot on the head.

It was imprisoned long ago
There is a vestige of stocks around its neck.

It was a cattle herder long ago
Its mouth shows signs of drinking butter milk.

Without sight, it can enter
Homage to the radiant one.

Without a leg, it can stand
Homage to the agile one.

No sooner than it is dead, it resurrects
Homage to the reincarnate Boddhisattava.

It is like a bridge when it is stretched
Admired by master craftsmen and their apprentice.

It is like a ladle when it is overturned
Admired by chefs and cooks.

It is like a bell when it is suspended
Admired by lamas and teachers.

All old women are surrounded by old men
Let such enclosing around be auspicious.

The ladle is surrounded by leaves (greens)
Let such enclosing around be auspicious.

The girls are surrounded by night prowlers[14]
Let such enclosing around be auspicious.

---

[12] Nag in Dzongkha.
[13] The great saint Naropa.
[14] Boys who visit their girl friends at night.

The hens are surrounded by roosters.
Let such enclosing around be auspicious.

The full length of his lewd autobiography, celebrating reproduction and fertility, was proclaimed in public. Throughout the festival, the clowns, protected by the masks, not only made obscene jokes and profane remarks on everything sacred, but became a counterpoint to the formal dances and rituals. They challenged the message of the formal dances and engaged in witty dialogues among themselves and with the audience and dancers. They played creative and impromptu roles, against the formal and exacting roles of the mask-dancers.

Throughout the festival, people were naturally in high spirits, which were further buoyed by the singchang they were served frequently. I and my friends went often to the four cellars, not so much to drink but to enjoy bantering with the young ladies. Singchang was tapped from several barrels in the front row while other barrels of singchang in the back rows slumbered to mature. As we went towards the cellars, which was always full of people, both young and old, I caught in the wind the rich and overwhelming perfume of evaporating singchang.

11

NO MORE FRAGRANT SMOKE FROM DONKARLA

The King was in Wangdecholing in 1950 when a messenger came from Paro with the sad news that Paro Penlop Tshering Penjor was seriously ill. Paro Penlop Tshering Penjor's father was King Ugyen Wangchuck's nephew; his mother was King Ugyen Wangchuck's daughter. There were two indigenous physicians and one doctor looking after his health, but they indicated that he would not recover. The unhappy news about his impending death was compounded by the concern over the vast assets and goods which might be lost if there was no orderly transition. Thus, Dronyer Jigme Dorji Wangchuck, the Crown Prince, was dispatched in great haste to Paro, accompanied by his secretary Pema Wangchuck. Some days after the dronyer reached Paro, Paro Penlop Tshering Penjor died. He was perhaps the longest serving Paro Penlop in history.

Tshering Penjor did not return even once to Lame Gonpa, where his mother Ashi Pedon and aunt Ashi Yangzom lived, after he took up the post. On appointed days during fine weather, Paro Penlop came to the peak of Donkarla above Paro Valley, while his mother or his aunt, who actually brought him up, came to the peak of Kitiphu above Jakar. These two peaks were face to face. Plumes of smoke, charged with sentiments, were sent up into the sky from each peak. He could not come to Lame Gonpa for the funeral of his mother or aunt, but he built several commemorative stupas, which were first of their kind in Bhutan, near Ugyen Pelri Palace, for his mother and aunt. Penlop Tshering Penjor had an eye for beautiful women and buildings. He built the Ugyen Pelri Palace in Paro, perhaps the most beautiful building a Bhutanese ever designed. He sent the gorap (gate controller) of Paro to Calcutta to broaden his architectural ideas before Ugyen Pelri Palace was constructed.

Penlop Tshering Penjor was given a grand funeral. Afterwards, Dronyer Jigme took charge of the responsibilities and continued to stay in Paro. He forwarded to the King in Wangdecholing massive records about the tangible legacies of Paro Penlop and how his personal inheritance was divided among his two wives and two children. Dronyer Jigme Dorji Wangchuck maintained regular correspondence with the King who admonished him in replies to be firm and just with the people in the West.

The following winter, the King decided to go to Paro himself. The royal entourage, which included the Elder Queen, arrived in Paro after night stopovers in Domkhar, Trongsa, Chendebji, Razawog, Samtengang, Wangduephodrang, Talodo and Chimithangkha. The morning after his arrival, the King inspected the stores and the bequeathments of Kusho Tshering Penjor, which consisted of antiques, books, treasures, and clothes (especially silk brocades). The dronyer was extremely conscious of his father's demand for meticulous records and strict administration and was therefore in command of enough details. He had even prepared, with alacrity, bulky inventory of the goods left behind by Tshering Penjor, and estimated the quantity of food which had been paid to the monastic community of Paro dzong in the past months he had been in Paro.

The entourage that came to Paro was a sizeable crowd, including almost all of the staff of the palace secretariat who were brought to continue the work on the tax reform of Paro. In the secretarial team were Lopon Kelzang Dawa, Lopon Thinley, Tangsibi Kesang, Yeshey Wangdi, Sonam Penjor, Omze Tenzin, Depung Kota, Namthere Penjor, Sengji Shintala and myself.

As soon as we got to Paro, our team, led by Lopon Thinley, threw ourselves at the reform of taxes in consultation with the gups and mangmis of Paro. This time, tax collections which accrued to the dzong were recorded in detail. Then the actual requirement of the dzong was estimated. The main objective was again to reduce the tax burden. There were not many foodstuff taxes that could be reduced, but there was substantial scope for cutting down peculiar taxes like the bark of daphne plant for making paper. Finally, circulars were sent to all the officials and the people informing them of the changes that had been introduced. The team left Paro without completing the tax reform, but we had acquired sufficient information, which we took with us to Wangdecholing. The work was later completed and the documents sent back to Paro for implementation.

As usual, when the King visited a place, people came to call on him from far and near. Gongzim Sonam Tobgye came all the way from Kalimpong. Others such as Ashi Bida and Ashi Gagey, the wives of the late Paro Penlop Tshering Penjor, came with impressive presents time and again. They either sent gifts of packed food, or brought it along with themselves. The custom of sending a banquet to influential people was quite popular and passionately practised. When family members of the late Paro Penlop called on the King, he demonstrated extraordinary filial kindness towards the son and daughter of Ashi Bida. Ashi Chimi W ingmo of Khangkho, the third wife of Paro Penlop was issued with a royal ordinance exempting her from all taxes. Her property was declared inviolate from encroachment by future government officials.

During the presence of His Majesty in Paro that winter, Dronyer Jigme Dorji Wangchuck was installed as the new Paro Penlop. The new Paro Penlop inherited the entire staff of the old one. The only exception was his personal secretary Pema Wangchuck who came with him from Wangdecholing.

It was in Paro that I had one of the worst punishments I got from a senior attendant. It was quite late in the night and I surmised that His Majesty would not look for me to read the Epic of Gesar to him. So I went down to the Bridge Tower to see my friend Omze Tenzin, who was going to leave the next day. My friend Tenzin used the old excuse that a member of his family in Kurtoe was in critical condition. Tenzin did not return to work in the palace ever again. It transpired that soon after I left Deyangkha that night, the King looked for me to have a reading session. I was furiously reprimanded the next morning and a senior attendant passed an order to whip me forty times. I was whipped with peach twigs until the whole bundle was expended. I was not quite through forty lashings before I convulsed intolerably and fell unconscious and was carried outside. While I was left in a room to recover from the shock, the new Paro Penlop, Jigme Dorji Wangchuck, who held me in great affection, inquired about my condition and made me have a large amount of scrambled eggs; it was believed that this would abate the pain from bleeding and injury.

Until the King left for Bumthang, there was ceaseless number of people who came to call on him with gifts. A usual gift was an entire carcass of pig. The carcasses of pigs needed to be carved into bacon and immediately transported, for storage and preservation, to Jelela which was at a higher elevation. Being winter, it was extremely cold in Jelela , where there was a mountain of accumulated pork. Those who usually lived in that lonely building on top of the mountain had gone elsewhere, except an old couple who looked after the meat store.

The King assigned me to organize the consignments of pork from the store. I was to bring these to Chimithangkha, where I would join the royal entourage on its journey towards Bumthang. I arrived in Jelela late at night. The storekeeper and I went into the attic where rows of bacon were kept holding burning resin wood for light. I neither weighed nor counted the numbers of bacon strings; it would have taken me a whole night. I decided to accept the pork as it was and graded and sorted them into large, medium and thin slices and put them separately into back-loads for the porters. Each back load was labelled with respect to the size of bacon and quantity within.

After packing the bacon slices, the old storekeeper and I decided to reward ourselves with pork curry and asked the old woman to cook. She was an absolutely miserable cook. The night in Jelela was abrasively cold, as it was the height of winter, and the old couple lent me their wretched, odorous and flea-infested blanket for the night. I hesitantly pulled it over my chest and slept as close to the fire as I could.

The pork was transported the next day by some twenty porters whom the old storekeeper had rounded up from villages in Paro early in the morning. The porters and I arrived in Chimithangkha, and I reported to His Majesty that there was a shortfall of several slices of bacon. This, I explained, stemmed from the debility of the storekeepers, who could not protect it from rodents and vermin.

On our way to Bumthang via Punakha, the entourage was received with a full-blown sedrang in Punakha. I recall the complex procession very vividly. It is worth recalling for the pains we took to form a spectacle.

The entourage had its lunch at Laptshagang. Descending the hills of Laptshagang, we came across a hill from where Punakha dzong was fully visible, and at that viewpoint, His Majesty got off his riding pony. When we reached the stupa on the hill, His Majesty the King put his robe on. Both Lopon Kelzang Wangdi, an unbelievably handsome monk of Punakha, and the King made a short prayer and prostrated three times towards the dzong. This spot on the hill stood at one hour's walking distance from the dzong. While His Majesty took a short rest after the prayer, the ceremonial procession was formed. Three of us - Darpon, Dayok and myself - organized the formation of ceremonial procession. All ordinary changgaps had to wear their silk ghos which we issued on the spot. Paw (heroes) put on their dancing attire. No one could move alone; all formed part of the procession. However, cooks - whether of kitchen of the King, high officials or other members of the entourage - were sent ahead of the ceremonial procession, and were thus excluded from it. With them also went the servants of the high officials. The children and wives of high officials formed the next segment of the advance team. This team and the ceremonial procession were separated by a gap of thirty minutes of walking time.

The first part of the ceremonial procession was a saddled white horse and a stable boy. The ponies carrying the stable chief and his luggage followed the white horse. This tiny group went at least thirty yards ahead of the main procession.

In strict order of precedence, the procession was formed as follows: one drummer, one bellman, a pair of jalingpas, two pairs of paw, one chokdar bearer with a flag with the imprint of the goddess of learning and twelve zodiac signs which would avert all accidents and evils, one tsendar bearer with a spear with frills around it which was thought to be the standard of the deity tsan, one rudar (a triangular standard) bearer and lhadar (white flag) bearer. Except for two pairs of paw, who wore silk ghos, the rest of the procession members wore red uniform ghos.

Then there were about nine horses on which were loaded parts of a big cannon, which now decorates the entrance of the Headquarters of the Royal Bhutan Army in Lungtenphu. The cannon was taken along wherever the entourage went. It took nine people to fire. Next came a pair of changgaps carrying chamshoe, a pair of changgaps carrying zongnga, a pair of changgaps with drinking water bottles, a horse burdened with Darpon's personal affects, and Darpon Parop Jaga on his horse and a pair of gunners (paddum).

Darpon bid the gunners to fire the guns at regular intervals during the ceremonial procession. The paddum dashed below the road and fired their guns and rushed back into the procession line. After the Darpon were a pair of changgaps with His Majesty's personal firearms. Then there were garpas with their bosses' guns, zingaps with their own firearms, officials with pistols, about twenty men dressed as traditional warriors with shields, helmets and swords, some garpas with His Majesty's ceremonial swords, a garpa with His Majesty's reading material (e.g. Epic of Gesar), a changgap with the box of damzey (sacred substances), a sungkhop (special priest of the King) or kadrep with jabgao (usually Lopon Kelzang Dawa carried the jabgao), the senior secretary of the King with the red seal (this was usually Lopon Thinley) and other officials. Officials were allowed to ride their ponies in the procession.

The officials were followed by the monks of Punakha who came to receive the King. They had their own musical instruments, and marched in a certain sequence. After the monks should have been the ministerial ranking officials resident in Punakha and their attendants (although this time, there was no minister). After the monks were four horses, each with one stable boy and a changgap, laden with His Majesty's personal affects.

In addition, there were about fifteen spare riding horses for the King led by a man each. Immediately after the riding horses were the chashumi of the King. The chashumi were physically powerful men: usually tall, big framed and heavy. Following the chashumis were a pair of monks who played the jaling, a pair of paw, the second kudrung of Punakha dzong, a Jangdue's (a deity) Kangjuedpa, a carrier of Jangdue's throne carpet, Jangdue's black riding pony, and a servant of Jangdue. It is believed that Jangdue of Drugo, who was deified as a god of war, was a Mongol general of the Gesar of Ling. Jangdue became a tutelar deity of the monarchy since the time of Deb Jigme Namgyel, who first had a dream about Jangdue.

In the dream, Jangdue told Deb Jigme Namgyel that he was destined to be his protector deity. Jangdue is depicted as black in complexion, wrapped in black clothes and riding a black horse. Deb Jigme Namgyel, a man of swarthy complexion, was advised to emulate his protector deity. He too wore black ghos, a black crown and rode on black horses, which brought him the popular title of the Black Regent. Jangdue was said to have appeared in Jigme Namgyel's dream on the night before the fatal day when he travelled from Simtokha to Punakha. Jangdue warned him not to undertake the journey. But Deb Jigme Namgyel discounted the significance of the dream because it was not vivid enough. Deb Jigme Namgyel was thrown off his yak at Lhungtshog and died from injury in Simtokha. King Ugyen Wangchuck's belief in Jangdue was reinforced by his personal Lama's advice that his fortune would be increased if he sought the protection of Jangdue.

It was believed that the invisible and immortal Jangdue was with the entourage every day wherever it went. That is why a riding pony was taken along for Jangdue. After the servant of Jangdue came: a changgap of the King carrying another bottle of water, a senior changgap carrying doma bata (betel nut container), a changgap with a silk carpet, and a changgap carrying the box containing the crown which the King put on as he came close to Punakha dzong.

His Majesty's riding steed was led by a chipon, who wore a khamar. He carried a horn decanter filled with araa. Around the riding pony of the King were four solidly built chashumi, followed by four fully armed chandaaps. Then there was a sungkhop, the person who prayed to the protective deity of the King and performed other placatory acts.

The ceremonial procession consisted of about three hundred

people, and so was spread out; each person had to walk at least three yards behind the other. Thus an impressively long column was formed.

As the paddum fired their guns, the monks appeared on the top of the dzong's roof. Trumpets, cymbals, and jalings blared throughout the valley. As the procession approached the second stupa opposite the dzong, the officials got off their horses. The four high lopons of the Punakha monk body were waiting there. Since the four lopons were of ministerial rank, other officials had to bow to them. The four high lopons offered ceremonial scarfs to His Majesty as he got near the stupa. He took his shiny yellow hat off at this point. Immediately after that, the four lopons joined the high officials' group in the ceremonial procession.

The King got off the horse at the base of the staircase near the dzong. He was met by the Je Khenpo, Samten Jamtsho, at the top of the staircase. They exchanged ceremonial scarves. The Je Khenpo and His Majesty prostrated thrice facing the tower. In front of the central tower of the dzong, a libation ceremony was performed for His Majesty. There were about five hundred monks lined up against the tower facing the King. As the libation ceremony started, the dance of the paw stopped together with the music from the roof top. They resumed again when the ceremony concluded. The music from the rooftop stopped only when the King and the Je Khenpo left for their respective rooms inside the dzong.

After the King took his seat inside the room of the Deb, Nyerchen and Darpon Yanglay introduced the shugdrel ceremony. Darpon Yanglay was by then the senior most attendant and an influential person in the court.

Although the entourage was in Punakha only for a week, the secretarial team launched tax reform of Punakha, just as we had done for Paro. During this exercise, reams of bark paper were kept within the royal chamber and issued strictly according to need. If paper was needed for writing royal decrees, which filled less than a full page, the Zimpon Nam tore a piece and gave it to the secretaries. Waste was not encouraged in the court of King Jigme Wangchuck.

The secretarial team, as always, led double lives even during our short stay in Punakha. We worked on tax reform during the day, and at night we dealt with a series of litigations. The senior secretaries conducted the trials whilst the younger ones recorded the proceedings. We invariably had to keep long hours at night because of lengthy arbitration, and this was made worse by the mid-night feasts forced upon us by the litigants who wanted to make us more well-disposed to their line of argument.

12

THE DOOR CLOSES

The entourage returned to Kinga Rabden whereupon a prolonged game of archery was started. It went on for a month with a few day's pause. Even during the previous winter, just before the entourage returned to Wangdecholing, a marathon archery contest was held. During a game of archery, an ominous incident brought the game to an untimely end.

Rukubji Dorji Gyetshen, who was one of the most talented archery players I ever saw, collapsed near the target and died a few moments later. He had both style and marksmanship. He was only in his early thirties when he died on the spot. He had just returned from his trip to Talo, the palace of Shabdrung, bringing a bundle of swords, which His Majesty gave away to all the garpas as customary gifts.

We were hopeful that nothing would happen to spoil our stay in Kinga Rabden the following year. However, it was not to be the case, as a few days after the game ended, His Majesty was troubled by chest pain and nausea. I believe that the tremendous pressure of getting entangled in the details of administration was a major factor in the deterioration of His Majesty's health. He personally supervised the execution of any important work and thus took upon himself onerous duties. For example, he was involved along with the secretaries, to a minute degree, in the auditing of the accounts of all dzongkhags and the reform of the taxation system, which remained his main preoccupation towards the end of his reign. His Majesty also possessed an overweening drive for perfection in etiquette. Indeed, his sensitivity about the maintenance of decorum by his courtiers and changgaps, required them to be absolutely perfect in matters of etiquette. The daily running of the palaces, including inspection of the records of the food store, further placed great strain on his health. The palaces were run efficiently and with a minimum wastage of material resources. He was a perfectionist who was compelled to mete out light corporal punishment, in the way teachers did sometimes to their promising pupils, to bring everyone to his usual high standards. However, he was as much respected as he was feared.

His Majesty seemed sometimes deeply concerned by the external situations affecting his country. Tibet was in the throes of a catastrophe. Waves of refugees, which began first as a trickle, came into Bhutan, some wishing to settle and others going further to Nepal and India. India had gained independence a few years ago and a new relationship had to be fostered. Yet there were very few able men beside the likes of Gongzim Sonam Tobgye, Dasho Phuntsho Wangdi of Lame Gonpa and Lopon Kelzang Dawa with whom to share his concerns about foreign relations.

The relationship with Tibetan officials at the border was less than happy. The pompous Tibetan Zongpons at Phari, with whom rice was bartered for salt, once wrote a letter which began with ungracious salutation "To Trongsa Penlopla".

When the entourage returned to Wangdecholing, His Majesty planned to reconstruct Wangdecholing Palace. In his reign, he had so far built the palaces of Tashicholing in Domkhar, Kinga Rabden and Samchiling. He issued a writ to the garpas of Mangde, Punakha, Haa, Kurtoe and Trongsa to come to work. Garpas of Trashigang were excluded because they were responsible for farming the estates in Bumthang. About three hundred garpas came to Wangdecholing to work, in response to the writ. They were deployed, under the overall charge of Zhemgang Zongpon Thinley Namgyel, half brother of the Queens, to extract timber from the mountains of Choskhor for an entire summer. Some of them floated the timber down the Chamkharchu where it was trapped at Wangdecholing. By the end of the summer, the meadows of Wangdecholing were blanketed with logs, beams and planks. I was one of those who maintained an attendance register for the workers, and those who were frequently absent were asked to be replaced by able bodied garpas from the same houses. However, the reconstruction was never launched, as events took a different turn.

Dasho Jigme Dorji Wangchuck was away in Paro as the new Paro Penlop during this period. The Elder Queen was also in Paro to witness and bless her son's marriage to Ashi Kesang. When the King was informed about the date of marriage in Paro, he sent a trader immediately to Lhasa to buy special ornaments and jewels as wedding presents for the bride. The trader was back from Lhasa in a fortnight with a golden jabgao, studded with turquoise, silk and many other things, which were dispatched to Paro. The day of wedding was celebrated in Wangdecholing with archery and dances.

But it was a year of evil omen. There was a mild gale which broke the arch of the tent in Wangdecholing and the King reckoned the incident to be ominous. A Tibetan lama, Drigung Khenpo, was engaged to perform a 'tra phap', a form of oracle. The lama held a mirror in which he read portents of the future. Though our mortal eyes did not see anything, the lama claimed that he saw a fire in the mirror which was doused when an image of a monk flitted across the mirror. The consequences of these sacred visions were lost on the Drigung Lama, and he worshipped further for their significance to be spelt in writing across the mirror. And behold! the lines were read by the lama, which I duly recorded, sitting by his side. But the lines were yet again incomprehensible at that time as they alluded to a snake. In hindsight, the signs seemed to make sense. It was prediction of His Majesty's sad demise the following year. He was born in the year of the snake.

The year also witnessed an outbreak of a peculiar skin disease. People got sores on their legs which did not heal on average for three months. The idea of falling sick for three months and being away from duty was too tempting for me. Whilst handling a bamboo basket one day, I bruised my ankle. On this cut, I trickled a drop of pus from an infected person. The next day, to my great delight, I discovered that my wound had turned septic and the ankle was swollen. There were endless drops of pus oozing out of it. I successfully became sick after three days and took to the leisurely life which I longed for. However, as the days wore on, the ulcer increased in its surface area and depth and took a serious turn. I became disabled for over a month during which time the King asked Mahaguru, a kadrep and an indigenous doctor, to see me.

Mahaguru came to see me with ten dres of rice, some meat and butter which His Majesty had graciously asked him to present to me. I was advised that the affected foot should be immersed in the river early in the morning for half an hour or so. I walked to the Chamkharchu early in the morning leaning heavily on a walking stick and followed this therapeutic prescription. The shore of the Chamkharchu assumed a strange spectacle of men and women assembled to dip their legs in the shivery and frosty mornings into the frothy river. No doubt, the whole troop of sick people were following the prescription originating from the same therapist. The treatment was not surprisingly ineffective.

Winter came, and the royal household moved to Kinga Rabden. I followed the entourage to Kinga Rabden a few weeks later, after I recovered from the wound. The King left, along with the Younger Queen and sixty changgaps, for the hot springs in Gaylegphug, then known as Hatisar. Dr Kabo, Lopon Thinley and I were part of the entourage. I accompanied the King in order to read the Epic of Gesar. Both Neoli Babu, the Commissioner of Southern Bhutan, and Gongzim Sonam Tobgye came to join the royal entourage in Gaylegphug, though Gongzim left after two days.

After His Majesty returned from the hot springs in Gaylegphug, he played archery but he had to take frequent rest during the game. His Majesty's health deteriorated and messages were carried through night and day to the Elder Queen and Paro Penlop in Kalimpong as well as to the Younger Queen.

Soon, the door of the chamber remained closed, even after the sun shone in the morning. This was a signal for the changgaps not to follow their routine. They were not to put their swords on for the day. There were more and more days when the swords remained stacked in the corridor and the door remained shut. More than three weeks passed.

As winter advanced, the King recovered. Relieved by the improved health of the King, the Younger Queen left for the hot springs in Gaylegphug. However, once again, His Majesty's health deteriorated, but this time inexorably. More messages were sent to the Elder Queen, Paro Penlop and the Younger Queen. The Younger Queen rode back from Gaylegphug, and in less than a week after her arrival, the reign of King Jigme Wangchuck came to an end. The Elder Queen and Ashi Kesang were to join the Paro Penlop in Kinga Rabden a bit later. Paro Penlop Jigme Dorji Wangchuck was still on his way from Kalimpong. He travelled by day and by night using a lamp. As he walked up the hills of Yudrongcholing on the last day of his journey, dusk fell and he arrived in Kinga Rabden late in night. He was late by two days. He went immediately to his father lying-in-state.

The young Lhalung Sungtrul, 20, presided over the interim ceremonies. In charge of everything for the moment was Dasho Thinley Namgyel, a half brother of the Queens, assisted by Gup Jangtu, Gup Leki, Haap Yangley, Thegila, Parop Darpon Jaga who was the chief of garpas, Gangteyp Agay Dorji and Urap Ngidup Namgay.

With the coming of the first Bhutanese month, it was time to move the cortege to Domkhar in Bumthang, where it again lay-in-state from the 2nd to the 5th Bhutanese month. It was thence moved to Wangdecholing for cremation in Kurje. The cortege was encased in the centre of a stupa-pyre which was set on fire. A hundred monks led by the Je Khenpo arrived from Punakha. Different groups sat praying on each side of the stupa: Je Khenpo on one side, Nimalung Lama Yeshey Pem on the second side, Chodrak Lama on the third side and Sungtrul on the fourth side. All the princes and princesses and thousands of his mourning subjects were present on the day of cremation. After the remains were committed to fire, the ashes and the debris were collected in small pieces of fabric and placed into the Chamkharchu by monks. One monk was ungentle in his manner: he rudely flung away debris and ashes. He was instantly rebuked by the King.

The new King and Queen Ashi Kesang made a week long sojourn in the hot springs of Dur after the cremation. I was the only member of the secretarial staff to leave for Dur with the King and the Queen. The royal couple rode yaks over the high passes where the air was very thin. Even yaks ran out of breath as they crossed the high treeless passes. The hottest of the springs was so close to the river that it was actually submerged by the river during the summer. It bubbled with sulfureous mist during the winter. The royal couple was in blissful love and always together, with their hands intertwined. Gup Leki managed the mess for the entourage and made me follow the old system of recording the daily food consumption. The food register was of no use. Instead of taking back the balance to Wangdecholing, on the day the entourage returned to Wangdecholing, the King distributed most of the excess food to the herders camped near the hot spring.

13

A NEW ERA BEGINS

One of the Paro Penlop's first acts was to announce, the day after he reached Kinga Rabden to see his father lying-in-state, that there would be continuity in the responsibilities and the positions of all his father's retainers and secretaries. It mitigated all the anxiety that the courtiers harboured about their services with the passing away of His Majesty. The composition and the ranks of the courtiers were preserved.

Soon after he reached Kinga Rabden, the new King, who was still the Paro Penlop, issued a royal decree to chiefs of every dzong that the seal of Trongsa Penlop had no legal force after the signified date and would be replaced by the newly chosen seal with the 'Druk' imprint. The late King Jigme Wangchuck occupied the dual positions of King of Bhutan and Penlop of Trongsa, and preferred to use the seal of Trongsa Penlop on his decrees and ordinances, making it the symbol of the King in his reign.

There was also a striking change in the style of working. The late King used to brief the secretaries standing in front of him; the new King allowed them to sit and take note and encouraged an open and direct communication whenever he had time. The amount of work for the secretaries increased. This new style of working brought about changes in the individual behaviour of the secretaries: His Majesty told us what he expected of us and then left us on our own. It bred a sense of challenge and responsibility. The secretaries were put in a separate flat in Kinga Rabden Palace. Lopon Thinley liaised between the new King and us, about our work. The thunderous grunt - wooh oop - that His late Majesty used to call the attendants was replaced by a soft whistle.

There was also a change in the form of emoluments for the courtiers and secretaries. Senior secretaries and courtiers were paid in cash instead of food commodities. Thus Lopon Kelzang Dawa, Lopon Thinley, Dr Kabo and Babu Chogyel were paid Rs. 200 a month. Tangsibi Kesang was paid Rs. 100 a month and Yeshey Wangdi was paid Rs. 80 a month. Both Sonam Penjor and I were paid at a modest rate of Rs. 60 a month. Those who were paid salary were ordered to abstain from eating in the common kitchen.

Several new appointments were made, all chosen from the ranks of secretaries and courtiers. In all, about eight persons were promoted and posted in various dzongkhags.

Sha Yabjee, a big and dark man, was made Wangdue Dronyer. Gup Jangtu, an old courtier was made Trongsa Dronyer. The highest official appointed by the third King in the wake of the passing away of the second King was Lopon Kelzang Dawa. Lopon Kelzang was conferred red scarf and posted as Dzongtshab of Paro, in place of Paro Penlop, with exceptionally broad powers. I recall His Majesty say that Kelzang Dawa must be made the highest official. However, Dzongtshab Kelzang Dawa's personal life became highly entangled and affected his public life. This was ultimately his undoing. In a complicated turn of event, both his brother and two wives became estranged from him and he felt deeply wronged by them. Though he took to a severe amount of drinking during his tenure as Paro

Dzongtshab, His Majesty was deeply sympathetic to his personal predicament. His Majesty turned a blind eye and allowed Dasho Kelzang Dawa to do as he wished until he died in the post in 1955 or so. His late Majesty showed unusual kindness to courtiers who had a long association with himself or his father and rewarded them with appropriate posts.

With the posting of Lopon Kelzang Dawa as the dzongtshab of Paro, Lopon Thinley assumed a far more pivotal position. He had been used to discharging the functions of Lopon Kelzang because of frequent absence of Lopon Kelzang Dawa on account of weakening health. Lopon Thinley had by then completely given up drinking.

We were most fascinated, for it was completely new to us, by the use of revenue and postal stamps which the new King ordered from Kalimpong. Three load of stamps were delivered in the first consignment. Revenue stamps were denominated in Rs. 5 and 50 paise. With his usual ingenuity, Lopon Thinley devised some rules about the uses of revenue stamps and postal stamps. Fifty paise stamps were used for postal services and Rs. 1 stamps for legal documents.

After his father's funeral rite was completed in Bumthang, His Majesty became preoccupied with moving his base from Wangdecholing to Paro. The plan to shift his residence from Bumthang to Paro must have been on his mind for quite some time. While he was in the hot spring of Dur, the Elder Queen Mother was away in her palace in Domkhar to sort the mobile assets to be taken away with them to Paro. The Younger Queen Mother had decided to stay on in Wangdecholing. The retainers expected a hectic time packing some of the moveable properties of the late King found in

Wangdecholing.

Nothing prepared them for what the young King did; it took everybody's breath away when he left all the goods that were there and gave for good the keys of the stores in Wangdecholing to the Younger Queen Mother, in a characteristic show of his generosity. Save four boxes of swords and some guns, he wanted to own nothing that was in the palace of Wangdecholing.

The Queen, the King and the Elder Queen Mother rode off to Paro. The departure of the immediate royal family and the loss of prestige of Bumthang as the capital produced a mood of hysteria and public melancholy in Bumthang and Trongsa. Even in remote villages of Bumthang, people wept bitterly when they heard the King had forever left their land. The garpas of Eastern Bhutan and the subjects in Bumthang were saddened by the change in the location of the capital from central to western Bhutan.

The King, who left for Paro in the 7th month, instructed some secretaries and retainers to follow him to Paro after visiting their own families. I was one of those who made the trip later. As I was going far away, I had two horses to carry my belongings, and a servant - Rinchen Tshering - to cook for me. I reached Wangduephodrang, which was administered by Dronyer Sha Yabjee, as its Tshechu (festival) was about to begin. I called on my old friend Sha Yabjee to replenish my food stock which was close to being exhausted. Sha Yabjee remembered that I was a keen mask dancer from our old days in Wangdecholing and Kinga Rabden. I was happy to break my journey and participate in the performance of the dance of stag and hounds and the dance of the hero and heroine.

I reached Paro to offer my services at a stage when feverish activities were under way for the forthcoming coronation of the King. The zingaps were building guest houses for the foreign delegates. Lopon Thinley assumed the co-ordinating role: instructing and organizing the preparations for the coronation. The King received his five silk scarves of noble colours from the shrine of Shabdrung in Punakha. The colour combination of the scarves was chosen by Jigme Namgyel, the great grand father of the King and used by all succeeding Kings at the time of their consecration. The King made the return trip between Paro and Punakha in four days. The entry of the King into Paro dzong was made with an elaborate sedrang and chipdrel. A musical band consisting of forty men was brought to Paro from India for the occasion by Haa Dungpa Jigme Dorji. They wore red jackets and white anklets. Lopon Thinley was the Chief of Protocol and I was his constant assistant, a position I occupied more or less till the end of his life.

Three days of celebration were declared. On the day of the coronation, the chipdrel or the procession was crammed within a short distance: from Deyangkha to the Paro dzong. The guns stationed at Namgay Zam went off at frequent intervals, as the procession lengthened towards the dzong. In the midst of the procession, we heard an erratic burst of fire. Some of us rushed down to the site and found the two gunmen horribly burnt. Around them were lying burnt magazines. They had overstuffed the barrel with gun powder. The magazines nearby had caught fire as they attempted to ignite the gun powder in the barrel of the gun.

Among those invited from outside were H. Dayal, the Gangtok Political Officer, the Chogyal of Sikkim, Representative of the Indian Prime Minister J. Nehru and the King's Indian friend Dinesh

Singh. The chief of each district and various representatives of the people were informed through a royal circular and they were present. The celebratory performances were shown on the lawn of the Paro Ugyen Pelri Palace. Towards the evening His Majesty and the guests returned to the dzong in a procession. Documentary films were shown in the open in the evenings by the Political Officer based in Gangtok.

Although he was crowned in Paro, the King wanted ultimately to live in Thimphu. He decided to build his palace in Dechencholing, then known as Kashinang. Thimphu Zimpon Rinchen Dorji (alias Jochu) and changgap Phuntshog Wangdi were deputed to supervise the construction. His Majesty chose to locate the capital in Thimphu because of its accessibility by motor road which was being constructed between Phuntsholing and Thimphu. Thimphu was much more accessible to foreign visitors even by mule track from Sikkim or India. His Majesty commanded garpas to prepare timber for the construction of Dechencholing Palace. He was inclined to construct the palace in Motithang but one of his kadreps, Tandin Dorji, who had his house there, suggested Dechencholing. Tandin Dorji of Kabjisa was one of His Majesty's most regular kadreps.

The King was invited to visit Delhi and left for India soon after the coronation in 1952. He chose several high officials to accompany him. The entourage included Dzongtshab Kelzang Dawa, Wangdue Dronyer Sha Yabjee, Lopon Thinley, Tangsibi Kesang, Paro Zimpon, Phuntshog Wangdi, Gelong Namdrul of Trongsa, Paro Solpon and Druk Zongpa, during whose incumbency the Drukgyel dzong was burnt down.

The King was going to be out of the country for a while and he gave options to the zingaps and courtiers to stay on in Paro or to go on a long home leave. Zingaps who wanted to go on an indefinite leave were going to be recalled selectively. I chose to take a vacation in spite of Lopon Thinley's advice to the contrary. I was joined by about eighty zingaps, who fell into a long line one morning to take leave en masse. His Majesty looked at the group from a balcony, and I made myself as inconspicuous as possible by mingling with the crowd consisting largely of zingaps. I felt I might not be allowed to go if I did not conceal myself partially in the crowd. I was struck by a persistent feeling of vast and inaccessible distance between Paro and my village. I did not want to be permanently away from home because the sense of distance involved was always difficult for many of us from central and eastern Bhutan to bear. The capital had shifted for good and if we were to continue in our calling, we feared that we might have to live in Western Bhutan. Most of us from eastern and central Bhutan found the idea of living in western Bhutan difficult in those days. Tenzin, my colleague from Trashigang, had left under a pretext in 1950. I wanted to follow suit.

I returned to my home which was by now entrusted to my younger brother and my wife. My constant absence from home and my wife had resulted in my wife being married bigamously by my younger brother Choni. When I got home, it was autumn, and my father was away at Tsamang in Monggar. He too had remarried a woman from Tsamang, some years after the death of my mother. When I reached home, it struck me that our family or household had not many cows left: the herd had dwindled to two. So I took it upon myself to go and buy cows from Trashigang, now governed by a friend of mine, Nyerchen Talip Rinzin. A nyerchen was indispensable in order to manage the taxes of this populous district. Trashigang Zongpon Dopola had died and no one had yet been appointed to the post. Talip Rinzin used to work with me as a courtier and we were on extremely good terms. Although I wished to buy several cows and heifers, I did not have enough money. I relied on the kindness of my friend, the nyerchen, to lend me some money or to arrange for the purchase of some cows on credit. I first went to Tsamang to see my father on my way to Trashigang. From there I took a circuitous route that took me to many places for pleasure.

Of all the places I have been in our country, the most memorable villages turned out to be the ones in Kurtoe. I had now only a distant memory of the people in some parts of Kurtoe which I had frequented in my childhood. I could remember them when I retreated into my memory: I saw the girls dancing, singing, laughing, drinking, weaving, cooking, suckling, winnowing, chatting, joking and flashing glances at me. But when I became conscious of such mental images stored so long ago, I was not really sure that they were smiling only at me. All of them must be married and bringing up children, I thought to myself. I tried to visualize their grown up faces; I could only see blurred images. I made up my mind to revisit them on my way to Trashigang. When I went round the villages to beg alms in my childhood I had nothing exciting but herbal incense powder to give them. However, I had some money on this trip, and I could present it to them for any generous hospitality.

I had by then come to be convinced of what made travel and stay in the villages enjoyable. Most changgaps, zingaps and secretaries who had spent many years in the court expected to be treated with some deference and stuffy hospitality when they were in the villages. Such expectation ruined the wonderful experience they might have had during their stay in the villages. It was a lesson, borne by my personal experience, that nothing succeeded like informality to make oneself come down to their level and launch a free wheeling conversation. This enabled me to build up instant relationship with complete strangers. Only then could one realize the true value of travel: to make friends met in such serendipitous contexts and enrich our experiences.

From Tsamang, I headed towards Lhuntsi, and then to Khoma and Pangkhar villages. I crossed the iron chain bridge that was down below Lhuntsi dzong. The iron chain bridge there, and next to Khoma village, were free from corrosion, although no one could tell when the enormous chains were made. The bridges swayed a lot in the wind and the people tried to tip-toe across them. But the horses, who were unloaded to help them across the bridges, tried to run, further increasing the amplitude of the vibrations.

The most memorable village on the whole trip was Pangkhar, where I had not been before. The village of Pangkhar stood on the hill. It usually took about three hours from Khoma village which is at the base of the mountain. But the climb was very strenuous and took much longer as we lurched up the steep gradient through chirpine woods, lemon grass openings and mixed oak forest on a bright day. We visited a holy cave used for meditation by Guru Rimpoche and Kema village on the way. We readily accepted gifts of cucumbers and pomegranates plucked freshly from village gardens as we passed by. These fruits were eaten without delay. Farmers were busy harvesting rice, amaranths, maize, fox tail millet, and chilly.

There were red patches of land around the houses, which we

discovered were masses of chilly drying in the sun. The air often smelt mildly of chillies, which was a pleasurable stimulus.

The sight of ripening fruits and fields, the addictive flavour of chilly and a slight pull in my stomach suddenly generated a craving for food. The hard climb to Pangkhar on an empty stomach triggered me to ponder what had remained one of the most erratic factors in my life: shifting sources of food. I did not have a cook when I worked in Wangdecholing, Kinga Rabden and Paro. I relied most of the time on my hosts in various places to cook for me; when they did, I did not like eating alone. As I had hoped to be a free man, no longer in the service of the court, I resolved at that moment that I should maintain a well stocked kitchen all the time. I must collect large quantities of kharang, and chillies to take home, I thought to myself.

The sudden concern for food security and the drive for food collection was quite momentary; it disappeared as soon as we got something to eat from the first house we came across in Pangkhar. We entered the house on the pretext of seeking drinking water, although the water was flowing right outside the village. We decided against staying in the house which relieved our hunger, as there was only an old couple there. We imposed ourselves gently on a more lively hostess whose house stood in a clustered group of houses. The village had a view of the entire valley and stood on the hill higher than the sky, a kind of location which I would always aim for if I could build a house for myself. She and her husband were threshing and winnowing wheat in the porch of their house.

"Are you threshing wheat? It is very windy." was my opening gambit, though it might have seemed self-evident unless one was blind. But opening remarks have to be perfunctory.

"Threshing wheat, today," she replied with a slow stare, "Are you coming from down below?"

"We came from Khoma via Kema. I am from Bumthang. I am going to Trashigang for cattle trading. Where will I reach today? I do not think there is any village further up where I could halt tonight." I said, dropping a hint that I would not like to go any further for the day.

"Are you a zingap?" She was pondering whether to invite us in or not. That was the crucial moment. She had to make up her mind quickly whether to let us go away or to invite us in. She took stock of us rapidly.

"Yes, I am a zingap. No, I used to be a zingap; I have stopped being one."

"Please come in for some tea. You must be tired and you might not have had lunch," she said with certain insight into our condition.

We showed the usual degree of modesty in not jumping at the offer. Without much conviction in my own statement, I said "We would not like to disturb your work. Harvesting period is a busy time of the year."

After she insisted a few more times, we followed her into the house where tea, araa and the evening meal were served in rapid succession. She apologized for not cooking any meat, an extremely scarce food item. She lamented that cattle mortality had been unusually low that year.

According to the custom of the village, the ladies of the village came to see us with a pitcher of araa each in the evening. Araa from different pitchers was emptied into an large earthen pot and heated with eggs and butter. Each person present in the house was served a very big ladle of araa so that the amount of araa drunk by each person was exactly equal. Araa that was left over was served in the second round and a third round and so forth, divided equally between the people present. We deferred our departure from Pangkhar for another day because of the warm hospitality which made us reluctant to leave. We were served araa several times the next day. The strength of the araa was comparatively weaker than the kind distilled in other parts of the country. For this reason, the habitual consumption of araa in this area did not result in serious intoxication. But the highly relaxed atmosphere it created helped the ladies enjoy themselves and give us great pleasure by serenading throughout the night. The number of songs they knew would have enabled them to sing incessantly for a week; it was only a question of having the capacity to indulge on the part of the guests.

On the second night, we pleaded with our hostesses to wind up the dancing and singing around midnight so that we could go to bed earlier than we did the night before. My hostess insisted that I also sing. I sang the song that I penned with a friend of mine some years ago. It had by then become quite popular but only a few knew about its origin:

I, the mountain lion beautified by the emerald mane
My heart yearns only for the snow mountains.
Although harsh fate brings me to haunt the rocky cliff
There is a wish for us to meet again soon.

I, the river which comes down from the mountain ranges

My heart yearns only for the Indian plains.
Although harsh fate makes me meander through different valleys
There is a wish for us to meet again soon.

I, the fleet footed horse of Zeling
My heart yearns only for the green grassland.
Although harsh fate makes me voyage around foreign places
There is a wish for us to meet again soon.

I, (Yeetro), the daughter of heavenly Drizang
My heart yearns only for you, my heart-friend.
Although harsh fate made him (husband King Norzang) go to war
There is a wish for us to meet again soon.

I, the golden honey bee of the valley
My heart yearns only for the taste of honey.
Although harsh fate makes me haunt the cliff
There is a wish for us to meet again soon.
I, the gomchen, who strives for the high peaks
My heart yearns only for religion.
Although harsh fate makes me haunt the worldly villages
There is a wish for us to meet again soon.

I, the young son, born to my mother
My heart yearns only for you, my heart-friend.
Although harsh fate makes me haunt other places

There is a wish for us to meet again soon.

It was hard for them to believe that I did not drink. For their satisfaction, I had to drink a little, and having done this, they forced upon me a little more the next time. I recall that by the morning of the second day, I was getting a sense of euphoria, not from drinks, but from the charm of the hostesses that seemed to overwhelm me. They were, in my mind, always associated with haunting tunes. At other times, I recall them sitting at their looms, weaving, where they acquired the creative authority of painters.

"I am unmarried" I felt tempted to say to a young woman. Such verbal indiscretions were committed frequently by young courtiers. The young woman opened up a little while she wove, with me sitting by her.

"It is very harsh to live in the village. It is so physically exhausting to work for most of the year in the field. Planting and weeding, clearing bushes, husking and grinding, harvesting, carrying goods on the back; it is never ending from morning to nightfall. Look at my rough hands." She showed a genuine wish to seek an escape from her rural life and I wished for a moment that I was unmarried. She shifted her gaze from me to the tapestry of design she was weaving.

"Indeed, that must be so. Our days are also sometimes tedious and fearful. Often, we get to sleep only around midnight and we have to go to work much before sun rise. Sometimes, I get a morbid dread of the regimen in the court. After working for a month or so, I cannot stand it and I then cannot help staying away for a few days pretending to be sick."

"But you do not have to work outdoors in wet weather. You do not have to carry heavy loads and walk alone through bristly footpaths in the forest. A dasho's wife does not have to do anything comparable. I hope to leave the place if I meet someone."

Our hostesses came to see us off and shared many rounds of drinks in a forest clearing at some distance from the village. I gave them a few betams each.

Crossing the mountain behind Pangkhar, I left for Tashi Yangtse to come out finally in Trashigang. In Trashigang, my friend Nyerchen Talip Rinzin was pleased to see me, for he at once mentioned various odd jobs in his office that I could do for him. He was not literate and needed all the help I could give him for a few months. There was a backlog of tax receipts and documents to be prepared as well as agreements to be drawn up between litigants during my stay with him for two months. When his staff adjudicated cases, fines were sometimes levied in terms of cows. Out of these fines paid in the form of cows, I bought four cows for rupees eighty each with the money I borrowed from Talip Rinzin. In addition, he was kind enough to present me with two cows as a token of our friendship and as payment for my services for two months. My servant, Rinchen Tshering, and I thus wended our way back at a sluggish rate with the mixed animal train of two horses and six cows.

On the way back, we went to Chaskhar to see Bao Gyeltshen. Several years ago, he had been engaged in a litigation in Wangdecholing and was short of money to pay the fine. I had lent him some money which I now wanted to be repaid in the form of a cow. I was able to persuade him to give me .two cows: one to discharge his debt and another on credit. Now the number of cows

185

grew to a respectable size: eight which became the core of the herd of my parental household.

While in Chaskhar, I came across another lot of jamtsham heifers being driven towards their winter pastures where they would join the herds. There were three men from Ura who had gone to Dungsam via Trashigang buying jatshams to augment their herds. They had taken more than a month to scout for sellers on their way to South-Eastern Bhutan. They were able to procure ten jatshams, each one from a different seller, before they looped their way back. But one of the jatsham had died from foot and mouth disease on the way, and they tried to sell the carcass to minimize their loss. One of the three went round the villages to look for interested buyers.

"My heifer died yesterday. Its carcass is in the paddy field. I have put foliage over it to prevent crows from scavenging. It died from an unknown disease," the carcass owner explained in a beguiling manner. He did not want anyone in the village to know that their herd was infected with foot and mouth disease. Their herd would be quarantined by the villagers immediately if they knew about the disease.

"I will be interested to buy if you sell the meat in parts instead of the carcass as a whole," said the villager who had worked out that the cheapest way to buy meat was to buy it in pieces.

"I do not have the stomach to see the butcher's knife go into my jatsham and the carcass being sliced into pieces. I was very fond of the jatsham. I will not handle the meat at all; you have to do it yourself. If you buy, it will have to be whole jatsham. It is there in the paddy field. I can't stand even its sight," said the carcass seller, trying to get rid of the whole dead cow. After a bit of haggling, the villager agreed to buy the whole carcass for Rs. 25. He had paid Rs. 90 for the live jatsham only ten days ago.

The three men from Ura hurried home, which still lay at eight days' distance, with their herd reduced to nine jatshams. Once again, after a few days, one of the jatshams collapsed from foot and mouth disease in the middle of a forest. The three men argued a great deal about the course of action to take over the afflicted jatsham. They were concerned that local villagers might know about it and detain them for several months. They wanted to avoid being caught in this situation, especially before crossing the bridge over Drangmechu. If they could get across the bridge over Drangmechu, they could find several alternative mule tracks to escape the quarantine. They abandoned the sick jatsham in the middle of the track. The three men drove rest of the herd as fast as they could till they crossed the bridge over Drangmechu. A day later, two of them returned to see the afflicted jatsham. Its health had not improved. In fact wide patches of skin over its nose and upper lip had started cracking and coming off. They hauled it deep into the forest, talked to it and left it to die. All three of them were emotionally numb from the loss of two cows when I met them in Chaskhar.

I was so anxious to avoid their herd that I decided to leave the same evening I met them. The journey was tediously slow, with the cows digressing endlessly beside the road. We finally reached Tsamang to meet my father but he had already left for home. To travel without being hindered by cows, I temporarily left the eight cows with my step-mother in Tsamang and we continued the journey home at a faster pace. The cows were later collected by a servant of my father.

I now looked forward to being part of the village life, with a realistic prospect of becoming a part time lama. My leave was open ended. As long as I was not recalled, it implied termination of court service. I was not asked to come back even after the return of His Majesty from India. A few days after my arrival in the village, I received a letter from Lopon Thinley conveying the displeasure of the King for going on leave without personally informing him and also saying that my services were not ardently required in the court. The tone of the letter produced a mixed feeling in me, but I was quite relieved that I was not asked to return. However, I received another letter a month or so later; I was not after all let off completely. The circular from His Majesty the King directed me to report immediately to the nyerchen and dronyer of Trongsa to become his secretary. Trongsa Dronyer Jangtu had kept an eye on me and submitted to the King that I would be an asset as their secretary; the King endorsed this readily. I left for Trongsa with great reluctance. For almost a year while I worked in Trongsa, I had free food but I was not paid any wage.

14

YEARS IN TRONGSA AND TRASHIGANG

Ibecame a secretary to both Dronyer Jangtu and Nyerchen Paybar while I was in Trongsa during 1953. Nyerchen Paybar, a monk of Trongsa, was absolutely incorruptible and was treated most affectionately by the King. He was a genius at organizing feasts, festivities and ceremonies.

Serving as a clerk in Trongsa dzong, I rarely ventured out into the village below. I slept in the dzong, which housed only the monks and other men. I used to live in a flat in the dzong with Gatu, the store-in-charge of Trongsa and a nephew of Lopon Paybar. I came to hear about Pema from Gatu, though I had not seen her yet. I was making my way out of the dzong once to wash one of my four ghos in the stream. Over the bridge, I met a her, also going to the stream. Dressed for the laundry she had bound her colourful kira much above her ankles. She wore a shallow bamboo sun hat as women do when they go for harvest. When she took it off near the stream, I was taken aback by an extraordinarily pleasant face. We launched into a lively conversation as we pounded our clothes on the rocks. We got a favourable opportunity to know each other, as we washed our clothes together for the whole day.

Some days after I met her, she removed my bedding from the dzong and took it to her place in Dangreynang. My busy but somewhat lonesome life led me to acquiesce to her audacious move. It would deliver me from the hermitage of the dzong. Thus, I came to be involved in an affair which I hoped would elude the notice of my wife living in Shingkhar. But, bad news travelled fast, carried by porters, muleteers, pilgrims and couriers from one place to another, and my own wife had heard the disturbing news of my affair in Trongsa. I received a letter, which did not openly say anything about my misdemeanour, but regretting a great deal about the loss of contact over several months. She pointed out obliquely that it would be appropriate for her and our daughter to be with me. She emphasized that she would be soon coming to join me in Trongsa, which first worried me and then began to alarm me, in view of her impending arrival, amidst my embarrassing relationship with Pema.

Lopon Paybar was fatherly to me, and he advised me against marrying Pema. Dronyer Jangtu also did not approve of my relationship, though his view was born more out of an enlightened motivation. Jangtu encouraged me to become his son-in-law. His daughter was with me frequently to learn how to read and write.

I was initially not aware that Pema was married to a soldier, who was away for sometime. Very soon, the affair was noticed by her husband when he was back in Trongsa. He brought an informal proceeding against me. I was financially saved by Lopon Paybar who paid the restitution for breaking up the marriage. Having paid the fine, Lopon Paybar wanted me to part with Pema. Separation appeared, at that time, quite unthinkable for both of us and we began to stand by each other against all odds.

My closest friend during my secretarial stint in Trongsa was Nubi Dungpa Nagphay, with whom I had gone on many expeditions to take census of cattle and yaks belonging to the royal household, when he was a changgap in Wangdecholing and Kinga Rabden. I borrowed his best gho on several occasions and was at his place whenever I found time to spare. Nagphay had two places in Trongsa: one in the dzong where women were barred from staying at night, and one outside the dzong where he housed his wife and family.

I was informed an evening that my wife had reached Trongsa and was putting up with Nagphay's family. It was understandably an exasperating moment for me.

The situation thus forced me to reconsider my own feelings quite a lot. As I dwelt more on my marriage and my affair, it seemed that I did not want either to marry Pema or continue being the husband of Pedon Wangmo. I was not sure how I could break out of my own predicament in either way. I wanted the unbiased advice of my father. So, the same evening my wife reached Trongsa, I fled, without informing anyone, to Shingkhar to see my father. Pema was so attached to me at that point that she could not be deterred from coming with me to Shingkhar. It got dark without moon by the time we reached Balingpang above Trongsa. There was a deserted cowshed in the forest and we decided to spend the night there. We got up at the crack of the dawn and reached Gyetsa early in the day. We continued our vigorous trek and as the sun was setting we were able to climb the mountain range of Tangsibi village. It was totally dark by the time we walked past Ura village.

My father had gone to bed when we reached home. I knocked on the gate and woke them up. As we entered the courtyard of our house, my father gave me the grave news that the police had come from Trongsa to apprehend us. To mislead the police, in case the police found his action suspicious, my father pretended that he was going to the big shrine room to light yet another butter lamp. Pema and I were led to the shrine and hidden there for the night. Predictably, my father denied that I had come to Shingkhar and deceived the police. The police therefore returned to Trongsa the next morning.

Soon after the police men were out of sight, my father and I sat down to consider what course of action we could take. I pleaded with my father to end my marriage to Pedon Wangmo, for I had been anyway away from her for most of my married life. In the compromise that was worked out between the two of us, she would be the sole wife of my younger brother Choni. With this solution in mind, my father left for Trongsa to bring her back and dissolve my marriage with her. Towards mid-day, my father followed the police, by the same route, to Trongsa. He suggested that Pema and I take a different route and reappear in Trongsa, as if we had never been home during this time. I was obviously to pretend that I had been in Trongsa all the while, hiding somewhere. Pema and I followed the second route, involving some deviation, to Trongsa via Shangmaiya, and reached my landlord's house in Trongsa at midnight.

Four days after I was found missing, I made myself publicly visible, whereupon, the authorities called and asked me to explain the situation. My father and I had reached a common understanding of how the incident should end. But we went through different starting and bargaining positions to lend credibility to the fabrication that we had never met. I argued that I would like to end my marriage to Pedon Wangmo. It was, I said, pointless to pretend that I was married because in practice I had been away for so long since I was married. The best compromise would be, I suggested, for her to marry my younger brother. My father, on the other hand, persuaded me in front of all other people, to take a conciliatory attitude and to protect the marriage. At the end, the compromise I suggested was worked out. She became the sole wife of my younger brother whereas I was now married to Pema. But my relationship with Pema was as ephemeral and shaky as could be imagined.

I was summoned once again to Dechencholing by the King after a year in Trongsa. I had Pema, her child from her previous husband and her sister living with me when I received the summons. I was reluctant to take her with me to Thimphu, as it would be too impractical. When I broke this news to her, I was astonished to know that she was resigned, and perhaps wanted to stay back without me. Our relationship came to an end as it began, without much hang-up. I decided to leave a few moveable goods I had accumulated at her place.

I travelled as fast as I could to Thimphu and called on Lopon Thinley. But he informed me that His Majesty was not in any way eager to give me an audience immediately upon arrival. In fact, Lopon Thinley advised me against seeking an audience with the King, for His Majesty was still indignant at my long absence from the court.

I was however commanded, through Lopon Thinley, to immediately call on Ashi Tashi, the elder sister of Her Majesty the Queen. In those days, Ashi Tashi enjoyed a reputation of being an extremely able and highly intelligent lady. The King had set up a working group led by Ashi Tashi to commute in-kind taxes to cash taxes in Trashigang district. I called on her in the Guest House in Dechencholing and was immediately pressed into service. Travel plans to go to Trashigang were prepared for a group of seven people

- Ashi Tashi, myself and five servants. We reached Trashigang with night halts in Talodo, Wangduephodrang, Ridha, Chendebji, Trongsa, Ura, Sengor, Dupthozam, Monggar, Sherizampa and Yayung. Makeshift camps were built for the group in Trashigang by Babu Karchung and Kotsha, an ex-soldier, who were the joint administrators of Trashigang. These two officials had succeeded Zongpon Dopola, who died soon after the passing away of the late King.

Ashi Tashi proved to be a skilful administrator and organizer. Her evenings between three and five were devoted to seeing sick people in the small clinic she set up in Trashigang. People came to call on her in the mornings.

Babu Kharpa and his colleague Karma were teaching in the school in Bidung. Babu Kharpa studied in Kalimpong while Karma was a class mate of the second King. Ashi Tashi brought Babu Kharpa from Bidung to Trashigang to become her kadrep.

The eighteen dungpas of Trashigang were invited to a meeting and all the potential clerks, mostly gomchens, were drafted to write land records (thrams). A gomchen (lay priest), Tend Dorji, also became a clerk and a kadrep of Ashi Tashi. Fifteen to sixteen clerks were constantly preparing thrams, led by Tend Dorji. Tend Dorji was given a permanent post as the secretary to an official in Trashigang dzong, and gradually rose to become the Director of the Antiquities Department. Even my friend Omze Drep Tenzin, who had resigned from His Majesty's secretarial staff and left Paro some years ago, was employed as one of the heads of the newly recruited clerks. Most of them were ex-monks who had left the monastery, distracted by prospects of marriages. Tenzin compiled the thrams and bound them into formidable looking land registers. After the clerks were briefed on assessing the land by visual estimation technique, they were dispersed among the dungkhags to prepare the thrams. Paam, Rangshikhar and Shagner were without a dungpa, and so I went to certify the land. The land area was estimated in units of langdo (an area taken a day by a pair of bullocks to plough). On the basis of the land area in a family's possession, the land holding tax was determined in cash for the first time. A copy of thram was deposited in the office of Trashigang administrators, Babu Karchung and Kheng Kotsha, with strict instruction that taxes were to be levied in accordance with the thrams. Ashi Tashi kept the King informed through fortnightly dispatches to Thimphu, and she received prompt replies. She always wrote to the King in her own hand and letters from the King were in Dzongkha. There were runner services from one dzong to another. The couriers were now the employees of dzongs whereas it used to be people from the villages.

The representatives of the people, such as the gups and chimis, were informed of the new tax reform which came to be regarded as kamtrel (dry tax) as opposed to the old lontrel (wet tax). Ashi Tashi mobilized public support for the move to introduce cash tax by first gaining the support of the community leaders. For instance, she was friendly with Akhoray, the wealthiest man of Merak and Sakteng, and he, in turn, convinced the people of Merak and Sakteng of the benefit of the kamtrel. The introduction of kamtrel was not always welcome. For example, a spokesman for Ozurung gewog opposed its introduction.

The collection of cash tax began in Merak by Phub Dorji (a servant of Ashi Tashi), Akhoray and myself. We were entertained lavishly for a week before we turned to other parts of Trashigang. The yield of tax was highest in Merak and Sakteng, the two places which were already to some extent monetized because of their trade with Tawang on the Indian side.

At the time we were there, Lopon Letho of Kheng and one of his friends came to Trashigang to recruit soldiers. The new recruits swelled the number of people who had to be fed from the mess I managed. The food stock dwindled because of the large number of people it had to support. We decided to live partially off the forest. A team of new recruits was sent quite frequently to hunt deer to replenish our food stock.

Another visitor was my uncle Phuntshog Wangdi. He arrived in Trashigang from Thimphu, accompanied by an Indian wireless operator with a few wireless sets. A wireless set was installed in a tent at the Chagzam (bridge) over the river in Trashigang. He and the operator had installed wireless sets in all the dzongkhags along the way: in Thimphu, Wangduephodrang, Chukha, Jakar, Lhuntsi and Kurzam.

Ashi Tashi, the author of the new system of taxation, returned to Thimphu after six months in Trashigang, although the rest of the team remained behind for another six months working closely with Babu Karchung and Kotsha. I also had to stay behind.

While she was in Trashigang, Ashi Tashi brought together the best weavers of the area and made them weave for her on contract, wage and share basis. For about five months, there were more than twelve weavers in the dzong. She used the textiles as gifts and parcels. Lhaki, then a young and beautiful widow of 34 whose husband, Zongpon Dopola, had died, was one of the women who came to weave for Ashi Tashi. I believe I was looked upon as a potential suitor. I found myself taking an interest in her. As Ashi Tashi was about to return to Thimphu, I had a steady relationship with Lhaki.

I sold Lhaki's oranges dutifully during our courtship. Every holiday, I drove Lhaki's caravan loaded with oranges to Guwahati. The oranges were sold for rupees. A certain shopkeeper in Guwahati hoarded betams. The betams could be bought for two rupees each and resold profitably in Kalimpong for four rupees each. Lhaki and I were proceeding to Kalimpong to exchange her betams for rupees when we were arrested by the police in Siliguri and our betams weighed and seized. The betams could not be recovered. We called on Dasho Jigme Palden, who was in Kalimpong, to complain about the seizure. He refused to render any assistance and was furious at me for engaging in such illicit trade. We returned to Trashigang, with all the hard earned money from the sale of oranges confiscated by the Indian police.

Half a year after the betams were confiscated in Siliguri, Lhaki regained them. The Bhutanese Lyonchen had very kindly interceded for their return by pretending that it was public money. Lhaki then went to Phari, a trading centre in Tibet, to spend the betams. She made a profit from the business, which permitted her to purchase four mules.

Lhaki and I returned to Thimphu and lived with my uncle Phuntshog Wangdi in Dechencholing. When Phuntshog Wangdi resigned prematurely, we built a house for ourselves in

197

Dechencholing. We had no child. But, I had, from her younger sister, a lovely son whom we brought up.

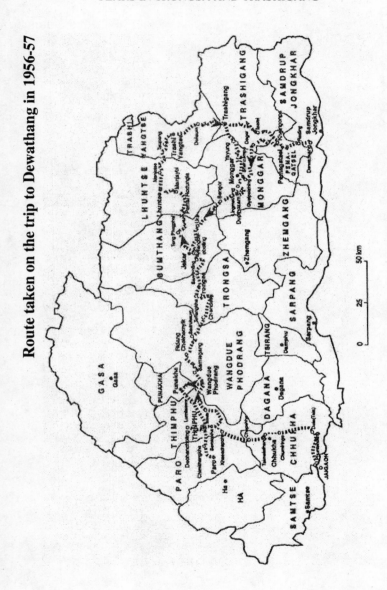

Route taken on the trip to Dewathang in 1956-57

15

VIEWS FROM MULE TRACKS

After I spent almost a year in Trashigang, I was summoned to return to Dechencholing in 1956. Dechencholing was then known as Kashinang. The principal work for the garpas in those days was gardening around the newly constructed palace. His Majesty was an indulgent and passionate gardener who not only loved flowers and plants but grew them. When they were not weeding the lawn, the garpas planted flowers and plants that His Majesty selected. As they mowed and weeded the lawn towards the upper end, weeds sprung again at the bottom of the garden. Maintaining the lawn became a perpetual work until the arrival of autumn stopped the growth. Garpas walked down to the villages in Thimphu to collect horse manure. When a garpa managed to deposit a back load of horse manure, he was rewarded inordinately with a kilogramme of butter or ten dres of rice.

Soon after I got back from Trashigang, I was granted an audience by the King in Dechencholing Palace after two years of being away from the court. All of my old colleagues - Lopon Thinley, Lopon Kesang of Tangsibi, Phub Dorji of Gangtey, Yeshey Wangdi and Sonam Penjor - welcomed me back into their fold. However, Sonam Penjor left us soon because he was appointed the Dungpa of Yangtse. After some years, he was given a higher post as Nyerchen of Trashigang. He died while he was the Nyerchen of

Monggar. Sonam Penjor had developed a good rapport with His Majesty when the latter was the Crown Prince. While Dronyer Jigme waited on His Majesty in the antechamber, Sonam Penjor kept him amused and absorbed by tales and anecdotes in his pleasing, but unaffected, style of conversation.

I could settle in Dechencholing quickly because my uncle Phuntshog Wangdi was by now Zimpon-Nam. He lived in a shack, which I shared, near the Palace. The shack was designed like a bungalow and had balconies and a spacious living room. We had a servant each to look after us. But the following year, my uncle resigned from his job to marry a half-sister of Lopon Thinley, and went to manage her estate in Pema Gatshel. Lopon Thinley, an astute match maker, arranged the marriage and pleaded with His Majesty to relieve my uncle.

When I reached Dechencholing, I found that the working environment had become much more complex. There was an increasingly clear delineation of responsibilities among the secretaries. There was a large room in the palace furnished with low tables swirling in papers and documents, next to which the secretaries were seated. Pulp paper and blue ink had replaced handmade bark paper and home-made black ink respectively. But as in our days in Kinga Rabden and Wangdecholing, there were litigants who came to Dechencholing directly, as there was no law saying that cases must be tried in dzongkhags first. So we - the courtiers and secretaries - still continued to adjudicate the cases brought before us in the evenings. The procedures for adjudication were simplified by Lopon Thinley. Nevertheless, the important framework of procedures remained intact. The most important aspect was that the minutes of the points and counterpoints, and the comments we made, were exhaustively noted and read to the King, sometimes in full, for his verdict.

Among other duties, I was asked to carry out the task so far done by Phub Dorji of Gangtey who was going to become the new private secretary to the Queen Mother. This consisted of jotting down ideas concerning criminal and civil laws which, off and on, came through to His Majesty when he was doing something else. There were already three such notebooks when I took over. It seemed that His Majesty incubated the ideas and thoughts which came to him in fragments and pieces in unlikely moments: while hunting, fishing or walking. His Majesty asked for me whenever a thought surfaced and seized him. I was to draft the ideas found in these notebooks in some coherent structure and form.

We faced mounting official queries from dzongkhags. The dzongkhags referred all untypical questions to the palace. There were inquiries about how to help families whose houses were destroyed by fire. His Majesty decreed that if houses were destroyed, Nu. 5,000 would be offered as compensation and 10% of the assessed value of the goods lost in fire would be paid.

One strand of our multifarious job which took most of our time was examining and certifying revenue accounts of each dzongkhag which were brought turn by turn to Dechencholing. The taxes were paid in cash only in Trashigang, since it was the first dzongkhag where in-kind taxes were commuted to cash taxes in 1955. This was followed by monetization of taxes in Haa and then gradually all over the country. The monetization of taxes was finally adopted throughout the country only in 1968. Other dzongkhags still continued to pay in-kind taxes, and we had to examine the books of in-kind tax income and expenditure. High officials of the dzongkhags had been paid in cash since 1953.

One of our tasks in Dechencholing was to release the monthly salaries for the high officials in the dzongkhags. Lower level officials were still being paid in-kind directly from in-kind taxes of the respective dzongkhags. We also sent the salaries of those who manned the wireless sets in various strategic points. Moreover, cash salary was disbursed to 'chubabu' or people who kept surveillance over water levels of major rivers in Bhutan to warn about potential floods in India. The estimate of their wages was sent to Gongzim Sonam Tobgye to get refunded by the Government of India.

For most of the secretarial staff, the work on tax reform continued. I recall from the accounts that the in-kind tax revenue in Zhongar, Lhuntsi, Dagana and Zhemgang was barely sufficient to defray the cost of feeding the monastic community and the lay officials.

The first National Assembly, presided over by Speaker Paro Dzongtshab Kelzang Dawa, took place in Punakha in 1953 while I was in Trashigang. The second session was held in 1957 in Paro. Dzongtshab Kelzang Dawa had passed away while I was in Trashigang and the post of Speaker was passed to Lopon Thinley. I was his assistant in all affairs, including the organization of the National Assembly. The main motions for the consideration of the session were: requisition of labour for motor road construction, conscription of soldiers, and review of draft laws of Thrimshung Chenmo (Supreme Laws). The Haa Dungpa Jigme Dorji addressed the National Assembly most frequently. The National Assembly met for ten consecutive days and resolved to provide labour for the construction of road between Trashigang and Samdrup Jongkhar; and between Thimphu and Phuntsholing. Other prominent people in that session of the National Assembly were Dratshang's Dorji Lopon, Pangpa Phentok, Miser Gup Sedo of Paro and Wang Gup Ngidup. A draft form of the legal code was put to the National Assembly for discussion. Important suggestions were noted. However, I believe that the Thrimshung would have been better without public debate because it was revised for the worse. This process continued for about three successive years of the National Assembly sessions. The King sat through the initial stages of discussion but left the National Assembly to decide most of the sections of the law. He was consulted when there was great disagreement and indecision. The Thrimshung was passed only in 1959.

The King left for a tour of southern Bhutan in the winter of 1956. Using Jaigoan which was fully wooded as the base, the King visited nearby places in the South including Phibsoo in Gaylegphug. Ashi Sonam Choden (born 1953), Ashi Dechen (born 1954), Dasho Jigme (born 1955) and the Queen joined him on the trip, but not on the next one to other dzongkhags in eastern Bhutan.

On the trip to eastern Bhutan, His Majesty was accompanied by about sixty soldiers in addition to the changgaps and secretarial staff consisting of Lopon Thinley, Tangsibi Kesang, Yeshey Wangdi and myself. A group of conversationalists (kadrep) also accompanied His Majesty. They included Thapoydrep Tshering, a monk; Kurtoep Nyerchen Drep Dendup, brother-in-law of the late Trashigang Zongpon Dopola; Gyem Dorji, the hunter; Lobzang

Dorji, Paap Yoeser, Gotu, Umteng Tshering, Trashigang Lobzang Dorji and Nubi Dungpa Nagphay. Each of them was a specialist in his own way. For example Kurtoep Dendup was a great hunter. He knew in minute detail the behaviours and habitats of wild animals. Thapoydrep Tshering was a blunt and forthright man. While other kadreps abounded with courteous phrases and suave manners, he talked to His Majesty as he spoke to others, lacing his words with curses. He also played hima (a kind of board game) against His Majesty. Lobzang Dorji, who had spent many years in Tibet, was a volatile but extraordinarily persuasive person. He spoke the most impeccable dzongkha I have ever heard.

Lopon Thinley was given the title of Chichap (Chief) for the duration of this trip and he took all the organizational and logistical decisions. Lopon Thinley had two extremely laid back servants. Consequently, I had to do a lot of things that should have been done by his servants. For example, I had to unfold his bedding in the tent and make his bed. I also had to check very frequently during the day whether the neck strap, belly-band and stirrup strap of his riding pony were securely fastened. Gaydon Thinley took his responsibilities far too seriously, and made rounds of the camp with a torch after everybody had gone to bed. He would slap people on the spot for shoddy work. I often liaised between Chichap Thinley and others, and, because of my close association with him, people regarded me occasionally with some trepidation.

A complete list of the caravan might have included a hundred ponies carrying food and clothes, two hundred people and ten mules carrying the tents. The muleteers and the mules had the most rigorous job. The tents were packed after the King left, but the muleteers had to overtake the main caravan to pitch the tents before the entourage got to the next camping spot. The muleteers and the advance party were equipped with wireless sets. Throughout the journey, the entourage was to be hosted by the dzongkhags where it was. However, the number of people swelled on the return journey to Thimphu via the direct lateral route. Many soldiers and retainers married during their brief stay in Lhuntsi, Bumthang and Trashigang and their new wives accompanied the entourage to Thimphu.

On the first day of the journey, the entourage got only as far as Simtokha from Dechencholing. As soon the camp was settled, the national flag was hoisted and a bugle sounded. This was done at every camp in the evening. The flag was square in shape and the dragon, instead of being diagonally placed, was straight. I was later commanded to redesign the flag as it is today.

The entourage travelled with night halts in Simtokha, Talodo, Tencholing, Samtengang, Ridha Choskhornyik, Sadruksum, Tshangkha, Trongsa, Samtenling, Wangdecholing, Tang Phogphai, Pumaiya in Rodungla, Kurtoe Menjaybi, Lhuntsi, Menjitse, Taupang near Trashiyangtse, Doksum, Trashigang, Tshatsi, Khairi Gonpa, and Rading before finally reaching Dewathang (see map of mule tracks on p. 244). There was a break in the journey of over a week each in Wangdecholing, Lhuntsi and Trashigang.

King Jigme Dorji Wangchuck inherited his father's extraordinary love for riding horses. The adungs and chandaaps were made to comb, brush and massage the horses. Of all the adungs, Khitu was His Majesty's favourite. He was far more gifted than his elder brother Khila. Both Khila and Khitu were the sons of a palace cook. Khitu was of medium build, dark, and superbly athletic and

207

graceful. His elder brother Khila was an able, eloquent and clever man. Both Khila and Khitu made a wonderful pair of mask dancers. It was on this trip, during the stopover in Wangdecholing, that Khila married Yangki who could sing quite well. Khila and Khitu rarely failed His Majesty in whatever assignment they were entrusted. According to their hereditary occupation, they were to become adungs or stable boys, an under-class. One reason, in my opinion, why Khila and Khitu were made close attendants or garpa, a position higher than adungs in the strict court hierarchy, was to demonstrate that the King did not differentiate between people of different social strata. His Majesty was breaking the values of class differentiation. Nevertheless, I believe, there was an undercurrent of resentment against Khila and Khitu because most of the garpas were drawn from a higher strata of society.

Kurtoe Menji was our first halt at a subtropical site. Chichap Thinley announced that petitions to seek land grants and alleviate hardships might be submitted to His Majesty. But to our great surprise, there were not many petitions on these issues. The people were interested only in bringing old, pending disputes to be settled and these were completed over a week's stay in Lhuntsi.

The entourage took rest for a whole month in Dewathang. The post of Zongpon of Dewathang and Pema Gatshel had fallen vacant after the death of its incumbent in the previous year and Babu Tashi was appointed to the post. Pema Gatshel was then part of the administrative unit known as Zhongar Dosum.

Her Majesty the Queen, the Crown Prince and princesses joined His Majesty in Dewathang. They drove from Kalimpong to Guwahati and rode on horse from Guwahati to Dewathang. The entire hill top was fenced off with bamboo mats and various play things were installed within the enclosure for the young Crown Prince and princesses.

A few days after the arrival of the Queen in Dewathang, my uncle Phuntshog Wangdi was asked to go to Calcutta to procure some goods for the royal family. Lopon Thinley gave permission for me to accompany my uncle on this trip. Our first night was spent in a shop in Rangia whose owner was known to my uncle. The journey from Rangia to Guwahati was my first experience of travelling in a bus. Both of us became thoroughly sick from the bus journey. We left by air for Calcutta the next day. My uncle, who had been to Calcutta before, bought clothes and other things which in all consisted of about five boxes.

Since both of us got extremely sick again while travelling in the plane from Guwahati to Calcutta, we decided to travel back by train. My uncle broke into a row with another passenger at Shelda Station as the passengers were crowding into the train. Fortunately, we met Dongachen, the Elder Queen Mother's trader, who placated the other person by thrusting a few rupees into his hand. At some point, my uncle and I had to evacuate the train on one side of the Ganges and cross the river by boat before getting on a train waiting on the other side. My uncle went to look for seats, leaving me to follow him with railway porters. After some moments, I lost sight of my uncle in the teeming crowd and began to panic. I shouted loudly after him 'Ashang, Ashang'. This amused the train of railway porters and I could hear them mimic me 'Ashang, Ashang.' We got off the train at Rangia and got on to a bus taking us to Guwahati. From there, we hired Bhutanese porters till Dewathang. We had just taken a week for the two way trip.

As I recalled a moment earlier, both Babu Tashi and Lopon Thinley were in Dewathang. However, their relationship had soured and an uneasy truce existed between them. The King was worried about the worsening relationship between them and intervened personally.

Lopon Thinley's father was Zhongar Zongpon Kunzang Wangdi but he was succeeded by Babu Tashi. At the time of taking the charge, Babu Tashi maintained that there were missing public properties. Lopon Thinley was offended by this allegation and jumped to the defence of his father's reputation.

I went to call on Babu Tashi to mend the relationship between the two. I reasserted that, he, Babu Tashi, was the teacher of my uncle who had fled and so I felt the same degree of respect for him as I felt for Lopon Thinley.

His Majesty was concerned with their disagreement and inquired into their case. His Majesty finally asked Lopon Thinley to make up for all missing goods which consisted of altar objects made of silver. His Majesty paid for the cost of replacement. I went to receive all the rejected silver goods including chalice, butter lamps and water cups. There were a large number of old, faded and worn out goods which were replaced by the King on behalf of Lopon Thinley. We had overlooked the possibility of a third person swapping the missing properties with worn out ones. It had indeed happened, although I came to know about it many years later. Babu Tashi was extremely pleased with my role in the negotiation with Lopon Thinley and presented me with a large quantity of food stuffs especially rice. Some months later, Babu Tashi was conferred with the honour of red scarf and made the Nyerchen of Trashigang.

After a month or so, Her Majesty the Queen, the princes, princesses and Haa Dungpa returned to Kalimpong via Guwahati. A few days later, His Majesty and the entourage also left for Thimphu by the lateral route.

Our journey was very smooth until we camped in Sadruksum Namdruksum. There, Wangduephodrang Nyerchen Gangteyp Rikela was the host. He was responsible for arranging food for all the retainers. Rikela had denied feed and fodder to some of the pack horses and this was reported in the evening to the King. Rikela was relieved instantly from his post.

The next evening in Tencholing, it was my friend, Dronyer Sha Yabjee of Wangduephodrang who fell foul of Lopon Thinley. Tencholing was then a wilderness full of heath; a patch of ground was cleared and levelled to pitch tents. When Lopon Thinley and I got on the camp site, Dronyer Sha Yabjee did not have the tent poles quite ready. Lopon Thinley got furious with Sha Yabjee and struck him with the rough side of his sword three times, before the sword shook off from its handle.

The tents were barely up when the King arrived and a welcome tea was served. As the Chichap Lopon Thinley was allocated a full pot of tea. Over tea, Lopon Thinley told me that there was a deeper reason for him to be high handed with my friend, Sha Yabjee who, with his red scarf status, was technically higher than Lopon Thinley himself in the hierarchy. Lopon Thinley justified his actions by saying that Sha Yabjee would have faced a greater misfortune like Rikela if Lopon Thinley had not taken out his anger on him. It was thus reasoned that Sha Yabjee had been saved from a greater risk of unknown proportion. Late at night, Dronyer Sha Yabjee called on Lopon Thinley to thank him for averting a personal disaster.

The tone of the evening might have continued to be sombre. Fortunately, I met an old colleague who was a changgap in the court. He had by now become a secretary to Sha Yabjee. He regaled us with lascivious account of his escapades around Wangduephodrang late into the night. I recall that he talked about his recent affair which involved a visit to his Tibetan girl friend under the cover of night. She lived in Sha Samtengang, some three hours trekking distance from the fortress of Wangduephodrang where he worked. The distance was not considered too far; he felt very enthusiastic about visiting her even though it would take about six hours to trek back and forth. He left by nightfall and planned to be back by day break. Serious suitors regularly walked at night over long distances. Some travelled at night on ponies. They left their ponies leashed to trees in the outskirts of the village. Those who trekked for long at night had to build up a great deal of stamina to be left with requisite energy at the end of the trek.

He began: "I had my supper with my colleagues and soon excused myself on a pretext. The night was overcast and the moon light was erratic. I was daunted from going by the prospect of rain. I thought that I would turn back at the point when it rained, but I would go as far as I could. It did not rain at all and after I crossed Rabuna, the moon shone more brightly. I could see the path more clearly and could walk fast. I was struck by a little bit of fear of bears and leopards when I walked through the creek below Chebashong and I found myself walking even faster and tripping often. The creek was notorious for sheltering bears. I thought I was inured to fear of wild animals but this was not so as yet. I found myself chanting mantras loudly, to which I rarely resorted. The noise would prevent the bears from colliding with me at road bends. I expected that the noise would give the bears enough time to back out of my way.

"As I walked in the dark, I began to recall many tales about people mauled by bears, particularly a recent incident involving one Dorji in Keta Bongo. Bears and boars were the bane of the farmers. They feasted on the crops, paying little attention to people who guarded the crops throughout the night. Dorji borrowed a match lock gun and sat on a platform in the millet field one night. He stuffed the gun powder and kept it ready to feed lead pellets into the barrel. The lead pellets were kept ready in the fold of his gho.

Dorji kept himself up throughout the night in front of a small fire, howling more fiercely than a dog to scare the wild animals away. When Dorji felt his throat drying, he pulled out from the fold of his gho a quarter of a betel nut with a paan (leaf taken with betel nut) to chew. The fold of his gho was a veritable bag containing many things including a handkerchief, wallet, cups, a sewing kit, a small knife, a match box, a tangle of cords and strings, blessed ointment for his arthritic knees, hat, keys, a pair of forceps to pull out his beard and moustache. The dawn was breaking: he could see the end of the field clearly.

Dorji got up on the platform to go home and looked at the tall heads of fox tail millet close by the platform. They were moving. He focused his eyes on the one of the stilts of the platform. A bear was actually trying to climb the post and was in an upright position against it. The bear looked straight into Dorji's eyes and opened its mouth. Dorji could see its tongue, throat and fangs. He felt nervous in spite of his preparedness for such an encounter throughout the night. He grabbed his match lock gun and turned it against the bear and aimed at its gaping mouth.

Suddenly, he lowered the gun for he had forgotten to load the pellet. He put his hand quickly into the fold of the gun to retrieve the pellet, inserted it into the barrel of the gun and fired into the mouth of the bear. The bear withdrew at once and dashed into the bushes. Dorji expected the bear to stagger and collapse. But the bear ran with alacrity towards the forest. It even looked back in an audacious manner at Dorji. It was an extraordinary bear, Dorji thought, quite intrigued. Dorji's hand unconsciously slipped into the fold of his gho for a piece of betel nut. Without looking at it, he tossed it into his mouth, rolled his tongue around it and tried to sink his teeth into it. His teeth nearly broke, because it was the lead pellet which should have been fired into the mouth of the bear. Instead, a piece of betel nut had been served to the bear early in the morning.

"I reached Samtengang before the people had gone to bed. Lights flickered through the windows and I could hear the murmurs of conversation in the house of my Tibetan girl friend. A few dogs came howling at me. Dogs were the biggest obstacles to successful visits; they roused the people from their sleep and made the family members wary and inhospitable. It seemed that my girl friend's family was not going to retire quickly, so I had to find a warm place to have a nap. It was a windy night in Samtengang. I could think of no better place than their ground floor which was used as a cattle pen.

I gently nudged the door open and looked inside from the

entrance. The pen was without a window. I could not see anything in the dark though I heard the cattle ruminating. Standing on the threshold on one leg, I stretched my other leg downwards. We normally assume the floor level not be too far down, but my leg did not come into contact with the floor surface. I stretched my leg further down without being able to find the ground. Then, it occurred to me that the floor of the pen had been mined deeply for manure, resulting in a very low floor level. Safe in the knowledge that the ground that would support me was not altogether missing, I jumped. I landed on something soft and unstable which pulled out immediately while making a shrill cry of alarm. The cattle made hissing sound produced by expulsion of pressurised air through their nostrils. I tumbled down on the ground. It was a pig who was badly disturbed by my landing. The commotion in the pen attracted the attention of the people upstairs. They were coming down in force led by my girl friend bearing a torch.

"It is the leopard that came yesterday," said one of them.

"The leopard is getting very bold. We were hardly asleep," answered a woman.

"It must be a leopard going for the pig. The dogs did not make a sound. The dogs have been totally cowered for some time now; it must be a leopard," commented another woman.

By the time they came to the entrance of the pen, I had hidden myself between the far end of the wall and a submissively weak cow, which was lying impervious to the commotion around it. Behind it I lay exactly aligned with its reclining body. I vigorously scratched its flank to provoke a severe itch that needed immediate relief which I provided. The cow stood very still, savouring the relief I gave, while the women looked around for signs of the big cat. The women finally withdrew from the cattle pen, satisfied that their timely intervention had prevented the cattle and the pig from coming to any harm.

After some time, it became quiet upstairs. I took a long rest in the cattle pen, to allow the women upstairs to fall asleep. Then I came out of the pen and scrambled up the ladder. With the help of my dagger that had an exceptionally hooked tip, I could release the wooden bolt of the commodious room where they all slept. The opening of the door, which made a lot of creaking noise if done in one push, was the most difficult part of the operation. It had to be done by imperceptible degrees and took me almost half an hour.

"Once inside the room, it was not useful to be a biped. I could step on things or bump into things in the dark if I walked, even though I was sure of the direction in which I should go as I knew where she usually slept. Crawling on all fours was far safer.

"I took off all the clothes I wore and wrapped them inside my gho. I put the gho on top of the tall wooden box beside her. The box had no lid and the gho sank to the bottom of the box. As soon as I found myself next to my girl friend, her aunt began to stir out of her bed. She was looking for some dry ferns and the match box. I got up naked and went to hide in the cavernous nook to the right side of the hearth. In retrospect, it was quite foolish of me to go there. Her aunt lit the fire which sent up a lot of smoke and also illuminated my front side completely. I stealthily spread both my palms on the soot on the wall and blackened the front part of my body and face as much as possible. I did it repeatedly so that I could merge into the dark background. I stood there unnoticed by her aunt, though I could see that my girl friend was biting the blanket to muffle her giggling. The problem began with smoke emission. I could hardly breathe. I was getting unwittingly 'smoked out' by her aunt. I dashed naked towards the door. Her aunt collapsed with fright at such a sight.

"Thus, I found myself strolling around the village naked on a frosty night. I contemplated retrieval of my clothes. It was not possible without her aunt seeing me. I considered various options. I could hide the next day in the forest and try to get back my clothes in the night. I could walk back to Wangduephodrang. I could not come to terms with the thought of walking naked over such a long way and meeting someone in that fashion in the morning. I hoped that my girl friend would foresee my odd situation and come to my rescue. But as I waited for a long time next to the ladder, I felt convinced that she was snugly asleep in her bed.

"I looked for a warmer place than the cattle pen as the wind picked up speed. Eventually, I found the mound of compost that had been taken out. I stuck my arm into the mound. It was very warm inside, though not as dry as I would have liked. I bore a big enough cavity in the mound and sat inside it; it was like a toxic chamber. The smell was quite overpowering. But I made up my mind to tolerate the fermented smell so as not to die of hypothermia. From time to time, I looked for signs of my girl friend. Only at the last crow of the rooster did she come out with my clothes."

16

FREEDOM OF SERFS AND PM NEHRU IN PARO

The King was extremely fond of mask dances and wanted to include more demanding ones in the forthcoming Thimphu Domchoe. I became the instructor for the mask dances for three months during which I introduced the most formal and rigorous of the dances - Dramitse Ngacham and Peleng Gengsum. Several garpas were recruited to perform mask dances and my friend, Nubi Dungpa Nagphay was appointed as the chief of mask dancers and granted the title of Champon Chichap. The lead dancers were Khila and Khitu who became the first and the last respectively in the line of dancers. Paro Geta Dungpa, a man with a breathtakingly rich and mellifluous voice, taught Damnyenchogyel, the most elegant and spectacular of the musical performances. The Domchoe, which was held in the 8th month of the Bhutanese calendar, was made into a special occasion to celebrate the formal entry of the Crown Prince Jigme Singye Wangchuck, who was about three years old, into the dzong. He moved in a procession from Dechencholing to Tashichodzong. The seat of the Crown Prince was flanked by those of the Queen, the King and the Chief Abbot of Bhutan, in the gallery.

His Majesty was now able to spare some time daily for gardening, riding and mask dances, pastimes which he found enjoyable after strenuous duties of state. After he got through his correspondence and other official duties, he would come to the garden. At the end of his garden in Dechencholing was the stable for his horses. The stable was no longer like a barn. His Majesty was so fond of his horses that the rebuilt stable was comparable to a human residence. The window frames were richly carved and painted, with motifs usually found on houses, verging on the appearance of a modest shrine. The stable also had striped wooden flooring. The head of each horse, looking out of the stable window, was visible like a picture bordered by a frame.

Beyond the stable was the lawn on which mask dancers rehearsed their shows every evening. His Majesty joined in the mask dance, especially when the high notes of the cymbals quickened and the blare of the long horns became more raging, calling for movements of lightning rushes and leaps, suggestive of the flight of a winged panther. During the downturn phase of the dance, when the movement became muffled and stealthy, His Majesty quietly withdrew to watch. It became a habit for His Majesty to visit and see, in a set order, the garden, the stable and horses, and the mask dances.

The King was about to make a landmark social reform: the freedom of the serfs. Although the serfs were known by many different terms, such as khey, jou, zaden, pongyer, and jaam, there were essentially two broad categories of serfs, namely drab and zab. Draba worked without any payment on the master's land in return for a piece of land allocated by the master for their own use. They cropped such a plot for themselves and worked the rest of their time on the land belonging to the master. Drab families did not pay any tax because they were only answerable to the master. Zab were in a worse situation: they worked entirely for the master who gave them only food and clothes.

As a prelude to this social reform, His Majesty issued royal ordinance that the serfs were to be called by some word other than the traditional derogatory terms, such as khey, jou or zaden. They were to be addressed as nangzen, a softer term which did not carry as much stigma as the other three words. The nobilities of Kurtoe had the largest number of serfs. A prominent household of Nai, for example, had more than a hundred serfs. Even from this underclass, a select few could rise to be maid servants and butlers in their adolescence, while the others worked on the land of the nobilities. Such select groups of indentured servants were known as zaden.

Almost a year after he issued the decree changing the nomenclature for the serfs, the King proclaimed manumission for all serfs. His Majesty decreed that they were free to leave their former masters without fear of recrimination. But they were forbidden to take any of their masters' moveable assets as well as to settle in the same gewog. They were promised gifts of land in other gewogs to give them a good start as free individuals. This was done so that they would not have to mingle awkwardly and embarrassingly with their former masters.

There was a considerable exodus of serfs from Wangduephodrang, Paro, Thimphu and Punakha. They converged, in masses, in Dechencholing to seek grants of land from His Majesty. His Majesty wanted to install most of them as full fledged tax paying households in Thimphu Dzongkhag, where the number of tax paying households had declined. It became obvious, when referring to thrams, that there had been more households in Thimphu district in the past. Their numbers were reduced either due to outbreaks of epidemics or acquittal of land and houses because of excessive tax burdens. In-kind revenue accruing to Thimphu dzong had fallen and the number of 'tsa tong' (empty land, not to be confused with free land) had increased. Free land was always preferred to tsa tong land because the 'tsa tong' land carried tax liability with it. The new settlers had to pay the amount of tax levied on its previous land holders.

His Majesty asked me and Dasho Dago to allocate land to the serfs who now flocked to Dechencholing. There was a good expanse of uncultivated land in Kabjisa near Chorten Nyingpa and Oysakha, which we found during survey. More and more serfs descended into the area as we distributed land, until the number of serfs exceeded the plots available for distribution. But we noticed that many households in that area were utilizing land which was not registered in their own thrams. We were therefore empowered to redistribute land from those illegal land holdings to the landless serfs. When all the uncultivated land for redistribution was exhausted, we began our exploration for resettlement areas in other parts of Western Bhutan. A suitable piece of land was found in Peteyri in Punakha, after rambling up and down the mountains for two days. Some forested areas of Peteyri bore signs of having been inhabited and cultivated at one stage in time. But the traces of terraced fields were now covered in dense undergrowth and trees, clearly indicating that it had been several generations or so since it reverted to wilderness. The water which was once conducted to Peteyri through an irrigation channel had been diverted in other directions.

The site in Peteyri was recommended for all the serfs from

Gaselo. As in Kurtoe, a few wealthy families of Gaselo had more than twenty to thirty serfs. The total number of serfs from Gaselo probably exceeded a thousand, and they were all settled in one area. Kabji Peteyri has become a dense, wide village since then. The people of Kabji Peteyri came to acknowledge their gratitude to me almost two decades later, in 1974, when I was constructing my cottage in Toebesa. They brought a luncheon feast for the construction workers in the time honoured tradition.

The majority of the serfs from Paro and a few from Punakha were awarded land in Pangrezam above Dechencholing, and Khasadrapchu. We were going about our work as usual in Pangrezam when the King, going for an evening ride, chanced to see us and inquired about the progress of our work. We reported that there was a strong preference for free land instead of 'tsa tong' land, because of the lack of tax on free land. We further reported that we were getting unavoidably caught up in disputes between the serfs and their former masters. The disputes were mostly about property such as houses of the serfs which they claimed were built by serfs and belonged to them. We were commanded to resolve the issues by asking the masters to compensate for the houses of the serfs. The compensations, however meagre, helped the serfs to establish themselves elsewhere.

The National Assembly was convened for the second time in 1957 to discuss the forthcoming visit of Indian Prime Minister Nehru. It was decided that the more articulate among the mangmis (people's representative in the National Assembly) would ask questions to Nehru from the floor. In the same session, the National Assembly resolved to establish a military centre in Tencholing with labour contributions raised from all around the country. Bahadur Namgay was the chief of army based in Tencholing. Bahadur Namgay was once dispatched to Southern Bhutan to overcome a group of insurgents against the royal government, and his success had made him prominent. He was soon promoted to major when a younger batch of captains like Penjor, Ugyen and Lam Dorji returned after their training from India.

I was assigned to work with them for about two months to devise dzongkhag equivalents of military drill commands. The translations could not be literal ones because they wanted especially masculine, assertive and short sounding words. To get the words of their choice, I referred to epics and scriptures for terrifying utterances with adequate etymology. Lopon Thinley was consulted frequently, though he seldom altered the phrases I coined or plucked out of scriptures. Lopon Thinley and I also discussed symbols or insignia of ranks for military personnel with the three captains. I was able to come up with tantric designs for the army flag and decorations used to denote hierarchy in the army. I was later to do the same for the police ensigns when Royal Bhutan Police was founded.

Lopon Thinley was appointed the Speaker of National Assembly and conferred the honour of the red scarf on the eve of Nehru's arrival. He had been a white scarf officer till then. His Majesty informed him through someone that he could come to receive Nehru in a red scarf the next day. He became a high official without any fanfare. Expectedly, he was one of the officials who had the privilege of having a group discussion with Nehru. Nehru remarked later that he regretted that this man (Gaydon Thinley) had not received adequate education to realize his full potential. He was to be addressed hence forth as Gaydon Thinley. I became His Majesty's de facto private secretary, after the promotion of Lopon Thinley to Gaydon.

As I mentioned earlier, the first Speaker of the National Assembly had died around 1955. Dasho Kelzang Dawa's fame had reached its zenith when he was appointed the first Speaker of the National Assembly held in Punakha. He died as Paro Dzongtshab. For a person who enjoyed certain degree of power and influence, he never used it to aggrandize himself: he was without a house of his own or large land holding. Nor did he unduly help his younger brother or his relatives. He was a selfless servant of the King. Among the personal affects he bequeathed were several ghos, swords and guns. Towards the end of his life, he began to drink heavily, a tendency which was atypical and unexpected in such an intelligent man. I felt odd to recollect the strange pattern in the habits of two great servants of the Kings. Gaydon Thinley could not resist regular and large amounts of alcohol in the early part of his life in Wangdecholing and Kinga Rabden, while Dasho Kelzang Dawa became less and less of a teetotaller towards the later part of his life in Paro.

Gaydon Thinley never had an able butler or servant in spite of attaining one of the highest positions in the country. I was his butler and aide all through the time I was attached to him. In fact, we shared the same cottage in Wangthangkha in Dechencholing.

As I came to assist Gaydon Thinley for much of his life, I learnt some of his drafting skills and manner of speech just as he had done as an apprentice to Lopon Kelzang Dawa. Gaydon Thinley's composition style embodied the most supple feltshig. His Majesty the King admired feltshig in its best forms, and I came to adopt this style of writing. Most of the Royal Kashos were drafted either by me or Gaydon Thinley. Although Gaydon Thinley was very resourceful, he was less familiar than me in the sphere of rituals, graphics and scriptural knowledge. Gaydon left it to me to judge the quality of paintings, idols and ceremonial standards.

Thimphu was now rife with news of Nehru's visit to Bhutan, for which a grand preparation had to be made. The members of the National Assembly, then known as mangmis, were summoned to Paro and worked for two months before the visit of Nehru. They were deployed to build temporary camps, repair mule tracks and extract more than four thousand flag poles which were erected along the footpath from Paro Gangteng to Paro dzong. A mangmi had to fell and bring two flag poles from the forest a day for about two months.

Riding horses for Nehru's delegation were sent as far as Gangtok. Nehru's entourage had to cross a piece of Chinese territory in Yatung and Chinese troops accompanied him to the Bhutanese border. Nehru was accompanied by his daughter Indira Gandhi and his aide Metha. Armed escorts, dressed in gho and fur hats, were despatched to Gangtok with horses and other high officials. In Paro, Nehru was welcomed from the Gangteng area to the Paro Ugyen Pelri Palace with a ceremonial procession. The second storey of the palace was refurbished for Nehru and his daughter Indira. Prime Minister Nehru and Indira formally called on the King and his family in Paro dzong the next day. Nehru brought along about thirty back loads of gifts, including telephones, toy cars and bicycles for the prince and princesses.

The King made a hundred soldiers, led by Zamadar Chencho, present a guard of honour, wearing buley and gho. After a discussion, the Prime Minister and his delegates visited the exhibitions of Bhutanese artefacts in the dzong. A fine selection of thangkhas (scroll paintings), metal goods, and armouries were put on display. Gaydon Thinley and I were put in charge of the exhibition consisting of the finest artefacts from Phajoding, Trashigang (near Yosepang) and other monasteries of Western Bhutan. These objects were returned to their respective places after Nehru left Bhutan.

Members of Nehru's delegation were taken around U-tse, Kuenrey, and Dukhang where the National Assembly was in session. The National Assembly presented a letter of thanks, done on scroll, to Nehru for his visit. Several eloquent spokesmen like Gup Jangtu and Sedo posed questions to Nehru.

Nehru hosted a dinner for the members of the National Assembly under bright light cast by six gas lamps. His Majesty, anticipating that they might be invited, had briefed them on table manners. Not withstanding this prudent advice, some of the members of the National Assembly departed with spoons, out of their admiration for the fine metal work, and furtively put a portion of pudding into their pockets to give a taste of pudding to the people at home.

Nehru spent a week in Paro during which he visited Shabjithang village and Taktsang monastery. He brought along documentary films which were shown to the people every evening during his stay. He asked people for tea one afternoon, and sponsored an expensive ritual in Paro Kyichu Lhakhang. Courtiers and the members of the National Assembly were impressed with his largess. He presented all the secretarial staff with a pen and a ball point each.

One day, Nehru addressed a public gathering from an unusually high dias erected for the occasion. Pema Wangchuck (later Lyonpo) was his interpreter, but his amplified voice began to tremble and stutter. After sometime, the King nudged away Pema Wangchuck and began to interpret Nehru's speech. Nehru said that His Majesty had invited him to visit Bhutan for the last four years, but he could not take up the offer because of problems in various parts of India that preoccupied him. He remarked in his speech on the wealth of jewellery of the ladies of Paro, the beauty of the landscape and the goodness of people. Questions were raised from amongst the public gathering. Most of them asked about Indian assistance to Bhutan.

After the speech to the public of Paro, Nehru hosted a tea reception for thousands of people who had come to listen to him. I recall that there were more people than nine sacks of biscuits could go round; after the biscuits ran out, a local snack made of pounded, roasted maize was served to the remaining crowd. On the day of their departure, there was a farewell procession and a large number of Bhutanese officials, including Sha Yabjee, Jangtu, Dasho Thinley Namgyel, Dranglab Thegila and Gaydon Thinley went to see off Nehru as far as Gangtok.

17

ON THE FAST LANE TO INDIA

In the winter following the visit of Prime Minister Nehru to Bhutan, King Jigme Dorji was invited on a reciprocal visit to India. The visit was to take place in the 12th lunar month. His Majesty planned to be in Calcutta for at least two months before the state visit which would start in Delhi. The Haa Dungpa had arranged for the immediate members of the royal family to stay at 2 Mayfair Road in Calcutta. Her Majesty the Queen, the Crown Prince and the princesses also went to spend the winter in Calcutta. On the trip to Calcutta, the entourage consisted of the Haa Dungpa, Gaydon Thinley, Paro Dzongtshab Bajo, Dr Tobgyel, Gelong Adangpa, Lt. Tshering, Lt. Wangdi, Khila and Shayngab Dendu. Gelong Adangpa, the court merchant, was posted in Calcutta to change rupees into dollars.

The other members of the entourage were put in accommodations some distance away from 2 Mayfair Road. I lived in a flat with Gaydon Thinley and Paro Dzongtshab Bajo. After some weeks, I was put in a separate flat near the Grand Hotel, as the private secretary to HM had to be nearby. In the other apartment in the same building lived Ashi Tesla Tsering Yangzom and her husband, the Haa Dungpa. She was a daughter of nobility - Tsarong Shapey - of Lhasa and had studied in Kalimpong before marrying the Haa Dungpa.

All of us reported to the King at 8 in the morning every day at 2 Mayfair Road and were let off if there was no further command. The bills for food and lodging were settled by Mr Lawrence Sitling, the Haa Dungpa's personal assistant.

During our stay in Calcutta, I learnt some Hindi words and came to like 'chapati', 'chicken tandoori', salad and 'dahi' (yogurt). I had the financial freedom to try a variety of food, as the bills were settled by Mr Lawrence. But my diet did not vary very much throughout my stay in Calcutta because the extent of my Hindi was limited to 'chapati', 'chicken tandoori', 'dahi' and a few other desperately necessary words.

Gaydon Thinley and Paro Dzongtshab were keen on sightseeing and went to visit the resort of Khitapur, taking me along. They also took me along to watch films and wrestling matches. The former bored me immediately and I could rarely sit through a show.

When the time finally came to go to Delhi, Her Majesty, the Crown Prince and princesses did not join the delegation. Those carrying on to Delhi were Gaydon Thinley, Paro Dzongtshab Bajo, Lawrence Sitling, Haa Dungpa, Khila, Dendu, Gelong Adangpa, me and two security officers. On the eve of departure for Delhi, security guards and a motorcade appeared around 2 Mayfair Road. There was a car for every two persons. The next morning at the airport, Gaydon Thinley was visibly frightened of flying though he suppressed his fear as much as possible. While walking towards the plane, I could see blasts of steam evaporating from his bald head. He slowed down as we came to the staircase leading us to the plane. While His Majesty was being welcomed aboard, Gaydon Thinley took a few steps aside to be away from the glare of attention. I was puzzled. His right hand deftly took out his wallet: then, he took out a 50 paise coin and tossed it in the sky. The coin fell, rolled a few paces and came to standstill on the tarmac of the taxiway, glistening in the sun. He had offered it to the heavens for a safe journey. Gaydon, who was sweating profusely even in the plane, was asked to come to the VIP section of the special plane, to assuage his fear.

The members of the entourage were briefed by the King, who said that bowing and cowing in deference to him should be avoided completely during this trip. They were to sit and eat near him, literally holding their heads high. Nevertheless, they cringed and withered, as if they were sitting near a big fire, whenever they stood near him. At Delhi Airport, there was a 21 gun salute. I followed Gaydon down the flight staircase. Nehru and his daughter, Indira Gandhi, could be seen amongst a sea of faces down below. As the King came down to the last rungs of the flight staircase, garland after garland landed on His Majesty, who hastily passed them on to us. The royal entourage was driven to Hyderabad House through avenues lined with the flags of Bhutan and India. In Hyderabad House, the rooms to be occupied had their names on the doors. Since I was designated as private secretary to HM the King, my room had an ample amount of stationery and a handsome writing desk. An electric fireplace, which gave the appearance of burning twigs and charcoal, emitted some heat in the corner of the room. The entourage had a quiet dinner in Hyderabad House amongst ourselves. For me, it was the first dinner shared at the same table with HM the King. It was easier to be equal in a foreign land, where tradition did not bind us.

The next day, the King called on President Rajendra Prasad. The meeting between the two heads of state was also attended by the Haa Dungpa, Paro Dzongtshab Bajo and Gaydon Thinley. Other Bhutanese officials were led up to the waiting room carrying gifts. The meeting, being in the nature of a courtesy call, lasted only for a short time. The programme for the next day included a visit to the Lok Sabbha. We were invited to witness, from the special gallery, the opening of the Lok Sabbha by President Rajendra Prasad who arrived in the state coach.

After the session, Nehru lead the delegation away to a nearby room for a brief rest before accompanying the group to a hotel for a lunch attended by a large number of guests. President Rajendra Prasad hosted a banquet in honour of the King. Speeches were delivered by both the leaders. I sat near Dr Tobgyel, who was my role model in table manners. His Majesty hosted a return banquet in Hyderabad House. Mr Lawrence and I went round Delhi distributing the invitation cards. I was introduced by Mr Lawrence as private secretary to the King. After a week in Delhi, the delegation returned to Calcutta, from whence they left for Hasimara by a chartered plane.

Gelong Adangpa and I were left behind in Calcutta to sort out the air transportation of goods from Calcutta to Hasimara. The air consignment was for Dechencholing Palace, and there were furniture, fabrics, crookeries, lamps, toiletries and many other things. The amount of goods was enough for two full air trips, and there was barely sufficient space for us in the plane; we sat crushed between the cargo.

The day we transported the air cargo from the airport to Jaigoan, where the royal entourage was camped, was very hot. I was riding a frisky mule, and in a bag on the mule was bottle of water. I took a large swig and spat it out immediately, as I felt a most biting sensation. Some of it fell on the mule who reared up and threw me to the ground. The bottle contained sulphuric acid. The day after this dangerous experience of nearly imbibing a mouthful of acid, the royal entourage, to which Adangpa and I were added, travelled to Thimphu by ponies. The route to Thimphu passed through Jaigoan, Dala, Chumi Ringo, Tsimalathang, Chapcha and Khasadrapchu, taking the entourage six days.

His Majesty wanted to separate his own accounts from that of the government and proposed this to the National Assembly in 1959. The King was scrupulous not to mix the revenue accruing to the government with his own. His accounts were maintained separately by Dranglab Kunzang, who had to oversee the produce from four large herds of cattle, rice estates of Botokha, Khawajara, Shelngana and Chebakha. Chogyal, who was a tutor to the King in Wangdecholing, had become Paro Tapon. After his stint as Paro Tapon, he was promoted to Tsipon with a red scarf and asked to separate the government revenue and expenditure from that of His Majesty's.

Both His Majesty and Tsipon Chogyal toiled for several weeks in a room using pebbles as their abacus. After many days of trying to balance the accounts, the aggregate sums computed by His Majesty and the Tsipon showed substantial discrepancy. They went through the sums again and again, but could not reconcile their estimates. I was with them to keep a record of their computation, which I did, at first, rather mechanically. But as they tried to verify the sums repeatedly, I paid great attention to their methods of calculation and was able to observe the errors they made. I noted down the wrong steps in silence and rewrote the whole corrected accounts at night.

The next day, at an appropriate moment, I ventured to suggest that wrong steps were taken at a point in the calculation with the stone abacus. His Majesty was, at first sceptical and then aggravated by my intervention. He went through my notes very carefully and was satisfied that my version of the accounts could be accepted. In a fit of joyful appreciation, he took off his gho and flung it to me as gift. A strict bifurcation between the property and income of the King and the government was established by 1961.

In 1961, the Rigney School was opened in Dechenphu, though it was later moved to Simtokha. Gaydon Thinley was responsible for producing textbooks, while Dilkhor Khentse was to run the school and be its principal. I and others were busy writing, copying and printing textbooks. The first students included Pem Dorji of Trongsa, Sangay Dorji and Peseling Khandu of Bumthang. In all, there were forty of them.

By 1962, the motor road between Thimphu and Phuntsholing was opened, constructed by gangs of labourers requisitioned from all over Bhutan. The labourers were managed by four labour officers who presented their accounts to His Majesty. The lapons often made savings out of the allocated funds, and the King made cash presents to those who made extraordinary savings. Lapon Tandin Dorji was very good at cutting expenditure, and he was rewarded monetarily several times. Sometimes even labourers and the palace secretaries got extra payments out of the savings.

The second King had sought British aid to open a wider and shorter trunk road between Pasakha and Thimphu via Chapcha and discussed the possibility with Dronyer Jigme Dorji Wangchuck (Crown Prince), Lopon Kelzang Dawa, and Gongzim Sonam Tobgye. The request for aid was most probably rejected. The second King then decided to open a more direct and safer mule track using local labour. The mule track road which was used then was circuitous and connected every small hamlet on the way. Dungyik Tangsibi Kesang and Kabji Tandin Dorji were deputed to open a more direct route. Dungyik Kesang was recalled by the second King to Wangdecholing after two years and substituted by Chandaap Phuntshog Wangdi. This new route later overlapped the motor highway between Phuntsholing and Thimphu, which was completed in 1962. With the opening of the motor roads between Thimphu and Phuntsholing, travellers could reach Thimphu in vehicles in a day in contrast to six days on foot, and the flow of distinguished visitors from India and abroad increased steadily. Dignitaries of many races, professions and nations came to call on His Majesty. They left, deeply impressed by his vision for his beautiful, rugged country and people.

18

TUMULTUOUS MID-SIXTIES

His Majesty at 34, that is in 1964, was a remarkably handsome and athletic man. His physical exertions, through long walks along mule tracks and excursions into the remote parts of the country, horsemanship, game hunting and gardening maintained his stamina and vigour. Indeed, His Majesty was insensible to physical discomfort and preferred simplicity to luxury. This was manifested in several ways. The furnishing in his room and the collection of his wardrobe, which consisted of very few foreign goods, were rathe r minimal. In fact, at a certain period of time, the number of ghos he wore regularly was kept at two of the same pattern - Bumthang matha. He used them alternatively until one of them got damaged by cigarette burn holes and needed replacing. His Majesty smoked a great deal.

I had the privilege of travelling many times in the back of the Mahendra jeep, in which His Majesty always travelled, and of which the hood was permanently stripped. His Majesty did not like cars and other vehicles. As the motor roads were not yet tarred, travelling without a hood meant a dust bath, but His Majesty seemed not in the least bothered by it. Indeed, His Majesty was, in my opinion, not troubled or in the least perturbed by bad weather while he travelled in his hoodless Mahendra jeep.

As memories of those days take hold of me, I find myself often remembering the day I sat next to a soldier in the back of the jeep with His Majesty, travelling from Wangduephodrang to Thimphu. The soldier was a magnificent singer whose company enthralled us till the end of our journey in torrential rain. As we drove past the forest above Thinleygang, it poured heavily and streams had formed instantly at regular points on the road. But His Majesty did not even look for his rain coat. Despite being wet all over, His Majesty appeared far away and transported, by the resonant voice of the soldier, to the experiences described by the music and lyric. As I recalled earlier, His Majesty was very fond of the rich repertoire of folk songs.

Among various sports, His Majesty was most formidable at shot put. Nobody among the young courtiers, palace staff and soldiers could beat him at it. He had perfected his techniques at the game and could out-do any taller or stronger person. As usual, one evening at around 4 pm, His Majesty came out to the lawns of Dechencholing Palace to practice shot put with several persons. He picked up the shot put, stepped back several paces and threw it with a forward movement of his body. The shot put landed as usual much further than anybody's throw. However, we noticed that His Majesty did not track the flight of the throw, but instead looked awkwardly backwards. In the next instant, he clutched his chest, doubled up with pain and had to be carried inside. Fortunately, Her Majesty the Queen and the Lyonchen were in Dechencholing at that time and doctors were flown in by a helicopter.

While His Majesty lay convalescing, he delegated his authority to the Lyonchen. He moved on a wheel chair and had to be helped to climb the staircase. I was deeply anguished to see His Majesty, for the first time, in such a circumstance and held several rounds of daylong prayers and rituals so that he could get well soon. Other people also, at their own expense, did similar things for his recovery. A Royal Command to the effect that the Lyonchen could issue ordinance was proclaimed and signed by the King, and accordingly the Lyonchen signed and issued directives for some four months. Dronchung Sangye Penjor took the place of Lyonchen when the latter left for tours. Senior secretaries and I were accountable to the Lyonchen, who immediately refurbished our office. The mattresses and low tables of Bhutanese design were replaced by chairs and tables. However, we were somewhat vexed when the Lyonchen transferred Gaydon Thinley to Wangduephodrang.

His Majesty soon left for Switzerland for medical care. During the absence of the King from Thimphu, the Lyonchen of Bhutan was assassinated. A gun shot fired through the window had caused fatal injury. A message about it was immediately sent to Switzerland. The days immediately after his assassination were absolutely confusing for us. Two days later, the King, although not fully recovered, returned from Switzerland, performing the last leg of the journey from Indian border town to Dechencholing by helicopter. Gaydon Thinley was recalled by Dronchung Sangye Penjor from Wangduephodrang.

His Majesty set up an Investigation Committee comprising of Gaydon Thinley, Dronchung Sangye Penjor, Thimphu Dzongda Japhak Dorji, Trongsa Dzongda Dawa Tshering and Commissioner Rinchen. Secretarial support to the committee consisted of three clerks including myself. The investigation was held in

Tashichodzong and every suspect and witness was brought in to throw light on the nebulous and baffling affair. Tsagay Jambay, the assassin was captured. Tandin Dorji, a kadrep of the King, was sent to escort Brigadier Namgay and Brigadier Bachu, the masterminds behind the conspiracy. The former was the chief of army and the latter a quarter master who lived in the police camp in Thimphu. Both of them were brought to Dechencholing, handcuffed and locked in huts behind the Palace of Dechencholing for about ten days. Brigadier Bachu was found with his dagger stuck into his vitals; he had disembowelled himself but could not die for a few days. The anarchic state that prevailed in Thimphu became calmer after the arrest of Brigadier Namgay.

As the days wore on, an increasing number of accused people and witnesses were called by the investigation committee. Three clerks to the investigation committee, which included me, drafted the minutes of the proceedings. There were others who visited the detained people to record inquiries. After some weeks, I could not attend the trial, because I had to go back to HM's Secretariat to resume my responsibility as a private secretary to the King, who had by then got well.

The trial of Brigadier Namgay and the principal culprits came to an end after several weeks. The task of summing up the charges against the culprits fell on Gaydon Thinley, and it took about two days to read the charges, before the verdict to execute him. The sentences of deaths were passed publicly in the central hall of Tashichodzong. Hundreds of people witnessed the trial from the galleries of the hall. Brigadier Namgay was extremely laconic and did not defend his actions or speak for himself. He accepted the retribution quite readily. The trial for others, conducted again by Gaydon Thinley, took another three months or so.

Brigadier Namgay and Gaydon Thinley were classmates in the school in Thinley Rabten in Bumthang in the thirties. Moreover, they were cousins. When Brigadier Namgay was a younger officer, they were on intimate terms. A few days before the death of Brigadier Namgay, Gaydon Thinley, as a friend and a relative, visited him in the prison. I accompanied Gaydon Thinley during his prison visits when he carried the best food and drinks for Brigadier Namgay. The content of the discussion, the tone and manner Gaydon adopted in the prison was naturally different from the ones during the inquest. Here in the prison, Gaydon Thinley and Brigadier Namgay spoke of the strange twist in their lives and how their early lives that began with countless possibilities of divergence and alternatives had brought them face to face as the judge and the condemned prisoner. While I sat listening to them, Gaydon Thinley finally came round to the main purpose of his visit which was to offer his deepest sympathy to Brigadier Namgay. However, Brigadier Namgay manifested admirable confidence and calm. I felt that he was not at all distracted by any fear of death during his few last days.

His Majesty lived in Paro Kyichu for most of the year 1965. His health once again began to trouble him and he had to leave for Switzerland. Gaydon Thinley was commanded to shoulder the burden of administration, from his base within Dechencholing Palace.

Two days after the departure of His Majesty, Colonel Penjor, a high official of the army, came to fetch me from Dechencholing, acting on the instruction of the interim Lyonchen Dasho Lhendup Dorji, then living in Paro Gangteng. When I reported there, I found the entire coterie of the Lyonchen and a large numbers of soldiers in Paro Gangteng. I was kept in isolation in a guest house in Paro Gangteng for a few days. Then, I was allowed to stay in the nearby village, provided I reported to Colonel Penjor every morning. I spent about eleven days in Paro. Colonel Penjor invited me fishing with him one day out in Drukgyel dzong, although I had never gone fishing. He was actually fishing for information. Colonel Penjor quizzed me on whether Brigadier Namgay had acted independently or had been instigated to carry out the assassination. That is, was there another mastermind behind Brigadier Namgay? I was quite taken back by the magnitude and gravity of his question, for which I did not have any answer. The next morning when I went as usual to Gangteng, I found the whole place deserted, except for a sentry, who told me that the interim Lyonchen, his friends and many top military officers had left for Calcutta the previous night. I returned to see Gaydon Thinley in Thimphu that afternoon. Throughout the period of crisis, Gaydon Thinley was becoming increasingly ill and bedridden. His throat was affected and his voice failed him; he could barely whisper. But he had to give direction from his bed.

Gaydon sent me to Paro to invite Paro Penlop Prince Namgyal Wangchuk for a meeting. I traced the Prince to the shores of Pachu, where he was blissfully fishing, near Yutsena village.

Meeting Prince Namgyal Wangchuk was always an instructive and uplifting experience. He had an added depth, like his brother, the King, who could not be fathomed easily. The Prince seemed most regal in his bearing and was equally respected in both towns and villages.

While the Prince cast the line with spoon bait again and again, I gave an account of events, as briefed by Gaydon. I was coming to the end of the briefing when a sizeable and magnificent trout could be seen struggling at the end of the line. He gently unhinged the wriggling trout from the hook as I proceeded to give the names of the military and civilian officials who fled Bhutan.

Prince Namgyal Wangchuk came immediately to Dechencholing. I conducted the Prince to a chair in Gaydon's bedroom when he reached Dechencholing. Once again, Gaydon asked me to recount the events, after which I withdrew from the meeting. Perhaps the Prince called Switzerland to inform the King about the flight of high officials. His Majesty arrived in Kyichu three days later by helicopter. He decided to live there for the time being. His health had greatly improved. In contrast, Gaydon Thinley's health was deteriorating rapidly. His Majesty was kind enough to command that the prayers and rituals for Gaydon's recovery should be held at the expense of the government.

Before the confusion created by the flight of many high military and civilian officials was fully resolved, it was alleged that a team of soldiers had gone to capture Yangki, the mistress of the King who lived in Bumthang, at the behest of interim Lyonchen Dasho Lhendup Dorji, who had by then found asylum in Kathmandu. To elude them, she had got as far as Gaylegphug before she was rescued. Yet again, an investigation team was set up to try the soldiers who had agreed to capture her.

In the turmoil and disarray in the army following the flight of many high military officials, Prince Namgyal Wangchuk was appointed commander-in-chief of the army. He was transferred from Paro and took his residence in Lungtenphu in Thimphu. I was on my way back from Lungtenphu after offering my felicitations to the Prince. I was driving an Indian Jeep and had a friend and his servants with me. I was steering the jeep out of a long line of vehicles parked on the edge of the untarred parking area. The parking area resembled a terrace on the slope. The ground was very dry and the traction was probably low. I watched the wheels turn while the vehicle reversed. There seemed to be some space left; I eased the pressure on the brake pedal. But I had overestimated the space left at the verge, bounded by steep slope. I saw the rear wheels go out of sight when I stamped on the brake. The vehicle tumbled down the hill, rolling twice on the way before it came to rest on the lower terrace. I was found in a coma with head and leg injuries and was hospitalized for nearly a month. My friend suffered a severe cut on his leg. But the servants had jumped out of the vehicle as it rolled down the hill.

A great deal had happened while I was in the hospital. But the most dismal thing to find when I came out of the hospital was that Gaydon's health was shattered almost completely. I was glad to be discharged from the hospital, particularly because of the opportunity I had to be by his side during his last days. Towards the end of his life, I was often with him, sometimes at the behest of His Majesty. His Majesty himself was at his side of Gaydon Thinley about three times. Though His Majesty knew that Gaydon Thinley's condition was irreversible, I recall His Majesty saying during one of his visits:

"I have always borne in my mind the good work you have been doing. You have been doing your work to the best of your ability and motives, from the time we were together in Wangdecholing. I will send you wherever there is treatment for you. You will get the best of medical attention, and you will surely get well. You should never doubt that you will not get well, as you eventually will. You must put your mind at rest about it. But you must ask me today for anything you want to be done to help you get over any domestic and personal problem you have. I wish to tell you that I am not doing this because you are not going to live. You will live. But I do not want you to be worried about anything during your illness."

It was in response to this generous offer that Gaydon Thinley asked for substantial agricultural land in Punakha, Wangduephodrang and Mendigang. These properties, which were part of government land, were granted free of cost.

After the passing away of Gaydon Thinley, we organized a state funeral for him. T. Jagar, who was hitherto Leykhung of Trashigang, was appointed Gaydon.

The following year, that is 1965, the Royal Advisory Council was instituted by the King, partly in response to the political crisis of the immediate past. The Royal Councillors consisted of Umteng Tshering as its Chairman, Geshey Tshewang as the representative of the monk body, Wang Ngidup as the representative of Western Bhutan, Chitala as the representative of the Eastern Bhutan, and Durga Das as the representative of Southern Bhutan. The honours for these high officials were conferred in Paro Kyichu, where His Majesty lived.

The day after the members of Royal Advisory Council were appointed, there was a bomb blast in Kyichu, intended for His Majesty. The King had his bed in the central shrine and his toilet was in a tent pitched outside. As he went out and walked towards the tent, it went up in explosion though he came to no harm. The blasted spot and the tattered tents were left untouched till the police dogs arrived from India. The next morning, His Majesty moved his residence into Paro dzong. Yet again there was an investigation committee consisting of Wangduephodrang Thrimpon Ngidup Namgay, the new Gaydon T. Jagar and members of the Royal Advisory Council. The police dogs tracked Shatu, who was incriminated and sentenced to life imprisonment. Shatu was released from the prison, as an act of general amnesty granted in 1972.

19

TWO SUBLIME VISITORS

Prime Minister Indira Gandhi visited Bhutan for two days in May, 1968. His Majesty vacated his rooms in Tashichodzong for Mrs Gandhi. He moved out to the cottage by the river, which later came to be called the Royal Cottage. This unassuming cottage by the river became his residence for the rest of his life. Every day a bevy of soldiers, almost forty to fifty, worked around the cottage planting trees and mowing the lawn. It was during this visit that Mrs Gandhi presented to the King a Cheetak helicopter. In her speech after His Majesty's, Mrs Gandhi remembered her earlier visit, in 1958, by mule track.

"As you reminded me, ten years ago I came with my father to this beautiful country. We passed through Chumbi Valley and through Haa. It took us many days. It was a long journey, and a difficult journey, during which we rode on mules and got acquainted with yaks. But it was an interesting journey, and for myself I can say that I enjoyed every moment of it. We were here for a few days only, but we were impressed by the warm welcome which you gave us, Your Majesty, and the friendship and the affection which your people showed us. This time I have come by helicopter taking less than an hour from Hasimara to Thimphu, and I hear that one can now come to Paro all the way by plane. The fastness of the journey and the better communication themselves show what great changes are coming about in Bhutan. Bhutan is progressing fast and I am glad that India is able to help in this progress."

Till the visit of Mrs Gandhi, there were no ministers in the government. Soon after Mrs Gandhi left Bhutan, the National Assembly met in Paro. It was proposed, and subsequently endorsed by the National Assembly, that a Council of Ministers should be formed and posts of ministers created, with Prince Namgyal Wangchuk as Minister of Industries, Trade, Commerce, Forest and Mines, Tsipon Chogyel as Minister of Finance, Gaydon T. Jagar as Home Minister. The following year, Secretary General of Development Dawa Tsering was made Minister of Development. After the appointment of Prince Namgyal Wangchuk as Minister of Trade, Commerce, Industries, Forest and Mines, the function of commander-in- chief reverted to the King. I organized the celebration of the honours for the ministers. However, on the day of celebration, I was also granted a red scarf though I continued to be the private secretary to the King. The responsibilities of the HM's Secretariat became less onerous after the creation of ministries.

The next assignment that involved me quite a lot was the preparation for the visit of His Holiness the Karmapa, who had founded a monastery in Rumtek in Sikkim since he left Tibet via Bumthang in the wake of Chinese occupation of Tibet. As many as six jeeps and a land rover were sent to Rumtek to invite His Holiness. The land rover was later presented to His Holiness by the King. The previous incarnation of His Holiness was a guru of King Jigme Wangchuck, and the relationship had continued down the generations. His Holiness gave public discourses in various places during his visit which lasted over a month. He visited Bumthang, where the fabulous Domkhar Palace was presented to him by the Elder Queen Mother. On his return from Bumthang to Thimphu, with his troupe of around fifty monks, His Holiness staged a classical Tibetan play in Tashichodzong courtyard. When the Karmapa left Bhutan, His Majesty offered him Nu. 100,000 and hoped that His Holiness would visit Bhutan every year. Indeed, he was to fulfill this request, as His Holiness visited Bhutan the following year.

The construction of Tashichodzong, which was begun in 1961 with a labour force of about two thousand people, was coming to a conclusion. Paap Yoser Lhendup (later Dasho Yoser) was its chief architect and engineer. He was assisted by two other architects, Mr Namchu Babu and Mr. Uttari. In 1963, Ngidu Dorji and I, both working in the same office, spent about two months redrawing and relabelling the blue print of the dzong in dzongkha. The blue print was prepared by Mr Uttari and Mr Namchu Babu and was a translation of the ideas of Paap Yoser and His Majesty. At the end of the assignment, His Majesty honoured us - Mr. Uttari, Namchu, myself and Ngidu Dorji - by inviting us to a private dinner. The King's security men were asked to dance for us after the dinner. Following the dance performance by the soldiers, His Majesty asked Uttari to sing. In the course of his performance, Uttari broke down. I was unable to realize how much the invitation had meant for Mr. Uttari. Perhaps, he was overwhelmed by the sense of change: the old dzong was being demolished as we finalized and celebrated the blue print for a new one.

The progress in the reconstruction of the dzong was quite slow as there were only about two thousand labourers at any given time.

There were no mechanical aids in construction, except a few trucks ferrying stones and timber.

His Majesty began to think about religious objects to fill up the new prayer hall for the monks, which could also be used as the Great Hall of the National Assembly. His Majesty therefore wanted to equip the place with a set of objects known as repositories or receptacles on three sacred planes: the body, the mind, and the speech. In this scheme, ten thousand small copper statues of Buddha were installed as repository of the sacred body. Fifty-one volumes of Kanjur and two-hundred volumes of Tenjur (commentaries on the teachings of Buddha) were produced in gold calligraphy as repository of the sacred speech. A chorten was built as the repository of the sacred mind.

The writing, begun in 1966, of fifty two out of one hundred volumes of Kanjur, in gold calligraphy, was completed in 1967. The original collection (written in the 18th century) belonged to the central monk body. The fifty two original volumes had been destroyed in a fire. Some sixty seven calligraphers were engaged for two years to write the missing fifty two volumes, using an enormous amount of gold. Gold calligraphy work on two hundred volumes of Tenjur was completed in 1968.

I was made responsible for the production of ten thousand copper images. I invited a well-known Nepali silversmith from Kathmandu and three local apprentices were assigned to help him. In quarter of a year, the silver smith and his local associates could produce only seven eight-inch statues of Buddha. The cost of a single statue came to about Nu. 700. At that rate of production, we would require over Nu. 7 million and three and a half centuries before we got ten thousand copper images. The solution was provided by my friend, Khorchen Trulku, who established a monastery in Dehra Dun after fleeing his home in Minduling in Tibet. He produced a sample for Nu. 200, which was approved by His Majesty for its excellent quality. At the end of negotiation, a contract was drawn up between Khorchen Trulku and the Finance Minister, in terms of which Khorchen Trulku would deliver ten thousand copper statues in three years. However, Gelong Nyerchen Drep alleged that I had a covert interest in the contract and that the statues could be bought for as little as Nu. 100. Though there was no truth in the allegation, the contract was reviewed. Khorchen Trulku simply had to give in for Nu. 100 per statue because his monastery had bought the raw material in stock and had already cast several thousand copper Buddha.

Tashichodzong took two years to demolish and six years to rebuild; and the work was completed in 1969. I submitted to His Majesty that it should be an occasion for celebration and also submitted how it might be done. There were three days of celebration with a day of mask and folk dances. One novel feature of the celebration was that the seven auspicious symbols of the King (queen, minister, chief warrior, gem, wheel, elephant, horse) were displayed live. An elephant was brought all the way from Manas to Thimphu. Fortunately, since it was summer, the elephant might not have found the weather in Thimphu too inhospitable.

Like other officials that year, I joined the firing practice every Saturday at Changlengmethang. The final firing test was held in Pangrezam, witnessed by the King himself. I was one of the best shots, and was presented with a sten carbine machine gun.

251

In 1970, my wife and I, Zhung Dronyer Shayngap Dendu and his wife were nominated to visit Osaka EXPO in Japan. We travelled via Calcutta, Bangkok and Hongkong. We arrived in Tokyo at night and were booked into Hotel New Otani. The Japanese government had hired a Sakyapa Lama, Sonam Jamtsho, as our interpreter. After a night halt in Tokyo and Kyoto, we left for Osaka by train. The three days in Osaka attending EXPO were an experience of an entirely different order. I found it simply difficult to cope with the strange sights of skyscrapers, bullet trains, automated offices, glass houses, tidy people, and the orderliness of everything. It was my first and last trip outside India.

In the winter of 1970, the entourage left for Kalapani, a coal mining area in Southern Bhutan. His Majesty was rarely in Thimphu for the traditional New Year. He was either in Punakha or in Southern Bhutan.

20

COMING HOME AT LAST

His Majesty invariably attended the Dantak Day celebration, which took place every year in February in Dewathang. An advance party was sent to receive the King in an Indian village near Kalapani. The Dantak officers were well aware of His Majesty's fondness for folk dances. They had a colourful folk dance party, waiting to burst into songs as soon as they saw the entourage at Rangia. Dantak Day had three main types of entertainment: duels or fights, dances, and dramas. His Majesty hosted one of the days of celebration and personally served food and drinks to the Dantak soldiers. As a change, one of the days, the entire entourage and regiments of Dantak soldiers left for a picnic on the Brahmaputra river during the celebration. All the boats on the river were hired by Dantak to host a 'floating lunch'.

A large number of functionaries shared transport all the way from Thimphu to attend the three day celebration at Dewathang, with stopovers at Chaselakha and Phuntsholing. I shared a jeep with Miss Yangden as she did not have a vehicle of her own. I was hardly left with any choice as to my travelling companion, because His Majesty included Miss Yangden in the official delegation and asked me to take her. Miss Yangden was then the dzongda Ramjam of Thimphu and the only woman high official. We met very often as our offices were close to each other.

By the time I arrived in Dewathang, my wife Lhaki, who was in Trashigang for most of that year, had heard an exaggerated account of my affair with Miss Yangden. When I drove from Dewathang to Trashigang to see her one evening, she refused to talk to me. Lhaki was deeply hurt by my affair and was hardly able to greet me pleasantly. I pleaded for my foibles. Our argument became quite heated and it seemed that the question of parting ways was coming to the fore. As I now look back at our heated conversation that night, both of us were moving away from reconciliation and playing brinkmanship. Early in the morning I returned to Dewathang. Lhaki followed me to Dewathang in a different vehicle. There was an official dinner in Dewathang in the evening. The seating arrangement again put me next to Miss Yangden. My wife came instantly to know about it. Under the circumstance, Lhaki was rightly infuriated by what might have seemed a heedless and provocative plan on my part, though I did not wish to offend her any further. I later heard that Yangki, the mistress of the King, orchestrated the breakdown of my marriage with Lhaki.

While we were in Dewathang, Lhaki deputed two intermediaries for three consecutive nights to seek clarification on my affair and my motives. The mediators were driving the marriage towards dissolution and I decided to acquiesce and end my marriage. She was rightfully going to claim her share of our property in Thimphu, and so she made off to Thimphu ahead of me. I passed on the keys of the house in Thimphu to her; and asked her to vacate the house and take all the things.

I arrived in Thimphu much later, via Gaylegphug, with the royal entourage. While I was in my office the next day, I received (predictably) a phone call from Lhaki about the division of property. I forfeited any claim to our household property; she received all of it, except the gun that belonged to the office. The house was put out on the market and the proceeds shared equally between us. It fetched Nu. 70,000. I rebuilt a house for myself out of my share of Nu. 35,000 on a plot which I got absolutely free.

During a visit of my uncle Phuntshog Wangdi to Thimphu, he broached the idea of a suitable bride. My uncle and Lyonpo Pema Wangchuck went to see Thimphu Zimpon Rinchen Dorji (alias Jochu) to seek the hand of his eldest daughter - Tshering Doma. Her father accepted the marriage proposal. She was recalled from Calcutta where she was doing a secretarial course. I was bordering on 42 when I remarried for the last time. She brought many fresh and broadening perspectives into my life. As she spoke and wrote English very well, she made up for one of the main deficiencies. Since my house was still being rebuilt, both I and my wife went to stay with my father-in-law in Zillukha, Thimphu. My father-in-law now took an uncontrollable interest in constructing the house for me, not withstanding the fact that the contract had already been given to Bachu Phuntsho.

However, misfortune was to visit me, along with the happiness and strength I found in my wife. A year after my marriage, my father-in-law fell into a coma and died suddenly one evening. My father-in-law was a keen building contractor at the time of his death. He had about eighty construction workers on his pay roll, and had received an advance of Nu. 90,000 to build three shops in the main avenue in Thimphu town. The foundations for the shops were barely laid, but there was a cash balance of only Nu. 51,000. I had to execute the contract fully on behalf of my father-in-law, which called for an additional expenditure of Nu. 100,000, excluding the cash balance of Nu. 51,000. I sank into debt of about Nu. 100,000 to complete the construction of three shops and also a house near the Thimphu town centre. I would have found it difficult in the extreme to repay the debt if His Majesty did not give me a cash gift of Nu. 40,000 to retire the debt.

Although my father-in-law's death left me buried deep in debt, he was not without other assets. He owned over twenty nine acres of paddy field in Bem Sisi in Punakha and held grazing rights over extensive pasture land. We could utilize the pasture, but our right over the paddy field was quite tenuous. The legal documents said that we would inherit it completely only on the death of Gelong Nyerchen Drep, my wife's maternal grandfather. According to an agreement signed between my father-in-law and Gelong Nyerchen Drep, my father-in-law had agreed to pay land taxes, while the produce from the land would accrue to Gelong Nyerchen Drep until his death. My father-in-law, and by extension my wife and I, would inherit the paddy field on the death of Gelong Nyerchen Drep.

I decided to utilize the pasture land immediately. I invested about Nu. 8,000 to buy twelve jatshams-cows, each costing Nu. 5,000 to Nu. 6,000. To boost the size of the herd, another dozen yangkooms (heifers) were imported from Rangia, India. After a year's gestation, the herd began to pay back. The dairy produce was regularly sold in the Thimphu grocery market. Unknown to me, my servant Rinchen Tshering had been making blaring announcement at the grocery market that "the cheese and butter on sale belong to Dasho Shingkhar Lam, the Secretary to His Majesty!" He perhaps did not enjoy the experience and wished to expose my petty business.

However, things began to take a disagreeable turn several years after our marriage. Gelong Nyerchen Drep repudiated the agreement. In a bold and unchallengeable move, he presented the pasture and paddy field to a powerful figure. Our hope of getting the land as well as the pasture was completely dashed. I now faced the strange problem of possessing a sizeable herd of cattle without a patch of pasture. Fortunately, I was able to negotiate the sale of my herd with an unexpected buyer: the central monastic body, who wanted to augment its communal herd.

21

THE FIFTH SPEAKER

At the beginning of the reign of the third King in 1952, Tangsibi Kesang, Yeshey Wangdi and myself were secretaries of the same rank. Yeshey was highly regarded by the second King. He was an able communicator. However, the third King was not fond of Yeshey Wangdi to the same degree. The third King had a keen eye for the elegant style in which the court circulars were drafted. Yeshey Wangdi had a slightly turgid style of writing; Tangsibi Kesang was certainly not better. Moreover, the relationship between Yeshey Wangdi and Tangsibi Kesang was covertly rancorous: Tangsibi Kesang disparaged Yeshey Wangdi in front of the third King. I think that Tangsibi Kesang's repeated remarks about Yeshey Wangdi finally influenced the third King to push him out of favour, and he left us to join the Ministry of Development as a translator. He died relatively young and bitter.

Tangsibi Kesang had progressed steadily in the official hierarchy since our days together in the court of the second King, who sent him to supervise road building gangs for half a year in 1950 or so, when mule tracks between Thimphu and Pasakha were widened and shortened. As I recalled earlier, he was also sent on a bangchen mission against the Zongpon of Trashigang, Dopola. He held a series of jobs in the reign of the third King. He was the auditor of accounts of the central monk body, a judge in the High

Court, a member of Central Accounting Office and the fourth Speaker of the National Assembly. Till the end of his life (which was brought about when he fell off a house by accident), he maintained a prodigal appetite. He was one of the very few persons I met who could eat five big portions of pork on an abnormally large heap of rice.

Dasho Kesang of Tangsibi was the Fourth Speaker of the National Assembly and his tenure lasted till 1970. As he completed his term, the question about who would succeed him exercised HM's and many peoples' minds. The position of the Speaker was, as one might naturally expect, one of great dignity, authority and stature associated with distinguished persons like Dasho Kelzang Dawa and Gaydon Thinley (the first and second speaker respectively). Though Dasho Kesang of Tangsibi could be re-elected, there was a desire for change. In the session in 1970, three candidates were nominated: myself as the representative of the officials; Drabey Lopon Tsewang Pem as the representative of the monk body; and Dasho Kolay Lam as the representative of the people. My candidature was put to His Majesty for his endorsement, before the election took place. I was told much later that His Majesty expressed some reservation about my suitability as the next Speaker. He remarked that I would always make a better work-horse in the office than a Speaker. However, at the end, I was formerly nominated and came out successful in the election.

Those of us working in the National Assembly including (my assistant Sangay Dorji) began to launch some simple changes, for the session in 1971, to streamline the structure, functions and procedures of the National Assembly. We could attempt to introduce only those changes which occurred to us in an obvious sort of way. We felt that the representation in the National Assembly could be made more proportional with respect to the number of gewogs. The gewogs of nearby dzongkhags such as Thimphu and Wangduephodrang had as many as eight chimis, whereas some of the remote gewogs in eastern Bhutan were rather insufficiently represented. The number of chimis representing a certain number of gewogs was roughly balanced and made more equal. To help identify the chimis from the audience, we introduced the medallion and rosette which the members of the National Assembly stuck on their gho lapels. Agendas were also drawn up to steer the Assembly's deliberations. Every member wishing to address the Assembly at length on a certain issue gave prior notice in writing and put it on the table of the Speaker everyday. He was then called upon by the Speaker to address the house, and the members could debate his issue immediately afterwards.

The morning of October 13th, the first day of the 35th session of the National Assembly, as I recall, was very bright and sunny. The night before, during which I stayed up very late working on my opening speech to the Assembly, was quite starry and frosty. I remember giving a few final touches to my speech towards the early hours, looking now and then at the starry skies, through the foliage of the juniper that was sprouting to obstruct the view from the window. While reading the speech, and at the same time supposing myself to be among the audience, I pondered briefly over a few points which seemed jarring.

I wondered whether I should speak about the lack of prejudice, and the need for the members of the National Assembly and the government officials to be free from bias. This objectivity had been a valuable characteristic which should be protected. At that point, I remember I heard a bell ringing faintly through the valley. It was the 4 am bell calling the monks in Thimphu dzong for their prayers. I felt that the point about officials and members being free from discrimination and bias seemed worth reinforcing in the National Assembly.

I also balked, while re-reading the speech, at whether I should dwell on the Karmic relationship between good intentions and actions on the one hand, and one's well-being on the other. The number of quotations and allusions to literary sources appeared to be excessive. On second thought, neither of these appeared to be out of place. After all, a critical perspective on one's own actions and motives, which is informed by the belief in Karmic causation, is essential whether one is a public official, representative of the public or peasant. Perhaps it was even more relevant in the life of public officials, who might possibly feel that the moral requirement which applied to individuals might not apply to them in their official capacities.

I also wondered whether my abstract of the history of Bhutan from Shabdrung to His Majesty Jigme Dorji Wangchuck was not labouring an obvious point. But then, I felt, I should bring once again to the attention of the members of the National Assembly all the good and the great things that came about through the figures of Guru Rimpoche, Shabdrung Ngawang Namgyel, Desi Jigme Namgyel and his direct descendants - the Kings of Bhutan.

A new dawn would break in an hour or so, and I rested in my bed only for a while before the alarm went off. My wife got up and made me a bowl of thin rice broth and some light breakfast. I went into the shrine room to make a short prayer before I got dressed fully in my ceremonial boots and gho, the red robe, and sword in silver scabbard, helped by my wife.

At that moment, I could hear the diesel engine of my metallic blue Toyota land cruiser racing and warming up, a procedure that needed meticulous observance especially following cold wintry nights. I arrived in the dzong courtyard a little early. Almost all the members of the National Assembly were present in the courtyard to await His Majesty's ceremonial entry into the dzong and the Great Hall of the National Assembly.

It was always a magnificent sight to see the Great Hall of the National Assembly, which was a giant chapel with more than a dozen towering pillars. On this occasion, the ceremonial opening of the session, it was filled by lines upon lines of people. The rhythmic sound of prayers and ritual music and the sight of people in ceremonial robes of white, red, scarlet, blue and orange sitting below the towering, shafted and fluted pillars, and soft chandelier lights were highly moving. His Majesty entered the hall and was seated on the throne placed immediately behind the Speaker's dias. I then took my place on the Speaker's dias. All the others present in the Great Hall sat all at once, as though they have been drilled to perform the bodily movement together. I then announced that His Majesty would immediately address the Assembly. It was always a humbling experience to hear His Majesty, as he would speak without help of so much as a note. His speeches were often recorded and transcribed, as it was with the speech on that occasion. His Majesty spoke:

"A few years ago in 1967 it was decided in the National Assembly that Bhutan should try and become a member of the United Nations. As a result of this, our friend the Government of India was informed of our hopes, and they, in turn, spoke to all members of the UN about our aims. On account of the assistance given to us by the Government of India in requesting the members of other countries of the UN to vote in favour of our admission, it seemed to us that we would probably be able to join successfully. A short time ago the Minister of Trade and Industry and the Minister of Development were sent to New York to assist our permanent representative, Lyonpo Sangye Penjor and his staff, on the occasion of our admission. The necessary number of votes were obtained because of the providence of Lord Buddha and the protection of our tutelar deities, and in particular due to the fortune you, the people of Bhutan, possess. At 1 o'clock on the morning of the 3rd day of the 8th month it became possible for us to join the UN, and so our ambition was attained in front of all the countries of the world, and I hope, on that account, you will be very pleased. Our admission was possible because of the support, both in terms of funding and lobby, of the Government of India, and for this we owe them our gratitude.

"Until today, our affairs were conducted like things done in our own secluded houses, and were done without being observed by others and did seem to be free of mistakes. However, having been admitted to the UN, we have left our own isolation and will be in the midst of other countries of the UN. Both our successes and failures will henceforth be noticed by other countries of the UN. As illustrated by the saying 'It is easy to be a monk though it is difficult to provide for the monk's needs', all of you are fully aware that our internal situation leaves much to be improved. Although we have joined the UN, there is hardly any possibility that the organization can alleviate all our hardships and plights. If we do not fully cooperate among ourselves and be united in our efforts to develop the country, we will be an affront to the country and also demean our country's international image. It will be extremely difficult for the country to be made strong by the government alone. In all our endeavours we have taken so far, we have been successful because of the unity and cooperation we have managed to foster. We must redouble our struggle. As a means of being dedicated to this country, you the members must be as imaginative as possible and suggest your views to the National Assembly. You must, further, communicate closely with the people and tap their views and report the main decisions in the following session of the Assembly.

"...As we have been admitted into the UN, it is necessary to interact and develop relations with other countries with disparate policies and sizes. While we launch cooperation with them, some nations will give us aid only to benefit our country and such aid will be of great utility to this country. Other countries will provide aid to serve their own ends and such kind of assistance will be harmful and dangerous. I feel that it will be risky to accept aid from many countries at the same time. The whole question of aid should be carefully examined by all of you during this session, so as to be absolutely clear on this issue. I would urge all of you to distinguish between the type of aid which should be accepted and which should be declined. Clarity of thinking on aid will be extremely vital for the sake of the country.

"...Today, we have a resident Indian Ambassador and our own

Ambassadors have been posted both in New York and New Delhi...Some of you may wonder why we have already exchanged Ambassadors with India when I have just said that other foreign missions will not be accepted in Bhutan for the time being...It is undesirable to confine our country to the medieval period while every country in the world is witnessing rapid changes everyday. Our country too must keep up with others if it has simultaneously to move towards the two-fold goals of immediate well-being and everlasting stability. Therefore, we have initiated development programmes. In doing so, we face constraints in both manpower and resources. We have, therefore, sought substantial aid from our friend and neighbour India. Given the scale of aid from India, it was necessary to have continuous negotiations with India. But it was difficult to send officers down to Delhi every time matters of national importance came up. Similar problems arose for Indian officials to visit Bhutan. The problem could be resolved only by exchanging missions, and now it has added to the ease of communication between us, enhancing the level of assistance from India. The extent of aid India has given us is known to all of you..."

In the same speech, His Majesty spoke about the creation of a relief fund for the refugees from East Pakistan, sheltering in Bengal. Further, His Majesty explained the reasons for committing Bhutan's vote for the admission of People's Republic of China into the UN.

He informed the house, in a tone which showed that he was overwhelmed by the occasion of their departure, that about twenty senior officials, after their distinguished services for over twenty years, were retiring of their own will. Nevertheless, a bright side of their resignation, His Majesty said, was that they would enrich the communities to which they would return during their retirement years. His words of farewell and appreciation were, as always, deeply stirring, for His Majesty had the surprising ability to empathise with people in moments of overwhelming emotions.

After the address by His Majesty, it was my turn to give the opening speech to the 35th session of the National Assembly. I adjusted the microphone which was placed, perhaps, too far away from the Speaker's dias on which I was sitting cross legged.

"Today is an auspicious day, with promising cosmic signs, to begin the 35th session of the National Assembly. We have opened the session with the most felicitous ceremonies. To quote Choje Drowai Gonpo:

For worthy events, let there be auspicious ceremonies,
And may we consecrate them with all favourable celebrations.

"There is hardly anything that you, the knowledgeable members of the National Assembly, do not know or have not heard about the National Assembly. However, some of the members were recently elected and I would like to acquaint them with the little that I consider should be said for their benefit, while refreshing the memory of the older members. As the line from Shaytring reminds us:

The marble on which the moonlight falls
Should it not sparkle with greater brightness?

"To begin with, our country - Druk Yul - is a sacred land blessed by Guru Rimpoche with a wealth of dharma and relics of treasures. In those days, the place was referred to as Lho Mon. But it was destined by Guru Rimpoche as a territory to be brought under the civilizing influence of Pelden Drukpa Rimpoche. Thus, laws were instituted in a lawless place and valleys were settled which were hitherto not inhabited. A religious state was founded under the order of Pelden Drukpa some 317 years ago, that is in 1652. Since then, successive chief abbots have come to the spiritual throne and about fifty six Desi have occupied the secular throne. During such period, the country was far from peaceful, and embroiled in internal strife brought about by discrimination and bias.

"Nevertheless, Desi Jigme Namgyel came to the secular throne, induced by the wishes and prayers of the higher beings, and banished the very word "internal strife" from our state of affairs. He further reunited the country and brought the luminous experience of peace to all the people.

"Moreover, his son His Majesty Ugyen Wangchuck was enthroned as the first King of Bhutan on the basis of collective choice and voice of the officials, people and monks. His Majesty ruled the country in a most benign manner for nineteen years, in accordance with the ten virtues of God's religion and the 16 virtues of man's religion which were once promoted by God King Tsongtsen Gampo.

"The next King, His Majesty Jigme Wangchuck, ruled the country for twenty years. His reign is well known for his patronage of Buddhism and the increase in the welfare of the people. He brought greater development to the nation by instituting schools and hospitals, and strengthened the security of the country by establishing defence forces. Although a number of development activities were initiated by His Majesty, there was a delay in the introduction of modern education. Hence, it seems that our country lagged far behind other nations. However, as a Buddhist country, the country has been fortunate to have the third King His Majesty Jigme Dorji Wangchuck, who has been on the throne for the last twenty years. Because he has greater love and affectation for his people than his own children, he has worked ceaselessly for the well-being of the people and security of the country. In doing do, he has promoted Buddhism and protected our rich tradition and heritage.

"Until he introduced reforms, people had to pay heavy taxes, in terms of both labour and material resources, in innumerable and immeasurable ways, to the gups, dungpas and authorities in the dzongkhags. None of these taxes have to be borne now; there is only a low cash tax. As a result, people today work only for their own livelihood. These developments are analogous to the standards and norms of other developed countries, and renders our country on a par with others. Like the emergence of paradise on earth, our country is now presentable to the world.

"There is a tremendous sense of gratitude among the people to the King for these benevolent acts, and the bond of faith and confidence between the King and the people will be forever intact. I honestly doubt whether the bond of faith and confidence between the King and the people which exists in Bhutan can be found anywhere else in the world. Because of this close bond of faith, confidence and loyalty between the King and the people, all our endeavours will be fulfilled, and we can step forward and join the ranks of other countries.

"In the bygone era of our ancestors, we did not gather together as we do today, to hold discussions among ourselves in the National Assembly. There is a proliferation of development programmes with every passing year, about which public discussion should take place. Even though the breadth of knowledge possessed by His Majesty is truly vast, he believes in the collective wisdom of the people rather than his own ideas and decisions. His approach is summed up in Legshay:

> Every small enterprise of the wise
> Is always realized through dialogue;
> Unwavering in it, it will be accomplished,
> But even failure will be admired.

"His Majesty believes strongly in consultation between the King, officials and the people to make decisions which will bring both long and short-term benefits to the country. With such hope in consultative decision making, His Majesty established the National Assembly in 1953, that is 18 years ago. With the establishment of the National Assembly, you are aware that the mode of working and decision-making have improved a great deal. To a great extent, the security of the nation and the welfare of the people have also been enhanced.

"We have hardly heard of the United Nations, and yet today, a small country such as ours was able to join the big and powerful nations of the world in that organization. It is an achievement which we celebrate, and lifts all our hearts. Our achievement owes much to the Gods which our parents have revered and in which we continue to have faith and belief. Nor have we forsaken the tutelar deities of our ancestors.

We continue to recognize the truth of the karmic relationship between present conditions and previous acts. We wish to preserve cooperation and unity that is made possible by the bond of faith and confidence between the King, ministers and the people. This unity and cooperation has contributed to all our successes, such as admission into the UN. Our progress is also due to the unstinting assistance, in terms of both manpower and resources, given by our neighbour India, to whom we are highly grateful.

"Unity and cooperation, not only in words but also in deeds, is absolutely vital. I would venture to say that the greatest threat to unity and cooperation is bias and discrimination. Discrimination among the people of a same country can arise if there is bias between east and west, and between centre and periphery. There can be organizational bias if we discriminate between the civil services and the armed force services, and between the mighty and the humble. We have never stooped to discrimination so far, and we must further refrain from even envisaging such practices. To this day, discrimination has not been our way, and we are sure it never will be.

"I would hazard to say that the different sects might become a basis of bias and discrimination. There are so many ways of practising the Buddhist teachings. Individuals can choose among different schools of Buddhism according to their aptitude and temperament. The different schools arose to meet different requirements of the individuals, but all of them are creations of Buddha. Nevertheless, because of a lack of common understanding on fundamental points in these different schools, a sect will be commended by some while denounced by others; practised by some while suppressed by others; and such attitudes will only create a rift in the common understanding and unity among the people. So, it is best to affirm the way of Buddhism that has been already spread among us in the time of our parents. To cite from Lugilabja:

> To all beings, the mercy of enlightened beings is impartial,
> Although the immaculate teachings of Buddha have no sect
> To pursue the sect which has flourished
> In the time of our ancestors is most prudent.

"Thus, instead of embracing additional sects, we should sustain the combination of old and new schools of Buddhism that have always prevailed in this country. In addition, we should affirm our belief in the powerful tutelar deities of these sects and teachings. The advent of other sects would impair the unity and cooperation that exist in the country. There is no doubt that the peace we enjoy in our country is the result of being a blessed Buddhist nation.

"As Buddhists, not only the clerics, but even the laymen, must be governed by the clear or correct view which is central to Buddhism. The clear and correct view is essentially comprised of faith in the three refuges, faith and confidence in higher beings and recognition of the truth of karmic experience and relationship. We are bound by a karmic chain. If one performs good deeds, one will be rewarded in similar terms, and if one does bad deeds, they will inevitably rebound on oneself, as Kuenkhen Longchenpa wrote:

The garuda which soars so high above the earth
Its shadow, for once, can not be perceived
But its body crumbles into four elements,
As it ripens (with karmic force) and the moment of (death) comes;
The shadow is particularly visible.

"It is an article of faith among us that we will experience good for good and bad for bad. There is hardly a member among us who do not believe in this moral law, and it is my deepest hope that nobody will discard this moral law. For if people are convinced of doing only what is good for oneself without concern for others, one will neither be able to serve this country nor fulfil the tasks that we have planned to carry out. Moreover, one's own present and future lives will be adversely and visibly affected. Scientific development has enabled many modernised countries to launch flights through the sky and penetrate deeply into the earth. Not withstanding these achievements, because they do not have unity and cooperation and do not believe in the karmic force, they face strife and war, epidemics and natural disasters and they are denied the peace and prosperity that we enjoy...

"Among the members gathered here today, some represent the monk body, some represent the officials of the government, and the others represent the public. Though we are drawn from various quarters, we are all citizens of the same nation. Those of you who come here as representatives of the public from different parts of the country have been hand-picked from the crowd and selected from the few, so that you are the best choice. I have boundless hope that you will be able to perceive the hardships of village life and render service to the government. You may be regarded as the keys that will unlock the door between the government and the people. You are aware of the tasks as well as the problems faced by the government, and these must be conveyed fully to the people. The government can not always perceive the problems the people have. It is your duty to reflect on the means to overcome the constraints and inform the government. That is why we recognize that it is important for us to exchange ideas in the National Assembly. Both the government and the people have enormous hope in you, as an instrument of progress. You are here at the unstinting expense of the government.

"Once you are in the Great Hall of the Assembly, irrespective of your status and power, all of you are equal as members of the National Assembly. In the context of national interest, you may speak in a forthright manner, without any hesitation. But you are all aware that we must neither express matters of personal interest nor say things based on status and wealth of someone. If our discussions are influenced by personal interest or our course of discussion take regard of inappropriate factors like wealth and status of the some people, we will be doing a disservice to the country. There is nothing of greater disservice, may I remind you, to the country than such acts. Moreover, while participating in a discussion, nobody should say something merely to echo others' arguments. To quote again from Legshay:

> The wise man can appraise for himself
> The fool imitates the others.

"One must assess the issue oneself and state frankly whether the proposition is acceptable or not. I would submit to the members not to waste time and the expenses of the public and government to come here to merely repeat points made by others.

"Another thing I wish to say is that should a question concerning the monk body arise, you should not react apathetically to it as though it does not at all concern you. If that is your attitude, we would rather not have a discussion in the National Assembly. The National Assembly is convened to seek the view of each person. You must resist the tendency to think that a view expressed by a member, who has been chosen by his people, is equally acceptable to yourself.

"If every person contributes an idea to an issue, we can successfully pursue whatever we set out to do. It is only a matter of taking your responsibility conscientiously; you can certainly contribute to the deliberations. Even an ordinary person will articulate his or her needs when it concerns him or herself. As each of you have been selected from among the masses, I have no doubt that everyone of you is highly capable of contributing to the discussion. It will be obligatory for each of us, who love our country, to even contemplate between moments of our sleep, in what way we can serve the country. Each of us must be motivated so highly to serve the country so that each of us will become a jewel of the nation.

"As regards myself, I possess neither the inborn intelligence nor knowledge acquired through education. It is only your confidence in my capacities which have led the Assembly to elect me as the Speaker. I am very grateful for this high honour. Although I lack scholarship and learning, which is a cause for my regret and ignorance, for more than half my life I have been happy and fortunate. It is due to the mercy of the Gods, the kindness of the country and the King that I owe my good life. I pledge all that I am capable of offering to the best of my abilities, including my life, to the service of the country and the King. Those of you present here today have displayed greater commitment to the service to the country than myself, and when I commit any error and omission, I hope that you will remind me about it so that it can be amended."

The conclusion of the National Assembly was celebrated for two days in Changlengmethang. His Majesty was inclined to have frequent festivities and merriment that year.

My inaugural address to the National Assembly was, I believe, well received. It renewed His Majesty's confidence in me in my new position, and the day after my inaugural speech was presented, I was appointed as a deputy minister. There was no ceremony for promotion; I was just asked to use the scarlet robe on the following day. I thus joined the privileged ranks of three other deputy ministers at that time: Pema Wangchuck, Kalyon Japhak Dorji and Zhung Dronyer Shayngap Dendu. In addition, there were five ministers: Lyonpo Dawa Tsering, Minister of Development; Lyonpo Chogyal, Minister of Finance; Tengye Lyonpo Prince Namgyal Wangchuk, Minister of Trade and Industries; Lyonpo T. Jagar, Minister of Home Affairs; and Lyonpo Sangye Penjor, Minister of Communications. I became a member of the Cabinet (Lhengyel Shungtshog). Soon, I was also appointed the secretary of the Cabinet, which met every Friday.

The National Assembly delegated to the Secretariat of the

National Assembly the task of drafting several rules to be submitted to the Assembly. The National Assembly in conjunction with the Royal Advisory Council (Lodey Tshogdey) framed a string of laws. Rules for the Speaker of the National Assembly, Motor Vehicle Act, Citizenship Act, Tourism and Customs Regulations, Entitlements Rules for Ministers, Deputy Ministers and Royal Family Members, were framed and passed by the National Assembly. In a short span of two years, from 1970 to 1972, more than ten sets of rules were passed.

During the session in November, 1968, His Majesty the King announced to the National Assembly that his term of office should be subjected to a vote of confidence by the National Assembly every three years. Document on this proposal was circulated to all the members so that they could discuss the issue in all the villages. It did not of course mean an end to the monarchy. As His Majesty told the members of the National Assembly, "I have a feeling that my last speech to the National Assembly was not clear to all of you. I did not say that the system of hereditary monarchy should be abolished. My intention was to empower the National Assembly to change by peaceful means any King, including myself, who is found unfit to rule the country." The vote of no-confidence was to become an instrument to enable the National Assembly to allow the reigning monarch to abdicate in favour of another member of the royal family, by a predefined order of succession to the throne. It was proposed as a mechanism for the Assembly to find an acceptable line of succession among the members of royal family.

For most of the members and the villagers, this proposition was too extreme to be agreeable. The need for a vote of no confidence for the monarch was rejected outright by three successive sessions of the National Assembly. Eventually, His Majesty compelled the National Assembly to cast a vote of confidence and adopt its outcome as a resolution. A second vote of confidence on His Majesty's rule was taken in the 23rd (spring) session of the National Assembly. On the day the vote of confidence was tabled, surprisingly, four votes against the King were found. I believe that the four votes against him were arranged by His Majesty with some of the members. As I went to His Majesty's office one afternoon, I could hear he was saying something in a rather soft voice. I stood by the door considering whether I should take a peek and clear my throat to reveal my presence behind the door-curtain. But His Majesty continued with his discussion and I could clearly hear what was being said. He said that the introduction of vote of confidence was perceived, by many people such as the Chogyal of Sikkim, to be a miscalculation. It was indeed an error of judgement, His Majesty said, on the part of his close friend, the Chogyal of Sikkim.

22

THE THUNDERBOLT FROM KENYA

In the winter of 1971, His Majesty left for Kenya on vacation. The trip was coupled with his treatment. On his return, the National Assembly was convened in April 1972. The session was dominated by the question as to whether the Crown Prince should be installed as Trongsa Penlop or Paro Penlop. There was a clear preference among the members of the National Assembly for the former. He planned to hold the coronation of Crown Prince Jigme Singye Wangchuck as the fourth King two years later. After the coronation, His Majesty planned to withdraw into the background and be concerned only with religious and cultural affairs. Her Majesty the Queen and the King often held long discussions either in Dechencholing Palace or the Royal Cottage about the investiture of the Trongsa Penlop.

His Majesty was again ailing, and it was clear that he would not be able to attend Dantak Day celebration in Dewathang. A new venue for the Dantak Day celebration was chosen; it was Changlengmethang. Dantak Day and the celebration of the installation of the Trongsa Penlop in Thimphu was combined into a week-long show. The organizers, including myself, faced immense difficulty in producing a sufficiently long programme to fill seven days.

Some days before leaving for Trongsa for the investiture ceremony, I had the privilege of being visited in my office by His Majesty and the Crown Prince. It was on this occasion that His Majesty reminded the Crown Prince that it would be very difficult to check the erosion of Driglam Namsha. At that time, His Majesty said that I was the reference point for such esoteric matters and commanded me to write a tract on Driglam Namsha. He said, however, that the gap in my knowledge would be the ceremonial procedures for the sacred part of the coronation, as he himself was the only one who had received guidance on it directly from the second King. I was highly honoured by his command, for I felt it was a measure of his regard for me.

The celebration in Changlengmethang was followed by preparation for the investiture ceremony in Trongsa. His Majesty the King, the Minister of Finance, and several officials including myself left for Trongsa. But His Majesty was in some pain throughout the stay in Trongsa. He lived in the same room in which he was born in Thripang in Trongsa. On the day the Crown Prince set out from Thimphu, he stopped for a night at Rukubji. I was sent from Trongsa to Rukubji to report on the details of the investiture ceremony which would take place the next day. I recall very clearly that as soon as the Crown Prince saw me, he inquired after his father's health. I returned to Trongsa on the same day to complete the preparation for the arrival of the Crown Prince in Trongsa at 10 am the next day. When the Crown Prince reached the premise of the dzong, he came out of a car and rode into the dzong on a white steed. Reminiscent of the custom during the arrival of second King from Bumthang, the notables of Bumthang and Trongsa called on the Crown Prince with offerings and gifts, which were reciprocated in equal measure.

His Majesty got up early on the day of the investiture ceremony. But he came back to Thripang to rest before the entire ceremony was over. The next day, several members of the royal family went to Jambay Lhakhang and Kurje in Bumthang to offer prayers, and they returned two days later. His Majesty could not accompany Bumthang because his condition was going from bad to worse.

The monsoon came early that year, threatening to wash away the road to Thimphu. Nevertheless, the entourage decided to return to Thimphu by road, instead of flying by helicopter. A day for departure was chosen, but at the last minute, His Majesty changed his mind and refused to leave. This scenario was repeated three times. Luggage was loaded in trucks and jeeps to be unloaded again in the afternoon. There were soldiers, officers, dancers and many others waiting to leave Trongsa. Eventually, they were given permission by the Trongsa Penlop to leave. His Majesty wanted to stay back until he got well and then go by road. Or else, he wished his life to come to an end at his beloved Thripang, where he was born 44 years ago. He was haunted by the Bhutanese notion that "one should die where one was born".

His Majesty relied more and more on pain killers, though it was not administered in sufficient doses. He wanted to have more than what his physicians - Dr Yonten and Dr Tobgyel - gave him. On the day of departure, he asked me to write a note absolving the doctors of their responsibility for giving him extra pain killers and to say that he was taking the pain killers on his own free will. He was not in a condition to sign the note when I took it to him. On the way back, the entourage spent the night in Rukubji. On the way to Rukubji, a land mass slipped just as the convoy reached Chagzam and was held up in the rain for an hour. That night, I went to submit the note for his signature. His Majesty was half-asleep. I thrust the note in front of him and he signed it with great effort. The signature was quite distorted. His condition became very critical that night. The next day, there was a road block at Nobding which held up the progress of the journey by another hour.

His Majesty did not agree easily to go abroad for treatment. All the members of the Royal Family, particularly Her Majesty the Queen Mother, Her Majesty the Queen, the Crown Prince and the princesses, pleaded with him to go, and after three nights in Thimphu, His Majesty left for Nairobi in Kenya. He was to rest there for a while before continuing his trip to Switzerland. Among many others, the entourage included the Queen Mother and the Trongsa Penlop.

Some nights after His Majesty left Phuntsholing, we received the news about his passing away. The Cabinet, chaired by the eldest princess HRH Sonam Choden, met to discuss the funeral. Prince Namgyal Wangchuk, the Tengyel Lyonpo, made decisions. I was given the charge of designing the casket and organizing some parts of the rituals which lasted for 49 days, the maximum necessary for the consciousness to move to an intermediate state. The casket in which His Majesty lay in state was placed in the Royal Cottage and encircled by offerings on all sides. Dasho Kolay Lam looked after the participants in the rituals. There was an army of monks and lamas, including His Holiness Dilkhor Khentse, in the tents which were pitched on the lawn of Royal Cottage. Throughout the 49 days of ceremony, dignitaries from many parts of the world came to pay their homage to the late King.

The Trongsa Penlop moved immediately into the upper floor of the Royal Cottage while His Majesty lay-in-state downstairs. The Cabinet appealed to the Trongsa Penlop to accept the reins of government immediately. The Trongsa Penlop was invited to a session of the Cabinet, and with a brief ceremony installed as the Head of the government. A full fledged coronation was to be held two years later.

While His Majesty lay-in-state in Thimphu from 23rd July to 19th October, the 37th session of the National Assembly was convened on 10th September. I addressed the National Assembly:

"The autumn session of the National Assembly in this, the Year of the Water Rat, is convened earlier than usual on account of an emergency. Although I feel hesitant to bring the news to the National Assembly, as you are all aware, there is no choice but to do it. The news about the calamity that I have to share with all of you is neither about the rise of an external enemy nor about the tragedy of an internal insurrection. Yet the gravity of the event that has taken place exceeds both of these mishaps. His Majesty, who was more indispensable to us than our own eyes and who was the jewel of our country, has been unexpectedly spirited away to the heavens. His demise, which took place despite his medical treatment and the rituals sponsored for his recovery, has left us in greater grief than that we would experience if our own hearts were to leave our breasts. The progenitor of our welfare and the noble trustee of our loyalty has left us behind, creating darkness at noon, and afflicting us with grief and remorse. Out of remembrance for His Late Majesty and with a deep anguish, I would like to recount briefly the achievements of His Late Majesty. His achievements are too numerous to be related and there is scarcely time to speak at length about them. Nevertheless, I would like to describe the most important achievements of His Late Majesty whose fond memory we cherish. As it has been said:

His knowledge was equal to that of all enlightened beings,
Our saviour, his benevolence surpassed that of all enlightened beings.

"His Late Majesty, who was, as far as this country is concerned, more merciful than a thousand enlightened beings and more kindly than one's parents, acceded to the throne in 1952. From the time he acceded to the throne, he constantly devoted himself to the advancement of the country and its people, without caring for his own health and life, and he persistently found ways and means to build this nation as much as any other nation in the world and make it more secure and stable than any other in the world. Since he acceded to the throne, he was so preoccupied with the affairs of the state that he was not idle for a single moment.

"His Late Majesty was a man of immense knowledge and intelligence. He believed in drawing on the prudence of the populace to run the country. Therefore, he established the National Assembly in 1953. Since this new mode of meeting among ourselves was introduced, it has met for thirty six successive sessions in which His Late Majesty graciously participated.

"If the governance of the country is not based on the rule of law, there will hardly be a distinction between right and wrong corresponding to acceptable and unacceptable actions respectively, and such a deficiency in law will be detrimental to the development of the country. We have important legal tracts composed by the authorities of antiquity, but their bearing is less clear on the acceptable and unacceptable activities in the contemporary society. His Majesty, therefore, took the burden of drafting a new Thrimshung with as many as seventeen sections, all by himself. The Thrimshung was examined and reviewed by this National Assembly for three successive years and was ratified in 1959. Hence, a sound legislature on which to base the integrity of the country was introduced, and the mighty and the humble were both made equal before law.

"The chief sources of hardship for people in the olden days were the heavy burdens of taxes in terms of both labour and material resources. The burden was inequitable: severe for some and trifling for others. Taxes were made equitable and uniform, and lowered to one quarter of what people used to pay. For convenience, by 1968, in-kind taxes were fully commuted to cash taxes, which were uniform and equitable. Conscripted labour tax was completely abolished. Moreover, as all of you will remember, in the last session of the National Assembly, His Majesty declared that taxes on (rural) people may be reduced, but never increased. I believe that a more kind hearted King as His Late Majesty will not be found anywhere else. We are enjoying a degree of peace and comfort that was never secured earlier.

"Among the developed nations of the world, the deployment of serfs and indentured servants is regarded as immoral, and was gradually abandoned. Here too, in a civilized nation, serfdom was annulled in 1956 by His Late Majesty, and the stigma associated with it was banished. He granted manumission to all the serfs and abolished discrimination among the precious lives of all human beings and rendered all the people equal, without regard to status. Accomplishing these common goals as well as forging unity and cooperation stems from this change which made all of us equal as precious human beings.

"Although there are many forms of government like democracy, monarchy and communism on the surface of the earth, a substantial number of countries adopt either democracy or monarchy, as these are the most popular forms of government. It was His Majesty's intention to devise a government which is an improvement on either of these two forms of government. In order to enhance the fundamental stability of the country, in 1970, His Majesty introduced a new form of government combining democracy and monarchy. A system of voting on ministerial candidates was introduced, and in 1968, His Majesty gave up his powers of making decisions to the National Assembly. There is no such remarkable precedence in the history of monarchies in the world, whereby a King surrendered his powers to the people for the sake of strengthening the security of the country.

"Until recently, we did not have an impressive capital. As this situation was absolutely disagreeable in keeping with the development trend in our country, the construction of the dzong was started in 1963, as the seat of all central secretariats and the central monk body. Both the outer features and the inner designs were based entirely on our own tradition. This befitting structure took about seven years and more than Nu 200 lakhs to build, and it now beautifies the country like an ornament.

"Favourable happenings, both short and long term, in the country are dependent ultimately on the precious teachings of the Buddha. As Shewalha said:

The only source of beneficence;
May the teachings last long.

"His Majesty considered it highly important to extend patronage to Buddhism, because it is the only path to eventual liberation as well as to the accumulation of transitory merit. In 1966, the golden calligraphic writing of Kanjur was commissioned. Further, golden calligraphic work on Tenjur, which was started in 1970, is almost complete. As bodily support or a repository of Buddhist teachings, ten thousand statues and a silken thangkha were made. As mind support or a repository of Buddhist teachings, three thousand chortens or stupas are being produced. Countless important temples and monasteries of this country were renovated. As the monastic community is central to the teachings of Buddhism, the strength of the central monk body was increased to 1,100. Many meditation centres and higher institutions were established. Countless prayers wheels of mantras were installed in addition to boundless offerings and donations, all of which were dedicated to the precious teachings of Buddhism.

"Above all, our isolated country continued to remain on the fringe of the world. Nothing was abundant; the revenue was not adequate to meet the expenditure of respective dzongkhags, let aside finance development. There was an acute scarcity of trained people. We faced an immense difficulty unlike any other country, because of the shortage of both manpower and resources. His Majesty had to travel abroad frequently to seek assistance to overcome these constraints.

"We have had long trade and cultural ties with our neighbour India. This friendship was strengthened considerably during the reign of His Late Majesty, especially in 1958, when Nehru was invited to Bhutan. This was the first time a Prime Minister came to Bhutan. Because of his visit, the friendship between the two countries became more steadfast. From 1961 onwards, the Government of India began to give assistance in terms of both manpower and resources, which enabled us to launch development activities.

"In 1962, a motor road was opened (from Phuntsholing to Thimphu) for the first time. With the exception of three districts in Southern Bhutan and three districts in the remote parts of Bhutan, ten districts in the country have been linked by motor road. It is apparent to everyone how beneficial the motor roads have become for both the government and the people.

"In 1963, Bhutan was able to join the Colombo Plan which made it possible for our country to strike up relationships with other countries and become known among them. This in turn led Bhutan to receive more aid. We are presently in the second year of our Third Five Year Plan. As priority is given to education in our development, about twenty thousand of our children are attending schools and getting an education, as though they were in a golden age. With regard to postal services, letters can be delivered within one to two hours, whereas it used to take several days and nights. In 1966, Bhutan joined the Universal Postal Union, and facilities for direct exchange of post with other countries became available.

"Likewise, the establishment of various organizations like the Department of Agriculture, Department of Animal Husbandry, Department of Health Services, Department of Forest, Department of Publicity, Department of Electricity and Department of Transport have been highly beneficial.

"To prevent our traditions from declining, a school of Buddhist studies was founded in Simtokha and an indigenous hospital was opened in Dechencholing. As all of you are aware, these activities do not merely arrest the decline of our traditions but provide very useful services to the people.

"In a similar manner, within the affairs of the government, several new bodies like the Royal Advisory Council, Council of Ministers, Planning Commission, High Court, Central Audit and Accounts Office (now Royal Audit Authority), Bank of Bhutan, various ministries, Royal Bhutan Army and Royal Bhutan Police were established. These institutions have strengthened the government and enhanced the capacity for developing the country.

"Many foreigners wish to visit our country to see the progress we are able to make. In 1968, Mrs Indira Gandhi was invited to Bhutan. In 1970 President of India V. V. Giri visited Bhutan, being the first time a Head of State visited Bhutan.

"Since 1969, Bhutan made efforts to get admission into the United Nations and in 1971 we were admitted as a full member. India was the first country with which Bhutan exchanged ambassadors. It has greatly facilitated communications between our two governments. Bhutan was the second country in the world to recognize the independence of Bangladesh. These achievements I mentioned and sound policies of the government have earned our country a certain favourable reputation.

"What I have related briefly to you concerning the major achievements of His Late Majesty attained in the last twenty one years of his reign is by no means based on hearsay. I have myself witnessed and experienced these things while I attended him continually since the day he acceded to the throne. History will reflect his achievements in detail, but I have submitted a summary of what I could recollect. It is entirely due to the benevolence of His Late Majesty that this country has experienced miraculous development in the last ten years. There has not been as benevolent a King as His Late Majesty in the history of Bhutan, and his benevolence cannot be forgotten in aeons to come. When we are left behind by such a benign King, we are plunged into the grief that is comparable to the grief felt by a mother whose only child is washed away by a turbulent river in flood. In his respectful memory, all of us who are present shall now stand in silence for three minutes.

"We have just paid homage to the memory of His Late Majesty, our benevolent King. If we continue to dwell on our grief and sorrow, such feelings will only grow. Although our grief will but continue, I feel that we can lessen it by reminding ourselves that all of us worked for him with absolute loyalty. We never acted contrary to his wishes or hurt his feelings. He was an emanation of a Bodhisattava, though due to our sullied intelligence, we had not be able to realize his true identity.

"He had foreseen that, for the time being, his predestined time for Bodhisattava acts had come to an end. Because he had foreseen the end of his life, he installed the Crown Prince as the Trongsa Penlop and also held a ceremony for the Trongsa Penlop on the throne in Tashichodzong.

"The significance of this investiture and throne ceremony was to give formal recognition to the heir-apparent and to remind all of us that, when he departs, the Crown Prince would be the next father of our welfare. In this respect, our fortunes have decreased by phuta but not by dre. Although His Late Majesty is no longer with us, the people of Bhutan are fortunate enough to have the Crown Prince Jigme Singye Wangchuck succeed him as the fourth hereditary King of Bhutan. We have no doubt that in His Majesty's reign, the safety of the country and the alleviation of the hardship of the people will be achieved on a scale much larger than that of the time of His Late Majesty.

"There is a further matter which I would like to submit to the members of the National Assembly. Other sessions of the National Assembly are important in themselves but this - 37th session - is the most important one. It marks the end of His Late Majesty's time, and the succession of the fourth hereditary King of Bhutan. Moreover, this is the first session after His Majesty has acceded to the throne. We must strive to think about our country more than ever, to hail the reign of His Majesty.

"Because of the wisdom and benevolence of His Late Majesty, we have made vast progress in terms of both immediate peace and long term security. But it is not enough just to express gratitude to him repeatedly. We must not only follow his actions and plans, but we must fulfill his valuable commands as though his words were as dear to us as our own lives, so that his heavenly soul will be gratified. If the commands of His Late Majesty were to vanish like a puff of breath in the air, it would represent nothing less than betrayal of the faith and loyalty between the King and the people. If the heavenly soul of His Majesty is not satisfied, little good will come to those of us left behind and the benefits of the services we have rendered to His Late Majesty in the past will be diminished. It is therefore vital for us to pursue development in a timely manner and, in particular, to keep alive the commands of His Late Majesty in the same way as we safeguard our own lives.

"We experience peace and comfort due to the blessed unity and cooperation that exists between all the peoples. We are like amicable members of a household and we ought to be selfless enough to think about the larger interest of the country. Above all, there is unblemished faith and loyalty between the King and the people. We have a culture where the ruler treats his people with more love and affection than his own offsprings, and where the people revere their King like a God and regard every act of the King as wise. The faith and loyalty between the King and the people is so constant that it can be hardly found anywhere else. We the subjects must now acknowledge ourselves as the subjects of one ruler and people of one nation, and unite and cooperate among ourselves.

We must duly realize the Sovereign as the King and demonstrate our faith and loyalty.

"As His Late Majesty has enjoined us, we must believe in the principle of causality and have faith in the gods worshipped in the days of our parents, and observe our customs and traditions. If we all concentrate as much as possible on the advancement of our country, it will become better and better. I am unable to speak well on these matters, but as all of you were chosen and selected from among the masses, you are highly informed. I am certain that you are able to perceive and hear much more than what I am able to say."

For the first time, His Majesty Jigme Singye Wangchuck addressed the National Assembly. His short speech on the inaugural day summed up everything that needed to be said. It betrayed his sharp and quick mind. Despite being only 17, he created a remarkable impression as a highly persuasive speaker, which became one of the hallmarks of his striking personality. The sudden shift in the burden of the state on his young shoulders had weighed rather heavily on His Majesty's mind. But we were left in no doubt about the enervating charisma and the determination he possessed. His Majesty again spoke on the closing day of the National Assembly:

"I wish to say today a few words to this Assembly. This Assembly in its 32nd session, had resolved that a Council of Regents, consisting of four members, should be appointed in the case of a minor monarch. I concurred with this resolution since I am not yet 21.

"You have, however, decided against such a Council and have vested in me the powers of a ruler. I have little experience but I shall rely upon the sound judgement of this august body, and endeavour to serve the nation to the best of my ability.

"Till now, all our achievements have been due to the selfless dedication and generosity of our Late King who led the country so nobly till he passed away.

"Our country's continued sovereignty and prosperity owes to the blessings of the Lord Buddha, our guardian deities and our forefathers. Also, we owe this to the strong and undefiled faith between the ruler, the monk body, the government and the people. Therefore, despite the fact that the source of our happiness and our beloved father has left us, if we continue to maintain this bond, it would enhance the national progress.

"His Late Majesty's principal wish was that this country should enjoy greater peace and prosperity. We can be confident that, if we keep this in mind and tread the path that he showed us, we will achieve our common goals."

23

A FUNERAL AND A CORONATION

The funeral cortege was kept in the Royal Cottage for about three months, while Kingkhor Lopon Jeda, the man who supervised the golden calligraphic writing of Kanjur, was assigned to build the monumental crematorium in Kurje in Bumthang. Some members of the National Assembly had proposed that the remains of His Majesty be preserved as a relic, unaware of the fact that His Majesty had expressed his wish to be cremated in the same spot where his father and grandfather were cremated.

I undertook the general coordination of the funeral procession and supervised all the carpentry work to mount the casket on a new lorry, which was impressively disguised as divine lodgings on wheels. Night halts were planned at Wangduephodrang and Trongsa for the procession of the cortege to Bumthang along with many receptions on the route to Bumthang Kurje. All the functionaries above the level of director left for Kurje with the funeral cortege. The convoy was led by a pilot, followed by my own jeep, which in turn was followed by the lorry containing the casket. Then, there were vehicles of the Trongsa Penlop and the members of the royal family, ministers, dashos and so forth, resulting in a convoy of over a hundred vehicles. The procession was delayed in Nobding for over an hour because the brand new lorry carrying the casket developed mechanical failure. I could hardly avoid developing a sense of absurdity. We had gone into extraordinary detail to think through the logistics and procured a new lorry for the trip.

The procession got to Trongsa in time in the evening and finally to Kurje the next day. During the three days trip to Kurje, the route was lined with innumerable people who came to bid farewell to His Late Majesty. Children stood on the best viewpoints by the road for a long time after the procession passed them, dazed by the earth shaking noise of the convoy and the bewildering spectacle of vehicles. Incense and herbal smoke, usually offered during purification or deity invocation rites, was produced everywhere along the route, and engulfed the procession as it passed like thick mist. People compared the loss they felt to the occurrence of a solar eclipse, the greatest cosmic breakdown, whose long umbra was crossing over them on that particular day.

The casket was placed in the old shrine of Kurje for three nights before it was encased in the crematorium built in the shape of a stupa. The crematorium was surrounded by groups of monks, lead by four distinguished lamas, including His Holiness the Karmapa. As flames lit the crematorium, they overshot and caught on the rafters of the roof. There was a danger that the roofs would collapse on the main crematorium structure before the casket was fully burnt. Fortunately, the fire fighting unit discreetly sprang into action and controlled the fire.

I took leave of His Majesty on the evening after the cremation was held. I, in my capacity as the Speaker of the National Assembly, and my assistant Sangay Dorji were invited by my counterpart Mr. Dhillon to visit India for twenty one days. The first items were to observe the Lok Sabbha in session and call on Mrs Gandhi, the

Prime Minister of India, during a short recess in the parliament. I also called on Foreign Minister Swaran Singh and many other high officials during the trip. My delegation hopped to Amritsar, Bombay, Bangalore, Madras, and Calcutta.

When I returned from my trip to India, the funeral services were completed and all the government officials were back in Thimphu. Now the attention shifted to the preliminary crowning of His Majesty in Punakha. I again had a considerable responsibility in preparing the ceremonial side of it. The whole of next year, that is 1973, was dominated by preparation for the public coronation on June 2, 1974. Prince Namgyal Wangchuk became the chairman of the Coronation Committee. Yet again I found myself, assisted by a few officers, with the responsibility of preparing its ceremonial side. Foreign Minister Lyonpo Dawa Tsering took charge of the invitation and protocol for over a hundred foreign dignitaries representing numerous countries.

The flattest piece of river bed in Thimphu, Changlengmethang was flattened further to be made into the main venue for public celebration during the coronation. On the side of the slope, semicircular open galleries overlooking the huge arena were built. This open theatre could provide seats to thirty to forty thousand people, the entire population of the city. On the side of the river which flowed through avenues of willow trees, several pavilions were built among which the most splendid one was the two storey royal pavilion.

There was also a great deal of renaming of houses and streets. In all these linguistic reconversions and other initiatives, Prince Namgyal Wangchuk was my constant support. Many guests would travel to Thimphu by road. Along the highway between Phuntsholing and Thimphu, many places had been named, for example, as Putiliveer and Kharbandi by road workers from India and Nepal. These were renamed in Dzongkha. Streets in Thimphu were also named. Finally, all houses belonging to royal family members were hired, renamed and turned into VVIP guest houses.

The throne room was substantially restored for the coronation. The silk upholstery was replaced by leopard skins, with patterns of spots. When the plan of the seating arrangement came up for discussion, the Coronation Committee faced a delicate matter: whether the Chief Abbot of Bhutan, the Je Khenpo, should occupy a higher throne than the three other incarnate lamas - Their Holinesses Karmapa, Khamtrul and Dilkhor Khentse. Eventually it was decided that the Je Khenpo would merit the second highest throne after His Majesty because of the special role he had during the coronation ceremony. The seats for the three high lamas and the Chogyal of Sikkim were made lower than that of the Je Khenpo but higher than those of the other guests.

I was involved quite extensively in the coordination of daily programmes for three days of public celebration, dovetailing the presentation of the army's guard of honour, mask and folk dances and other ceremonies in both the dzong and in Changlengmethang stadium. Nearer the date of coronation, we were breathlessly busy with the mock ceremonies in the dzong and Changlengmethang. The mock ceremonies were held to replicate the actual situation as precisely as possible and included proxies for guests. It was so necessary to go through mock sessions, not only to measure the time taken for each part of the ceremony, but to spot any minute detail we might have overlooked in our general concentration on major parts of the event.

There were so many things to do before the coronation that I did not sleep for two consecutive nights. The general excitement of the coronation had decreased my sensitivity to fatigue that I went through the preparatory days in an elevated mood. I returned late in the evening and as I sat down, I suddenly collapsed from exhaustion. But I was reinvigorated enough by next morning to go back to work.

On the day of coronation, His Majesty the King drove in a motorcade from Dechencholing Palace. The route to the dzong was lined with flags. A sedrang was located on the roof top of a house in Langjophakha. The guests were already waiting in the courtyard of the dzong. His Majesty took a guard of honour outside the entrance to the dzong and marched into the dzong.

A marchang offering was made in the courtyard of the dzong while the Je Khenpo and the King stood there for a while. The welcoming ceremony in the courtyard with marchang was a very moving and elaborate one. Then the King and Je Khenpo marched up the corridor and the staircase to the Throne Room and prostrated thrice before the shrine. The Je Khenpo took the scarf from the altar and offered it to the King, who wore it round his shoulders. His Majesty sat on the throne, and the Je Khenpo offered the crown to the King. The Je Khenpo retraced his steps to sit on his own throne next to the King's. The three lamas - Karmapa, Dilkhor Khentse, Khamtrul - were lead to their seats from the lounge. Then the members of the royal family and the foreign dignitaries were ushered into the Throne Room. The shugdrel ceremony was set to go when Lyonpo Dawa Tsering found two foreign dignitaries missing. He rushed out and fetched them. The ceremony was followed by the presentation of gifts by the guests. There were so many guests that gift presentation lasted from 9 o'clock in the morning to 2 o'clock in the afternoon.

The next day the guests and the public were entertained in Changlengmethang. The arrival of the King in Changlengmethang was followed by the inspection of the guard of honour from a slow moving jeep. His Majesty then addressed the public and presented a gold medal each to the foreign dignitaries. He gave ample sign of his prodigious capacity for leadership at the time of delivering his Coronation Address. He wrote himself and it contained several key ideas that have unfolded as policies since then:

"Two years ago when my father passed away, all the dratshangs (monk bodies), officials and you, my people, placed your trust in me and made me King. During the short while that I have been on the Throne, I have not been able to render any great service to our country. However, I offer my pledge today that I shall endeavour to serve our beloved country and people with integrity and to the best of my ability.

"From year to year, Bhutan is receiving increasing financial and technical assistance from many countries. Among them, we have received the greatest assistance from our good friend India. Although the process of socio-economic development was initiated in our country only a few years ago, we have achieved tremendous progress within a short span of time. In spite of this progress, our present internal revenue cannot meet even a fraction of our government expenditure. Therefore, the most important task before us at present is to achieve economic self-reliance to ensure the continued progress of our country in the future. Bhutan has a small population, abundant land and rich natural resources and sound planning on our part will enable us to realize our aim of economic self-reliance in the near future.

"As far as you, my people, are concerned, you should not adopt the attitude that whatever is required to be done for your welfare will be done entirely by the government. On the contrary, a little effort on the part will be much more effective than a great deal of effort on the part of the government. If the government and people join hands and work with determination, our people will achieve prosperity and our nation will become strong and stable.

"In earlier times, when our country was passing through a critical period and our people were suffering greatly due to civil wars and internal strife, Ugyen Wangchuck was unanimously elected as the first hereditary King of Bhutan on December 17, 1907, ushering in period of great peace and happiness for Bhutan. The fact that our country continues to enjoy peace and stability is due to the blessings of our deities and the great loyalty and devotion shown by the dratshangs, officials and people of our Kingdom.

"The only message I have to convey to you today, my people, is that if everyone of us consider ourselves Bhutanese, and think and act as one, and if we have faith in the Triple Gem, our Glorious Kingdom of Bhutan will grow from strength to strength and achieve prosperity, peace and happiness.

"Today we are extremely happy to have with us representative of friendly countries and other guests to participate in our celebrations. To you, my people, and to all our guests, I offer my Tashi Delek."

The foreign dignitaries left Bhutan either by helicopter or by road on the third day of the celebration. The royal family members and the high officials mingled in the tents in Changlengmethang for lunch in joyous mood. I breathed a sigh of relief at the end of that day for up to that point I had a crucial role orchestrating the ceremonies and programmes. Prisoners were freed and prisons made empty on the occasion of coronation. A number of people who left Bhutan during the short upheaval in 1964 were pardoned and re-entered Bhutan.

However, my career had reached its pinnacle around the same time. My term as the Speaker of the National Assembly was over soon after the coronation. I referred this to His Majesty and Home Minister Lyonpo T. Jagar. Yangpai Lopon Ngidup, who had long ago been the third Speaker of the National Assembly, was appointed as my successor. I felt that a heavy burden had been lifted on the day I gave up the responsibility of the Speaker. But I continued to be one of the thirty representatives of the government in the National Assembly. In my farewell speech to the National Assembly, I pointed out that no speaker in the history of the National Assembly had such a burden. A King had passed away; a new one was installed. I felt enormous satisfaction that there was no perceptible failure on my part during all this crucial transition.

24

HANGING UP THE SWORD

I was the Secretary of Royal Secretariat till 1985. This was a position to which I was appointed during the reign of Late King Jigme Dorji Wangchuck. I had the good fortune to continue in this capacity even after the untimely passing away of the King in 1972. But it would be fair to say that I was the Secretary only in a nominal sense after the passing away of King Jigme Dorji Wangchuck; for I did not deal with any issue of major importance. Before 1974, I had to participate frequently in meetings, an attendance that became necessary because of the multiple posts I held. I was Secretary of the Royal Secretariat, Secretary of Lhengyel Shungtshog (Cabinet) and the Speaker of the National Assembly. But after 1974 I found myself with more time on my hands. I felt that I should refrain from participating, as I had no valuable suggestions to make. The lack of a demanding assignment naturally began to wear on me and as it stretched into years, it was difficult for me, not to develop an increasing sense of dissipation, which had to be overcome.

In 1976, Thimphu abounded with unsettling rumours about an intrigue that could endanger the safety of the state. A mysterious and tense mood swept over Thimphu. It was to usher in a short period of bewilderment for me and my family. For three months, I could not attend my office, as I came under suspicion. My family faced this period, which was disorienting, with great courage and show of love. At the end of three months, which seemed interminable, I was cleared of any involvement or role. As a measure of my vindication, I had once again the good fortune to be reinstated in my original post in the Royal Secretariat. But as before, I had a great deal of time to confront myself while I sat alone. The years between 1976 and 1985 were the most uncertain and tedious for me.

I had naturally pondered often over my resignation in those years when a sense of despondency overcame me. I realized then that I had reached the pinnacle of my career sometime ago. I considered many questions. I had only three years to go before I would reach the age of retirement at sixty. I faced a certain predicament in coming to terms with the question of whether I should leave my public service before superannuation. I strongly felt that others should not consider my resignation as something done out of disappointment. It was important to remind myself that one should bear uncertainty lightly, and not do anything that might be taken as an action of a disaffected person. While I proposed to resign from the civil service, I did not wish my resignation to be construed as desertion of the civil service, which was in general starved of manpower.

Several of my close friends were concerned enough to discuss my intention to take an early retirement. Their views were similar; I should continue to work until superannuation. But I could not acquiesce to this suggestion, however sympathetic it might have been, as I could not see how I could come to terms with as many years as three without doing anything worthwhile. I felt that my resignation could allow me to do something worthy. However, I felt that one of their reasons to persuade me to stay on, which they were reluctant to state openly, was the possibility for my career to rise further under a more fortunate circumstance that might come about in the course of time. But I could not again see myself as a person who deliberately courted a greater position as a matter of time, instead of a constantly useful role in the government.

I had also to consider whether it would be worth clinging on to my entitlement of a deputy minister for another three years. I was entitled till then to services of two servants, one chauffeur and a monthly salary of Nu 2,000. As it is apparent from this, in those days, my pay and allowances and other privileges were sufficient for a decent living for my family, but not in any way enough to put away a substantial amount for the future. I would have very little on which I could live the remaining part of my years, if it had not been for the kindness of the Late King who made grants and gifts to me from time to time. I faced several difficult situations arising out of demands for unforeseen expenditures during funerals of my close relatives, obligations to discharge debts incurred by my relatives who died prematurely, or settlement of my own divorces. When I found myself in such situations, the Late King Jigme Dorji Wangchuck whom I served the longest part of my life, mitigated my financial constraints through sheer generosity.

I would have become a quite well-to-do person if I had not given away some of the land I acquired to my parental home. These fields were mainly in eastern and central Bhutan. I felt that I was bound by tradition to purchase a certain amount of land for my parental home which was not in any way very well endowed. Besides, I had my first wife, whom I divorced, and her daughter living there. I would also have become better off if I had seized all the materialistic opportunities that came my way. I must confess that I was not aware until much later of the easy way in which officials could become wealthy by investing in land.

For example, at one time, King Jigme Dorji Wangchuck granted me land title at a nominal cost for a sizeable part of rice terraces in Bajo in Wangduephodrang. I gratefully declined the gift because I did not see at that time the remotest possibility for me or my relatives (who came from an alpine district) to farm the paddy fields in Wangduephodrang, a sub-tropical valley. My contemporaries, however, were very prudent and pounced on the opportunity. In those days one had to walk for a week from my parental home in Bumthang to Wangduephodrang, and it seemed to me that travelling with ponies as pack-animals would continue in my time. I then wrote off the possibility that it would be easy to travel from one end of Bhutan to another by motor roads in a matter of two decades. Having never travelled abroad to see the change in other parts of the world, I could not, at that time, anticipate the rapidity of development in Bhutan, especially with the construction of motor road. I could not at all conceive how easy it would become to travel; travel by ponies seemed the only way for the ordinary people.

On another occasion, I was given the opportunity to fence off a large part of bush area around my house in Thimphu as my own property. I again refused to accept this area as my land holding, because I did not see any advantage in laying claim to a bush area. The bush area regenerated with thorny thickets around boulders; I did not see any obvious use for it. In twenty years, the same bush area gained colossal economic value and is now populated with buildings.

On both accounts, which were by no means all the experiences I had of similar kind, I did not foresee that the land value would rise so sharply so soon after I denied these properties to myself. Now, when I reflect on these incidences, my responses to these opportunities seem quite preposterous.

Nevertheless, I had a house of my own in Thimphu and a cottage in Toebesa with a certain amount of land around them. It used to be quite customary for a family to have two houses: one in Thimphu for summer and one in the Puna-Wangdue valley for winter. I had two cars, a rarity in those days, and a small herd of cattle, which was quite common. The small herd produced enough diary goods for the consumption of my family. I was confident that I would make some money out of the odd commercial assignments and artistic commissions. I was consulted quite frequently to do various things like painting, drafting, sculpting, carving, designing houses and dresses and tailoring draperies and tents, and small commissions of this sort would once again develop my aptitudes in these fields. My wife was also regarded even then as an enterprising person. So the question of livelihood after retirement did not weigh so heavily on my mind, and we felt that we could bring up our four children and give them education in schools with some reputation in Kalimpong and Darjeeling, even after my retirement.

However, there was also at one stage a distinct possibility that my responsibility would be changed, and I might be considered for a post to take charge of cultural affairs, art and architecture. This kind suggestion was made to me from several quarters as an engagement very compatible with my own inclination. I found the suggestion indeed attractive as I had an intrinsic interest in the arts and cultural affairs. It was kindly put to me that the art and architectural design of the Bhutanese Temple in Bodh Gaya in India, to be built by the Royal Government of Bhutan, might be entrusted to me. I could not, however, raise my hopes too high as I began to learn that there were other constraints that needed to be taken into account in order to employ me in a different capacity. I took up the issue of retirement from all angles and arrived at the conclusion that I must hand in my resignation.

In my letter of resignation to the Royal Civil Service Commission, which was then headed by the western educated son of late Gaydon Thinley, I wrote that I wanted to start a new life for myself as a lama of which I was a reincarnation. I felt that I had reached a phase in life when the call of religion seemed very strong. Having resigned, I collected all my retirement benefits: my gratuity of Nu. 40,000, provident fund repayment of Nu. 60,000 and incentive for accepting redundancy of Nu. 40,000. Redundancy incentive was a given to those who resigned before reaching the period of superannuation.

As I completed the formalities of resignation, I prepared myself to welcome my able and young successor, Wangchen, an early morning in autumn. The stars were appropriate for him to be installed as the new Secretary, and for me to leave. I received him at the corridor and led him to my rectangular office in the South East wing of Tashichodzong as the first rays of the sun shone through its tall windows. After an auspicious ceremony, my successor was appointed as Secretary to His Majesty. The room became lively with people coming to felicitate my successor, as I sat next to him.

Here in this room, I had worked for one and a half decades. I would always remember its sober elegance and brightness. From one of its giant windows facing the East I could have a view of the modest Royal Cottage next to the river; beyond, I could see the rice terraces which had turned golden in autumn. This particular view lightened my mood and I often used to enjoy it, although it was not as stupendous as the one from the palace in Kinga Rabden or Trongsa dzong. The opposite wall of the valley rose steeply from the rice terraces next to the narrow river bed. Through other windows facing South, I could see the town of Thimphu and Changangkha Lhakhang. A grove of poplars and willows rose up to the level of windows, their tops almost touching the windows. This view, which had been pleasing in the past, now began to excite a measure of sadness in me. I had to repress my feelings at that time, for the train of my thoughts was taking me to some fine as well as exacting moments I had in the office.

While the room crackled with a degree of hushed excitement not common in the office, I discreetly gathered my private files to go. I took my last glance at the room as I withdrew quietly from it, after wishing my successor the best. I made my way along the long corridor and heard my own footsteps echo with those of others. The wooden floor of the corridor gleamed; it was scrubbed daily with a weed and rags which lent the floor a brownish colour and left a mild fragrance.

I climbed down the wooden staircase into the courtyard. The morning sun lit half of the central tower and the stone court yard in front. I surveyed this view standing for a moment on the landing of the staircase. I recall that at that moment I became aware of the bellow of the jaling and the hum of pigeons filling the cloisters. Although it was usual for monks to play the jaling at this time of the morning, the effect of the note was quite overwhelming for me that morning. At the far end of the courtyard where the high central tower of the dzong stood, I could see first a few and then more and more people arriving for work. Cleaners, monks, and policemen hurriedly crossed the court yard. A few bushes of chrysanthemums stood under the lone cherry tree in the court yard.

I crossed the court yard and the cloisters, descended two more staircases before I came out of the dzong. The guards at the entrance came to attention and saluted as I passed them. People strolling for work in the opposite direction bowed, and came to a standstill for a moment, in deference to my position displayed by the scarlet robe and the ceremonial sword. They stopped by the side of the road, leaving the whole stretch in front momentarily to me. I walked past the lines of poplars from which pale yellow leaves drifted and dropped rustling around me. I felt the bracing air touch my closely cropped head and the chill grip my bare knees. When I finally came to the restricted parking bay where my car was, I unbuckled my ceremonial sword and folded the scarlet robe of deputy minister that I wore.

Here I ended my career spanning forty two years. I was never to pick up the ceremonial sword again. I had expected to feel a sense of disarray, at any rate for some days, at my own resignation. I was, as many would have remarked, cutting myself off from a reassuring and powerful body. But as I shelved my ceremonial sword at home afterwards, I began to feel an immediate relief from something like a heavy curfew on my mind. A welcome sense of respite came over me. I was somewhat astonished by the fact that I had not been able to assess till then the extent of my own disguised gloom that had lasted far too long.

The end of my public career was marked by a farewell dinner by my able successor, Wangchen. I was presented with two Tibetan rugs, one table, and a white scarf symbolizing pure good wishes. My successor, a far sighted, quiet and inscrutable young man, who happened to be from a village next to mine, spoke such kind words that I felt my usual equanimity leaving me. It was my turn to say a few word of thanks to those present at the dinner for their unexpected gesture that made me all the more touched:

"I am now approaching an age when religion has a stronger appeal and prayers demand more time than they do at a younger age. Spending as I did almost forty years in the service of the government, it is time for me to make a fresh start. I was brought up as a lay Buddhist priest till I was summoned to become part of the mass of servants in the royal household. A new turn in one's life is difficult to adapt to; but I shall pick up, in a manner of speaking, the thread of my religious life where I left it almost forty two years ago. I was about 16 when all of a sudden the course of my life was diverted from the vocation of a lama to a servant of the government. It was no doubt my fate that I should become a servant of the government by accident and contingency at so early an age, and remain thereafter as one for so long. During this long period, I had the privilege to offer continuously whatever abilities I happened to have, to the service of three successive kings, from the second to the fourth. I feel it was a distinct honour that is hardly available to most servants of the government, however long they have been associated with public life. We have changed in the last three decades more than we did in the last three centuries. in the course of my public life. In the course of my public life, I have been a witness to the revolution to which I could not make significant contributions.

"I will never be able to repay the kindness and generosity owed to my mentors and patrons especially Their Majesties. But I derive great satisfaction from my belief that I have not committed any error in the course of my duty. It is not so much with the things I have accomplished on my own as the commands I have executed fully that I feel pleased. As far as I can recall, whatever I have done has not come under any reproach. I have always endeavoured to maintain common decency and honour in whatever I did. It was also my good fortune that I have not disappointed Their Majesties the Kings while discharging my duties. That is not to say that I was alone able to carry out the wishes of Their Majesties. I have had again the good fortune to work with a group of people, as my immediate staff, with the highest devotion to Their Majesties. I would pray for my successor that the same harmonious relationship would flourish between him and the staff of Royal Secretariat. I would like to ask the staff I am leaving behind to give the same support to my successor that you have given me.

"... Now I end my public career today, and I hope to devote more of my time to prayers and worship. But I am leaving public life, not this valley or town. Although I am assimilated in the collectivist lifestyle of our villages as much as any other peasant, I can hardly revert to my village. I will continue to be here in this town or valley till my old age, and if I happen to fall on difficult times, I hope that all of you who remain with the state will be sympathetic to me. If I happen to fall on difficult times, then I hope that your kindness will again prevail and you will come to my assistance."

25

ENVOI

The following is an imaginary press release:

Shingkhar Lam Kunzang Wangchuck, who resigned in October 1985, was Secretary of the Royal Secretariat. He belonged to a generation of courtiers, with roots in the villages, who were turned into high function'aries with the growth of the government and administration.

He was born on 1st February 1928, the eldest of three children. Both his sister and brother died in their fifties. Shingkhar Lam is the reincarnation of the lama of Wamtshespa as well as a hereditary lama of Shingkhar Village in Bumthang. Buddhism, and the arts it spawned, remained an abiding interest throughout his life both as an academic subject and a faith. His interest in Buddhism influenced his everyday life even while he was a rising public figure. He was always impressed by the subtleties of Buddhist literature and art, and cultivated friendships with many lamas, painters and sculptors. Such relationships sustained his spiritual, ritual and theological inquiries.

His skills ranged from painting to architecture. He received his education from the age of five till sixteen from several scholars. His father and uncle taught him until he acquired basic literacy, and he pursued his studies in grammar further with the eminent scholar, Lopon Norbu Wangchuck. He had both initiations from a Zogchen lama who arrived in Bhutan from Kham in Tibet, when he was about eleven. Though such doors of educational opportunities were open to him, he did not grow in material comfort, because his parents were not wealthy. He was brought up, by all accounts, to follow a pattern of life fairly common to the provincial lamas who were partially itinerant, leading their priestly proteges on alm rounds to warmer places in winter, while they were part farmers and part lamas in their own localities.

Very early on, the course of his life was to became totally unpredictable. Unexpected events intruded upon his life again and again. In 1944, Shingkhar Lam was indentured first as a retainer, and later turned into a clerk among the secretarial staff of King Jigme Wangchuck at the age of 18. He was recruited to fill the place of a court servant, his uncle, who went missing.

Shingkhar Lam served the second King for eight years till His Majesty's passing away in 1952. During this period, the elder secretaries came to appreciate his abilities. In those days (when Dzongkha typewriters were at least forty years away), he drafted court documents faster than anybody else, as he had the quickest scribe among the clerks. He possessed an uncommonly gifted style and clarity of expression.

Those years brought him to the notice of the Crown Prince, later King Jigme Dorji Wangchuck, who was to look upon him always with kindness and affection. Like many other persons associated with the royal household, Shingkhar Lam continued to serve the succeeding King, His Majesty Jigme Dorji Wangchuck, as a member of his private secretarial staff from 1952 to 1964. After the death of Gaydon Thinley, in 1964, with whom he had been associated for a long time, Shingkhar Lam became Private Secretary to the King. The honour of the red robe, which brought the title of Dasho with it, was conferred much later in 1968.

Although Shingkhar Lam travelled widely in the country, he has been beyond towns in the Indo-Bhutan border only thrice: the first time in 1957 to Calcutta, the second time as part of the Royal entourage in 1959 to Delhi, and the third time in 1972 at the invitation of the Speaker of Indian Parliament, Mr G. S. Dhillon. The only other country he visited was Japan where he went to attend Expo'70, an international trade fair held in Osaka. Because he could neither speak or write English, he did not go on other trips abroad.

His linguistic handicap perhaps circumscribed the breadth of his relationships among many people, especially expatriates with whom dealings were on a rapid increase. His direct reach and personal influence among these people was also reduced. His views therefore might have come to have only limited hold among the public policy makers after the late seventies, when the mass of officials communicating in English increased substantially. Had he been tutored to learn English, his career could have become even more adaptable and taken off in an altogether different direction. The colleagues who outlasted him as officials spoke and wrote English. But this shortcoming did not diminish his own role in many spheres where he could draw on his indigenous erudition and grasp of local situations.

Dasho Shingkhar Lam was elected as the Speaker of the National Assembly in its 34th session in 1971. Soon after his election as the Speaker of the National Assembly, he was conferred with the honour of the scarlet robe by King Jigme Dorji Wangchuck on 6th May 1971. He was concurrently the Speaker of the National Assembly, the Secretary of Royal Secretariat and the Secretary of Lhengyel Shungtshog, a unique combination of positions in which he continued till the 40th session of the National Assembly in 1974. His maiden address to the National Assembly is still remembered as a powerful one touching on fundamental issues. His speech delivered on the occasion of the third King's demise will, however, be rediscovered by future speakers, not only as a moving tribute to the Late King, but as a paragon of public speech exploiting a wide range of native idioms and techniques.

His command over many issues was quite prodigious, though his humility and moral sensitivity, both esteemed characteristics of a Buddhist, did not encourage him at all to promote his own superior abilities in the face of people who thought they knew better.

He rarely failed to astonish people with his incomparable craftsmanship and technical abilities. His office life might have impaired his craftsmanship. After a long period of frozen creativity, his talents seemed to thaw once again during his old age, as he found the opportunity to pray, worship, paint, write, draw, pursue mask-dance, design and sculpture.

However he always tended to discount his importance and achievements during his career. His sense of modesty did not allow him to reveal his contributions to national life, and he did not point to any specific policy he shaped. Shingkhar Lam was a master of restraint and always inclined to understate. Indeed, the understatement which he conveyed through his speech as well as general comportment, marked by humility, came to be regarded as a hallmark that set him apart. His mannerisms almost bordered on the obsequious. But he behaved in the same way with one and all which lent sincerity to his personality. When he spoke, his upper frame stooped forward in a position of courtesy and attentiveness, and he spoke in a soft tone. His delicate manner of speech was inimitable, though some tried to emulate him. The closely-cropped head, which is so typical of the Bhutanese, brought out the contours of his oval shaped head and somehow heightened the entrenched impression of his modesty and sensibility that prevailed. He spoke always in a low tone and sounded in a peculiar way both grave and graceful. It was the voice of a man who had witnessed events from a broader perspective of having a thousand eyes, and whose views were tempered by the middle path. He took everything seriously inspite of realizing the cosmic unimportance of every event'.

BIOGRAPHICAL MILESTONES

1928   Kunzang Wangchuck alias Dasho Shingkhar Lam born.

1932   Installed as reincarnation of Lama of Wamtshespa, Chokey Dorji.

1933   Started tutoring from uncle Jigme Dorji.

1936   Started tutoring from father Kenchog Gyeltshen.

1938   Construction of house in Shingkhar.

1939   Study and benediction from Lama Drupgyud Rimpoche in Tharpaling monastery in Bumthang.

1940   Benediction from Kanjur Lama, the bogus god man from Tibet, in Kurje and his visit to Ura.

1943   Retreat for prayers with father in monastery at Garkhai, Shingkhar.

1944   Flight of uncle Sonam Tenzin and conscription as tozep.

1945   Death of mother Pema Tshoki.

1945   Tutoring from Lopon Norbu Wangchuk in Domkhar.

1946   Trip to Northern Choskhor for census of cattle and yaks.

1947   Trip to Longtey and Gangtey for census of cattle and yaks.

1947   Trip to Haa with His Majesty who went to meet Political Officer from Gangtok, Sikkim.

1947   Investiture of Crown Prince Jigme Dorji Wangchuck as Trongsa Dronyer.

1950   Death of Paro Penlop Tshering Penjor.

1950   Installation of Crown Prince Jigme Dorji Wangchuck as Paro Penlop.

1952	Death of the Second King Jigme Wangchuck in Kinga Rabden.
1952	Coronation of the Third King Jigme Dorji Wangchuck in Paro.
1952	Resignation from the court and leave for home.
1953	The first National Assembly session convened in Punakha.
1953	Recruited as clerk to Lopon Paybar and Dronyer Jangtu of Trongsa dzong.
1955	Summoned to Thimphu by His Majesty Jigme Dorji Wangchuck and sent to Trashigang to assist Ashi Tashi.
1956	Summoned to Thimphu by His Majesty from Trashigang.
1956	On tours with His Majesty from Thimphu to Trashigang.
1957	Return of the Royal Entourage to Thimphu via Dewathang.
1957	Celebration of Crown Prince Jigme Singye Wangchuck's entry into Tashichodzong.
1957	Training of mask dancers in summer in Tashichodzong.
1957	The second National Assembly session convened. Yearly National Assembly started.
1958	Declaration of the freedom of serfs.
1958	Visit of PM Nehru, Prime Minister of India.
1959	Thrimshung Chenmo (Supreme Laws) passed by the National Assembly.
1959	State visit of HM the King to India.
1960	Tencholing military camp established in Wangduephodrang.
1961	Rigney School established in Wangditsi, Thimphu.
1962	Road opened between Thimphu and Phuntsholing.

BIOGRAPHICAL MILESTONES

1963 Reconstruction of Tashichodzong started.

1964 Lyonchen Jigme Dorji assassinated.

1964 Involved in jeep accident at Lungtenphu, Thimphu.

1965 Royal Advisory Council and Royal Bhutan Police established.

1966 Gilded calligraphy of Kanjur for Tashichodzong started.

1968 Finance and Home Ministers appointed.

1968 Awarded red scarf and appointed as Secretary to His Majesty.

1968 State Visit of Prime Minister Mrs. Indira Gandhi.

1970 Visited Osaka to see Expo'70.

1971 Appointed as Speaker of National Assembly.

1972 Investiture of Crown Prince Jigme Singye Wangchuck as Trongsa Penlop.

1972 Third King Jigme Dorji Wangchuck passed away in Nairobi, Kenya.

1973 Appointed Deputy Chairman of the Coronation Committee.

1974 Coronation of the Fourth King Jigme Singye Wangchuck.

1974 End of tenure as Speaker of the National Assembly.

1978 Death of father Lama Kenchog Gyeltshen in Thimphu.

1985 Resigned from civil service.

GLOSSARY OF DZONGKHA TERMS

Adung, Livery, stable boy, riding assistant

Agay, Grandfather or elderly man

Araa, Home made whisky usually distilled from barley or wheat

Ashang, Maternal uncle

Ashi, Title for a woman of nobility or aristocracy

Atsara, Clown with a red, big-nosed mask

Aum, Lady

Bangchen, Literally one with power, men sent by the court to levy fines and penalties

Bangchung, Bamboo plates, baskets

Banyer, Cattle master

Benda/khodrup, Types of butter tax

Betam, Silver coin

Bodhisattava, Enlightened beings

Boob, Three pieces of textile to make one kira or gho

Buley, Fashionable flat circular hat woven out of bamboo

Chagabao, An older type of gun

Changgap, Butlers, valets and men in waiting

Champon Chichap Chief of the mask dancers

Chandaap, Security men

Chang, Ale, alcohol

Chashumi, Personal aide to the King

Cheta Kasho, Circular related to taxation

Chichap, Chief

Chimi, Member of the National Assembly. They were earlier known as mangmi

Chorten, Stupa, monument

Darpon, Chief of the attendants

Dasho, Title of a red scarf official

Dayok, Assistant to the darpon

Debi Zimpon Nam, Chamberlain to the Deb

Desi, Civil ruler of Bhutan before the monarchy

Dojab, Overseer of loads

Doma, Betel nut

Domchoe, Festivals in Punakha and Thimphu

Drami, drami, zab, drab, Serfs

Dramnyen, Guitar like instrument with seven strings

Dratshang, Monk body in general

Dres, Measure of volume roughly equivalent to 1.67 kg

Driglam Namsha, Code of disciplined behaviour

Dronyer, Guest master

Drupgho, Gho entitlement for the chief carpenter/ architect and mason given when the construction of a house is completed.

Dungkhag, Sub-division of a district

Dungpa, Administrator of a dungkhag

Dungthrim, Judge in a dungkhag

Dungyik, Clerk

Dzong, Fortress

Dzongda, Civil administrator of a district

Dzongkha, National language

Dzongkhag, District

Dzongtshab, Representative of the King in the district

Feltshig, Written language which is a mixture of national language and choskay, the classical Tibetan

Garuda, Mythical bird which feeds on snakes

Gelong, Ordained monk

Gendup, Central monk body

Gewog, Collection of villages

Gho, Gent's dress

Gomchen, Priest

Gongzim, Senior Chamberlain to the King

Gonpo, Protective deities

Gorap, Gate controller

Gung, Household

Gup (goop), High rank of an attendant

Gup, Headman of a block

Hima, A type of chess game which is now extinct

Jaling, A clarinet like musical instrument

Jatsham, yangkoom, Breeds of cow

Je Khenpo, Chief Abbot of Bhutan

Kadrep, Conversation companions

Kalyon, Chief minister in olden days, but now refers only to Chairman of Royal Advisory Council

Kamtrel, Cash tax

Kanjur, 100 volumes (together with 12 volumes of Bum) of canonical collection of Buddhist scriptures

Karchey, Flour made out of roasted wheat

Kasho, Court circular or Royal Decree

Keptang, Wheat or buckwheat pancake

Khamar, Red scarf with white band in the middle, worn earlier by the head of a family indicating that it was a tax payer

Kharang, Semi ground maize food

Khurwa, Buckwheat pancake, staple diet of Bumthang

Kira, Lady's dress

Kusho, Term of respect for the King and Paro Penlop Tshering Penjor

Kutshab, Representative, ambassador

La, Mountain pass

Lagho, Gho entitlement for the chief carpenter/ architect and mason to replace the ones worn out during construction

Langdo, An area which can be ploughed by a pair of bullock in a day

Lapon, Labour officer

Lasey, Snacks taken just before crossing a high pass

Lhakhang, Temple

Lontrel, In-kind tax

Lopon, Teacher (also used to refer to anyone as a term of respect)

Lyonpo, Minister

Mangmi, Representative of the people in the National Assembly as they were called in 1950s

Mani, Rotating prayer wheel

Marchang, Drinks libation ceremony

Matam, Coin

Mewang, Dzong cleaner

Monpa, A person who belong to Mon people in central Bhutan

Neten, An abbot of a regional monk body

Nyerchen, Store master in a dzong with the rank of red scarf

Nyerpa, Store master managing the estates of aristocracies

Nyikem, Red scarf officials

Paan, Leaf taken with betel nut and lime paste

Paddum, Canon, soldiers who fire canons

Pangoleng garpa, Men from eastern Bhutan who were requisitioned to work in buckwheat fields of royal estates in Bumthang

Penlop, Governor of a region consisting of several districts

Phuta, Measure of volume

Rabdey, Monk bodies of Trongsa, Paro and Wangduephodrang

Rabjungpa, Monk bodies of Dagana, Lhuntsi and Trashigang

Ramjam, Deputy to a red scarf official

Rigney, Arts and letters

Rimpoche, Term of respect for a high lama

Sang, Measure of weight

Sedrang, Ceremonial reception

Shabdrung, Term used to refer to the Founder of Bhutan and his reincarnations

Shamdrel, A dish (almost extinct) of many ingredients

Shanyer, Meat master

Shung, Central, government

Singchang, Beer made out of wheat

GLOSSARY OF DZONGKHA TERMS

Solpon, Solyok, Palace chef

Suma, Households who did not pay any tax to their dzongkhags but paid directly to some aristocracies (e.g. Lame Gonpa, Wangdecholing, Wangdecholing Ama, Ashi Phuntsho Choden etc.)

Tangti, Small hand drum

Tapon, Chief of stable

Tenjur, Canonical collection of Buddhist treatises and commentarial works

Thangkha, Scroll painting

Thojab, Grain tax based on land output

Thram, Land register

Thrimpon, Judge

Thrimshung Chenmo, Laws enacted in 1958

Torma, Ritual offering or effigies

Tozep, Lowest of the attendants who were entitled to meals from the common kitchen

Trelpa, Households who were liable to pay taxes

Trolthak, A type of textile tax, known as Kheng as 'kapey tsatroe'

Trulku, Reincarnate lama

Tsanyer, Fodder master

Tshechu, Festival which normally begins on the 10th of a lunar month

Tshogpon, Speaker of the National Assembly

Tsipon, Chief finance officer

Tsuna, Lime paste taken with betel nut and paan

Wang, Blessing, initiation

Wangyon, Literally, levy for blessing: but generally understood as taxes

Woola, Labour service or tax

Yathra, Colourful woollen textile of Bumthang

Zangtam, Copper coin

Zaw, Sizzled rice snack

Zingap, Menial worker

Zongpon, Fort governor of a district

Zurpa, Splinter household which is yet to pay taxes